DAWN OF TRIBULATION

Other Books by D.I. Telbat

The COIL Series: Christian Suspense
The COIL Legacy Series: Christian Suspense
COIL Legacy Collection: 3 Books in 1 Volume
The RESOLUTION Series: America's Last Days
The STEADFAST Series: America's Last Days
STEADFAST Collection: 6 Novellas in 1 Volume
Last Dawn Series: America's Last Days
Leeward Set: Where Christians Dare
Never Lost Series: Trafficking Rescue Novels

Arabian Variable
Called To Gobi
God's Colonel
Soldier of Hope
Short Story Collections

DAWN OF TRIBULATION

America's Last Days

BOOK FOUR OF THE LAST DAWN SERIES

D.I. TELBAT

IN SEASON PUBLICATIONS
USA

Printed in the United States of America

DAWN OF TRIBULATION: America's Last Days
/ D.I. Telbat -- 1st ed.

Categories: Futuristic Christian Fiction;
Christian Suspense

D.I. Telbat / In Season Publications
https://ditelbat.com
https://books2read.com/DITelbat

ISBN 978-1-7371777-9-1

Cover Design by Streetlight Graphics

To those who reach for eternity,
for those who are willing to forego the temporary.

Acknowledgements

Publishing a series takes a special type of endurance from a whole team of editors, readers, and advisors. Friends and family have continued to faithfully offer direction as this COIL adventure continues to unfold (since 2004). Thanks to Dee for editing and promoting through yet another novel. Others have again shared in the work, finding errors, and/or offering valuable feedback. My gratitude is extended to our group of appreciated Beta Readers for their personal and helpful touch. May God bless each one of you for your faithful service to the Telbat Team.

Character Sketch

Alice Prine - A black one-armed woman who leads and scouts for the group of Christian refugees. She carries a steel walking stick, and her loyalty is unshakeable.

Andy "Runner" Radner - The son of Eric Radner, Wyoming survivalist and leader of a Christian homestead. Now, Andy has become a ruthless bounty hunter, accompanied by his Labrador, also named Runner.

Annette Caspertein - She was married to Titus in San Diego until his death from the Meridia Virus. The mother of Levi now is the wife of Rudy Caspertein in Colorado. She yearns for the day when she'll see her son again.

Brian Steelman - Once a Federation Enforcer, this new believer becomes a leader with and companion to Levi Caspertein during their march westward.

Chen Li - Nathan's wife who was once a strong COIL operative, faithfully enduring hardship and trial under harsh regimes, has grown weak and fearful.

Chloe Azmaveth - COIL's original public relations officer, now in her late sixties. Her experience spans from field operations to strategic planning for the refugees traveling west.

Jenna Dowler - The blind daughter of Corban Dowler and once code-named Radiant Shade, she is the gentle backbone of faith and perseverance in the band of travelers.

Kip Brogdon - The son of a Pacific States general, this missions-minded believer, along with wife Mia, bravely faces any persecution to share the gospel. He once assumed the name Serval, and founded the Servalites, a passive missionary corps across the southern United States.

Lena Travers - Once a Federation Enforcer, this ruthless woman has been humbled through a debilitating disfigurement; now accompanies Levi Caspertein in leadership of the refugees.

Levi Caspertein - Witty son of the infamous arms dealer, Titus Caspertein, also known as the Serval. As a Special Forces operator, he leads a small band of refugees from New York toward Colorado where there is rumored to be safe haven from persecution.

Milo Rotham - Once a colonel in the Federation Citizen Army, this ambitious soldier has joined the march west. He is just beginning to understand the value of the believers around him.

Miranda Nelson - Thirty-year-old native of Chicago; this believer has a one-track mind for the Last Days—and has an eye for Rex Caspertein.

Mia Trimble Brogdon – Daughter of Wynter Caspertein and Wes Trimble, and wife of Kip Brogdon. This young woman has committed herself to her husband's frightening goal of sharing the gospel across a dangerous America.

Nathan Isaacson - Also known as Eagle Eyes; husband of Chen Li and original leader of COIL's most dependable Special Forces team.

Rex Caspertein - Bear-sized son of Rudy Caspertein & cousin to Levi; leads a small band of believers westward toward Colorado.

Rudy Caspertein - The aged seismologist, now married to Annette, whose influence and stand for Christ in CO draws believers together and brings the attention of oppressors.

Trapper Sullivan - This homesteader and rancher helps Rudy Caspertein teach and lead the believers in Colorado; father of Wayne Sullivan, mayor of Meeker, Colorado.

Veronika Kane - OPT Advocate from Denver; wears a red and black cape in her ruthless enforcement of the Oath of Solidarity.

Vorca - The Native American nursemaid for young Caleb, both now part of the Caspertein family in Colorado.

Wayne Sullivan - The son of Trapper Sullivan, this mayor in Colorado disdains the faith of his father and prefers the new movement of the OPT.

Glossary

COIL – Commission of International Laborers; founded by ex-CIA Agent Corban Dowler to aid Christians under persecution; teams of undercover Christian Special Forces using only non-lethal weapons in rescue missions and protecting believers from Satan's wiles.

Servalites – a passive missionary corps operating across the southern United States.

One Planet Trust – Called the OPT; a global movement that is uniting governments through radio communication and the Oath of Solidarity; based on science, solidarity, success, and unity; penalty of death for anyone who resists.

Pan-Day – the general reference to the time when the Meridia Virus began to wipe out one hundred million Americans. The Meridia Virus was introduced at the end of *Distant Harm*, Book Three of *The COIL Legacy*.

Travel Route

Dawn of Tribulation
D.I. Telbat
Pan-Day America + 20 Years

1. Erwin, TN
2. Ellijay, GA
3. Boaz, AL
4. Red Bay, AL
5. Marks, MS
6. Paris, AR
7. Oklahoma
8. Moab, UT

9. Grand Junction, CO
10. Meeker, CO
11. Laramie Mtns, WY
12. Yellowstone Nat'l Park
13. Nebraska
14. Iowa
15. Illinois

A Note from the Author

Dear Friend,

This book was written in the midst of the Covid pandemic. Its first pages begin where the last book ended—the same night, the same hour. I typed a large portion of this while I was under quarantine for the virus myself. *Dawn of Tribulation* seems eerily and appropriately placed in this time of America's last days. The Meridia Virus (fictional) was scripted into the story ten years ago, but I couldn't have guessed the final pages of this adventure would mingle with the spreading of Covid and the strife of globalistic ambitions in real life.

If you have followed the COIL books from the first novel, *Dark Liaison*, you will notice that this concluding book has remained true to the calling and character of the COIL cause for Christ. Many beloved friends were lost along the way, but it's been my pleasure to include some of the original players in these final pages.

When I think back to the first few COIL books, I think of how far Jenna Dowler has come, how much Chloe Azmaveth has grown, and what challenges the Casperteins have overcome. Nathan Isaacson was a featured character in several books, and I rejoice with you to see him standing at the end as he stood at the beginning.

In this concluding novel, there is the inclusion of Andy Radner whose bounty hunter appearance occurred in the previous novel, *Dawn of Subjection*. Many of you read *The Steadfast Series* in which his father Eric Radner's story stretched over six novellas during the same

Meridia Virus aftermath. Similarly, references to *The Resolution Series* (featuring Wes, Wynter, and Mia Trimble) has been included here as well.

For years, I had hoped to merge all these mighty COIL actors and series into a single timeline. Now, in *Dawn of Tribulation*, it is complete. I hope you notice something about eternal hope in their lives by the way they overcome through their faith in a mighty and gracious God.

There are a number of real towns and cities I lightly featured in this book, but outside of their geography and perhaps a tourist attraction, the details and character of each location are entirely fictionalized. My goal was to give the reader a glimpse of a lost society clinging to dying hopes and dreams in every locale. Meanwhile, pilgrims who believe in Jesus Christ remain vulnerable—yet show themselves undeniably confident in their Savior's arms.

For those who anticipate more COIL books after this, I hope not to disappoint you! I have plans, as long as the Lord tarries, to return to that span of twenty years after the pandemic when Levi was growing up in San Diego, learning from his father, Titus, and facing challenges with the Brogdon family and the Pacific States. There are twenty years' worth of adventures to share from the lives of Titus, Levi, Annette, Mia, and Oleg!

As I write this, it's early 2021. There are many conflicts around us right now. As believers, may our eyes remain on the fight that truly matters in this world and the next. If we have energy, may it be spent sharing the gospel and saving souls. It ain't easy, as Titus and Levi Caspertein have been known to say, but it will be worth it. The God of the Bible is with us. Consider 2 Timothy 4:1-5.

May God be praised through this work,

David Telbat

Chapter One

Levi Caspertein stood poised in the Tennessee forest as the sky slowly brightened. It was the middle of the night in the Cherokee National Forest, so the illumination that started at the treetops drew Levi's eyes from the creature he'd cornered in a thicket. Darkness continued to fade until full daylight shined upon the forest floor.

The bushes rustled, and Levi returned his gaze to the ground. Two little eyes shimmered not three feet away. Holding his jacket in front of him, he slipped his hands inside the sleeves, then pounced on what he now identified as an adult rabbit. He trapped the furry animal under his coat and clutched it tightly as it kicked and squirmed. Rolling onto his back, Levi held the rabbit against his chest as it screamed an unearthly sound, matching the phenomenon that was occurring in the sky over the eastern continent of North America.

Far above, the rumble of meteors streaked across the black backdrop. A dozen icy space rocks burned like white flares, lower and brighter than Levi had seen before. And so many all at once!

They soared out of sight beyond the treetops. Their thunder faded to a rumble, then to silence. The rabbit stopped screaming, and darkness once again settled upon the forest. Levi stared wide-eyed at the sky as several Bible passages came to mind, verses that warned the world of the wrath and tribulation to come. There would be signs in the sky, but Levi didn't need to fear. The Lord was coming for His Church one day soon. What he'd just witnessed was nothing compared to what the Bible said would unfold during the Tribulation.

Sitting upright in the midst of the thicket, Levi carefully kept the rabbit wrapped in his coat. The meteor shower was worthy of some marveling, but he had more pressing matters to attend to that night.

With a yank, he tore his rifle sling from the bramble and rose to his feet. After thirty minutes of hunting, he'd finally caught a wild animal to use in his plan. Now, it was time to commence with his scheme. Lena Travers had been kidnapped, and he wasn't leaving Tennessee without her.

That was, if the bounty hunter called Runner—the man with the tomahawk—hadn't already killed her to spite him.

Levi moved up the mountain slope but angled toward the eastern ridge so he didn't approach directly to where he believed Runner was hiding. It was no mystery why Runner had taken Lena. Lena was nothing to Runner. No, Runner was using Lena as bait. The stranger had been hired by the Federation to kill Levi, and Lena was merely the tool the killer was using to bait him in.

Wrapping the rabbit tighter, Levi held the animal in his left arm as he swung his battle rifle off his right shoulder. He tried not to think of the skilled predator who was waiting for him, expecting him. Although Levi had spared Runner's life once, he didn't expect the killer to return the favor.

Since he'd given his heavy pack to Nathan Isaacson and Brian Steelman, who were escorting Chen Li and Jenna Dowler, Levi wasn't burdened with anything but the canteen on his belt as he crept uphill through trees and under boughs. He placed his feet with caution, pausing at lengthy intervals, his taut muscles trembling as he listened in the dark. If Lena was still alive, she might try to make a noise to warn him, even though her mouth was too injured to communicate in words.

An hour passed, and Levi sensed the ground leveling off as he reached the peak of the mountain. For ten minutes, he stood motionless, listening, his eyes wide, feeling the rabbit slowing its breathing inside the jacket. Levi sniffed the breeze, praying for God to guide his senses in the seconds to come . . .

Then he heard it—a sound to his right perhaps twenty yards away. Judging by the starlight, a stand of young trees rose about thirty feet high. They grew close together, offering cover for Runner and his black Labrador.

The sound he'd heard had been so slight, his mind almost convinced him that he hadn't heard anything at all. But, no. An arm had moved across a branch, or the dog that Runner used for tracking and hunting had shifted on her paws.

Levi eased the jacket from his chest but gripped the bundle firmly in his left hand. His movements were agonizingly slow—a necessary caution against making any noise. If the rabbit squealed or cried out now, he would be finished. Runner carried only a tomahawk, but it was all the killer needed.

Holding his breath, Levi hung his left arm at his side. Then, he swung his arm back, and with an underarm throw, he tossed his jacket with the rabbit into the sky. He could only vaguely see the shadow against the stars as it arced into the tops of the saplings nearby.

He imagined the rabbit panicking from the sudden weightlessness. It could make all the noise it wanted to now, and it did—as soon as the jacket and rabbit tumbled through the branches. Levi would've smiled at the ruckus if Lena's life wasn't hanging in the balance.

Shouldering his rifle, he aimed at the stand of young trees. The instant he heard a dog growl, he opened fire, raking the trees with gel-tranqs, his non-lethal tranquilizer rounds. His flashing muzzle was leveled about chest high. Then he took a second sweep across the saplings, this time a little lower.

After half his magazine was exhausted, Levi dove to the right, rolled over his shoulder, and came up on one knee. Poised, he listened past the echo of his gunfire that rolled across the Tennessee landscape.

Bushes whipped along the ground to his left. Levi guessed the noise was too swift to be a person. Sure enough, an instant later he heard the soft bounding of the rabbit, followed by the dog's excited snort. Rabbit and canine disappeared off the mountaintop in a flurry of movement and barks.

But the stand of trees nearby wasn't quiet, either. Someone moved. Levi licked his lips, his finger on the trigger. Runner may have hidden himself well inside the saplings, but now he couldn't get himself out without making more noise.

"Aah!" came a cry. It was Lena!

Levi didn't move. He was still learning to interpret her throaty sounds, and she was still learning to communicate without a mandible, which had been shot off by Colonel Milo Rotham back in New York City.

"Aah-ah!" she called again.

Cupping his mouth with his hand, Levi turned his head to throw his voice to the side.

"Is Runner down?"

"Ah. Ah-hah-ah."

He rose to his feet and sighed.

"Hang on. I'm coming to you."

As he moved toward the trees, he kept his rifle leveled, now prepared to tranq even the dog if she returned. With one arm, he pushed his way into the branches until Lena clutched his ammo vest. He let his rifle hang on its sling and held her in return. She sobbed in her throaty way, gasping mixed with whining.

"You're safe now. Where's Runner?"

"Aah." In the darkness, she directed his hand to the ground.

He knelt and felt the slender body of the young bounty hunter. Using both hands, he found the man's tomahawk still in his grip. Lena also searched the unconscious man, her hands crossing over Levi's. From inside Runner's buckskins, Lena drew a book, and from his belt, she yanked the .22 pistol she'd had on her when she'd been captured. Levi gently touched his Bible as she pushed it toward him.

"No, you can keep carrying it. I'm just glad we got it back." He reached inside his own vest. "Here. I found something that belongs to you as well."

He gave her the lace veil she'd used to cover her disfigured face since taking it from a bridal shop in New Jersey.

"Take this. It's Runner's pack." He handed the bundle to her. "Watch out for that mutt. It ain't easy moving in the dark knowing that dog can see us better than we can see her."

With Runner held awkwardly in his arms, Levi plowed his way back out to the clearing and lay Runner on the ground.

"You see those meteors a couple hours ago?" He gathered fuel for a fire, using Runner's tomahawk to hack off a couple dead branches. "Never seen anything like that before."

"Aah."

"It's just the beginning, Lena. The closer we get to the Tribulation, I think we'll see more of that stuff. Maybe earthquakes, too. I wonder how the rest of the world is reacting to it all."

In minutes, the fire was lit, and Levi added more sticks until there was enough light to illuminate the small clearing.

"All right. Let's see how you're holding up. I know he jumped you after sundown."

He moved to her side to check her face. She'd already wrapped her mouth and neck with the bridal lace, so now he removed it. With her hands in her lap, she surrendered to his touch. After all, he'd saved her life weeks earlier after she'd been injured.

From his neck, he untied a bandana and wet it with his canteen to wash blood from her nostrils.

"Looks like he got you across the bridge of the nose here. You might have a couple black eyes for a few days."

He tucked her loose blonde hair back to check her neck and ears, all while her blue eyes watched him.

"Aah?" she asked.

"You'll live. Definitely a broken nose." He wrapped her head with the lace to cover her mouth. "Don't worry. You're not as ugly as me yet."

She slapped his arm as he returned to his side of the fire.

"Watch for that dog." He picked through Runner's small pack. "She fell for my rabbit trick, but that doesn't mean she'll appreciate me manhandling her master."

He found Runner's crossbow. Weeks earlier, Levi had disarmed the hunter of his six arrows, which he'd had in his pack. Now he took the crossbow, which had a short stock no longer than his arm.

Lena pointed to Levi's canteen. It was near empty, but he tossed it to her anyway.

"This guy hasn't taken my hints to leave us alone," Levi said, "so we're going to leave him with only his buckskins this time. Maybe that'll slow him down."

"Aah." She turned suddenly to the darkness. "Aah!"

Levi rose to his feet and aimed his rifle over the fire at two diamonds shining ten feet away.

"Carefully, Lena, come to my side of the fire. Get behind me. I've tranqed dogs before. They don't always go to sleep as fast as people."

Instead, Lena slapped her thigh.

"Aah. Aah-ah!"

The dog padded forward, sniffed Lena's hand, then investigated her unconscious master, Runner. After a moment, she returned to Lena's touch, who pet the animal's black coat.

"Okay." Levi sighed. "Interesting turn of events. The killer guard-dog isn't such a killer after all."

"Ah." Lena nuzzled the Lab and roughed her mane. "Aah-ah?"

Levi lowered his rifle and continued to search Runner and his property.

"Depending on how quickly Nathan leads the others west, we're at least a half-day behind them. How do you feel about covering a few miles right now before we find some shelter?"

"Ah." She nodded, then glanced at the dog. "Aah?"

Levi looked up from Runner's pack into the pleading eyes of both Lena and the dog.

"Seriously? Take the man's dog, too?" Levi stuffed Runner's knife into his own waistband. "Well, I guess we're stripping him of everything else. What'll you call her?"

"Auggie." She ruffled the dog's neck.

"Auggie?" Levi shrugged, knowing the sounds Lena could make with her throat were limited. "Auggie it is. But we don't even know if she'll come with us when we get going."

"Aah-ah."

Finally, Levi dropped Runner's empty pack into the fire.

"I've taken everything this guy's used to hunt me and Jenna the past few weeks. I don't know what more to do. He might still come after us."

"Ah." Lena made the shape of a pistol with her fingers.

"Yeah, we'll tranq him again, but I don't want to keep tranqing the guy. You ready?"

He added a log to the fire to keep any forest predators at bay while Runner slept off the tranquilizer. Then he backed away from the fire, seeing if Auggie would follow Lena. The dog didn't even look back but ran ahead of Lena as if to scout the way for her new master. Or she had the scent of another critter.

"Runner isn't going to be happy when he wakes up." Levi chuckled. "I'm not sure if we're discouraging him or antagonizing him."

"Aah."

"You're right. It's his choice. Time will tell."

Nathan Isaacson noticed the birds circling from a couple miles away before he spotted the slaughter on the highway. He didn't immediately warn his wife, Chen Li, but he glanced back at Brian Steelman where he was leading the pack horse next to blind Jenna Dowler. Brian was a wary-eyed Boston man, an ex-Enforcer for the Federation, and Nathan had learned to rely on the tall man in his mid-forties. As expected, Brian lifted his head, signaling that he was alert.

Jenna was reciting several Psalms from memory where she walked with a hand on the mare's mane. The horse plodded along comfortably on the littered highway, her back burdened with all the travelers' gear, including Levi's hefty pack that he'd brought from San Diego.

Being married for more than twenty years, Nathan smiled at his wife, Chen Li, a Hong Kong native. She had been an elite COIL operative in her prime, but her undercover years in the Bowery had softened her physically and emotionally. Her faith was unwavering, but Nathan had noticed the stoic resolve of his lovely wife had cracked under the years of suffering, fear, and secrecy.

She smiled back, and Nathan saw the love in her eyes behind the weariness. Daily, they'd lived with the threat of capture at the hands of enemies known and unknown. And daily, they affirmed their love for one another, knowing any day could be their last. They knew heaven awaited them, but they'd made an agreement to pass from this earth with a bond as strong as the first day they'd repeated their vows before their God, friends, and fellow saints.

That shared moment touched Nathan's soul, for he knew the next moment wasn't promised.

"Let's take a break here," Nathan voiced, and pointed to tall grass on the shoulder of the rural highway. He started to lead the way, though his eyes were squinting ahead at the debris up the highway. "Levi and Lena can't be far behind now."

"Nathan Isaacson!" Jenna snapped. He'd learned to measure the blind woman's aggravation with his leadership by the title she used for him. "I may be blind, but I still have a nose. What is it? Why are we pulling off here? What do you see? I can smell it on the wind."

"What's she talking about?" Chen Li stopped on the edge of the pavement.

"That." Brian gestured up the highway, then leaned toward Jenna. "Buzzards are circling over something dead up the highway. About two hundred yards."

"Then why are we stopping here?" Jenna continued. "Don't tell me it's for Levi and Lena. Take us up there, Nathan. We're not squeamish."

Biting his tongue, Nathan walked ahead. He knew Jenna wasn't squeamish, but he was thinking of his wife, and guarding her from looking unnecessarily upon more human carnage.

He counted the bodies before he reached them. The stench was overpowering.

"Stay back!" Nathan ordered his friends. This time, he didn't leave it up for debate. Once he saw Brian had stopped the horse, Nathan went on alone.

Instead of checking out the dead, he studied the untrimmed vegetation that choked the highway there, and even the leafy oak trees nearby. He had no doubt the five travelers had been ambushed, and the highwaymen could still be waiting nearby for more victims.

But the trees were quiet and the grass was still, so he walked among the dead—four men and one woman. Whatever possessions they'd carried were gone. Everything had been plundered.

Nathan walked back to his three companions and slid out the entrenching shovel that Levi kept tethered to his pack.

"It's that guy Shaker and Lisbon and three others." He moved his rifle to his back. "Hon, why don't you and Jenna wait here with the horse while Brian and I bury them."

"Is Tyra with them?" Chen Li's voice broke. "Do you see a wheelbarrow?"

"No wheelbarrow." Nathan set his free hand on his wife's shoulder. "There's a woman, a little on the older side—dirty blonde hair, some shoestring necklaces, one of them is a cross."

"That's her." Chen Li covered her mouth and turned her face into Nathan's chest.

Nathan noticed that Jenna's usual serene face was twitching behind her grimy sunglasses.

"You okay, Jenna?" he asked as Brian took the shovel and his rifle, an antique .308 caliber, and went to take care of the dead. "I know you two traveled with Shaker for a couple weeks."

"Next time you tell us to stay back," Jenna said softly, her right hand petting the horse's neck, "we'll stay back. I'll stay back."

"Thank you." Nathan thought Jenna now understood that Chen Li was too fragile for this, even if the blind woman wasn't. "Let the horse graze while we do this. Once they're in the ground, we'll call you both up. Maybe we can sing something over their graves. And when I say *we*, I mean you two, Jenna and Chen Li. No one wants to hear my gravelly voice. This day is sad enough already."

He left his wife in Jenna's hands, then joined Brian, who'd begun to excavate the shallow ditch beside the highway. After a few minutes, Nathan took a turn with the small shovel, and the younger man watched the highway for danger.

"Smoke ahead," Brian announced.

Nathan stood and gazed to the west. Black smoke billowed far away.

"That's no campfire," Nathan said. "That looks like a whole town."

"It's the Plains Zone." Brian checked his rifle, which held only five gel-tranq cartridges. "We left one war zone for another, it looks like."

"Maybe we should head south and go around." Nathan continued to dig. "Avoid whatever's ahead. Or we could be the next ones to be buried on this highway."

"We'll leave some markers for Levi along the way." Brian stepped into the middle of the highway to gaze east.

"You were with these people for a little while, right?" Nathan set the shovel aside so he and Brian could move the bodies into the grave. "Levi and I shared the gospel with Shaker and Lisbon. They didn't seem to respond."

"These others were the same," Brian said. "I'm learning it's totally different when a Christian dies. It's not the same kind of ending. Or sadness."

"For a Christian, death is a graduation, a new beginning. For a non-Christian, it's like an eternal end. I prefer a funeral for believers. It's hard to know what to say, otherwise. Like today. Five lives lived but were perhaps wasted. How do you celebrate them for ignoring their Savior their whole lives? Or like Shaker—victimizing people all these years?"

"I don't want you to mourn me." Brian wiped his hands on the grass, the dead now in the trench. "Most of my life, I lived for myself, but I'm God's now."

"I know you are, Brian. That's why I'd celebrate your death if I had to, but I'd rather live beside you to celebrate our lives a little longer."

"No complaints here."

They covered the bodies, leaving a mound of earth in the ditch. Brian plucked some white daisies from the roadside and laid them on the mound. Nathan called Chen Li and Jenna to join them. The horse continued to graze while they all stood over the site.

"You think Levi and Lena will think one of us is buried here?" Brian asked.

"We'll leave a fish sign a few yards up the road," Nathan said. "He'll understand we're still on the move."

Jenna sang a hymn she'd written herself, something fitting to remember the lost as well as to honor Jesus Christ.

"It's a long way to Colorado," Nathan said to Brian as they headed onto the highway. "If I go before you, I don't want you to mourn me, either."

"The only weeping there'll be over your grave," Brian said, "will be from my attempt to sing. My voice is no better than yours. But I promise to lay down some daisies for you."

Andy "Runner" Radner opened his eyes to the crackling fire a few feet away. That's strange, he thought. He couldn't remember lighting a fire. And in the middle of a clearing? Normally, he hid his lit campfires in the shelter of trees and foliage.

He sat up and felt an ache high on his chest, just below his collar bone. Then, his memory flooded back. The woman with the deformed face had been his prisoner. High above the town of Erwin, far up in the mountains of eastern Tennessee, he had laid a trap for Levi Caspertein. But the welt on his chest told the rest of the story. Levi had shot him with one of those cursed tranquilizer rounds!

Weakly, he climbed to his feet and glanced about for Runner, the dog who shared his name. This wasn't the first time the high-spirited black Labrador had let him down. He had a mind to beat some ferocity back into the dog that was supposed to help him hunt their prey and guard against danger. But at least this Lab he'd picked up a couple years earlier was better than some he'd had.

Snarling at the flames, Andy reached into the fire and plucked what was left of the nylon material that had been his backpack. Only then did he realize that the knife and sheath on his belt were gone, as was his tomahawk he'd had in his hand while waiting in ambush.

Turning in a circle, he whistled twice for Runner and listened to the night, but only the mountain breeze swished through the treetops. It was a lonely sound. Runner was gone. She'd really left him this time. He could feel it. Levi wouldn't kill a person since it was against his religion, but maybe he had killed the hunting dog. That was pure cruelty!

Andy sat cross-legged in front of the fire, his anger intensifying from the helplessness he felt against the stranger who continued to best him. All of the other victims he'd been hired to kill had died easier. He'd never been taunted by a target like this! It was humiliating. Although Andy knew his tracking and hunting abilities were better than anyone's on the planet, he couldn't find an edge against Levi.

This was way beyond a contract with the Appalachian Federation. Andy wasn't even thinking about killing Jenna Dowler, the blind woman from New York. Now, he wanted only to find Levi and defy the ridiculous rumors that the man was supernaturally protected by God.

"I don't believe it," Andy stated softly, and he spit into the fire. Then he spoke louder. "I don't believe that nonsense! I don't believe it! You hear me? I don't believe it!"

He leaped to his feet to kick and stomp at the wood and ashes. In seconds, he'd spread the embers across the clearing. Panting and sweating in the warm night air, he watched the coals catch fire on the dry grass, then pine needles snapped as the white heat claimed them.

"I don't care."

Andy turned his back to the growing fire as the wind pitched it over the ridge, igniting a tree on the edge of the clearing. The light of the fire grew, which cast eerie shadows in front of him as he descended the mountain, nothing in his hands since Levi had relieved him of every possession.

From a distance, he paused and looked back at the mountain. It was fully ablaze now, tearing southward through the trees at a walking pace. He'd never started a forest fire before. Something about it seemed like a breach of nature, like he'd crossed a threshold by allowing it to spread. It was out of control now. The destruction couldn't be contained. It was beautiful, powerful, and horrible all at once. It would devour every living thing until it exhausted itself or came up against a river or lake.

The fire was himself, Andy realized. He was a man without a people, now blowing where circumstance led him, surrendering himself to the destructive calling he'd accepted after first realizing as a teenager the power he felt when taking an animal's life. Hunting people had come later, but of course, he'd had to leave River Camp and his adoptive father and mother after that. Eric and Gretchen Radner couldn't contain him. He was a wildfire, destined to wreak havoc across America!

No longer was he Runner. He was now Fire Runner.

As he reached the bottom of the mountain, he imagined introducing himself to strangers as Fire Runner. Would it terrify them? It was a mystical name, a name that spoke of both deadliness and terror. Many others on the roads he'd traveled had made up their own handles as well. Originally, he'd shared his dog's name, but this was a new era. His dog had been either stolen or killed. So now he would be Fire Runner, bringing devastation like an uncontrollable fire wherever he ran. Until he killed Levi Caspertein.

Navigating by the stars, he walked west through the forest, now thinking of surviving long enough to get down the road and find Levi. His hatchet and knife had been taken, but Andy couldn't remember living any other way but on the edge of the wild. His father had taught him about every edible plant and root. Before Andy's eighth birthday, he recalled Eric had taken him into Wyoming's mountains and taught him to survive if he were ever lost. He could build and start a fire with only sticks, catch fish in a river by using a rock trap, snares for squirrels, and bolos for turkeys. Andy knew how to use the forest to his advantage.

And that wasn't all. His heart beat faster at the memory of Eric teaching him about poisonous plants to avoid. It was so Andy would never eat things like death camas, an onion-like plant with leaves like grass. Or hemlock, which grew around swamps and wet meadows. And Andy had already seen chinaberry trees in the distance. Levi may have disarmed him, but Andy had other weapons he could gather, all to bring a painful and ultimate end to Levi Caspertein.

Maybe Levi thought his antics were amusing, but Andy wasn't amused. Every time the coward toyed with him, Andy felt like Levi wasn't taking him seriously. Nothing irritated him more than people thinking he was insignificant. Maybe his father wanted to live quietly in their Wyoming hideaway, but Andy was a killer—uncontained, raging, powerful, and horrible!

He was Fire Runner!

Rex Caspertein stood afar off from the caravan of two hundred people. From his vantage point off Interstate 80, he could see every man, woman, and child traipse along the paved lanes, heading west toward Colorado.

It'd been two weeks since the forty Lake Erie refugees had joined the hundred Christian escapees from New York

City. And in the last two weeks, sixty more had joined, one or two families at a time. Several of the newcomers had firearms, but Rex had given them each a warning before they joined the caravan: he was in charge. The only lethal weapons allowed would be used for hunting. Anyone who didn't want the protection of the Christians' non-lethal battle rifles could find someone else to travel with.

But no one had argued, and Rex was thankful there hadn't been any serious conflicts. Food and water were in constant scarcity, so anyone with a long gun was kept busy hunting dogs and deer. The canines were the offspring of domestic animals loosed around Pan-Day. Every breed of mongrel now prowled like wild animals during the day and lurked on the fringes of their campfires at night. No one had been attacked, but Rex kept even the latrines lit and guarded at night.

"Rex, you there?"

It was Alice Prine, the one-armed black woman who preferred to take point every day. She wore one of the two radio headsets, keeping Rex informed of what was ahead.

"I'm here. What's up?"

He gazed past the caravan toward the border of Illinois, which couldn't be far ahead. Lake Michigan's coastline wasn't visible, but he'd seen gulls and low-flying geese all morning.

"We've got incoming foot traffic coming straight at us. Maybe eighty or ninety people."

"Well, tell them they're going the wrong way." Rex chuckled and walked quickly toward the head of the caravan to coordinate the men and women God had provided for him to escort to safety. "Are they hostiles?"

"They look like us. But they're headed east."

"Pull back to us," he ordered. "I don't want you facing them alone. Help us cover the people."

He reached the front and signaled Scooter away from a conversation he was having with a gray-haired woman in overalls. Scooter was a middle-aged Mexican who'd been a COIL operative. His thinning crewcut no longer stood perfectly as he said it had in his youth.

"Travelers coming our way," Rex told the older man once they were away from the others. News of strangers could cause a panic. "Can you lead us off to the field on the right to rest until they pass?"

"You got it." Scooter jogged ahead.

Next, Rex located Bruno, another old COIL operative, and approached him where he was walking next to ex-Colonel Milo Rotham.

"Spread out to cover," he told them. "Incoming travelers, Alice says."

The two men separated, each with their own battle rifle. Although Rotham had recently been hunting them, when his military unit had been decimated by an Iowa militia, he'd taken refuge from the Plains Zone dangers by joining the Christians.

"Trouble?" Chloe Azmaveth asked as she drew up to walk beside him.

He'd learned to rely on the COIL intelligence officer, now approaching her seventh decade. Her dark curls flowed from under a baseball cap.

"Hope not. Just some travelers. Scooter's leading us off the freeway."

Chloe turned away and signaled Nick Zoft, the chubby ex-mayor from Hackensack, with whom she often paired up for guard duty. He wasn't an athletic man, but Rex had found the man dependable if not skilled with a rifle, and his faith as a witness for Christ was unshakable.

Rex caught the eye of Taylor Tharp, a smaller version of Bruno, and Hank Lowery, a balding nutritionist from New York. Both were family men walking with their wives, but they immediately hustled away to take up guard positions off the interstate.

"Where do you want me?" ex-Sergeant Sean Harris asked, his rifle already in his hands. His wiry eyebrows had been the butt of much jesting from some of the men, but Sean had a good sense of humor, though he wasn't yet a believer.

"Take the south side," Rex said, "and don't hide. I want them to see we're armed and alert."

"Who is it?"

"I hope peaceful people."

The caravan wound off the pavement into a field overgrown now by knee-high brown grass. Word had spread that something was happening, so conversation between the two hundred people diminished to nervous whispers, and the tension passed even to the few animals among them. Two milk goats, Ruth and Naomi, and a pair of pack horses perked their ears, fully alert.

Once in the field, the people bunched up naturally, and the eight shooters stood at a distance of one hundred yards, spread out and encircling the people. Rex and Chloe had taught them this defensive formation. Even though they had only a few rifles, their positioning would be a challenge for even a stronger force to overcome. Those with hunting rifles in the group knelt or sat in the grass. Their rifles were held tightly, but if Rex saw them panic and raise their weapons to kill, he intended to tranq them before they could shoot at a stranger. No one would be killed by the people he was responsible for, not if he could help it. He didn't need to worry about the hundred Christians acting unsuitably, but the other hundred . . . he wasn't sure about.

Alice reached the main group and took up a position behind and to the north of the refugees. Chloe joined Rex's side at the edge of the interstate, and as they had braced for danger together a dozen times before, Chloe held binoculars to her eyes.

"They're not armed," Chloe reported. "I don't see a single rifle. There's a lot of them, though. They're filling both lanes. I think there's a second wave farther back. Yeah. They're coming around the next bend in the road."

"It's expected," Rex mumbled and browsed the sky. The night before, they'd all woken to the meteor shower far on the eastern horizon. "We're in the last days. We can't be the only displaced people on the highways."

When the strangers drew close enough to talk to, Rex raised his hand and smiled in greeting. He expected them to stop and talk, but instead, they just streamed past. Their clothes were worn, their shoes unworthy for the road, and their packs were too small to carry necessary provisions.

"Where are you coming from?" Chloe ventured at the downcast faces.

"Chicago," said a man with a bandage on his head. "We're not waiting for the OPT to crack down any further. Thousands are leaving the city."

The man drifted on with the flow of people.

"Excuse me." Rex grabbed a lone man in a tattered coat. The man stopped and looked up as if he was only now aware of strangers on the roadside. "What's the OPT?"

"Some new government." He had a backpack with a taped strap, which wouldn't last two days of stress. "Something Europe is organizing."

"Europe?" Chloe gasped. "Did they get satellite comms operating or something?"

"I don't know."

"What does OPT stand for?" she pressed

"I don't remember."

The man moved on.

"Can anyone tell us what's happening in Chicago?" Rex shouted over the heads of the last dozen travelers.

A young woman in a head scarf, her cheeks rosy from the march, drew up to Rex and Chloe. Her posture was straight, and her eyes were bright.

"What do you want to know?"

"What's this OPT? Some new government?" Rex gestured to the two hundred refugees. "We're from out east. We haven't heard."

"It's the One Planet Trust. I heard over the radio about it popping up. They're trying to unite the world under one government."

"One Planet Trust?" Chloe glanced at Rex, then stepped closer to the young lady. "They pushed you out of the city?"

"No, they were trying to keep us there. We're leaving voluntarily." She scoffed. "I didn't survive all these years just to get the mark of the beast now!"

"Mark of the beast?" Rex tilted his head. "You know the Book of Revelation?"

"Of course I do. I'm no fool. I know what's happening. First, they came with their Oath of Solidarity with the Meridia Virus vaccine, then they wanted to tell us which god to worship."

"You sound like you might be a Christian." Chloe held her hand out toward the refugees. "We're mostly Christians here."

"Then you don't want to go west or south." The woman hefted her pack farther up her back. "What I hear is the OPT is already pretty popular on the West Coast. It's a real craze, spreading by radio. Like before Pan-Day, everyone was calling for peace and unity. But it's not the kind of peace and unity that lasts forever. Know what I mean?"

"You don't want to go east, either!" Chloe stated. "Ohio is having Meridia Virus outbreaks, and the Federation kills all the Christians they can find. Your people need to know that."

Rex turned to see the travelers from Chicago walk steadily eastward.

"I don't know where else to go but east." The woman sighed. "What're you guys gonna do now?"

"Meeker is a quiet town in a remote part of Colorado." Rex nodded at Chloe. "We've got livestock, water, and plenty of room to avoid civilization."

"I don't think anyone's safe." The woman looked from Rex to Chloe. "I'm telling you, everything was fine for years. Then those with radios said they were talking to the West Coast, the south, and the East Coast. Everyone got excited about social recovery. It sounded like globalist talk that'll lead to that Anti-Christ guy. So, I heard others were leaving and I took off with them."

"I'm Rex Caspertein." Rex let his rifle hang on its sling. "You can call me Rex. This is Chloe. You shake?"

She checked the skin on his hand.

"You guys seem healthy." She gripped his hand and gave a hearty shake. "Miranda Nelson. You don't mind if I throw in with you guys then? Colorado sounds better than going east into the unknown."

"It's no trouble. We'll get back on the road in a few minutes, so rest your feet."

Rex watched her walk resolutely over to the two hundred and sit down next to Shailene Tharp, Taylor's wife. The two were immediately visiting, and Shailene introduced her to others seated nearby. Miranda was pretty, Rex admired, but he especially liked her outspoken attitude about the end times. She reminded him of Lyla Caspertein, Levi's wife who was killed weeks earlier by a Federation refugee. Although none of the young ladies in the group had caught his eye before, Miranda Nelson was someone that—

"Earth to Rex," Chloe called, and nudged his arm. "You heard what she said. We may not even be safe in Colorado. You know how those social movements before Pan-Day captured the hearts of every little town. If this OPT stuff is catching on, we could be dealing with a whole new problem."

"I wouldn't know where else to take us but back home to Meeker. What do you suggest?"

"Meeker. But we need to be ready for whatever this OPT stuff is all about. One Planet Trust? It really does sound like something straight out of the Bible, like your fiancée said."

"Miranda's not—" Rex held up his finger, unsuccessfully holding back his smile. "That's not fair, Chloe. I have other things to worry about."

"I'm glad one of us knows that," she teased, and walked onto the interstate to intercept the next wave of Chicago travelers. "I'm going to see what else I can find out. Go ahead without me. I'll catch up."

He waved his acknowledgement as she turned to walk beside leaders of the second group. They appeared as the first: undersupplied and unhealthy. Miranda was the healthiest Rex had noticed out of them all. They wouldn't make it a hundred miles, he guessed. Most of them would stop at the next ghost town, already exhausted. Although he wanted to warn them about dangers on the road ahead, he wasn't sure he had a better solution for them.

"Definitely the last days," he mumbled, and shouted to his shooters to come on in. It was almost twelve hundred miles to Meeker still. As if the miles weren't enough of an obstacle, now they had the OPT to avoid.

"I'm not that bright, Lord," he prayed as he walked into the field. "Give me the mouth and the marbles in my hard head to get everyone there safely."

☩

Rudy Caspertein cast the fly into the middle of Colorado's White River and let it drift down to a hole where he knew rainbow trout were hiding. He glanced at the sun and wiped his brow as the heat seemed to hinder the biting. It was time he headed back to town, anyway. The weekly Bible study for the Meeker community was out at Trapper Sullivan's ranch that evening, and he was leading the small group through the latter chapters of

Acts. A little more prayer before the presentation seemed in order.

Smiling, Rudy reeled in the fly, and realized that even when he could get alone like this with God, he didn't stop praying. Now approaching seventy, he'd learned the secret to peace and joy in a tumultuous world: constant communion with an omnipresent God.

Wagging a finger at the wily trout, he hooked the fly to the rod handle.

"Another day . . ."

He'd fished that part of the river a couple years earlier, so he knew there were fish there. However, he usually only caught and released. The fish all had cancer and worms, like most of the deer in the nearby ranges. Although the growths could be cut out, and the worms could be removed from the meat, Rudy couldn't bring himself to eat diseased meat, even though it was cooked well and probably safe. Twenty years earlier in Alaska, he'd eaten raw bear and seal meat, but those had been leaner times.

The lazy White River wound down the valley, creating great swaths, but Rudy cut across the field where one of the sheep dogs rose suddenly from a mid-morning nap and rousted the grazing sheep. Two other dogs stretched and yawned, then padded up to Rudy for a pat on their heads. With wolves and lions on the rise, the dogs had been raised from birth to guard the sheep, which, with the cattle on the plateau, were the livelihood of the town of Meeker, population six hundred. The four dogs were more vigilant than twenty human shepherds. They never took a day off, and their noses never stopped testing the wind.

Rudy was wondering how he could fit that into an analogy of God's vigilance and Christ's shepherding hand over His people—when he noticed Dathan Tentmaker's broad frame approaching him from town. Although Rudy was inches taller than the bearded black man, Dathan was an imposing figure and dependable leader in the community. Since Levi had recruited the ex-colonel out of the Federation, Dathan's faith had been steadily strengthened by other leaders in the local fellowship. His artistic skills—expressed in murals around town—left no one in Meeker ignorant of characters and stories in the Bible.

"Visitors in town," Dathan said once he was close enough. The man in his forties fell in beside Rudy. "Your wife sent me to bring you to the hotel."

"We've had visitors before." Rudy stopped and looked down at Dathan. "What kind of visitors? And why's my wife in town? She wasn't going into town today."

"They're people from Denver." Dathan shook his head. "You're not going to like what they're saying. Half the town is in the street or sitting on the courthouse lawn. Wayne Sullivan wants you there, too."

Rudy continued walking, his heading now toward town instead of toward the rimrock where he'd moved into a cabin with Annette, his brother's widow. They'd been married only six months, but she'd been a Christian and a Caspertein for over twenty years already, so their familiarity and closeness had blossomed without barriers.

"I'm no town leader." Rudy growled under his breath. "How many times do I have to tell them to leave me out of their administrations?"

"You might want to be in on this one." Dathan's legs were shorter, so he skipped every few steps to keep up. "You feed the town and keep them safe, so you're a leader whether you want to be or not."

Frowning, Rudy said nothing more until they reached Main Street and Hotel Meeker came into sight. People were crowded in front of the steps all the way across the street to the courthouse. Some of the buildings had been torn down and rebuilt since Pan-Day, but the courthouse and hotel remained, though the latter had been remodeled and needed fresh paint.

Five horses were hitched to the flagpole in front of the courthouse where someone had brought a few gallons of water for the animals. Rudy noticed three of the horses were saddled, and the other two carried packs. Three visitors with two pack horses? They must've been planning quite a trip with so much gear.

"What's going on, Mr. Caspertein?" asked a young man in the crowd. "Why are they here?"

"Tell them to go back to where they came from, Rudy!" ordered an older resident of Meeker. Her hair had fallen out, but Annette had made a wig for her from donated hair. "Tell them we're God-fearing, not man-fearing!"

Rudy touched the woman's shoulder in passing but said nothing.

The crowd parted for Rudy to approach the hotel, with Dathan on his heels. Near the front, he came upon Annette. Even in her sixties, she was still beautiful with dark, wavy hair and bold, piercing eyes. Rudy hadn't known her during her modeling days, but he wouldn't change anything about the woman she'd been—and the mother she'd become to everyone in White River Valley.

But Rudy read worry in her eyes. He bowed down to kiss her cheek, hoping to communicate some confidence to her, but he was a little unbalanced as well by the official visitors from Denver.

"Vorca?" He offered his fly pole to the hefty Native American woman somewhere in her early twenties. A toddler, who was at her side, had one hand in his mouth and the other held Vorca's plump hand. The woman had come from the mountains of California, but she still spoke no English. Only young Caleb, close to two-years-old, seemed to understand her native language, but Rudy had accepted her as one of the family when Levi had traveled east, leaving her and Caleb behind with them.

"Please, everyone!" Rudy raised his hand to the townspeople, many of whom were his employees, fellow Christians, and neighbors. Some he'd met only a year earlier, when a wave of refugees had arrived from the

Federation. Others, he'd taught Bible lessons to or baptized in the river. "Find some shade and water. I hope to come back in a few minutes with the answers you need."

With Dathan, Rudy followed his wife inside the hotel, which remained occupied by several permanent residents upstairs, but the downstairs had hosted small town parties. It was likely if the three visitors from Denver didn't want to stay with one of the families in town, they'd find comfortable lodging in the rooms above—even running water and electricity.

He found the small lobby, decorated with rugs and a head-mount of an elk, where the Meeker town council now stood against the wall. The council consisted of two men and two women, and Mayor Wayne Sullivan, the ambitious son of rancher Trapper Sullivan.

A woman with straight blonde hair that framed her stern face rose from a chair. A red and black cape was draped over her shoulders and reached down to her knees. It was covered in horsehair, but the visitor had a way about her that made her seem poised regardless. Immediately, she flipped the cape from her neck and held it out to a balding and muscled fifty-year-old man in army fatigues. Another man, also in fatigues, stood at her side. He was thinner with a severe underbite, causing his lower jaw to thrust forward.

"Finally. Rudy Caspertein, I presume?" she asked. "Then we can get started without repeating myself. I am Advocate Veronika Kane. These are my companions, Defender Imus and Defender Bisset."

"Wait." Rudy held up his hand. "I'm just coming in from the river, and you've been riding from a distance. I know I could use a seat while you tell me how both those men's first name is Defender."

"Can we get some more chairs brought in?" Mayor Sullivan asked his council members.

The formal woman folded her hands and waited as the room shuffled around and made space for folding chairs. In the commotion, Rudy leaned in to speak with the mayor.

"Anything you want to tell me, Wayne?"

The tall, slender man, usually with a ready smile, shook his head. Rudy had known him as a youth who had always followed the other boys, rarely taking initiative, especially in the shadow of Rex.

"The radio's been telling us people were coming from the capital, but not what they were coming for, so I didn't want to alarm anyone."

"Have you seen the street?" Rudy dropped his bulk into a chair. "They're alarmed, son."

"Now, as I was saying," the woman started again, still standing with her two men in fatigues, "I am Advocate Veronika Kane, and I am here to—"

"I'm sorry, Ms. Kane." Rudy held out his palms. "Maybe you're used to all this formality and whatnot, but I'm just an old Arkansas boy who needs to run through the pleasantries of introductions. If you've been waiting for us all to come together, and you're strangers from another place, that would make us the hosts and you the guests, wouldn't it?"

"Well . . ." Kane nodded once. "You are correct, Mr. Caspertein. We are your guests."

"Then why are you three standing there like you're some officials telling us what's what? Have a seat. Relax. Can we get you some water or something to eat?"

"Very well." Kane seated herself on the edge of an armchair that had as much dog hair on it as her cape had horsehair. The two in fatigues sat on folding chairs against the wall. "Does this please you, Mr. Caspertein?"

"Did the mayor offer you something to drink?"

"He did. And I will tell you what I told him. We have seventeen more towns to visit after this one. I'm sorry if I'm brisk, sir, but it's out of efficiency, not intentional impropriety."

"You're forgiven." Rudy grinned and offered his hand. "And call me Rudy. I'm nobody official, so you can drop the mister. Maybe I shouldn't even be here. Mayor Sullivan is capable of taking care of Meeker with the council."

"My purpose here," she said, acknowledging the mayor, then addressed Rudy directly, "extends beyond what is official. You were requested, sir, because you are a man of influence to guide the masses toward what is best for everyone."

"Guide the masses?" Rudy narrowed his eyes. "Interesting wording. I'm listening."

"Europe has successfully launched three geosynchronous communication satellites in an effort to restore communication with North America. Messages were relayed via HAM radios to the rest of us. Humanity is on the comeback, Mr., uh, Rudy. We are already decades ahead of pre-Pan-Day thinking. Society will be restructured in such a way that solidarity and science will fortify our success and our future. Nature and unity will light the way forward. We cannot afford to make the mistakes of the past. Advocates like myself are initiating the new plan, and Defenders like Imus and Bisset here will ensure every community that has survived the virus is uniquely ushered into the Trust."

"The Trust?" Rudy took a deep breath. "That sounds like a fraternity."

"It's a movement. Certainly not a government in the conventional sense. It's an agreement of solidarity, which Europe has proposed for all of humanity. It's unreasonable to reject what may be humanity's greatest potential and certain survival. There are some specifics regarding authority still being decided upon, but I've been given the responsibility to inform western Colorado of the opportunities of working together with the international community once again. Denver is even preparing a fleet of vehicles to help us meet more frequently, so we won't have to rely on horses much longer."

"Interesting." Rudy leaned back in the chair, its hinges creaking. From his peripheral vision, he noticed that everyone seemed to be watching him for a reaction. "You're using very careful wording, I understand, and I appreciate your . . . frankness."

"Thank you, Rudy."

"It's been my experience that movements don't come with authority—unless there's a consequence involved for going against the movement. What's the consequence of not going along with the movement?"

"Well . . ." Kane glanced at the others. "The consequences for not standing with those who seek life would naturally be death. No one would ever want that. What we're offering is too good to refuse. Anyone who doesn't want to be involved with the OPT must not want to live in support of the planet."

"The OPT?" Rudy tilted his head.

"One Planet Trust."

"Interesting. And whoever doesn't want to go along with the OPT automatically chooses to die? The OPT will enforce that somehow?"

"No one would ever choose that, Rudy." The woman scoffed. "The OPT is a way of life that improves everything around the world. New governments are adopting the Oath without any difficulty. Reports are flooding in of its success. The Oath ensures the survival of us all."

"Survival from death?" Rudy frowned. "What is the Oath?"

"It's the Oath of Solidarity." Kane offered Rudy a manila envelope. "We're providing two laminated copies for every community to start with. We're asking that everyone in your town takes the Oath. I'm here to appoint one OPT Advocate and one OPT Defender to coordinate this community's transition. We're hoping you will volunteer to be the Advocate, Rudy."

"Interesting." Rudy opened the envelope and withdrew two laminated pages. He passed one to Mayor Sullivan and held up the second so Annette and Dathan could read it with him.

One Planet Trust (OPT)

An international movement to unite the people of the world in social recovery.

Oath of Solidarity:

1. Solidarity unlocks humanity's greatest potential and survival.
   (Rejecting solidarity is rejecting humanity.)

2. Science determines our hope in the future stability of our race.
   (Denying hope in science is a denial of a future.)

3. Success is the evidence of our unity.
   (Refusing to participate in success is refusing to unify.)

4. Death is the logical penalty to rejecting life.
   (Refusing to uphold the OPT Oath of Solidarity will result in exclusion from markets, medicine, and the rest of mankind.)

"Unity will light the way!"

"So, there's a death penalty attached to refusing the Oath." Rudy passed the page to Annette and folded his hands in his lap. "A death penalty for not joining up with this . . . movement. Sounds a lot like the days before Pan-Day, when society and the press destroyed your name, business, and your family if you didn't go along with whatever movement someone was demonstrating for or against."

"Well, this is different." Kane lowered her head. "To reject the Oath is to reject life. You read it all, right? Every day, we either choose life or we choose death. By standing on this Oath, we agree together to make these principles our common bond."

"Oh, yes, I read it all. It's concise and transparent." Rudy pressed his lips together, hoping he didn't make a scene, but realizing he couldn't ignore what was being presented to his friends and family. "I'm probably the least likely to volunteer to be an OPT Advocate for Meeker, Colorado."

"Why? I don't understand. You're in a position to help this community see the wisdom of embracing the next age of humanity. You could begin by taking a census of OPT Oath-takers."

"If I affirm the points of this Oath, I'd be rejecting the opposite position."

"What's so wrong with that?"

"Well, for one, I don't believe that solidarity unlocks humanity's greatest potential or survival. I think that's ridiculous."

"What?" Kane blinked, her pale skin turning a shade darker.

"Yeah, I believe Jesus Christ came as the Son of God in the flesh and unlocked humanity's potential through the Holy Spirit—our survival beyond sin and death through the gift of eternal life."

"Bah!" blurted the woman, then she covered her mouth and recovered her composure. "But that's so absurd! I mean, Jesus is a fairy tale. You're welcome to enjoy any beliefs you want, even if it's in Jesus, but not at the expense of the safety of others."

"Exactly. You see my hope in the God of the Bible to be a contradiction to humanity's safety and hope in itself. I agree. The two are mutually exclusive. Both cannot coexist."

"But, then, you don't believe in science as the answer to our race's stability? What about the Meridia Virus? The environment and the longevity of life?"

"Ms. Kane, I'm a scientist, a leading seismologist on the world stage when the virus was dropped on us. What you're calling science is an attempt to make sense of laws in the physical universe. The origin of the study of science was an exercise to better understand the God who set those laws in motion. Science explains how and what happens, but the Word of God reveals who makes science happen, who holds all things together, and why He created everything. Again, my hope is in the Originator of science, not the processes the Creator put in order. That would be like falling in love with the picture of my wife instead of my wife in person."

Kane opened her mouth twice, but closed it and raised her head, apparently struggling to find the words.

"Maybe I can help you," Dathan said from behind Rudy. "I was part of the Appalachian Federation until a year ago. The Federation has said for nearly twenty years what this Oath says. Different words, but it's the same idea. None of these ideas actually work, and now you're trying to do this on a global level? These people took me in. This town would've died a long time ago if not for the Christian love that has been shown to every person in Meeker. You are not our enemy, uh, Advocate Kane, even though you choose to trust in humanity's ideas or sciences. We hope you don't see us as an enemy because we choose to continue to care for this community with the love and grace of Jesus Christ."

"You're my new public relations manager!" Rudy slapped Dathan's knee. "Couldn't have said it better myself."

"Do these two men speak for your whole community?" Kane asked, gazing intently at Mayor Sullivan. "The community of Meeker refuses to even receive OPT appointees? You have no idea how perplexing this is. Over sixty towns in Colorado have been reached with this good news, and you're the first and only community refusing to coordinate medicine and trade with us?"

"Correction," Annette said. "I'm sorry, but that's not true. We're not refusing anything but to agree where your hope rests. You're the one who is telling us that our view of the Creator isn't allowed."

"Uh, Rudy?" Mayor Sullivan rose to his feet. "No offense, everyone, but as elected mayor of Meeker, I'd like to hear Ms. Kane out."

Rudy nodded.

"Then I don't think I'm necessary here any longer. Ms. Kane, any expenses, supplies, or room and board you need, I'll cover the cost as long as you're in Meeker." Rudy stood and held his hand out to Annette. "I have a Bible study tonight with your father, Mayor. You remember the family and neighbors around you as you agree to take an Oath to put the rest of us to death."

Dathan started to rise, but Rudy set a heavy hand on his friend's shoulder, forcing him to stay in his seat. The two men locked eyes for a moment, and Dathan seemed to understand. Rudy wanted him to stay and listen, and give his report to him later.

In the hallway to the front door, Annette pulled Rudy to a stop where they were alone.

"What are we going to do?" she whispered.

"Warn the people. Stand for Jesus. And live until they kill us." Rudy shrugged. "We really don't have to change anything about what we've always done."

"The whole world is . . . uniting! It's prophecy." She touched her fingertips to her lips. "The boys—our boys—will be coming back to all of this?"

"Rex and Levi know their Bibles." Rudy embraced his wife. "And they're Casperteins. If this OPT wants to tackle Rex and Levi when they roll into town, that's their choice. And just for the record, if that happens, I wouldn't put my money on the OPT."

Chapter Two

Lena Travers focused her eye as she looked through Levi's battle rifle scope. The stock of the weapon was stained with the man's sweat and blood from the last year of turmoil and travel.

"He's almost within range," Levi said from where he lay prone beside her. "Wind's at about three knots from the west. You've got this."

Auggie, Runner's Labrador, lay on the other side of her. The dog's head was up, fully alert, facing her with ears perked. Runner had trained the canine to hunt, but Lena had never owned a more affectionate dog. The cold night before, as she and Levi had spent the night in the forest without good shelter, Auggie had lain between man and woman, licking their faces while they laughed.

Perfectly framed in the rifle scope, Runner walked up the rural, forested highway. They were somewhere in the Great Smokey Mountains of southeastern Tennessee, and Runner was still pursuing them. Even though Levi had stripped the bounty hunter of his possessions and weapons, the hunter had made more. Lena could see through the scope that he now carried a walking stick, and the stick appeared to be sharpened on the upper end.

She pulled the trigger. The rifle boomed, and Auggie yelped and flinched away.

"Auggie?" Lena reached for the Lab, who returned to her side, head down and tail between her legs. "Aah-ah."

The dog licked her face, returning Lena's reassurance that she was still loved regardless of the rifle's loud noise.

"Focus, Lena," Levi said, his brow steady against a pair of binoculars. Since they'd left their packs with

Nathan and the horse, they had only bare essentials. "It looks like you hit him in the lower leg or foot. You didn't gauge for distance, but you hit him somewhere, because he's not getting up."

Lena checked her target through the scope.

"Aah."

What a shot—nearly six hundred yards! It was twice the distance she'd ever fired a rifle in the Army before Pan-Day, or for the Federation the last few years. And now with gel-tranqs—at a moving target!

"All right. Let's get going while the gettin's good." Levi climbed to his feet.

Lena gave him his rifle and ruffled Auggie's hair. The dog returned to her wagging personality.

"Auggie!" Lena shouted, and gestured with her arm for the dog to go hunt. "Gah!"

The dog spun around, maybe even smiling, and raced into the forest.

"This guy's not giving up." Levi stuffed his binoculars into his vest pocket as he eyed the northern mountain ranges. There was smoke up there. Far away, a forest fire was burning across the ridge. "We've tranqed him twice in the last two days. What more do we need to do for him to get the message?"

They walked side by side down the highway. Lena was content in not responding to the man who had saved her life three times now. First, he'd nursed her through her face injury after Colonel Milo Rotham had shot her. Then he'd saved her from being whipped to death in Allentown. Finally, he had rescued her from the mountaintop above Erwin, where Runner had held her as bait, his tomahawk against her neck.

She was content not to speak because she'd come to realize that God had given her a gift by taking her mouth from her. The gift had been for her silence, her brokenness. No longer could she argue, protest, curse, or command. Now, she submitted to Levi's lead and trusted

God's sovereign hand. With every book of the Bible she read, she felt more connected to God's people historically, all because of her new abnormality. God had allowed her to lose her mouth, and since God was loving and sovereign, she knew now that losing her mouth was for her best.

The highway wound out of the mountains from where they could see the green forests of North Carolina and the rolling valleys of Georgia. On the southern slope of the mountains, the highway split at a crossroads. The roadway had been swept clean of needles, leaves, and dirt, leaving the Christian symbol of a fish pointing farther south rather than at the highway to the east.

"They've got their reasons," Levi said as he joined Lena in erasing the sign Nathan had left for them. He'd previously left other signs as well. "It ain't easy going south when you're trying to go west, but they have our gear, so we're bound to follow them."

"Aah."

Going over to the other highway, Lena knelt to create a new sign on the road. Levi stood over her, hands on his hips a moment, before he joined her.

"I don't care if you refuse to talk to me," he joked. "Your brains more than make up for your silence. If we can't discourage Runner, maybe we can misdirect him."

Lena was thrilled that he understood her idea without needing to explain. They'd left the last two fish signs in place. Now, the one they'd leave in place would hopefully convince Runner he was still tracking them successfully.

They spent a few more minutes leaving obvious tracks in the western direction, then cut through the trees to rejoin the southern route of their friends. Instead of walking down the middle of the road, they strolled together along the shoulder where Levi pointed out different plants, edible or medicinal, sometimes collecting them to put in his pocket. Lena gathered linden flowers for tea and oak bark for a concoction to use on their feet at night. Levi seemed to know endless remedies, but he said his mother and wife were the real experts.

That evening, they strung up a hide off the highway behind an abandoned garage where Levi could keep an eye on their backtrail and Lena could wash in a brook through the trees.

Barefooted, Lena returned from the brook and built a small fire. Auggie brought in a rabbit to add to the squirrel that Lena had shot around noon. She skinned the animals and put them on a spit. Then she tried to apply the oak ointment to her feet while Auggie licked it off.

"As far as I can tell, he's nowhere back there," Levi reported as he returned from the highway. "It's too dark now, so once we're finished with the fire, we'll douse it to make sure he's not able to track us here while we're sleeping. Maybe we really threw him off. I watched the highway where I could see for miles, and nothing was moving at all."

Levi had spoken most of the day, so he seemed content to sit quietly and stare at the fire as Lena pulled the Bible from her coat and read to herself. This business in the Book of Philippians was something she wanted to ponder. *Everything that was gain was really loss?* Lena could relate to that. The Bible was an ancient book, but it was still a book about her whole life.

They put out the fire and called Auggie to lay between them. Auggie was thrilled to be the center of attention, but Lena felt a yearning in her own heart to be closer to Levi. The dog was between them for warmth, but also because Levi was a married man. By summer's end, Levi and Lyla would be reunited in Meeker, and Lena would be left alone once again. Maybe she'd only have Auggie for the rest of her life. The following day, they'd probably catch up with Nathan and the others, and she'd no longer have Levi to herself.

She prayed to God that He would help purify her desires, and hugged Auggie even closer. Auggie licked her tears in return, and the three slept soundly.

Nathan led his party of four and their pack horse into the mountain community of Ellijay, Georgia. Outside the town surrounded by low mountain ridges, the travelers found orchards of apples, but they weren't in season. Nevertheless, signs that must've been posted in the last year—since their paint was still bright—welcomed visitors into Ellijay for cider, seasonal produce, and wines.

The town buildings were spread out, and there was no hint of fire damage or looting from the recent or distant past. The few people about didn't seem afraid of the four as they passed a church with a steeple and moved into the center of the town. A hitching post had been fashioned on the side of one street where a type of general store was manned, its front door open. Horse manure littered the otherwise clean street, so Nathan guessed their mare wasn't the only horse around, and he wouldn't need to defend her from locals who had a taste for horse meat.

"Levi can't be far behind now, right?" Chen Li asked as she cautiously eyed the dozen townspeople in sight.

"No, not far now." Nathan caught Brian's eye, and nodded at his rifle. "Let's see what we can trade for food and information, huh, Chen Li?"

He held out his hand to his wife, and she took it as they stepped away.

"We'll stay with the horse," Brian volunteered for Jenna, but Nathan noticed the man hook his thumb under the sling of his old rifle on his shoulder. "Don't be long."

Before Nathan went into the general store, he wanted a better look around the town. He was a little irritated that his friends seemed so eager for Levi to rejoin them, as if Nathan couldn't handle whatever Levi could. However, he found himself imagining how Levi would naturally read a town by a few pieces of information. Humbling himself, Nathan admitted to himself that Levi had a slightly better instinct with these things. What seemed safe, could actually be a trap. What seemed dangerous, could actually be friendly. During their previous adventures together, he'd noticed that Levi would use all possible situations—even his own blunders—for the glory of God.

Between buildings, many of them in disrepair, evergreen trees were growing, and more apple trees sprinkled the lawns of old businesses. Judging by the people outside and the houses where locals frequented, no more than a hundred people probably lived in Ellijay.

"What do you think?" Nathan stopped Chen Li in front of an old travel agency office where a sign now read, "Ellijay OPT Administration." The red letters were punctuated by a large arrow pointing at the open door. "Seems pretty quiet, huh?"

"Seems so. A pretty town. They even removed all the cars we usually see rusting along streets."

"Towed them all west of town," a voice said. It belonged to a young man who stood against the door frame of the administration office. He had gray eyes, was clean-shaven, and wore suspenders. "Ellijay has its share of challenges, but I'm glad you've noticed that we've made an effort to take care of her."

Another man, older and taller, his hair in a ponytail, exited the office and stood against the outside of the building. Nathan didn't miss the semi-automatic handgun in a leather holster on his hip.

"My name's Nathan. This is my wife, Chen Li. We're passing through, heading west, hoping to stock up on food supplies. We have a few things to trade."

Nathan thought of Levi's large pack of supplies on the horse, which gave them an abundance. They had an extra pair of field glasses, a skinning knife, a pair of trousers, and a wind-up watch. Though Nathan had been collecting lighters along the way, he wasn't ready to trade them yet.

"We'd be glad to help you out. I'm OPT Advocate Carter." He offered his hand to Nathan, who shook it. "This is Miller, OPT Defender of the Oath. You understand we'll need to trade under the OPT regulations."

Chen Li squeezed his hand, whether intentional or not, Nathan didn't know.

"Those are terms I'm not familiar with," Nathan said, "but I'm a Christian man. We submit to the laws of the land."

"You're a Christian?" The one that Carter had called Defender Miller stood up a little straighter. "So, are you Servalites?"

"Servalites?" Nathan frowned and tilted his head. "Hmm, I've never heard that word before. No, I'm not a Servalite."

"How long have you guys been on the road?" Carter asked. His hands appeared manicured, and his gray eyes took on a shrewd gaze.

Immediately, Nathan glanced back down the street at the horse where Brian and Jenna were sitting on the curb. Something indeed was amiss in Ellijay, and Brian wasn't on his feet to help him. Levi would've been alert and prepared!

"A few weeks." Nathan let go of Chen Li's hand so he could flip his rifle into action if necessary. "There was a town burning up in Tennessee, and some travelers a few days back needed burial. We were hoping to avoid whatever strife there was along the way. Maybe you'd better tell us what this OPT is."

"I'd rather show you. It's a pretty simple Oath." Carter walked into the office and returned seconds later with a laminated page. "There were some religious people called Servalites who came through here the last few weeks. They refused to take the Oath, and since I'm the OPT Advocate, I called on Miller here to arrest them. It's been a difficult but necessary adjustment—for the greater good. It's the new normal, like they used to say about how the virus forced us to change our lives, but not everyone is finding their place. I'm sure you'll have no problem."

Nathan accepted the laminated Oath and held it with Chen Li as they read the four points to themselves. A great sinking feeling developed within his chest as he read about the One Planet Trust's standard for solidarity, science, success, and the penalty for rejecting the Oath.

He felt Chen Li's eyes on his face, probably wondering how he was going to react. There was no question that they couldn't agree to such a pledge. The only question was, how were they supposed to get out of town without being arrested?

"So, you two are this OPT's representatives?" Nathan passed the Oath sheet back to Carter.

"Every town has an Advocate and Defender, and everyone who's taken the Oath already has agreed to uphold it. We all have to stand together. You understand."

"What happened to those people you arrested recently?" Nathan asked. "You called them Servalites?"

"There's a basement we use for holding people. Our jail fell apart years ago. So, we held them for a few days. Two others we've held a little longer." Carter's eyes narrowed. "The Oath is clear about the penalty. We're just trying to stick to regulations and hoping others comply so it doesn't put us in a bad place."

"And this bad place, uh, means you kill these, uh . . .?"

"Servalites," Miller said. "And it wasn't our decision to execute them. They insisted by their own free will to die by refusing to take the Oath. It's practically a compass-sionate execution we give them. I say strangle them. Carter prefers hanging. Some of the people said to do it by stoning, so the rest of the town is part of the enforcing. We're learning together."

"Enforcing." Nathan took a breath. "The Appalachian Federation has laws like this, imposed by people called Enforcers. They called the thousands of people they killed executions as well."

"You're not going to take the Oath, are you?" Miller asked in a low voice.

Pausing, Nathan measured the man's posture, guessing the next words out of his mouth would mean life or death. After all his years in violent lands, it was coming down to this quiet town to call him to stand for God or fall for man. He swallowed slowly, praying in his heart for God to give him strength for whatever came.

"No, I'm not going to—"

Chen Li stepped back as Miller reached for his holster. Nathan flipped the rifle off his shoulder and swung it level. But Miller was faster. He fired twice into Nathan's body at point-blank range. Stumbling backwards from the impact, Nathan found his body wasn't cooperating as he tried to keep his balance. A vacant feeling of loss seemed to bore through his insides. The back of his head hit the pavement, and when he looked down at himself, he saw blood oozing from his chest.

Miller stepped closer, his gun aimed at Chen Li, but he held his fire and roughly confiscated Nathan's rifle.

Nathan gasped as Chen Li huddled over him, weeping and calling his name, her small hands inadequate to stop the blood pouring out of him.

"There's . . . no pain." Nathan panted, resting his head on the ground. "I'm . . . paralyzed, Chen Li . . ."

"Don't move, Nate!" Chen Li's mouth fumbled for words. "I just have to—"

Brian's rifle boomed from down the street, and Advocate Carter was struck hard, then he fell.

Miller charged down the street, firing his pistol until he also was tranquilized by Brian. Nathan's head rolled left and right, watching the scene unfold, but in a strangely detached way. He was dying. This was it. It was his turn to go where billions had gone before him. Only Chen Li . . .

Townspeople were running toward them, some with weapons. Brian was close, but now he retreated to the horse and Jenna. No, the horse was down, kicking through its own death struggle. It must have been struck by a bullet. Jenna tentatively felt her way out into the street where Brian reached her and took her hand. In a hurry to flee with her, Brian turned too quickly, and Jenna went down. Hardly stopping, Brian pulled the blind woman over his shoulder and ran away.

An instant later, the townspeople were upon Nathan and Chen Li. Two other men stood close to Nathan's head where they were aiming hunting rifles at him. Others ran down the street in pursuit of Brian and Jenna.

"Don't fight them. I love you, Chen Li," Nathan mumbled to her as she cried and held out her hand to him while people were dragging her away.

He stared at the sky. It was blue. Tears ran from his eyes, but he smiled. It wasn't that bad. Eternity awaited. He'd made it. He was going to meet his Lord. This was the end. And the beginning. The others would come soon . . .

Andy Radner missed his dog, Runner, but that wasn't why there were tears in his eyes. He wiped furiously at the moisture on his face, then hobbled a few more steps down the highway. His foot caught on a crack in the pavement, and he pitched forward. As he fell, he tossed clear a spear he'd fashioned from a walking stick and his crutch that he'd cut from a forked branch. The sticks clattered across the debris-strewn highway, and he landed hard on his hands, bruising his palms.

He rolled onto his side and lay there staring at his palms as the aches from his whole body made him feel like giving up. Levi Caspertein was to blame for every woe he felt—from his loss of property to his broken foot.

The top of his foot had been struck by a single tranquilizer round, but since he wore soft-soled, hide boots, sewn by his own hand, the impact of the gelatin bullet hadn't just tranquilized him—it had also broken a small bone in his foot! Walking on it was excruciating.

To make matters worse, the branch he'd cut and made into a crutch to help him walk had rubbed his armpit raw. And he was starving. He couldn't track Levi and gather food at the same time. Both activities would've been difficult for a healthy person, but he was now far from healthy. Hungry, lonely, bruised, broken, and exhausted, he closed his eyes, wishing he would've never taken the contract to kill Levi Caspertein and Jenna Dowler.

It wasn't fair that he'd had so much bad luck since leaving New York. A few times, he'd felt the exhilaration of the hunt and the rapture of power with his prey so close. But mostly, he'd experienced loss. Now, he had nothing. He was lucky Levi had left him with his moccasin boots!

Andy sat up and stared at his throbbing left foot. It was swollen to the point that he dared not untie the laces to examine it. From the swelling, he might never get the boot on again, and how would he move without a boot? Then he'd need two crutches, not just one!

The Christians were going to Meeker, Colorado. He remembered Jenna Dowler admitting that much to her travel companions a couple weeks earlier, when Andy had joined their band as if he were a common traveler. Nathan, Levi, and the others weren't moving westward too swiftly, but it was still too fast for Andy with his broken foot. But he didn't want to go back west! Colorado was just one state south of where he'd been raised in Wyoming. After more than two years of proving himself as a deadly bounty hunter, he'd finally arrived in the east. Why return home?

To kill. He realized that was the only answer. The Federation might never allow him to receive citizenship and the status he wanted if he returned to New York without completing the job he'd been sent to do. That Colonel Rotham who'd given him his targets wasn't a merciful man. Andy had been just a little intimidated by him back at the Bowery. He didn't want to test the man's patience against the failure of a very clear order: put Levi Caspertein and Jenna Dowler in the ground.

Thinking of how life was so cruel, Andy brushed his hands over the weeds that grew from cracks in the pavement. He'd run away from River Camp to become a mighty man in the east. Now, he was just a weed, tranquilized as often as Levi wanted. Like a weed, he was at the mercy of the man he wished to kill.

In his fury, he tore at a blade of grass and plucked it out by the root. He tossed it onto the surface of the highway and watched it lie there. That was him. Just a weed. Helpless now that he had no supplies or mobility.

Sighing, he realized what he had to do to survive, even if it was humiliating. He needed to crawl into the forest and recuperate. With what he would find in the trees, he could rebuild his life, even though it would mean abandoning the hunt for Levi and Jenna. If he set traps for rabbits and mice, picked the right plants, and found a water source, he would regain his health in a matter of weeks.

Rather than walk like a man, he crawled off the highway into the ditch. He took his spear and crutch with him—his only possessions besides a few plants he'd collected and stuffed into his clothes. In the ditch, he plucked from a pocket the bulbs of a death camas plant, like a small onion. Poisoning Levi was off the table. Now, he'd need to collect wild potatoes and edible leaves for himself—anything that would sustain him. And a shelter— something with a roof would keep him dry during the next rain.

Then he saw them. Two travelers on the highway coming from the east. Andy lay flat off the pavement in the grass. He shifted his wooden spear to his right hand. With his left, he tossed his crutch a few feet away onto the pavement. The crutch had been obviously fashioned by someone's hand, and it would draw a traveler to it, like bait.

Andy licked his lips. Even crippled on one foot, he was still a devious predator. Even if he couldn't travel right now, he could still ambush travelers, take their gear, and roll their bodies into the mud on the other side of the highway. Yes, this would be easier than setting loop-snares for rabbits in the woods. People were dumber and easier prey. They'd have food and gear!

The two drew closer. Andy studied them. A middle-aged man with a gnarled face and light beard, and a boy of about ten. Both had packs and walking sticks, but Andy guessed if he could catch the man by surprise . . .

He poised lower in the grass, his chin on the ground, his hand wrapped around the end of the spear, ready to thrust.

"It doesn't matter, Willy," the man said. "Real men aren't afraid of that kind of work, even if it takes a year to finish. What's this here? Someone must've dropped it."

Holding his breath, Andy lunged forward. The man was close, approaching the crutch. Thousands of times while growing up, Andy had used spears for play or for hunting. He was proficient with any handheld weapon. But at that split second, his spear tip glanced off the man's own walking stick, blocking Andy's thrust altogether.

Realizing his mistake, Andy rolled over and positioned himself for another strike. But now he'd lost the element of surprise, and the man was armed with his own staff.

"Willy, stay back!" the man shouted as both travelers danced away. He held his staff in both hands, his forearms thick and his shoulders muscled. "Call out if you see any others."

"There's no one, Dad. What should I do?"

"Take off your pack, son, and set it in the next lane. Free yourself of the burden."

The father dropped his own pack and circled to the right, well out of reach of Andy's spear. He rose to his knees, suddenly noticing the way the man held his staff. This traveler wasn't afraid.

"I'm ready, Dad!" Willy shouted, the wiry boy bravely holding his smaller walking stick like his father held his. "What now?"

Andy glanced left and right, measuring the father's intentions. He'd positioned Andy between the two, and he could do nothing about it since he couldn't maneuver on his feet.

"When I go for him, Willy," the father said, "you strike from your side. Don't get too close! You just let him have it as soon as your old man moves in. You ready?"

Gasping at their brashness, Andy couldn't believe they were voicing their strategy aloud, but the father seemed to understand that their ambusher wasn't worthy of fear. Now, Andy accepted that he'd become the defender and not the attacker. On his knees, he shuffled backwards farther, trying to keep them both in front of him. But the man waded into the grass of the ditch and closed in on the right. The boy, with fear on his face, gulped nervously and drew nearer on the left.

Desperately, Andy thrust at the man's thick legs. It was a wild attempt, but he was cornered. The man slammed his staff against his leg, trapping Andy's spear against his shin. With his other leg, the man kicked firmly, snapping Andy's spear in the middle like a hinge.

Faster than Andy could flinch away, the boy struck him a glancing blow to the skull.

"That's how you do it, Willy!" the father praised, and ripped Andy's spear completely away from him. "Again! Let him have it, boy!"

Andy raised his arms to ward off the blows, but the boy was an expert batter. When Andy guarded his head, the youth swung horizontally at his torso. When Andy guarded his torso, the staff walloped his head.

Finally, after a dozen bruising blows, one landed hard on Andy's left ear. He sprawled into the grass at the edge of the highway, his sense of direction and balance completely lost.

The man was on him in an instant, rolling Andy onto his belly and shoving his face into the dirt. Choking on roots, Andy felt the boy attack his legs as the man tied his wrists behind his back.

"That's good, Willy." The traveler stepped back, then dragged Andy roughly into the highway. "Let him know you're in control. Cursed bushwhackers have no respect for anyone."

The boy wearied of beating Andy, and Andy had ceased to respond to the battery. His broken foot was now one wound among two-dozen welts and bruises—too many to feel individually.

"You handled him like a real man, Willy." The man patted his son on the shoulder. "I'm proud of you. He didn't have a chance, once you started on him."

"Yeah. He didn't have a chance!" The boy gripped and re-gripped his staff. "Now what?"

Andy barely breathed as he lay on his side, blood leaking across his face from his ear and cheek.

The man knelt next to him and jabbed him in the shoulder.

"What's your name?"

"Andy."

He closed his eyes. Why had he told him his real name? He'd been telling everyone he was Runner for two years. And now, he was supposed to be Fire Runner! There was no fear to be had by the name of Andy!

"Well, Andy, I'm Dwight Storch, and this is my son, Willy. You done picked the wrong victims on this highway, boy. It just so happened that our packs were getting heavy. Come on. On your feet."

"I can't!" Andy tried to shake off the man's firm grip on his buckskin shirt. In an instant, he was upright, standing on one foot, the other supporting little weight. "My foot's broken."

"Not too broken to keep from attacking strangers." He gestured to his son. "Willy, get your pack."

"No, I can't walk!" Andy shrieked.

But Dwight slapped him into submission, then strapped the boy's pack onto his front, and a heavier pack onto his shoulders. Still, Andy's hands were tightly bound behind his back.

"There!" Dwight laughed. "How's he look, son?"

"Like a mule."

"Please, I—"

"Quiet!" Dwight raised the end of his staff threateningly. "Not another peep! Mules don't complain. You'll carry what we give you, or Willy won't stop giving you the business end of his walking stick. Will you, Willy?"

"I'll give him the business, Dad!"

"If you don't march, I'll beat you myself. Now, get! Willy, keep him moving."

Andy's eyes bulged as the boy whacked the back of his legs. Limping forward, a cry escaped Andy's throat. The weight on his broken foot sent splintering pain shooting up his calf.

"That's how you do it, Willy. Stay on him. Get him moving like that team of horses the Howards used to have. Let him know who's boss."

The boy hit him again, but Andy didn't respond. He just limped ahead faster. Andy blinked through the tears, the road barely visible through his anguish. The weight on his slender frame threatened to fold his spine in two and buckle his knees. Trying to ignore the pain in his foot and everywhere else, he vaguely realized he was moving west.

Maybe he would intercept Levi after all. But unless he could free himself of his present horrors, he'd be in no shape to face the wily blond man who'd broken his foot in the first place!

On a cool, sunny morning, Rex Caspertein knelt in the green grass beside Interstate 80 south of Chicago. Abandoned houses and burned buildings littered the otherwise empty landscape. But in the median between east and westbound lanes, the two hundred refugees huddled in hiding.

"They're all going east," Alice reported in his ear through the comm.

Rex could see the six armored vehicles as well, all laden with men brandishing assault rifles. They were moving slowly up the on-ramp to the interstate. He guessed they were giving chase to those who'd fled their city. The One Planet Trust seemed to take the rejection of their Oath very personal.

"Caspertein!" Milo Rotham called from behind Rex.

Turning his head, Rex acknowledged the ex-colonel of the Federation pointing up the median. Other refugees looked as well, and several cried out. The Chicago Defenders of the OPT hadn't turned toward them, or seemed to even notice them, but a toddler had escaped his parents' clutches. The child of two or three years was bundled in several layers of clothing and was running toward the open freeway!

"Rotham!" Rex snapped his fingers. "Get him!"

The limber man darted in a crouch up the median. Rex checked the distance between the child and the convoy of six vehicles, now a quarter-mile away. But if any of the soldiers looked back . . .

Rex signaled with one hand for the refugees to huddle lower on the ground among their possessions. Even the goats and horses had been coaxed to lie on their sides where they were comforted with gentle words by their owners. Only the COIL personnel with rifles in their hands remained on their knees. The people had bunched up when they'd stopped walking, so they weren't strung out like usual. This way, it was easier for him to give orders to them as one. Alice was the only person out of sight, a little northward, and he had her on the comm.

"Get ready," Rex stated to his marksmen. He knew they were already prepared, but that was his way of letting them know he saw no way around the inevitable conflict, since Rotham was about to be seen recovering the child.

When the shooters among the refugees nodded their readiness, Rex's eyes fell upon Miranda Nelson, the tall Chicago native whose bold eyes stared back at him.

"I can shoot," she said from where she lay on the ground next to the goats, Ruth and Naomi. "Give me a rifle, and you'll see I can shoot."

"When the shooting starts," Rex hollered for the people, "Miranda will guide you behind the shooters. Stay together!"

She nodded, accepting her orders. He wouldn't have minded the thirty-year-old survivalist at his side with a rifle, but they had no more COIL rifles. Instead, she could lead the others so his riflemen could focus on their defense.

Rex faced east in time to see the toddler wander far out into the middle lane of the interstate. The child might not have been noticed, but now Rotham was darting out to recover the wayward youngster.

The brake lights of the last vehicle went red. They'd been spotted. It didn't matter that they weren't the escapees from Chicago the armed men were looking for. Rex understood that in these last days in America, anyone who didn't side with a world order would be deemed a threat. The OPT wasn't to be denied absolute control over the hearts and minds of the people.

"That's it!" Rex rose to his feet. There was no point hiding now. "Miranda, move everyone west over that embankment. Now! Go, everyone, move!"

They all scrambled, except for his shooters and the parents of the child that Rotham was returning with, the boy wailing in his arms.

"Chloe, I want you far on our right flank." Rex pointed south. "Everyone else, spread out between me and Chloe. Hold your fire unless you have a clear shot to tranq someone."

He ejected the gel-tranq magazine from his battle rifle and inserted a magazine from his vest—a full clip of phosphorus acid rounds from the arsenal Levi had brought from San Diego.

"Alice, we're setting up a firing line," Rex notified through the comm as he walked onto the interstate. "I'll be hitting them with phos first. How's your angle on our left flank?"

"Not great, but I can see them turning around toward you."

"Bruno, Scooter!" Rex called to the older veterans. "Flank them on the right. Taylor and Hank, watch over the families. Alice, try to get behind them once I stop their convoy."

Scooter and Bruno jogged off to the right, beyond Chloe, who was retying her hair under her hat, preparing for battle.

Rex kneeled on the pavement and rested his elbow on his knee. He steadied his breathing, trying to set aside the pressure of protecting his people from certain death. The one hundred Christians with him would never take the OPT Oath. They'd withstood the cages and threats of the Federation, so he was certain they wouldn't succumb to the latest demands for loyalty to science or nature or worship of humanity.

He fired the first phos round at the leading armored vehicle's left tire. The tire blew and the plated car swerved and stopped.

As the second vehicle, a Suburban, came into sight, Rex shot its front left tire as well. It was pulled into the first vehicle, and a medium-speed collision reached his ears. The other four vehicles swung wide around the first two, gaining speed at just over three hundred yards.

Continuing with the phos rounds, he shot the third, fourth, and fifth vehicles, but they kept driving within two hundred and fifty yards before they lurched and veered across the lanes. Axles were broken. Engines were smoking. Drivers could no longer control their vehicles as gears ground to a halt.

Only the sixth vehicle, a Humvee, was unscathed, yet it was behind the litter of disabled vehicles. Rex didn't have a shot at where it was parked. As soon as he saw soldiers piling out of their vehicles, he ran to the north side of the interstate for better cover.

Sean Harris, Nick Zoft, and Chloe opened fire. As soon as Rex switched back to gel-tranqs, he sighted through his scope at the gunmen he could spot from his angle. However, he held his fire for a few more seconds as the three shooters on his right drew the attention of the Chicago militants. Their focus on Chloe gave him time to move even farther north, closer to where he thought Alice was moving to flank them.

"Ah!" cried Sean Harris as he was struck and fell.

Rex almost ran to the old sergeant, but Nick Zoft let his rifle hang on the sling and saw to the wounded man. That left Chloe alone and exposed, receiving all the gunfire. The pressure was too much for the ex-Mossad operative. She dropped to her belly to reload out of sight.

But then Scooter and Bruno's rifles blasted from the east! The two had hustled to get around the vehicles, and now the OPT Defenders were caught exposed. Simultaneously, Alice's rifle boomed from the north, catching the gunmen in a crossfire.

Choosing that instant, Rex opened fire and advanced from a third side. Though he was alone, closer, and more exposed than his other shooters, he knew the Defenders would be in a panic now, realizing they'd been out-maneuvered by a smaller fighting force.

Another gun barked to his right, and Rex glanced over to see Rotham had returned to the fight after securing the child with his parents. Angling toward one another, Rex and Milo approached the same combatants on the west side of the disabled vehicles. Since they had no frontal targets, they skipped gel-tranqs off the pavement under the vehicles into the Defenders' legs.

Alice broke cover on Rex's left, firing wildly with her one arm, her walking staff fastened to her back. Though she may not have been hitting anything, the handful of remaining OPT Defenders in the shelter of their vehicles shifted frantically for cover—too unsettled to aim and fire effectively.

Rex halted and allowed Milo, Scooter, and Bruno—the most experienced—to mop up the last conscious Defenders. From his vantage point, Rex could see Chloe and Nick treating Sean's wound. Sean's wound concerned Rex since the man wasn't yet a believer. His death now would be far from a joyous occasion since he was still in rejection of his Savior.

Farther west, Rex could see a few heads of the two hundred men, women, and children relying on him.

"Thank you, Lord," Rex prayed. "If we're all still here, I guess You're not done with us yet."

The shooting stopped, and he moved a little closer to the vehicles. The three COIL men were collecting gear and weapons.

"Thirty-two by my count," Alice said as she approached Rex. "Their fuel tanks are full, and that last Humvee is still operational. Any reason we can't, uh, acquire it?"

The black woman smiled mischievously.

"No reason I can think of. Tell Milo to load up extra tires and fuel, then drive it around to the people."

"You saying you don't think I can drive a stick?"

He frowned at the stump of her left arm, knowing she was teasing him.

"I have no doubt you'd figure it out, but I need you back on point. We're not waiting around to see if these boys called for reinforcements from downtown."

Rex walked back down the highway where Miranda was the first to climb over the embankment.

"Everyone's safe and sound," she reported as she adjusted her head scarf, "except for one of the horses. Took one in the rump before we could get her to lay down. It's deep in the hip. Looks bad."

"Then we'll have to put her down. Have the men butcher it as fast as they can. We need to move out in an hour."

"You're forgetting I just joined y'all yesterday." She held out her empty hands. "Why would you think they're ready to take orders from me?"

"Well, you just led them to safety. They'll listen. One more thing." He closed the gap between them until he was certain she would hear. "What kind of military does Chicago have? Six trucks and thirty-two men is all, I hope?"

"No, they have a whole compound of trucks that fills a parking structure on Wabash Avenue. But they won't send anyone after us. You want to know what they'll do?" She set a hand on his chest, looking up with concern into his face. "They'll figure out where we're going and radio ahead. Everyone's communicating now. For two decades, we had radio silence. And now everyone's talking. It's like the forces of darkness are gathering."

"Who's between us and Colorado to intercept us? Do you know?"

"I don't know, but this is it, Rex." She drew back. "America's last days. There's nowhere for the righteous to hide but under the wings of the Almighty!"

"Until the Lord comes for us," he added.

"Yes, there's always that." She smiled and returned to the people.

Rex oversaw the loading of refugee gear into the Humvee, including three-quarters of the horse that had to be put down. Sean's bullet wound was high in his right shoulder, so he wasn't any use as a shooter for a while.

"You did this just so you could sit down on the job, didn't you?" Rex joked as he held the door of the Humvee for the wounded man. Chloe had removed the bullet, and Nick had fashioned a sling for him. "Just keep it in low gear and creep along behind us. You're our rear guard."

"At least you found some use for me." Sean winced. "And you didn't put me down like that horse."

"The horse is edible. You'd just be all gristle." Rex patted the top of the Humvee. "Besides, you can't die until you have the assurance you're at peace with God before you meet Him."

"Can't I just trust you about that religious stuff?"

"Nope. It doesn't count until you trust Him yourself."

Rex approached a young pregnant woman and her husband, who Chloe had said were believers from Erie.

"There's room only for her in the passenger seat," Rex told the husband, then addressed the woman. "The driver is Sean, and he's not yet right with Jesus Christ. Give him both barrels, if you know what I mean."

"Challenge accepted!" She laughed.

Her husband opted to walk next to the Humvee since it would be crawling along at walking speed behind the foot travelers.

"More radios," Milo informed, holding open a pack of collected handhelds from the convoy. "We destroyed their weapons. What do you want to do with these? I have six."

"Keep one for yourself," Rex said as Chloe led the people west again on the interstate. "And give the other five to Sean, Taylor, Scooter, Bruno, and Chloe."

"What about your new friend?" Milo asked.

"What new friend?"

"That Miranda cutie who turns red whenever she's around you."

"Oh, I see how it is." He chuckled as they walked together after the refugees. "Remind me why you're not carrying Naomi right now? Maybe if you had more to carry, you'd have less to say."

"Message received, Caspertein." He moved ahead with the radios. "But romance isn't dead just because we're out here in the Plains Zone."

"We get shot at too much for romance."

Rex stopped and stood in the freeway for several minutes, looking back the way they'd come. Only by the grace of God had more of them not been shot. They'd lost Lyla Caspertein and Brian Steelman hundreds of miles back, and only God knew what would happen hundreds of miles ahead. Getting to Colorado seemed so unlikely, now that OPT towns would be communicating with one another about their demise.

"We need a couple more Casperteins to even the score," he said to himself, thinking of Levi, his cousin, and Rudy, his father. "Bring us together, Lord."

He walked after the refugees, his rifle in his hands.

As a seismologist, Rudy Caspertein knew not to panic when he was awakened in the night by an earthquake. But Annette's reaction beside him in the bed was much different.

"Rudy!" She grabbed at his arm as he moved from the bed.

"Come on." He calmly pulled her with him. "It's growing. It's a big one! Vorca, get Caleb!"

He plucked Annette's tattered robe from a hook as they moved from the bedroom of the log cabin. In the darkness, objects from shelves clattered to the floor while the cookware in the cabinets rattled.

They reached the front door, their knees unsteady as the ground swayed and rolled beneath them. Still in her nightgown, Vorca held Caleb, and to their credit, neither made a peep. Rudy escorted them outside into the crisp air. He immediately turned and listened to his cabin logs grind together, crack, and shift. Years earlier, he'd responded to a monster earthquake in Alaska, but he felt this was something different, something deeper.

He helped Annette into her bathrobe, then knelt on the ground where the sheep had grazed just that week, nibbling at the young grass. Not far away, the sheep dogs barked, and Rudy imagined the herders rounding up the flock for safety from the unknown.

"This isn't normal, is it?" Annette asked.

Rudy realized he'd been counting in his head since leaving his bed—*forty-seven, forty-eight, forty-nine* . . .

"No, this isn't normal."

A new sound—above the shifting and swaying of natural and manmade structures—reached their ears. Thunder rolled across the Colorado landscape. It came from the north, and with a chill, Rudy stood in only his pajama bottoms and gazed at the northern sky. Annette rose to her feet to cling to him as the ground swayed less but still rumbled like a settling lion. Far away, lightning crackled and black clouds roiled upward with flashes of light in brilliant colors.

"What is it?"

"God help us, and God help Wyoming," Rudy whispered. "It's got to be the volcano—Yellowstone. It's finally erupting. The whole park sits over the mouth of a two-million-acre volcano. This is it, the one scientists have been predicting for decades."

"Are we safe here? How far away are we from it?"

"Put it this way. If it were small, we wouldn't be able to see those clouds on fire. The fact that we can see it erupting from here means the ash is going high, maybe even into the stratosphere. Depending on how much and how high, it could spread ash around the world. It could block out the sun, if it's the big one."

"It's like the Bible says—the sun darkened and the moon turned to blood. How bad will the—"

"Get down!" Rudy pulled her and Vorca to the ground again, then shielded their bodies with his own. An instant later, a hot wind tore over the rimrock above, then passed like a wave down the White River Valley.

For a few moments, Rudy heard nothing stir between his cabin and the town of Meeker, and he thought the sheep and dogs had all been killed. The rimrock above had surely protected most of the town from the blast, though the cattle were up on the plateau, and the sheep were out in the meadow.

But an instant later, dogs started barking again. At least some of the animals had survived.

"We're almost four hundred miles away." Rudy drew Annette with him. "The blast shouldn't have been that strong. That was like an atomic blast wave."

"What about the people up north?"

"I don't know. Maybe people in the mountains survived, but within fifty miles of that, the forests and rocks probably would've been disintegrated to dust. First with the OPT and their Oath of Solidarity, and now with the world's largest volcano erupting? God's not playing around. The end is near."

Rudy lit a couple lanterns as smaller aftershocks shook the ground, and Annette checked their food and water supplies.

"Water line must've burst," Annette announced from the kitchen. "You feel like digging up the pipes from the well again?"

"That's not all." Rudy pushed against the outer wall of the cabin. "I'll need to do a lot more with these logs than just re-caulk them before winter. This whole side collapsed. Wait a minute. What's that?"

Rudy ran outside again, Annette on his heels. They stared northwest once more at the boiling red, gray, and orange clouds.

"It's coming this way!" Annette cried.

"It's an ash cloud, probably heavier particles that didn't get tossed into the atmosphere. Could be radioactive. We'll need suits and masks from town. I know where they're stored."

"The sky's on fire!"

"No, that's just lightning and a reflection off the clouds. It's a fire, but it's on the ground. The forests must be burning up north. We've probably lost all the cattle on the upper plateau. The ash'll fall and kill the grass. It'll pollute the lakes if not the rivers. The sheep won't last without food. Wildlife could die off in the area in a matter of weeks."

"We've got grain for the horses."

"That won't last long. Come on. The ash'll start to fall here soon."

Inside the cabin, they tied handkerchiefs around their faces, then walked hand-in-hand to town, with Vorca and Caleb following. As they walked, the ash began to fall, some pieces lighter than cotton but as big as Rudy's hand.

"I haven't worn a mask since those months after the virus pandemic," Annette said. "You think our boys are okay?"

"They're Casperteins." Rudy smiled. "And they're Christians. Don't worry yourself. They're safe in the Lord's hands, whatever's happening."

Rudy didn't know what else to say to console her, but she seemed to receive it. If not for their faith in the God of the Bible, Rudy wasn't sure how they could've coped emotionally.

In town, everyone was in the streets, scarves and masks over their faces and glasses on their eyes. They stared at the northern sky, which was displayed in red and orange with occasional flashes of lightning higher up in the black, billowing cloud.

Old Man Trapper Sullivan rode a buckboard into town, drawn by a single quarter horse. Rudy helped the rancher down to stand with them in the street.

"Matthew 24:7?" Trapper asked.

"I'd say so." Rudy held up his palm as the ash fell. Already, the pavement was covered. "The livestock?"

"Saw some cattle in Anderson's Gulch. No saying what happened on the flat top. Wouldn't be surprised if that gust of wind pushed some right into the gorge. They were all exposed up there, Rudy."

The tall son of Trapper, Mayor Wayne Sullivan, moved through the crowd and stopped in front of Trapper.

"Hey, Dad. The house okay?"

"She'll hold."

The mayor nodded at Rudy and Annette.

"We had a fire at the RV park. Something electrical, but everyone made it out. That wind pushed a couple homes clean off their blocks."

"It was the blast wave from the volcano," Rudy said. "Not wind."

"What volcano?" Wayne asked.

"Yellowstone, son," Trapper said. "What do you think this ash is from?"

"Just a freak storm or something." Wayne shielded his eyes and looked skyward. "A volcano?"

"Everything in the valley could die now," Rudy said to Trapper. "We should get everyone we can together and butcher whatever animals died. We have some canned fruit and vegetables in the cabin, but whatever meat we don't salt and smoke—we'll be low on food in no time."

"We just have to wait for it to rain," Wayne said. "Everything'll be fine."

"A little rain will wash some ash away, sure," Rudy said, "but it could be in the stratosphere now, which is above the clouds. And this close to the eruption site, that ash could keep falling for days. I knew a guy who wrote his master's thesis on Yellowstone's volatility. Something this big changes the climate around the world. Without meteorological data streaming, we won't know what to expect from the weather in the coming months. I recommend heading south, Trapper."

"It's not going to get that bad." Wayne chuckled. "You're overreacting, Rudy. I mean, come on. Volcanos have erupted before."

"Nothing like this, Wayne. You'd better prepare the people you're responsible for. You'll need a plan to feed them and get them water."

"The OPT will help us." Wayne shrugged. "That's one good thing about belonging to a planet-wide community now. We'll be safe regardless."

"I belong to Jesus Christ's body of believers and nothing else," Rudy stated with some force. "I've got a hunch that your OPT people are going to be fighting to stay alive themselves. Whatever resources remain, there'll be killing for it as food and drinkable water disappears."

"You're getting a little ahead of yourself, aren't you?" Wayne chuckled again. "I know you don't think much of me joining the OPT, Rudy. Or you, Dad. But I'm telling you guys, these OPT people are going to come through for us. You've just got to keep the faith."

"I'm not putting any faith in some one world government!" Trapper barked. "Boy, you need to wake up. If I didn't know any better, I'd think you clean forgot the Bible you were raised on!"

"Well, I've grown up since those days." Wayne pulled up his pants. "Now I'm an Advocate for the OPT. Advocate Veronica Kane will be back in a few days to receive a roster of this town's Oath-takers. I know you guys will see things my way by then. Or else."

"Or else?" Trapper frowned over his bandana. "Boy, who do you think you're talking to?"

"When Kane comes back, she'll be coming with force! She said you old fashioned Christians would stir up trouble."

"There was a day you called yourself a Christian, son," Trapper said sadly. He gestured with his thumb at Rudy. "This man taught you himself. You know better."

"You're right." Wayne got into his father's face. "I do know better!"

Rudy wanted to put the mayor over his knee, and he guessed he could have done so without much difficulty, but instead, Rudy pointed to the sky.

"Hey, Wayne, did you notice the sunrise?" Rudy asked him.

Wayne scoffed.

"Funny," Wayne said. "It's pitch black. It's the middle of the night."

"No." Rudy responded. "The sun rose an hour ago. It's daylight above that ash. Look at your feet. You're standing up to your ankles in it. Are you going to ask the OPT to make the sun shine?"

"What?" Wayne looked from the sky to his feet. "I don't believe this!"

"You'd better believe it, because it'll only get worse for those who don't put their trust in God for His salvation. Maybe your end will be this ash, or maybe it'll be something else. You've taken a bad step into this OPT stuff, but there's still time for you. God's not giving up on you yet, son, but His patience is running thin."

Wayne's eyes seemed wider, but then he shook his head and walked away.

"You think he's telling the truth?" Annette asked. "That the OPT will be back?"

"I suspect so. Sorry, Trapper, but your son signed on with the devil himself."

"We'd better get to those cattle." Trapper brushed the ash from the top of his bald head. "It'll be a busy few days putting meat up."

"Come with me to get some protective gear," Rudy offered, "and I'll meet you at your place in a couple days. I'll pass the word and we believers will come together. We'll come up with a plan, maybe head south if the ash doesn't stop by then."

From the hardware store, Rudy and Annette rounded up several suits and biohazard masks with face shields. They walked Trapper to his buckboard and helped him climb up.

"I never thought I'd live to see this start to happen," Trapper said. "This must mean the Tribulation is coming upon us, huh?"

"When the virus hit our country, people never thought they'd witness that, either." Rudy put his arm around Annette. "We either got ready for the end or grew complacent. We're still seeing the beginning of birth pangs."

"Maranatha," Trapper said, and slapped the reins.

"Maranatha." Rudy waved in the darkness, then looked down at Annette. "Wayne's not going to get anyone ready for food shortages, and I've got a mind to head south where there's some wild game still living. What do you think, Mrs. Caspertein?"

"You'd really leave all this?"

"When Christ comes, we'll be leaving it all anyway." Rudy turned to Dathan Tentmaker in the crowded street. "Can you get your things together and go out to help Trapper for a few days, Dathan? None of us should be alone right now."

"I won't argue with that. Be glad to," Dathan said as he shook Rudy's hand.

Together, Rudy walked with Annette, Vorca, and Caleb back to the cabin, but the sun remained hidden behind the black clouds.

Chapter Three

L evi and Lena walked into the quiet town of Ellijay, Georgia, while the mist was still rising from the dew on the green hillsides. Auggie's tail wagged as she darted from their side into the grass, her nose to the ground. She was in heaven, exploring new lands and chasing meadow creatures on either side of the rural highway.

"Seems a peaceful place." Levi scuffed his boot at the prints on the dusty pavement. "Looks like Nathan came through here just last night. Nice to camp near a place like this, unless they found room and board."

"Aah," Lena agreed, then clapped her hands for Auggie to come to her. "Auggie!"

Auggie seemed to grasp the woman's communication better than Levi did, and he chuckled as Lena pointed at a white-painted house. Bounding away, Auggie went off to investigate. Birds nesting on the ground took flight as their gentle habitat was unsettled by the playful dog.

"I guess they're not early risers," Levi observed as they passed a general store on the main street. He tested the front door. "They must be around if they're locking their doors. All the glass is still in the windows, too."

"Aah." Lena's handgun was already in her hand, but Levi wasn't as concerned about the yawn-worthy town. Until he saw the tracks in the dust.

"That's strange." He stopped and studied footprints up and down the street. "Shell casings. And see how the prints are spaced out? Quite a few people were running in that direction. And this here . . . ."

He glanced up and slid his rifle off his shoulder to hold it in his hands.

"Aah?"

"Those are Jenna's boot prints! She moved off in that direction. These six or seven people were running after her. And these, I think, are Brian's boots, right?"

Lena aimed her pistol at the oval prints of the pack horse that led to a black stain on the dusty street. It looked like oil, but Levi knew it was blood. Drag marks showed that the horse had been skidded away.

"Get to the other side of the street and be ready for anything!"

She hustled to the far side and crouched. Auggie ceased her investigations of a chicken coop and perked her ears, watching Lena for a cue about yet undetected danger.

Levi moved alongside the buildings, past the hitching post, until he arrived at a small office marked, "Ellijay OPT Administration." A red arrow pointed at the door, but Levi was more concerned about another red stain on the street. It was smaller. Like from a human. He did the math. If Jenna and Brian had run northeast, that left Nathan and Chen Li unaccounted for.

He was about to move past the little office when he peered through the window, checking for danger. Instead, he saw his own backpack and other gear laying in a heap against a wall. It was all that had been on the pack horse, which Levi had left with Nathan before going after Lena.

Leveling his rifle, he first aimed at the nearby buildings, then the roofs, and even the distant chapel steeple, expecting to find the heads of ambushers spying on them. But nothing moved. He took a deep and rugged breath, his nostrils flaring, his anger barely contained.

The door to the administration building was unlocked. He ducked inside and whistled for Lena to join him. Auggie beat her across the street, and Levi closed the door once the three were inside.

"Aah!" Lena gasped as she noticed their own gear.

Levi crossed the room to a desk and picked up a COIL battle rifle that had blood on its black steel stock. But worse, a green ammo vest was soaked with blood, smelling ghastly. He brushed his fingers over the untouched magazines still in their pouches.

"Come here." He turned Lena around to fit her arms through the vest armholes. Then he turned her to zip up the front. "You can wash it out later, but for now, you're getting a weapon upgrade."

He took the silenced pistol from her and instead put the confiscated rifle into her hands.

"Aah?"

"It was Nathan's. Check the load. I don't even think he got off a shot. The holes in your new vest tell us why."

As Lena fit the sling over her head and checked the weapon, Levi went to their gear to inventory what remained. His pack seemed to have been rifled through, but it was intact. He didn't find Brian's homemade pack among the belongings, so he must've still had it with him. Jenna's small backpack was there, so he stuffed it into the larger one that was Nathan's. Chen Li's light pack he fastened to the outside of his own, which was still a hefty fifty pounds, including the entrenching shovel, camping gear, and food supplies.

"Aah!" Lena alerted.

Levi rushed to the window and looked out.

"Lower your gun." He drew the .22. "It's just one man. No noise to wake up the town. He doesn't look armed. Get back."

Together, they pressed themselves against the wall. The instant the stranger reached for the door handle, Levi yanked open the door himself, then grabbed the slender man by his suspenders and hurled him inside. Levi holstered his pistol, closed the door, and pursued the scrambler across the room. His face was clean-shaven, his pants pressed, his hair freshly barbered.

"Please! Wait!" Cornered and crouching against the wall, he held up his soft hands to Levi's advancing fury. The man's eyes settled on the rifle that hung from the sling off Levi's shoulder. "You're with the others. I can help you!"

Levi made a slow act of drawing the five-inch skinning knife from his hip. The tip freed itself from the sheath with a twang sound.

"You have ten seconds to tell me what happened." He didn't move to let the man climb to his feet. "Lena, watch the window."

"No one else is coming." The man in suspenders kept his hands raised defensively above his face. "They're all up at Miller's house. Two of your, uh, . . . friends locked themselves inside last night. We were trying to get them out all this time. It's all a misunderstanding. I was just trying to welcome them into the OPT."

"OPT?"

"The One Planet Trust. It's a new direction for America, for the whole world. It's on every radio. Every town is on board. We're just spreading the good news."

"What're you talking about?" Levi blinked, thinking back to past towns. "I've never heard of this OPT."

"Neither had your friends. It's just a few weeks old, so people are still figuring out that it's nothing but a positive move for us all."

"Explain." Levi waved the knife threateningly, though he already clutched a gel-tranq in his left hand. "Quickly!"

"The desk! On the desk. The Oath of Solidarity. It's so simple. I don't know why your friends panicked. All they had to do was take the Oath. Your friends went for their guns, then Miller—"

"Don't move!" Levi went to the desk and found the laminated page. He read through the Oath's four points, including the penalty of death. "You're killing people over this?"

"Well, we just started. We're supposed to, I mean, execute people who refuse to work together."

"This isn't working together." Levi tucked the page into his vest. "This is demanding loyalty to a cause that could conflict with people's consciences. How many have you executed?"

"Uh. Defender Miller just started a few days ago. The penalty is strangulation. To save on bullets."

"How many people?"

"Seven, counting the one last night. One of your friends. But it wasn't me! I'm sorry. I tried to stop them!"

"Yeah?" Levi growled. "I doubt it! Who died in the street? That was no strangling!"

"It was a big guy with . . . one of those rifles. He had all that stuff with him."

"So, the one this Miller strangled was a woman? Chinese?"

The man answered with only a trembling jaw and a rough swallow.

"Lena, are we clear?"

"Aah."

Levi sat on the edge of the desk. He struggled to think straight. Deep down, he wanted to scream and burn the town down, but he needed to think! And pray. His heart broke as he let his imagination stray to Chen Li's execution after Nathan had been slaughtered in the street.

"Where is Miller's house?" Levi asked, his voice now reflecting his hurt and the compassion he felt for his companions. "Where are my two friends holed up? Point. Which direction?"

"Um. That way." The man indicated southeast. "Do you want the others, too?"

"What others?"

"The ones still in the basement. The last two Servalites. I talked Miller into giving them until today to decide if they'd take the Oath or not. We've had them longer than the others, trying to break through their stubbornness."

"Did you say Servalites?" Levi rose from the desk. "There are Servalites here?"

"Yes. Um. There were six we arrested first. Christians trying to tell us not to cooperate with the OPT. So, we had to arrest them. And then two more came a few days later. A man and a woman."

"Where are they?"

"A basement. In that direction. A blue house. I . . . can take you there and help you."

"Yeah. Like you helped my friends."

Levi sheathed his knife, then pushed aside the man's hands to jab him in the shoulder with the gel-tranq. The man slumped unconsciously, and Levi moved to Nathan's pack, hefting it into his arms.

"I know this is heavy, but I can't carry it with mine."

Lena gave him her back and bowed under the weight of the pack. He fastened the straps on her front over the ammo vest, then nodded at her.

"You can leave town to wait for us, or you can risk getting shot by these OPT animals."

"Aah!" She scoffed and gave him an accusatory glare.

"I had to make the offer." He set his own pack on the desk, then struggled into the straps with Lena's help. "It ain't easy facing a town full of killers who think they're doing humanity a favor by killing you. These Servalites are from a Christian missionary group my cousin Mia and her fiancé started last year. They were in Colorado and New Mexico last I heard but spreading east. They're Christians if they're Servalites, so we can't leave town without them."

"Aah." She nodded sharply.

"Okay. We'll go to this basement jail to get the Servalites first, then go get Jenna and Brian at this Miller's place." He sighed at Auggie who was panting, looking from him to Lena. "I guess it's just the three of us. No barking and no shooting until we have to."

Levi exited the administration building first. His eyes lingered a moment on the stain of blood from Nathan. His friend and brother was gone. The man about whom his father had told him many stories—the servant and hero for Jesus Christ—had been murdered on the street. A military or some rogue force hadn't killed him. No, he'd been martyred by simple townspeople who'd signed on to the latest movement to unify under the banner of human determination and pride in self-accomplishment.

He moved southwest, the drawn and silenced handgun at his side, ready to raise and fire. Moving stealthily and swiftly was a challenge with their heavy packs, but Levi knew if they didn't take their gear with them now, they'd have to abandon it altogether once a ruckus started.

Auggie ran ahead, her head up instead of her nose down, as if she were taking point.

Leaving the shops of Main Street behind, Levi studied each residence for a basement. Many appeared to be lived in, and many had basements. Then he saw the blue house. It was the most dilapidated in the neighborhood, but it had a basement. There were red painted letters above the door that read, *Detention.*

Levi didn't lead Lena directly to the detention center. Instead, he moved to the right, angling toward the side of the house.

"Aah," Lena called.

He looked back and followed her gaze down and across the street. There were several abandoned houses with overgrown yards along the avenue. Two hundred yards away, numerous men with hunting rifles were milling around in front of a house.

"That's got to be Miller's place." Levi held up two fingers. "That's our second target this morning."

His eyes swept the neighborhood, checking past trees and beyond empty yards, praying no one looked their way or noticed them creeping toward the blue house.

A moment later, they reached the front corner. Levi surveyed the town from their new perspective.

"I know you can shoot, but we're not here to prove anything," he said in a low voice. "We're both angry, but no shooting, got it?"

"Ah."

"I'll clear this house, but from here on, we cover each other. We'll leap-frog up to Miller's place as soon as I come out. Then it'll be time to shoot. We'll stay apart so no one will catch us together, and we'll be able to cover each other. That tree up the street—can you reach it and hold that position?"

"Aah." She started forward, but he grabbed her pack and pulled her back, turning her to face him.

"If this is it for us, die well, not with hate but with compassion in your heart. These people have done what they've done because they're ignorant. Remember where you came from. If someone hadn't shown us compassion, we'd still be clueless and lost ourselves, still hurting people and God Himself."

"Aah." She thrust her finger into his chest. "Hah-aha ah-hah!"

"Yes, me, too. Shoot straight. See you soon."

Walking stiffly, she crossed the street and went into the next yard. Levi could tell she was struggling to restrain herself. Though she was closest to him, Jenna and Chen Li had become her sisters in a short time, and losing them had struck her deeply. Eighty yards away, she reached the sturdy elm and leaned against it. When she looked back at him, she nodded. She was exposed and in the open, except for the tree she sheltered behind.

Unbuckling his recovered backpack, Levi left it beside the wall of the blue house, but around the corner. He kept his rifle on the sling hanging down his side, but the sidearm was now his primary weapon, which he checked again. It contained only nine shots. Silence was his plan, but he couldn't imagine escaping the town without raising the booming battle rifle at some point.

The loud clap of a screen door nearby made him jump. About fifty yards away, a woman carried a metal pail from her house to a wide pen. Probably hogs, Levi guessed. Thankfully, the woman didn't look in his direction.

He moved around the corner and hopped onto the doorstep of the blue house. Without his pack, he was able to move unencumbered. Lightly, he rapped twice on the door, then turned the handle. It was unlocked. Acting like he owned the place, he pushed the door inward and stepped onto an ugly orange shag carpet. Levi swung the door closed with his left and fired his pistol with his right. A cap-wearing man in an office chair slumped forward onto his desk. His head lay inches before a thick novel he'd been reading. The yellowed pages flipped freely like a fan.

Levi silently moved across the carpet past the desk and into a back room where a queen-sized bed frame had been stripped of its mattress. The frame was leaning against an outer wall, and leather restraints had been fastened to the corners of the frame. Ellijay wasn't the peaceful, innocent town it seemed to be.

Next, Levi cleared the bathroom, which hadn't been cleaned in ages, and another bedroom where mildewed boxes were stacked to the stained ceiling.

Finding a wooden door to the basement, he unhooked the latch on the outside and opened the door. There was an orange light bulb to light the wooden stairs. It was clearly a dungeon. The odor was a telltale sign of a bathroom or inadequate ventilation.

Moving down the stairs, he prayed Lena didn't get too antsy about him taking so much time inside. He hadn't worked with her long, but she seemed disciplined enough to endure the tension of time and danger.

One more light bulb glowed in the basement room, but it wasn't enough to illuminate the interior of the two dark cells against the far wall. The cells seemed to be metal cages with thick iron bars welded across the front.

"Hey, Servalites," he called softly, remaining near the foot of the stairs where he could keep an eye on the door above. "You guys still alive in there?"

Someone stirred in the cell on the right, and straw shifted on the floor as a bearded, curly-haired man of medium height appeared behind the bars. His face was shadowed further by black eyes and a bloodied cheek-bone. They'd obviously beaten him and held him longer than just a few days.

"You good to go?" Levi asked. "We're getting you out of here. Who else is down here? Hey! Come on, buddy. Let's not wait for the rapture, huh? It ain't easy, but we need to roll now!"

Someone in the other cage crawled up to the bars. Long, filthy blonde hair hung in front of what Levi figured was a woman's face.

"On your feet." Levi checked the door at the top of the stairs, then crossed the basement to a double-bar lock on the wall. He hinged one lever up to open the first cell, then the other. "Come on. Shake it off and let's go!"

He jerked on the man's door twice before it opened with a rusty squeak. The man had been leaning on the front, so he fell into Levi's arms. Levi used one arm to hold the shorter man and holstered his gun.

"You've got to stand for me. Can you do that? Yeah? Can you walk? Hello, can you understand me?"

The man's eyes blinked rapidly, and one grimy hand pawed across Levi's face.

"Are you . . . real?" the man asked hoarsely.

"Real as rain, buddy, and it's gonna rain bullets if we don't get outta town. Can you make it up the stairs? Crawl if you have to. I'll get your friend here."

The man seemed overwhelmed by emotion, and he didn't answer as he sobbed in Levi's arms. Levi got him started walking toward the stairs, then he returned and tore open the second cage door. A woman lay on the straw floor with a bucket of waste in the corner.

"Come on, sister." Levi was glad to see her clothes were in one piece, though she wore only a simple cotton t-shirt and trousers. The OPT people had probably not abused them too badly since they'd tried to get the couple to agree to the Oath. "Hang on to me. That's it. I've got you. Good thing you're not too heavy, because I ain't too strong."

She was bone-thin, but she still had a little strength. He felt her arms around his neck as he gathered her up.

He caught up to the released man halfway up the stairs where he was crawling too slowly for Levi. Passing the man against the wall, Levi emerged from the dim dungeon into the living room. He laid the woman on the carpet, then returned for the man to help him stand upright as he emerged from the stairway.

From the desk, Levi fetched a gallon jug of water. The man was still weeping, now holding who must've been his wife. Levi coaxed the man to take a few gulps of water from the jug, and intentionally splashed water onto his bruised face.

"That's it." Levi wiped his hand across the man's upturned face while his eyes were closed. "Pull yourself together. You got a name? Is this your wife? You're Servalites, right? I'm a Christian, too. My name is Levi. Get ready to go. We're about to get out of here, but you've gotta help me out."

Levi went to the woman who seemed to be in worse shape, but she greedily drank from the jug until he forced it away from her to keep her from getting sick.

"Hold your head back," he encouraged, and like the man, she submitted her face to the baptism of water and his hand wiping her soiled hair out of her face. "You're gonna be okay. You've got shoes and clothes. That's enough to run away with, so now we're—"

His voice trailed off and he dropped the jug. With both hands, he took the woman's face and turned it to the light of the window. Beside him, the weeping man tried to cling to him. It would've been awkward if Levi hadn't realized quite suddenly that these two weren't strangers at all!

"You guys!" His own gasps and laughter accompanied his grasping at them both. He kissed their faces and held them tightly, one in each arm. *"It's you! It's really you! Mia? Kip?* Come on, brother. Are you okay now?"

Chuckling, Levi roused Kip Brogdon, a young man he'd known since a teen—the one who'd founded the Servalites. And his cousin Mia! She sobbed against his chest, her filthy nails clutching his ammo vest.

"We've got to do this later." Levi wiped his own eyes. "People are waiting on us. Come on. Stand up."

He pulled them each to their feet. Underweight and malnourished, they swayed where he held them by their arms.

"Are you listening? Come on, you two. It ain't easy getting ripped out of that sewer downstairs, but I know you two are as tough as any Caspertein."

"You . . . came for us," Kip said. "I can't believe it."

"Well, to be fair, I only stumbled across you. Thought you were some regular Servalites. Didn't know you were *the* Servalites!"

"Levi . . .?" Mia touched his face.

"Okay, we ready? We're going outside and to the left. I can't carry both of you. Kip! Are you listening?"

"I'm okay. I'm okay." The man straightened up. "Out and to the left. I'll help Mia."

"Good. Soldier up." He went to the door and gripped the handle. "It's about to get real serious. Ready?"

"Ready," they both said, but they didn't look ready in their frail state.

Levi opened the door enough to show his face. The instant Lena noticed him, she waved once with her left hand.

"Let's go." Levi led the way outside and stood with his back to the few people down the street at Miller's as Kip and Mia emerged. "That way. Go around the corner and stop."

They stepped off the doorstep and rounded the corner. Kip tripped over Levi's pack and pulled Mia down with him. But out of sight now, they gathered themselves as Levi studied the situation at Miller's place. Nine men, at least three with rifles, and at least two with sidearms. If Jenna and Brian were trapped inside, then more townspeople were probably around back, completing the siege.

"All right, listen up." Levi knelt in front of Kip and Mia. "This is my pack. Remember this old thing? You've got to take this with you. Drag it, carry it together, whatever you've got to do, but you need to get into those woods over there. See?"

They gazed westward.

"We can do it." Kip nodded at Mia. "Where are you going?"

"Stick this in your waistband just in case." Levi gave Kip the pistol. "You've got eight shots left. I've got to go get Jenna."

"Wait!" Mia touched his arm. "Jenna? *Your* Jenna?"

"Yes, my Jenna. She's not alone. As soon as I can get her, we'll find you in the woods. Stay out of sight. Go. Get moving!"

He helped them lift the heavy pack, and sharing its weight, they traipsed across the grass toward a span of forest over one hundred yards away. When they were halfway there, he sighed and raised his rifle to his shoulder. With two fingers, he signaled Lena. She waved him forward.

"Can't die now, Lord," he mumbled as he walked out into the street toward the Miller's place. "Too many people counting on me."

When he was even with Lena, he cupped his hand to yell to her.

"Pick your targets. Let's get our people out."

She gave him a thumbs-up. Being a military woman, she'd know that picking her targets meant to fire at enemies on her side. Nine men were in sight. That was four and a half apiece, with more probably behind the house. But Brian would most likely join the fight from inside as soon as it started. Three against maybe fifteen or twenty. Auggie was lying at Lena's feet, her head raised and panting, not quite the vicious dog Runner had raised her to be.

Though Levi had no cover, he felt confident as he approached the siege situation at the end of the avenue. The people of Ellijay weren't hardened survivalists or experienced soldiers. He could see that much from their choice of weapons. Since they were far removed from a large city, their exposure to the criminal element after Pan-Day had probably been limited. However, they'd thrown in with evil company. Levi knew he wasn't responsible as their judge, but he certainly didn't mind putting them on their knees for their indiscretions.

Nathan and Chen Li were gone, and under sudden and dreadful circumstances. But Levi withheld his wrath lest he exchange his gel-tranqs for the lethal rounds he used only for hunting. His weeks of traveling, joking, and fellowshipping with Nathan would have to be continued in heaven since his untimely death had stolen him from Levi's side.

Levi approached within forty yards of those surrounding the Miller house before one man with a checkered shirt turned. While the man stood in shock at the sight of a sizeable armed gunman approaching him, Levi gazed down his sights and fired at the man's chest.

His checkered shirt split open from the gel-tranq, and his feet left the ground. Before he landed on his back, Levi pivoted and fired again. Since he'd fought gun battles against enemies who were greater in number, he wasn't daunted by being outnumbered now. But the close proximity of those with rifles did cause him some pressure.

A bullet zipped past Levi's head, and a third gunman stumbled backwards as Lena engaged the enemy. The armed men were tranqed first, and only one managed to fire a shot at the only target he could see—that bullet smacked the dirt at Levi's feet. Even though the men who remained standing had no visible weapons, Levi and Lena seemed to agree that no one was worth the risk. They tranqed them without discrimination.

An instant later, men ran around both sides of Miller's house. Levi fired at the two on the right, even as a man with a hunting rifle fired at him from the hip. Searing heat branded Levi's side over his ribs, and he spun sideways to the ground as more guns blasted at him. He rolled over twice and scrambled to his knees, only to find his rifle had swiveled around backwards in his hands. It was pointing in the wrong direction!

Glass shattered from a window of Miller's house. For an instant, Levi knelt defenselessly as Brian from the window and Lena from the tree finished off the remaining shooters. Levi flipped his rifle around and flinched from the pain in his side as he rose to his feet. Blood ran down his hip as he swept the yard for any final foes.

"Let's go, Brian!" Levi called.

Rather than use his own belt, Levi unbuckled the belt of a fallen man. He fit the belt over his own ribs and lower chest, tightening it until he could breathe only with his belly. The pressure would stem the flow of blood until he could have the wound dressed.

Brian emerged first from the doorway, then led Jenna cautiously into the yard. He carried only his makeshift sack on his back and his antique rifle in his arms. Jenna carried nothing since her pack had been left with the horse, though Levi had since recovered it.

"They shot up Nathan yesterday," Brian said as he reached Levi, "but we weren't leaving without Chen Li."

"They already killed her. Jenna, you good?"

"As good as can be expected. Is Lena with you?"

"She's across the field watching over us with Nate's rifle. We freed a couple more Christians. Brian, they're in that direction in the woods, and they're in rough shape, so take care of them."

"Where are you going?" Brian asked.

"I'm not done with this town yet." Levi nodded at two townspeople who stood in front of their residence back by Main Street. "Go ahead. We'll be right behind you."

"Thank God you came." Brian's lips trembled. "I was running on empty. We walked right into them yesterday. Nathan didn't get a chance to—"

"I know." Levi clenched his teeth until his emotion passed. "We're sheep among wolves. Nathan knew that, too. Chen Li was spared from going on without him, if we can look at it that way. They've graduated. Get going. We'll be just a few minutes behind you."

Levi surveyed the town as Brian guided Jenna across the clearing toward the trees. Still, the two townspeople stood in their yard, watching.

Leaving Miller's yard, Levi walked up the street until he'd joined Lena and Auggie at the tree.

"Aah." She nodded at his bleeding side.

"It's nothing." He eyed the observers two lots away. "Cover me? I want to talk to them."

"Aah." She turned with her rifle to lean against the tree in the new direction. "Auggie, gha!"

The dog understood and joined Levi's side as he moved his rifle to his back. He didn't know why she'd sent Auggie with him since the dog was such a gentle creature. Auggie was only good for tracking animals, but Levi appreciated the company, and she certainly gloried in any perceived mission. However, a few yards from the tree, Auggie caught the scent of some critter and ran off to investigate.

Levi raised his right hand in greeting as he drew near to the two people. They turned out to be a man and woman in their thirties, wearing jeans and flannels, and were unarmed. The man's hair was unevenly cut, and the woman appeared to be homely, plump, and a little timid, since she stepped behind her husband.

"Your friends aren't dead." Levi stopped ten yards from them. "We just tranquilized them so we could recover our people and get away. We could've killed all of you, like you did to our people and our pack horse. But the love of Jesus who died for us compels us to show you grace. When those guys wake up, you tell them that they made a mistake, siding with this OPT stuff. You guys aren't thinking about eternity, and one day you'll stand before God Almighty to answer for this sinfulness. Your only hope is to put your faith in God's compassion. Otherwise, you'll know nothing but wrath and death for eternity. God's not messing around. I'm leaving you in His hands. He's the one you'll answer to for killing my friends. They were innocent and caring. You tell that to those others. You'll tell them?"

"Yeah." The young man nodded. "I'll tell them."

"It ain't easy choosing eternal matters over what seems so scary in this world," Levi said, "but you can't be so close-minded. Find a Bible and read it. It's God's Word to your heart. Don't live another day without making sure you're ready to die and face Him."

They said nothing more, only watched him, so he backed away a few steps, then returned to Lena. Auggie joined them at the tree.

"I gave them the gospel." Levi sighed. "This is one broken town to do what they've done to us and others. If this OPT stuff is really spreading, we'll probably see more towns like this."

"Aah-hah." Lena wiped at her face and Auggie whined against her leg.

"Yeah." Levi exhaled long. "Colorado is still a long ways away."

They crossed the street, then walked abreast across the clearing. Brian stood at the edge of the forest, watching the town and waiting for them.

"They'll call ahead," Brian said. "Wherever we go now, wherever the OPT is running the towns, we'll be attacked."

"If it's for Christ's sake," Levi said, putting his hand on the older soldier's shoulder, "then we have to be okay with it. If I had a choice, I'd rather they attack *us*, because we know what we're getting into—rather than people being attacked who aren't trained to handle this type of aggression."

Once in the trees, he found Jenna leaning against a stump, and Mia and Kip had collapsed on the ground over Levi's pack.

"Lena, can you watch the town?" He took Nathan's pack off her shoulders and eased it to the ground. "We'll make a very brief camp here to eat and divide up the gear we need to carry."

"Jenna and I haven't slept for a day and a half," Brian said.

"We're not here to sleep." Levi understood Brian was more concerned about Jenna than himself. Her head was bowed where she held onto the stump. She seemed already asleep. "We need to head cross-country and put some distance between us and this disaster."

"Jenna?" Mia used her husband's bony shoulder to climb to her feet. "I can't believe it's you."

"I'm sorry." Jenna said as she lifted her head. "I . . . don't recognize your voice."

Levi supported his cousin as she moved to Jenna's stump.

"We've never met." Mia knelt and took the blind woman's hand. "It's you. Levi found you. He really found you!"

Mia hugged Jenna and wept. Jenna held the young woman for a few moments, then their mutual weakness forced them to sit on the ground and hold each other.

"It's me, Mia," she finally managed. "I'm Wynter and Wes Trimble's daughter. Though I'm Mia Brogdon, now."

"Mia?" Jenna gasped. "Levi's little Mia?"

Levi left them to dote over one another as he gathered wood for a small fire. Once it was lit, and a dented pot from his pack was heating water, he checked on Lena.

"Is all quiet?" He came up behind her.

"Aah." She didn't look back from where she rested her rifle in the fork of a young tree. "Aah-ah?"

"You and I are the only ones rested and healthy to travel right now, but they'll just have to dig deep. Even if all we can do is get a couple miles into the hills, we can rest then for a few days and heal up."

"Aah-hah!"

"Yeah, yeah. Me, too." He touched his side. "I think God allows bullets to graze me just to remind me I'm not as invincible as I think I am."

"Aah."

Auggie sneezed twice and lifted her muzzle from some rodent's burrow. After seeing Lena was stationary, the dog went back to digging out a root system.

"Those boys'll be waking up in about ten minutes," Levi said. "I don't think they'll follow us right away, but if they do, let them have it. We need a good hour to get ourselves in order here to travel."

"Aah."

Levi returned to the fire where the four others had gathered and prepared a small meal. His heart was heavy, feeling very deeply the loss of Nathan and Chen Li, but for the others, he needed to hold himself together. He would have to grieve later.

He roused Kip from sleep and gave him a cup of thick broth with pieces of meat from one of Auggie's kills, and potatoes Nathan had stuffed in his pack. Brian ate slowly, and Jenna and Mia ate quickly over their tins. Levi took Lena a cup and watched the clearing near town as she ate by trickling broth into her throat. When she was finished, she replaced her bridal lace and took up her rifle again. She nodded to Levi like she wanted him to leave her to her guardianship.

"It suits you." He inspected Nathan's rifle, the sling over her head and shoulder. "Nathan would approve."

She looked away, and he walked back to camp. Next, he needed to divide Nathan's heavy pack between Lena, Jenna, and Brian. Mia and Kip were in no condition to carry much, since walking was hard enough on them. Levi guessed that before the day was over, he might be carrying one of them as well as their gear. He left his own pack as it was, and managed to separate the goods, leaving Brian with the heaviest items in Nathan's pack. Lena would take Brian's sack, and Lena's backpack was stuffed to bursting with extra clothes for everyone and a climbing rope, if they had to cross a river. Chen Li's pack was left inside his own.

No one complained or groaned when Levi pushed dirt onto the fire, but he saw the look on their faces.

"It ain't easy when you've got nothing left in the tank." One at a time, he helped them to their feet. "Brian, lead us out, heading west. Let's find a creek or spring in the woods, and we can make camp for a couple days. We've got all summer to get to Meeker. Kip, Mia, you two follow Brian. Jenna, I've got you."

He whistled for Lena and Auggie, then took hold of Jenna's upper arm to guide her through the forest behind Mia and Kip.

"How're you holding up?" Jenna asked Levi a few feet out of camp. "I smell blood. It's fresh."

"I bled a little, but it's mostly just a scratch." He steered her around a fallen log, then lifted her over a boulder covered in moss. "We have graver things to worry about than a few scratches."

"Did Chen Li go quickly?"

Levi hesitated to answer. He didn't want to think about it, but then he remembered who he was talking to. This was Radiant Shade. She had more nerve than all of them combined, and she needed to know. This was how she carried their memories and sacrifices.

"There was a dungeon in that detention house, and a torture rack. The guy I questioned said she was strangled, sometime after some Servalites were executed."

"Servalites. Interesting name. Your father's, I take it?"

"Actually, Kip started it last year." Levi chuckled. "If you want to hear a crazy story about God doing a miracle in someone's life . . ."

As they walked, he told her how Kip had assaulted Mia in San Diego and gotten her pregnant, then chased her halfway across the country. Kip had come to Christ in the desert, while dying of the Meridia Virus. But God had healed him, all to become the leader of the Servalites. Mia had taken a leap of faith, forgiven him, and joined his side, then Levi had continued east with his wife, Rex, and Alice.

"I can't wait to meet them all," Jenna said. "But Levi, where's Mia's child if they had a baby together?"

"The timing, Jenna, hasn't exactly been right for that conversation. Mia knows something about survival, and Kip was an elite soldier for his father the general, but they both look like they've been in a concentration camp for weeks. A baby couldn't survive what they must've been through."

"You think they've been through more than what Ellijay put them through?"

"They've had it hard for a long time." Levi paused and smiled, his heart aching. "But that doesn't mean God hasn't used their hardship for all kinds of good purposes. I mean, they were holding out for Christ in the hands of a wicked town. They left their mark on that place, not just their blood."

Brian slowly led the way across a highway and up a mountainside. Close behind him, Mia and Kip slipped and struggled. When one of them fell, the other helped them up. Jenna stumbled over rocks and branches on the uneven ground, but Levi held her firmly, and more than once he grabbed her with both hands to hold her upright, so she never fell to the ground.

He didn't look back at Lena, but he knew she was watching their backtrail and coming along at her own pace. Auggie darted ahead, left, right, and then returned to stare back at her—so Levi knew she wasn't far behind.

On a hillside burned free of brush and even sticks, Brian dropped to his knees and tasted the water of a stream no wider than his foot.

"It's fresh," he announced, and rolled to his side, his head bowed, his limbs not able to move any farther.

Levi understood he'd pushed them as far as they could go, even if they were only two miles west and above the town of Ellijay.

"We'll camp here," he said, and directed Jenna to Brian's exhausted form so she had someone to rely on. Levi dropped his pack and drew his shovel from a strap.

"Can you scout around while you gather firewood?" he asked Lena as she arrived. Her eyes were clear and wide above her veil. "I'm going to carve a little flat ground out of this slope."

She slapped her thigh to draw Auggie's attention, then she walked uphill.

Flames from a forest fire, Levi guessed, then rain had cleared the hillside bare of foliage. Even grass had been swept clean from the topsoil. The clay that remained, however, was soft and moist, and he made quick work of digging out a place to lay for each of them, so they wouldn't roll downhill while asleep. Right then, they were silent and already dozing wherever they slumped, so Levi worked around them, content to serve those who couldn't help themselves.

As he finished each sleeping place, he laid out tarps and sleeping bags or blankets, then helped each person to their bed. Brian was the last, and the man clutched Levi's sleeve as Levi took his coat from him.

"This isn't the first time you've carried my carcass to rest a little easier. Remember?"

"You can carry me next time. Rest up. There'll be meat on the fire when you wake up."

Between the sleeping travelers, Levi excavated a circular shelf for the fire. Lena arrived, wisely gathering dry sticks rather than anything green to burn, so minimal smoke would be sent skyward. From the stream, they refilled all their containers and placed a pot on the fire.

"Aah." Lena touched Levi's side, making him flinch.

Without argument, he stripped off his coat and shirt, and raised his arm for her to inspect the bullet wound. It wasn't the first time she'd doctored him. The gash was too wide to stitch, but deep enough to dress and wrap with white oak bark as antiseptic. Then, so he could move without shifting the dressing, she tightened the belt around his chest until he gasped. She helped him into another shirt from Jenna's pack, then took his blood-soaked shirt to the stream.

He looked after her, thinking of Lyla. Lena was so different than his outspoken Lyla, but her care with a stern hand left him thinking of and praying for his wife. Both women had treated him and helped him through wounds and challenges, but neither had overstepped so that his role as a man was undermined. It was hard not to pity Lena. She was growing so attached to him, but he couldn't keep reminding her of Lyla without hurting her feelings. Levi felt she needed a man of her own, but that seemed to be unlikely since she was so disfigured.

The sky darkened, and Levi stood to watch as a gray sheet of clouds floated across the blue canvas. Far higher than he'd ever seen lightning crackle, he watched white and blue static snap against the dark background.

"I've never seen clouds like that before," he said to Lena. She hung his wet shirt on a tree branch. "I'm gonna hunt around a little. You'll watch camp?"

She drew her notepad—which had been finally recovered from the gear Nathan had carried—and she scribbled a note.

"Will we make it?" he read, then gave her back the pad. "For now, I think we will. But life in this world is always an uncertainty. That's why we stay connected to our Savior every minute, from the heart. One day, it'll be you and me in Nathan and Chen Li's shoes. For God, we die without regret. There's no shame or fear in death for us, because we've been made right by our Lord. Don't worry about that day, all right? When it happens, we'll be ready."

The lines deepened at the corners of her eyes, and Levi realized that she was smiling.

Andy knew he was dying. The boy called Willy struck him again and again with his stout walking stick, but Andy no longer felt the blows. That's how he knew he was dying. He'd become numb to the pain, numb to caring, numb to life.

From where Andy lay in the mud, Dwight Storch grabbed him by the collar and lifted him within inches of his face.

"This animal is done-in, Willy." Dwight dropped Andy back into the mud. "That's how you break a coward, son. Not with prison and not with fines. You break 'em with a heavy hand. Come on. Let's get outta this rain. You hungry?"

"What about him, Dad?" Willy asked.

"He's not going anywhere. You done beat the fight right outta him. I doubt he could even crawl back to the highway. Get your pack. We've got an early morning tomorrow—without him."

Willy struck Andy again, forcing Andy onto his face in the mud as the boy wrestled his pack off Andy's back.

Andy thought about leaving his face right there in the mud. In a single breath, he could inhale water and soil into his lungs. Since he was too exhausted to cough, he'd suffocate in a couple short minutes. All of his misery could soon be over—his numbness, his suffering.

But he turned his head and took a breath of moldy air. Rain pattered on his cheek. For the first time in days, he was alone. No child wounding him, welting his body. No father giving his son twisted counsel on how to inflict upon him the most amount of distress. Father and son were right about one thing: Andy regretted ever trying to ambush those two travelers!

He drifted to sleep where he lay, then woke hours later in darkness. The rain had stopped, but he shivered where he lay in the puddle. After rolling over, he sat up and acknowledged a building nearby. A light shimmered in a window. As much as he wanted to beg strangers for mercy, warmth, and a little food, he wanted more to escape the man and boy who'd enslaved him. Though they'd given him water, they hadn't fed him in days. Four days? Maybe two? Time had blurred in his mind as the abuse had stretched on and on.

Using his elbows, he pulled himself into the weeds at the side of the driveway where he'd been laying. He plowed with his head through the wet vegetation, his eyes closed, hoping he could put enough distance behind him that his captors truly wouldn't bother with him in the morning.

He came up against metal fencing—maybe an animal pen. The odor of dung replaced the smell of rotting vegetation. In the darkness, Andy clawed his way up the fencing, which turned out to be only three feet high. Since his left foot was too numb to use, he pushed off the ground with his right, and tumbled into the pen. When he landed, it was elbow first into deep mud. No, not mud, but sludge and sewage. *That smell . . .*

A pig snorted nearby. Defenseless and weak, he shuddered at the thought of a domesticated boar attacking him. Even short, eight-month-old swine could outweigh a man, and their strength was incomparable.

But the animal didn't rush him. Andy crawled through the suctioning filth until he sensed he'd entered some sort of enclosure. He whimpered audibly as he sensed more than one pig inside, avoiding the wet weather. Warmth was all he wanted.

His lightly bearded cheek brushed up against one pig's bristly backside. He pushed deeper, and the pig barely shifted as Andy found himself in a back corner, his legs trailing along the wall. It was too dark to see, but he could hear about five animals breathing. The smell, musty and foul, would've made him vomit if he had any energy to heave.

He woke to daylight. Pain throbbed through his whole body from the beatings and forced marches on a broken foot. One of the pigs tugged at the boot on his left foot. The sole was already torn and hanging off. The pig was merely finishing the job.

Andy didn't move to defend himself, partly because he wasn't sure he could. Five pigs—monstrous two- or three-year-olds—foraged in the larger pen area. The one on his foot moved up to investigate his face, and Andy swatted the snout away. The sow returned to his foot. If the animal attacked, he wouldn't have been able to escape.

Sludge clung to his buckskins. He shifted on his elbow, still cramped in the back of the low shed. His stomach no longer ached for food, but he knew he was starving. And thirsty. His tongue was swollen and sticky.

The pig won his boot sole and flipped the leather away like a dog playing with a dead mouse. The four-hundred-pound sow snorted and circled the sole and bumped into the other rooting pigs. Before long, all of them were playing bumper-pig in their stumpy way.

Lifting his head, Andy checked his foot, but he couldn't judge its condition without removing the wool sock. Some feeling had returned. The skin felt tight, but he couldn't tell if he was wiggling his toes or not.

A tall figure moved beyond the wire fence. The pigs abandoned their playing, snorted in unison, and hurried to a feeding trough across the pen. It was thirty feet from Andy's mud bed inside the plywood shelter.

A man with a bucket dumped slop down the length of the trough. The pigs went wild, their muzzles chomping, their hooves prancing as they nudged each other left and right for the best gobbling position.

The man, in a denim jacket and black trousers, didn't stick around, but departed on a trail through an overgrown garden back to a two-story house. Andy now realized it had to be more than a mere residence since there was a sign out front, though it faced outward where he couldn't read it. Some kind of store or something.

The pigs were finished in sixty seconds, then they started to fight each other to investigate other sections of the trough. One spied Andy, and she trotted toward him. Andy knew the animal's appetite had been whetted, and he was the only edible thing left in the pen. He clenched his teeth and sat up. Without a weapon, there was no way he could fight off a grown pig. He couldn't even stand! The beast was all muscle and fat, outweighing him by hundreds of pounds.

"You had your chance in the night!" he growled, banking on him being human and the pig being dumber, unable to calculate Andy's defenselessness. Instead of slapping her when she drew close, he pushed her away, directing her snout elsewhere. For now, he would be spared, but if the animals got aggressive, he'd be in trouble. It was time to leave the pen.

Rather than lay back down in the shelter of the roof, he rocked three times before pushing himself to his hands and knees. His thighs each felt like a giant charley horse, and his back and ribs felt bruised and fractured, every muscle strained, every bone on fire.

He crawled slowly out of the shelter and looked around. The fence was only three feet high, but it would be a challenge to climb, unless he stood on his good foot and fell over it.

The other pigs steered clear of him as he moved through six inches of muck and managed to reach the feeding trough. He leaned against the fence, his elbow on the trough lip, and eyed the puddle of rainwater gathering in a corner.

"This is not happening," he mumbled, but not even the pigs looked up from their foraging.

Tears streamed down Andy's cheeks at the thought of what he was about to do. If he wanted to live, he had no choice. He had to get something in his belly, and he was dying of thirst.

Leaning over the puddle of dirty water, he sipped at it until it was gone. Then, his eye fell on something the pigs hadn't eaten, a lump about the size of his fist. He grabbed it, wiped it the best he could, and found it was a chunk of old cabbage. Unless he ate, he'd have no strength to heal or crawl away to hide somewhere else.

His gut convulsed against the trough, but he was determined to live on garbage rather than die with nothing at all. With resolve, he gnawed on the chunk of vegetable until it was completely gone.

He glared at the pigs. No, it couldn't be, he thought with a sudden chill. It wasn't possible that God was in this moment. But the memory was there, and he couldn't shut it out. It was a Bible story Eric had told him, something about a selfish son who had taken what was his and ran away into the world. After failing, the son had gone so far as to eating pig's food.

"The poorest, laziest people in Dad's River Camp would never eat pig slop," Andy thought to himself. Bowing his head, he wept.

Home? No. He couldn't. He hated River Camp and everything the Christians blindly devoted their lives to. Leaving River Camp was the best thing he could've done. *But pig slop?*

Sighing, he realized Wyoming was too far away for him to return. He might never recover physically to ever travel again, anyway.

Little flakes of snow floated down on the still morning air. He opened his palm to catch the snowflake. But the flake didn't melt. Wait. Snow this far south? He lifted his palm to his face and studied the flake. *Ash?*

The flakes fell all around him, and with them came an acrid odor he could smell even over the stench of the pigs. It was like no ash he'd ever known, and he'd been around campfires his whole life. This wasn't ash from a fire. This was something else.

Like a nuisance on his conscience, more ideas from the Bible came to mind. Eric had told him about things like plagues and famines, earthquakes and disasters that would one day happen to the earth. Christians might even die from natural disasters or be killed from persecution, but they had nothing to fear if they had placed their confidence in Jesus Christ. But Andy thought it was nuts to believe such nonsense. Disasters happened all the time around the world. It didn't mean anything.

But still, he'd never heard of ash falling from the sky in North America . . .

Miranda Nelson stood at the edge of a small crowd of men and women who all talked at once. In the middle was the mountain of a man, Rex Caspertein, listening to their complaints and concerns with much more patience than Miranda felt she'd have in his place.

Outside the crowd, seated on the ash-covered freeway lanes, were the refugee women and children. Their faces were covered by masks, especially their mouths. Some wore glasses or goggles to protect their eyes from the acrid-smelling residue. The rest had cut slits in scarves or head wraps to see through. The ash continued to fall like snow, covering the tracks the travelers had left on the highway.

"We can't keep going west!" a man stated to Rex. "We're going right into the mouth of the volcano! Next, it won't be ash; it'll be lava!"

"It'll be safer for us to the north," another urged. "Let's go where it's cooler."

"I say we have to leave the highway," a woman pleaded. "Think of the children!"

But Rex said nothing. From her angle, Miranda couldn't see his eyes through his ash-coated goggles. She was wearing wrap-around sunglasses that protected her eyes enough. Every few minutes, she shook her head free from the black and gray cotton-like substance that was landing on her head scarf.

There had been several aftershocks in the last couple of days since the huge quake. No one had known from where the earthquake originated until the day before, when the ash had begun to fall. The people who Rex called COIL operatives had gathered and determined that Yellowstone must've finally erupted.

Heading west seemed too dangerous with such a natural disaster unfolding, but there were dangers from the OPT in every direction. To complicate matters, only half of the refugees with them were Christians. That meant the other half of the group were responding to the dangers without their fear in check by faith in a Savior and God Almighty.

"Everything will change now," said the woman named Chloe. She'd walked up to stand next to Miranda, watching the animated crowd with her. The woman's curly flowing hair was catching all the ash that fell on her shoulders and down her back. "We can't expect the world to stay the same after this."

"Nothing changes for me." Miranda glanced at Chloe's face. "I'm not arguing. I'm just saying we're believers. We know what's coming, so we know what to expect—Christ. Some volcano or more earthquakes changes nothing."

"Everyone wants Rex to lead them in a different direction. We'll all have to decide individually where we should go."

"There's no decision for me." Miranda shook her head free of ash. "Listen to me. I'm sounding stubborn, but I don't mean it like that. I set myself to going with you guys, so wherever you COIL people go, I go. My view is vertical anyway, so I'll just hang out until then."

"A vertical view?" Chloe smiled. "I like that. Maybe I've lived for so long based on the conditions of others, I just see change happening based on what everyone decides today. You've survived alone for years, so maybe deciding what you'll do is easier."

Miranda surveyed some of the calmly-seated people on the pavement, then turned to Chloe.

"We can't live our lives based on what these people want to do, if they want to go in an unreasonable direction."

"That depends."

Frowning, Miranda turned back to Rex. Chloe couldn't be right, she thought. The people will either do what Rex tells them to do, or they'll go their own way and suffer the consequences.

She left Chloe, not wanting to argue with the short-sighted woman, and noticed one-armed Alice watching from further away. Miranda had sensed a kinship with the slender black woman the first time they'd met. Alice was quiet, but Rex put a lot of trust in her. And she seemed to rely on Rex's leadership with unflinching loyalty.

"What do you think will happen now?" Miranda asked the stoic woman who held her staff in her hand, her pack and rifle strapped to her back. "We keep going, right? Colorado?"

"I hope so." Alice sighed. "That's the only place I know of to meet up with an old friend."

"Who? If you don't mind me asking."

"You've heard us talking about him before—Levi." Alice lifted her head, her eyes hidden behind goggles. "I'd be with him now, except he asked me to stay with Rex and help the refugees."

"So, Levi's like a boyfriend or something?"

"Boyfriend?" Alice scoffed. "No, Levi's married. Was. He probably still thinks his wife, Lyla, is alive. I'm old enough to be his mother, but I love him like a . . . soldier loves her general who's saved her life a dozen times."

"Rex has talked about him like that, too. A real hero."

"He stayed back in New York to help a blind sister in the faith."

"I've heard the refugees call her Radiant Shade." Miranda held up her palm to the ash. "My whole life has been spent relying on myself. I've never really relied on anyone like I'm doing now, or like you have with Levi."

"These people didn't know Levi, even though he saved all their lives. The first night we met, Levi cut off my arm."

"On purpose?" Miranda eyed the woman's stump. "I mean, he didn't mean to, did he?"

"Of course, he meant to. I was gunshot and bleeding out. He cut it off and cauterized the blood vessels to save my life. Then he carried me down a mountain with a baby named Caleb. We crossed a desert together. I don't want much in this life, but I've asked God if I can walk beside Levi again."

"I've seen the way you lead with Rex. Levi must really be something. I mean, more than Rex, though?"

"You'll see. When we get to Meeker." Alice shifted her staff, planting it again on the ground. "And I don't lead with Rex. Chloe and Rex lead us. I just back their play."

"So, you trust Chloe as well?"

"As much as I do Rex."

"She says we might change directions now that the people want to go a different course."

"These COIL people are natural shepherds." Alice spoke with admiration. "If they can't convince everyone to go in a safe direction, then they might accompany them in a dangerous direction."

"So, that sounds sort of foolish."

"Sacrifice might seem foolish, I guess, from one perspective. Some might think Jesus was foolish when He put Himself in danger for us."

"Oh, I didn't mean it like that."

"I think you didn't realize you included Him when you said it," Alice said. "You have a lot to learn about caring for people like Jesus did, Miranda. You could learn from veteran shepherds like Chloe. Caring for people isn't approving of their ways even if they're moving in a bad direction."

Miranda raised her hand and opened her mouth to respond, but Alice walked away. The one-armed woman moved down the interstate and used binoculars to gaze through the falling ash, but she probably couldn't see far.

"Maybe I'm the foolish one," Miranda mumbled to herself, realizing she was arguing with people who'd been guardians over souls for decades. Chloe was right. She'd been living in Chicago, focused on herself staying alive since her parents had died during Pan-Day. Getting ready for heaven had been her parents' whole plan for her. But Alice had gotten through to her. Jesus certainly hadn't been focused on just returning to heaven. There'd been nothing safe about going to the cross for wayward sinners, but He'd done that anyway.

With arms raised, Rex was speaking to the people. Miranda returned to Chloe's side as Rex left the dispersing crowd to talk to the veteran shepherd, as Alice called her.

"I told them we can take an hour to pray and decide what to do," he said. He waved in the other COIL people. "Did you hear their arguments?"

"Yeah, I got the gist of it," Chloe said. Like a mother might do, she reached out and brushed ash from his beard. "What are our options as you see them?"

Rex waited until the others with tranq guns arrived to their huddle. Miranda hadn't been one of them for long, but they didn't dismiss her. She guessed it was because she was a believer. Much to Miranda's surprise, Chloe hooked her arm around her elbow, even though they'd recently disagreed. In response, Miranda used her other hand to hold Chloe's arm. It seemed Chloe had moved past Miranda's foolish opinions. She wondered if she might've stood that same way, arm in arm with her mother, if she were still alive. The COIL operators had welcomed her as family!

However, even after everyone had gathered shoulder to shoulder, Rex was silent, his head bowed. With the ash falling and in the atmosphere of uncertainty, Miranda felt strangely saddened for her new friends. They'd been through so much more than she, and so much change was being forced upon them.

Behind their scarfs and face coverings, a couple people sniffled, and most of the others bowed their heads with Rex. Miranda waited for someone to speak, but no one did right away. It was an odd prayer meeting, and she admired the believers for their quiet devotion to God and His will. There was no fanfare or prayer meeting announcement. This was simply their natural way to heal and prepare and respond.

But then she recalled that not all were believers in the circle. Sean Harris, who some called Sarge, was a short, gruff man with wiry eyebrows. Hank Lowery's wife had said the old sergeant from the Federation wasn't yet a believer. The same went for ex-Colonel Milo Rotham, his squished face hidden behind a thin handkerchief. Miranda could see his eyes, like hers, watching Rex and the others in their silence.

"We're not alone," Rex finally said, and lifted his head.

Miranda nodded, staring up at this bearded giant, realizing that she sensed God's very presence at that moment as well. She knew God was omnipresent, but sometimes, in moments of weakness or decision, He made Himself known more clearly.

"The people are restless," Rex continued, his voice low but strong for those few. Behind Taylor and Hank, their wives stood close, listening as well. "I believe God is giving us three directions to choose from. I can't tell you which to choose. Some of the men and women have already chosen. They may want me to go with them, but I'm settled on going to Meeker.

"Meeker is closer to Yellowstone, so it'll be hard to find water and game if the ash keeps falling. If you go with me, it ain't gonna be easy, as my cousin would say. But it's the only direction in which I think I'll find my dad. If Levi's still alive, he may show up there with Nathan, Chen Li, and Jenna, too. Some of you may owe your lives to them, but that doesn't mean you have to go with me. I also have to go on to Meeker for Levi, because he doesn't yet know what happened to his wife in Pennsylvania."

"I have to see him about that, too, Rex," Milo said through his handkerchief. "I'm going to Meeker with you."

Rex nodded at the ex-officer, but no one else seemed to have decided just yet. Except Miranda. Whatever other options existed, she didn't want to leave Rex, even if it meant going into the ashen hell of Colorado.

"The safest route for the people may be to go north."
Rex sighed. "I think there'll be less ash toward the
northern end of Wisconsin. Whoever goes that way should
keep going into Canada, though, even though the winter
will be harsh. I'd like to send all of you that way, but I
know not all the people will go. Continuing to Meeker
could be the death of us all. There's a chance that Canada
might even be free of the OPT. I can almost certainly
assure you that we'll face more of the OPT going west."

"We'll take them north, Rex," Bruno said softly, then
tugged Scooter's scarf from his mouth. "And if that's
Scooter under all those protective layers, he'll go with me.
We wouldn't know what to do without each other."

"I'd protest to leading anyone, if anyone would
listen." Scooter readjusted his scarf, then elbowed Bruno
in the gut. "But I'll chaperone this big guy to make sure he
goes far enough north and doesn't shy away from a little
frostbite."

"Then I know those who go with you will be in good
hands." Rex paused, waiting for more volunteers, but no
one else spoke right away. "There's quite a push to go
south as well. Some of the men who have hunting rifles
want to go fight the OPT wherever they can set up a
resistance. Many of them are from the Illinois group. I
wouldn't encourage any believers to throw in with the
violence they're planning."

"The strength we have left should be expressed in
love," Nick Zoft said, "not warfare."

"Well said, Nick. So, my friends, those are our
options, I think. Sorry if I can't offer you more. If Levi
were here, maybe he'd just send the OPT running somehow, and we'd see a different outcome. Then again, the
world is going the way the Lord said it would, and we just
need to spiritually stand in it, not fight it with our flesh.
We fight on our knees."

"We'll take our families north," Taylor said for
himself and Hank, who nodded beside him.

"I'm up for the challenge of going west with you, Rex." Sean offered his hand to Rex. "But I'm going to see the people from New York through to Canada. I think it's what Nathan would want from me. I promised him. If you see him in Meeker, tell him I did my part like I said I would. That would mean a lot to me."

"To Canada." Nick nodded, chuckling nervously, as if he knew the hardships ahead.

"Alice is with me," Rex said, "so you guys might want to have a new point-person walking out front. We'll leave you all the radios. We won't need them."

"I need to see Nathan and Chen Li again," Chloe said. "And I won't sleep in peace until I see Jenna and Levi safe and sound."

"And who knows who else Levi has picked up along his way, right?" Rex chuckled. "Where we're going, we won't have anything to feed Ruth and Naomi, so you guys take both the goats and the rest of the animals."

"Only if I don't have to milk the goats," Scooter said. "One of them keeps nibbling on my ears at night. Unless that's been Bruno."

Bruno roared with laughter and jostled with his smaller friend.

"Okay, let's brief the others and see who else is going north or south." Rex clapped his hands. "We'll all head out in the morning after we pray together, huh?"

The group shook hands and dispersed. Miranda waited until the others left, then she approached Rex.

"I'd like to go west with you."

"Really?" He brushed ash out of his beard again. "You know it's going to be about the worst trip you could ever take? This ash is probably killing everything. It'll be hard going, a solid month and a half of marching through wasteland. There'll be a lot of death, too. Our only hope is to reach the mountains where the volcanic devastation may be less, but there's no way to know yet."

"I finally found people I like—you, Chloe, and Alice. I'm not leaving you guys." She tried to read him through his facial covering. "I won't slow you up. And I'd kind of like to see what all the buzz is about your cousin."

"Levi?" Rex grunted. "You two are actually alike—all boldness and confidence. He'll love you."

"What about you?" Miranda held her breath when he went silent, studying her through her glasses.

"I'm less about boldness and confidence, and more about blunder and crawling."

"That wasn't my question, Rex Caspertein."

"Of course, I, uh, love you, too." His voice was shaky. "You're my sister in the faith, right?"

"Hmm. Not very smooth." She patted his arm. "Maybe we can turn your blundering and crawling into boldness and confidence along our journey, huh?"

She walked away, her heart light while he stuttered after her. No suitors had approached her in Chicago. No one had wanted a head-strong Christian nuisance with an eye for America's last days. But Rex was an easy target for her heart. If these were their last months on earth, she didn't mind spending them with the giant Caspertein man.

Chapter Four

R udy Caspertein looked for the sun that early Colorado morning, but the overcast sky hid the orange ball. Of course, it wasn't actually overcast. Now, five days after the Yellowstone eruption, Rudy realized he might never see the blue sky again.

He tested the straps on the three pack horses hitched outside his partially-collapsed log home. The violent aftershocks had forced them as a family to sleep outside the last few nights. Rudy had set up a wall tent in the yard between the hay barn and the house where he, Annette, Vorca, and Caleb could sleep. Now that same wall tent was folded and stowed on the first pack horse, along with large containers of water and food for the four travelers. The next two horses carried hay, grain, and more water.

"That's everything," Annette said as she set a second heavy backpack on the ground. She'd gathered the last of the items they wanted to take from inside the house. "It's sad to see it all go, isn't it? We weren't here together long, but so many memories. Good memories."

Together, they pet the head and neck of the lead pack horse. They'd talked the evening before about what animals to take on their journey away from the ash. Most of the livestock would die soon. Only a few riding horses had been brought in to be fed and watered at the house.

"When we run out of food for them," Rudy said, "we'll need to butcher the critters on the road. But maybe we'll reach Moab before that, and there'll be graze land."

"Yeah, maybe." Annette didn't sound too hopeful. She turned and lifted Rudy's pack for him. "We're witnessing the end of everything. It's hard to imagine there'll be much left after this for God to bring the tribulation years upon America."

"After this, there won't be a recognizable America." He fit his arms into the straps, buckled the chest strap, then lifted Annette's pack for her. "Many people have known that America's not in Bible prophecy. Now we know why. It started with a pandemic, led to a collapse, and then all the internal strife and death. Europe, Africa, and Asia will still be the focus of prophetic events, just like they've always been. Vorca, you ready?"

The Native American woman had already fit her own pack onto her back. If she were any other woman in her early twenties, Rudy would've checked the contents of her pack to ensure she'd packed only the essentials. But this was Vorca. Annette had shared many stories of the young woman's survival skills she'd put to use crossing half the country a year earlier.

Vorca jabbered in her native language. It sounded like she was scolding him, but Rudy had learned to exercise patience with the woman. She lifted Caleb into his arms. Rudy was tall enough to set Caleb on the mountain of gear on the lead horse. He settled into a pocket the child couldn't easily fall out of. Caleb responded to Vorca in her own language, then he squealed with delight.

"Horsey!" He slapped the nearest jug of water like a drum. "Go, horsey!"

Lastly, Rudy adjusted Caleb's tied mask on his face, made from a bandana sewn by Annette.

"He's a Caspertein all right." Rudy took the lead rope. "All he can think about is the adventure ahead."

"Don't single him out." Annette bumped her shoulder into her husband as they started forward. "All you men love a good survival challenge. If Rex and Levi were here, you three would be having the time of your lives."

"I'm too old to be having the time of my life." He leaned toward her. "And too married."

Annette laughed under her own mask and fit sunglasses over her eyes to ward off the ash.

"We may die soon," Annette said, "but at least it'll be with a smile on our faces—ribbing each other to the grave."

"*Ribbing?* I see my vernacular is rubbing off on you."

She didn't respond. Instead, she touched his arm.

"Rudy? Where are the others?"

Not far ahead at the edge of town, they saw only one figure instead of the four or five that Rudy expected to join them on their southern journey.

"I only see Trapper." Rudy glanced down an empty street of Meeker. The ash had piled deep overnight. "No one's outside. Maybe the others changed their minds. This lighter-colored ash is probably less dangerous."

"Trapper doesn't have any gear with him!" Annette slowed her pace. "What if we're alone?"

"We're four Casperteins accompanied by the Lord." Rudy tried to sound optimistic. "We're never alone. The others are probably waiting for us on the other end of town."

"No, I don't like this, Rudy."

"Fast, horsey!" Caleb roused, which brought a string of correction from Vorca.

Rudy slowed the horse train to a stop in front of Trapper and passed the lead rope to Annette so he could shake the older man's hand. Trapper waited with only one riding horse, the animal's muzzle wrapped lightly with mosquito netting.

"I expected to see you with your gear and a few other pack horses, Trap." Rudy didn't like what he read on his neighbor's face. "This isn't what we settled on just last night. We're under the gun, my friend, quite literally, in fact."

"That's why I've decided to stay." Trapper lowered his eyes. "Don't make this harder than it already is, Rudy."

He heard Annette sigh loudly behind him. No, it wasn't a sigh, but a growl under her breath.

"So? Is that why Dathan isn't here either?" Rudy didn't bother to disguise his frustration. "How about Gail and Tilda? They heard you were cancelling and that discouraged them as well?"

"My son came by the house last night after you left."

"What's Mayor Wayne have to do with us leaving, Trap?"

"Rudy, he's my son."

It was Rudy's turn to sigh, but now with patience in tow.

"You're right. I'm sorry. What did Wayne have to say?"

"He's been instructed by his OPT superiors to begin making arrests, especially in the shadow of this latest catastrophe. Denver doesn't want insurrection added to the unrest and fear many towns are feeling."

"Arrests for people who refuse to take the Oath, I assume?" Rudy thought of the four battle rifles he'd packed on the lead horse, with enough ammo to supply a military unit. "Maybe I'll need my rifle sooner than I thought."

"I told him you were leaving, and he promised he wouldn't bother you if you didn't let anyone else see you. Deep down, he fears you and doesn't want to have to face your family. He'd appreciate it if you went around town to the west."

"We're going down Main Street, Trapper. What about you?"

"He said I'd be left alone, if I wanted to stay."

"And what about the Oath?"

"As long as he's Advocate, he said I won't be made to take it."

"That may not be up to him. That Kane lady from Denver will be checking lists and rosters."

"I'm also thinking of your boys, Rudy."

"What do Rex and Levi have to do with this? They can take care of themselves. You know that. They're both good marksmen and fine Christians."

"But who in town will tell them where you guys have gone? Besides, Rudy, I'm too old to go all the way to Moab. I'd love to find a nice canyon to die in on the Colorado River, but this is my home. I'll stick around. If your boys show up, I'll warn them away from Wayne and send them south after you."

"Thank you, Trapper." Annette brushed past Rudy and embraced the man. "You're risking your life for our family to be together."

"Well, some of it is selfish." Trapper chuckled. "I'd like to think Wayne could be softening. He might step away from the OPT. Eventually."

"We can pray for that." Annette returned to the horse.

"So, Wayne and his OPT buddies in town have begun to make arrests? Interesting." Rudy turned and glared at the town. "That might explain the absence of Dathan and the ladies. The question is, did Wayne say anything about starting to enact the penalty phase of the Oath? Has he begun executions?"

"He didn't say anything about that. I'm sure he wouldn't, Rudy. I'm sure—"

"The OPT is driving now, Trap." Rudy walked back to the lead horse and unbuckled a bed roll above a water jug. "We can't be sure of anyone who's taken their side, especially those in leadership. I was hoping we wouldn't need these for a few more weeks, but here we are."

He passed a rifle to Annette, and an ammo vest full of magazines. She expertly checked the chamber and hung the weapon over her shoulder. Rudy had fired guns since he'd been a youth growing up with Wynter and Titus in Arkansas, but these were the COIL battle rifles—bullpups with a range of six hundred yards. Annette had come from San Diego carrying the rifle, so she was more of an expert than he was.

"Go home, Trapper." Rudy zipped up his own ammo vest. "I send my love with you, and I'm grateful for any message you're able to pass on to the boys, but now we need to focus on others who need saving."

"I'm sorry, Rudy." The man hung his head. "I've let you down. I've let the OPT divide us. I'm just an old—"

"Stop it." Rudy suddenly embraced the man in one of his bear hugs. He hugged the man tightly until he felt Trapper shudder for air. Then he held him at arm's length. "We're not divided spiritually, only moving in different directions physically. I know you'd never take the Oath. Even if it's not quite the mark of the beast yet, it's probably its predecessor. I know your heart, brother. We may be parting ways abruptly this morning, but we'll meet in the air one way or another."

"Thank you, Rudy." The man's goggles fogged up. "Thank you."

Rudy waited for Trapper to start back to his ranch on horseback. He was glad he and his elder brother in the faith hadn't parted ways with hostility, even though it wasn't an ideal situation. When Trapper was a distance away, Rudy turned to Vorca. He took the lead rope from his wife and gave it to the plump native woman.

"Take Caleb and the horses," he instructed, gesturing widely with his arms, "and stop and wait for us on the south end of town. Okay? Uh, Annette?"

More slowly, Annette instructed Vorca, but Vorca only stared blankly back, before she rattled something in her strange language, which set Caleb to his own jabbering. But without further deliberation, Vorca led the horses away to the west.

"Will we ever see those two again?" Rudy joked, looking after the animals and his two adopted family members. "It's hard to tell with her sometimes."

"She'll be fine." Annette hoisted her rifle higher. "What about us?"

"Levi took back the town a year ago. Now, we take our people back from the town—and get out of town."

"Sounds great. How?"

"Can you cover me from the side of Hotel Meeker? Just stay on ground level, because we'll need to leave in a hurry."

"No one's going to shoot us will they, Rudy?" Annette looked away. "These are people we know—who know us!"

"Most of the Christians have left already. Gail and Tilda are in their eighties. They've lived in Meeker half their lives, but it seems no one is standing up to Wayne. No one's off-limits to the OPT, and Wayne is the OPT now."

Annette walked stiffly over to Highway 13 to get behind Hotel Meeker. With the gun in her arms, there was no misreading her intentions. She was ready for battle. Rudy spent a few seconds steeling himself in the Lord's grace—whether they lived or died in the next few minutes—then he walked up Main Street. A few blocks later, he stopped in the street. The courthouse was on his right, and the hotel was on his left.

He wasn't surprised that Dathan had been arrested, since he was so outspoken about his new faith and he lived in town. And he wasn't too popular with some of the traditionalists since he was an outsider and an ex-Federation officer. The Christian refugees who'd lived there a year had welcomed him and even discipled him, but now many of them had left, fleeing the certain wrath of the OPT.

Besides Dathan, Gail and Tilda were also left in Rudy's hands. Neither woman would dare turn their backs on their loving Savior. They were all who were left in Meeker who'd wanted to leave before the devastating ash ruined resources too much to travel at all.

Silently, Annette crept up the alley alongside the hotel and stopped at the corner where she remained in some cover. The ash was falling now in smaller particles. It blocked out the sun, giving a dusk-feel, but Rudy could still see a few blocks away to at least 11th Street.

He turned to face the courthouse. Two men with rifles exited the front doors in which the glass had been replaced by plywood years before. They aimed their rifles at Rudy and took up positions on either side of the door. Then, Mayor Wayne Sullivan emerged from the building to stand at his full height, his black mask and glasses seeming oversized on his narrow face.

"I thought I might see you here," Wayne yelled, his voice muffled, "even though I thought you'd agreed to leave."

"You know why I'm here." Rudy didn't shift his rifle upward, even though it was in his hands. All he had to do was pivot, raise it, and fire. "I'm not leaving without my people and their belongings."

If they shot him right there, he didn't doubt that Annette would charge their guns and get shot herself. Maybe this was a ten-man job, not a two-gun solution.

"This is an OPT precinct now, Mr. Caspertein." Wayne crossed his arms. "Do you want to join them in a cell? I'm giving you a chance to leave."

"No, you have it wrong, son." Rudy tried to measure the angles. Was he blocking his wife's shot? "I'm giving you a chance to bring out my people. A year ago, my boys took this town back from the Federation. The same is about to happen to you, if you don't lower your weapons."

"I know Levi and Rex aren't here any longer." Wayne pulled down his mask to show his smile. "Who's going to take the town? You? I'm not a boy anymore, Rudy, and you're not my Sunday school teacher. I'm in charge now. I'm the mayor! And I'm the OPT Advocate of Meeker."

Rudy shrugged his shoulders, which was his signal, and a rifle boomed behind him. A bullet zipped past his ear like a hornet, and he dropped to one knee. Before he could raise his own rifle, and before the second gunman could locate her, Annette fired again. Both men on either side of Wayne crumbled, unconscious.

Wayne stuttered and backed up into the door of the courthouse. Rudy grunted as he rose to his feet then approached Wayne. Up close, Rudy looked down at the mayor.

"I don't need you conscious to get them out of here. What'll it be, Wayne?"

"I'll . . . get them." Wayne frowned and raised his hands in front of his face. "You never said you had any backup."

"We're Casperteins." Rudy chuckled. "We shouldn't have to tell anyone that."

Rudy followed Wayne into the courthouse and found it empty and dark. They moved to the rear where the holding cells were occupied by three people—Dathan Tentmaker, Gail, and Tilda. Only Gail and Tilda rose from their benches where they'd been praying.

"He resisted." Wayne used a heavy brass key to unlock Dathan's cell. "It's not my fault, Rudy."

Taking the key from Wayne, Rudy shoved the man into the cell as Dathan moaned and rolled his head on the concrete bench. The muscled ex-colonel had wrapped his torso in his own long-sleeve thermal, but his wounds had bled through the rough bandage.

"You came for me." Dathan closed his eyes as Rudy set this hand on his friend's forehead. "You didn't need to bother, Rudy. I'm done in."

"Can you walk? Or ride?" Rudy's other hand trembled over the bloody shirt, indecisive whether to examine the wound or to let it be. "I can put you on one of the horses."

"I . . . wouldn't make it." Dathan coughed. Fluid had filled at least one lung. "This is my last stop, even if it's not my final destination. Give me this honor."

"Honor?" Rudy smiled as a tear dropped on the man's shoulder. "You remembered that lesson."

"There's no shame in dying for Christ. I'll never take an Oath that rejects the Savior as being my only hope. I may be a young believer, but I won't break."

"You're a giant of the faith in God's Book, Dathan."

"Get Gail and Tilda out of here. Just take my gear, would you? I don't want my Bible in the OPT's hands."

Rudy took a deep breath, his eyes locked with Dathan's. Levi had won the man's loyalty a year earlier, but God had won the man's heart. And from the Bible studies over the last months, Rudy had taught the privilege of enduring persecution for the sake of Christ. Dathan was ready, Rudy saw, and he almost desired to stay and die with him under the OPT's hand.

"We have a chance to live free, so we will." Rudy patted the man's shoulder. "I'll get the others on their way. And I'll carry your gear myself if the horses won't. They're already groaning under all our furniture. You know, the piano, a sofa, an armoire . . . You don't have any of those in your pack, do you?"

"Don't make me laugh. It hurts too much. Go. And don't pity me."

"Pity you? You're about to leave a witness to the OPT that'll get you an extra crown in heaven. We envy a hero. We don't pity him."

"If you ever see Levi again, thank him for me, for giving me a chance. I hope I didn't waste it."

"You didn't, Dathan. The murals you painted have marked this town permanently. Your life touched us all." Rudy backed out of the cell, pulling Wayne with him. "Save me a place at the table."

Dathan weakly raised his hand but said nothing more.

Outside the cells, Rudy noticed confiscated gear piled against the wall. He spotted a pack with a Bible on top that obviously belonged to Dathan. The two elderly ladies' gear was next to Dathan's.

Rudy unlocked the women's cell and held it wide for them to exit.

"Is Dathan all right?" asked Gail, a sturdy woman with white, curly hair. Her quick humor and servant's hands had cared for every citizen of Meeker at some point before and since Pan-Day. "He was shot when he got in front of Wayne's men as we were trying to get away to meet you at the crossroads."

"He'll be staying here to leave a final testimony," Rudy said.

Their silence indicated that they understood the bold faith of Dathan as he faced death at the hands of his executioners.

Wayne didn't fight Rudy as he directed him inside the cell.

"You won't get far," the mayor said. "I'll report this to Advocate Kane, and she'll send troops after you. They're already getting those trucks running. No seed of sedition against humanity's survival will be allowed to take root."

"Haven't you seen that ash outside?" Rudy slammed the cell door and spoke through the side of the door. "The OPT isn't determining anything at all. God is bringing humanity to its knees, and that's exactly where you should be—on your knees!"

Rudy slapped the door with his palm, hoping he made Wayne jump, then he turned his back to the cells. He was met by Tilda's slender frame, her goggles already around her neck. The resolute woman from Missouri had been visiting her friend, Gail, when Pan-Day had struck, and she'd stayed in Colorado with her ever since.

"How are the others?" Tilda asked, her free hand on his chest, which was nearly as high as the short woman could reach. "They're standing?"

"Yes, the few believers who're staying in town— they're standing. And Dathan will be with them in the end." He looked to Gail, whose four hand-sewn quilts were rolled and fastened above and below a conventional backpack. "With all those quilts, we won't have to worry about sleeping on the hard, rocky ground."

"These aren't for the ground." Gail fit her glasses over her face. "We don't know who else we'll meet on the road who won't have any sleeping bags. They can at least wrap themselves in a quilt to make do."

"Of course." Rudy eyed Tilda's pack, hoping it contained more practical gear, but Rudy had known he'd need to have enough supplies on horseback for all of them. He picked up Dathan's hefty pack and swung it over his left shoulder as he stuck the Bible in his coat. "Let's head out, ladies. Annette is waiting outside."

Rudy led them out. When they emerged from the courthouse, he again lifted his battle rifle into firing position, but the two Defenders were still laying where they'd fallen. Bending down, he collected their eye glasses from them so his group would have extras on their trip. As he stood, he waved to Annette, and she waved back, letting him know the way was clear.

He walked into the street and noticed several citizens in their windows or on the edges of the street, but none were there to resist his departure. These were friends, even a few believers from the local body. They'd decided to remain in Meeker for different reasons, and Wayne would certainly seek them out one at a time.

"See you soon, Rudy," said an older gentleman, his scoliosis having twisted his spine. "Any day now."

"See you, Otis." Rudy knew the disabled man would be rounded up in a day or two and executed, but his eyes were on eternity. "You guys finish well."

Others waved or stood and watched solemnly as they left.

Gail and Tilda walked arm in arm behind him, their footfalls like whispers in the ash. Annette followed farther back on the left side of the street, her posture revealing that she was in defensive mode. They passed 13th Street, then approached the Meeker Ditch where the sheepdog competitions had taken place every year out in the meadow. There, Vorca led the horses into sight, with Caleb sitting high like a prince on his stallion.

It was about two hundred miles to Moab where they hoped to find a narrow canyon with grass and clean water. It seemed doubtful they'd find anywhere that the ash hadn't fallen, but Rudy had to try. He was protective about Caleb, not willing for the child to fall into the hands of the OPT. And something kept him hopeful about seeing Rex and Levi again, even though leaving Meeker made that more unlikely.

He stopped and waited for Annette to catch up as the others plodded ahead. Annette was crying by the time she reached Rudy. When he took her hand in his, she leaned against him and they strolled along together. If he'd been alone, Rudy thought he might've stopped and looked back. But Meeker was in his past now. He didn't need to look back. His home in the White River Valley was gone, covered in poisonous ash, left in the determined hands of the OPT.

Mia Brogdon held onto her husband's arm as they traipsed through the trees of a forest in either Georgia or Alabama. Sometimes, she kept Kip on his feet, and then there were miles that Kip had kept her upright. She didn't pay much attention to the roads or signs when they happened across them. All she focused on was the broad back of her cousin leading them west. Levi's pack was heaped high, carrying the weight that usually two men would carry, but his pace was still fast enough that he needed to stop and wait for them every fifty yards or so.

Behind her, Brian Steelman guided Jenna through the woodland. There was no opportunity to converse since Brian was steadily informing Jenna of what obstacles lay ahead. During the two days that Levi had allowed them to recover above Ellijay, Mia had listened to Jenna's story of infiltrating the Federation, lasting over ten years. But Mia hadn't shared her and Kip's story with anyone yet. That was partly from trying to gain her strength after so much abuse, but also the loss they'd suffered was still too painful to talk about.

But her loss wasn't the only loss in their band of six. She'd never seen Levi so quiet. Having grown up with her older cousin, she'd known him only as an energetic, skinny, young man who'd marched beside his father for years. Their trek from California over a year earlier seemed like ten years ago. The people Levi had gone east to save were either dead or had gone farther north. Only Jenna remained. And Brian Steelman, who Mia remembered as a wounded man in a western town.

Levi crouched behind a tree, and Mia pulled Kip to a stop behind Levi. Only then did she note their surroundings. Since she hadn't been paying attention, she hadn't realized they'd entered some southern community. She remembered coming this way with other Servalites a few months earlier. There was a large lake nearby, and friendly people.

Friendly! The people of Ellijay had seemed friendly at first as well, right up until they saw the Servalites as an anti-human threat since they wouldn't sign the Oath of Solidarity.

Jenna huddled against Mia as Brian left her in Mia's care. Brian hopped over a bush and clumsily fell into Levi. Mia could see that Brian's rifle was decades old, but she remembered he was a fine marksman. The mute, masked woman with a battle rifle moved like a ghost about twenty yards north, parallel to Levi. Lena looked to Levi for a signal, and Mia smiled with pride.

"What're you smiling about?" Kip asked, his breath coming in short gasps.

Mia straightened her face. Indeed, how could she smile after their heartbreak, their tragedy?

"I was just watching everyone rely on Levi. It reminded me of California. The Casperteins held San Diego together—what was left of the city, anyway."

"Yeah, I remember. Dad was concerned about Titus' influence, but he also used Titus as an ally to build up the military. Those were good years."

"I want to hear about those good years," Jenna said softly, easing forward.

"They weren't all good years, Jenna," Mia sighed. "I lived in fear of being forced to become someone's wife. Titus wouldn't let me go anywhere alone. But Levi—"

"You're smiling again." Kip's fingers, with dirty nails, touched her jaw. "I've missed that smile."

"It feels shameful to smile." She looked away. "It feels wrong."

"I don't think God wants us to grieve forever, Mia. The Servalites are still here. God isn't finished using us. We can use our sorrow to help others through their sorrow."

Mia felt like objecting to his hopes to serve again when they were so broken, but he drew her into an embrace before she could respond.

"I think we're here," Levi said to Brian, a weathered map in his hand. "It's Guntersville. The lake is that way."

"See if they've got clean water?" Brian shook his canteen. "The others are out, too."

"If there are people," Levi said, "there's water. Maybe they filter it free of the ash if there's not an underground well nearby. At least the ash is thinning now. Let's be careful. No repeats of Ellijay. Locked and loaded."

"No arguments from me." Brian checked his rifle. Though he'd been exhausted coming out of Ellijay, Mia could see the man was back to full strength. "How do you want to do this?"

"I'll go in and scout around that lodge there with the sign out front. You guys cover me. If it's safe, I'll wave you forward."

"You sure you want to put yourself out there like that?" Brian pet the dog they called Auggie as she nuzzled him. "Maybe we should wait until dark."

"It ain't easy drawing fire in the daylight." Levi slapped Brian's shoulder, chuckling as he moved from his cover. "It wouldn't be courage unless there were risks."

"Yep, he hasn't changed after all," Mia joked to Jenna. "He still thinks it's heroic getting shot at first."

"Describe what he's walking into," Jenna said. "And what are our escape routes?"

"Are you still thinking strategically after all this time?" Mia asked. "You know you're not in New York anymore."

"I try not to be an unnecessary burden on anyone." Jenna shifted on her knees. "If we can think ahead and stay out of danger, we keep men like Levi safe from having to rescue us all the time."

"But I wonder if he'd have anything to do if he wasn't putting his life on the line for us all the time." Mia laughed, then caught herself when she heard the strange sound. It was the sound of joy. "Okay, what he called the lodge is a big building, two stories, and paneled. Maybe an old hotel. There's a sign out front that welcomes travelers. I see a garden off to the right. There's some corn and rows of other vegetables. And next to that, I think there's a big pen farther off the road."

"Tell me about the roads."

"Okay, there's the highway in front of us, and then the driveway that goes off to the lodge and toward what must be the lake. Levi is nearly to the front porch of the lodge now. Lena is off to the right and moving closer to the garden to cover Levi. How do you guys know her again?"

"Oh, that's a wonderful story." Jenna sighed. "About fifteen years ago—"

"A story for another time, please?" Brian suggested from where he aimed his rifle. "If things get ugly, we're moving farther back into the trees, so get ready."

Mia didn't like Brian telling them what to do. This was Levi's show. He gave the orders. She leaned on Kip's shoulder to see Levi over Brian's head and shoulders.

"Levi's talking to someone at the front door," she whispered to Jenna. "I can't see who it is, but Levi has his rifle under his arm, ready to fire. I've seen him like that a hundred times. All blue eyes and smiles, but he could still shoot the head off a rattler without blinking at a hundred yards."

"Wait." Jenna titled her head. "The snake wasn't blinking, or Levi wasn't blinking? Who's not blinking when the shot takes place?"

Mia couldn't hold back her burst of laughter. Jenna shushed her but laughed no less abruptly.

"Ladies, please!" Brian scolded.

Mia took a breath to fire back at the new guy, but Kip set his hand on hers, and she knew what he was saying. Kip could do that. He wasn't a talker, except when he was preaching, but a single gesture from him could express a whole speech. Although Mia wasn't taking orders from anyone but Levi, Kip was her husband, and before God, she listened to him even when she least wanted to.

Outside the lodge and next to the garden, Levi stood with two strangers. He waved his friends forward, and Mia sighed with relief that it seemed they'd be sleeping indoors and out of the ash for a change. Since she and Kip had run from Ellijay days earlier with nothing but their soiled clothes, they'd been relying on Levi and his people for fresh clothes, sleeping blankets, and shelter. Tears came to Mia's eyes at the thought of a hot bath in the lodge. She was as tough as any other traveler, but she had her limits for the rugged living the men seemed to enjoy as a test of their willpower.

"Stay alert," Brian instructed her, Kip, and Jenna. "And stay behind me. Be ready to run at any minute."

"I guess this is just the world we live in now," Mia said as she took Jenna's hand and placed it on her shoulder. "We're ready to run everywhere we arrive."

"Everywhere until heaven," Jenna said.

Mia felt the rebuff. Lack of sleep, comfort, and safety had worn on her mind. Before Ellijay, she and Kip had led groups of Servalites into dozens of towns throughout the South. Now, after barely surviving an execution when others had perished—it brought out her pessimism.

They crossed the highway behind Brian, and Mia noticed Lena had remained in the trees, covering them. She was like one-armed Alice had been a year earlier—guarded, loyal to Levi, reclusive. But instead of missing an arm, most of her mouth was missing. Mia had seen the woman's face when her veil had dropped in camp a few days earlier. God seemed to unexpectedly use different kinds of needy people, Mia pondered, and they seemed to rally around Levi, who welcome them as assets.

Moving up the driveway, they entered the yard where Levi met them alone. Lena walked up briskly behind them yet kept her back to the wall of garden vegetation, the rifle in her hands, her eyes checking their surroundings.

"We can stay here for the night," Levi said. "It ain't easy sleeping in the devil's lair, but that's the way it is now. The OPT has already claimed Guntersville, but this guy says he's sympathetic to our plight. Lena, hang around out here. I'll spell you at nightfall. Brian, I'll wake you after midnight for your turn at watch. If they come for us, we'll at least have someone out here to warn us."

"How quickly can I get into a tub?" Mia blurted, then realized there was a man present who wasn't a relative, but Brian didn't react to her familiarity. "It's been a couple months."

"Rooms and food for everyone," Levi said, "but this isn't a safe place. The town is just up the shore a few blocks, and the owner, Marshall Moore, says they're already arresting people who won't sign the Oath. The locals, at least."

"I can't be silent about the Good News, Levi," Kip said, his weak frame swaying. But his gaze was fierce. "They still need to hear the gospel."

"Kip, I expect no less from you." Levi smiled warmly. "Just remember, Marshall may be sympathetic, but everyone in this town has already signed the Oath. It's a lot to break through, but the Lord favors your style."

"Wait." Jenna raised her hand. "You're encouraging us to be outspoken about Christ? Even with all the danger?"

"I'd rather we keep a low profile," Brian said.

"We could move quietly and safely through Guntersville, I suppose," Levi offered, winking at Kip, "and leave the citizens without an option for eternal life."

"I'm just saying that we live to share with others if we remain under cover," Jenna said. Mia felt the blind woman's body tense beside her. "We didn't last twenty years in the Federation by needlessly exposing ourselves to danger."

"That depends on whose needs you're talking about," Kip said, his voice soft, his head low. "Mia and I need medical attention and to get our health back, but Marshall and this house need Jesus. One need outweighs the other need."

"Yes, I guess I'm used to covert Christianity," Jenna conceded. "It sustained Christians in the city, but the needs are different out here."

"There's a time and place for both methods," Levi declared with authority like what Mia remembered his father having. "Caution doesn't mean silence. It just means we share Christ with an understanding of the dangers. We're sheep among wolves, my friends. Make no mistake about that, even if we carry weapons. At no time do we tape our mouths shut, and at no time do we act like wolves against wolves. Share openly. Lena's got our backs."

He signaled to Lena.

"Aah." She patted the stock of her rifle, then turned and walked into the trees at the edge of the highway.

Levi led them through the front door of the lodge into a spacious great room with a wood floor and large, round rugs spaced evenly where furniture was strangely missing. Only a dining table and ten wooden chairs furnished the area. A wide kitchen on the far side was occupied by a thin woman, her blonde hair piled atop her head.

"Your rooms are ready." Marshall Moore was a kind-faced man with thin white hair and shining blue eyes. He clasped his hands. "Clean sheets on the beds, candles on the dressers. Three matches are all I can spare per room."

"This is a hotel?" Jenna reached for the owner's hand. He hesitantly accepted her touch, seeming to recognize her blind condition. "God bless you for caring for strangers like this."

"Uh, of course. But, uh, it's not, you know, free." He looked to Levi. "I'd rather settle up now if we could? My daughter and I haven't had but a couple of guests for two weeks, a man and his son. We have expenses, too, you understand."

"Thanks to Nathan . . ." Levi unzipped a pocket on his pack and withdrew a cloth-wrapped bundle. "Everywhere he and I went since New York, he would search cars and kitchen drawers for these babies. That should cover our stay, I hope."

Marshall received the bundle, loosened the knot, and cradled the sudden overflow of an assortment of lighters—about thirty of them.

"Lighters!" He hustled to the dining table and let them fall on the surface. One at a time, he shook them close to his ear. "They're not empty. Are they full?"

"We refilled them with lighter fluid—all of them." Levi clapped the man on the back. "This squares us for three rooms and a meal?"

"And a hot bath," Mia inserted.

"Of course!" Marshall walked into the kitchen. "Susan, look! Lighters! Two dozen of them."

The young woman wiped her hands on her waist rag and faced their guests.

"You may be able to buy off my father," she hissed, "but you're endangering us. The OPT is no joke! They're trying to bring back the American dream, and people like you are standing against that."

"Oh, my sister." Mia left Jenna on Kip's arm and went to the kitchen. "We know the OPT means well. They're frightened and hopeful all at once. But sometimes in the most frightful moments, we ignore the most obvious. Look at us. You and I are about the same age. We're too young to remember how globalism was a rancid decay all over the world before Pan-Day. Maybe it's familiar to people, so they're returning to it now in their hour of desperation. But we shouldn't ignore the more basic needs we all have inside us. Spiritual needs. Needs that only God can fulfill when we consider eternity."

"I'm not listening to this." The woman's jaw muscles clenched. "You're throwing away this country's only chance at rebuilding our society. That makes you the enemy. Now get out of my face. I'll cook for you because you've paid us, but I don't have to listen to any of your preaching."

"Okay." Mia backed away. "My name is Mia. The OPT tortured me and killed my baby. My cousin rescued me a week ago after I no longer wanted to live. That's the OPT you think is restoring the American dream."

Mia returned to Jenna's side.

"I was going to ask you about the little one," Levi said, "when the time seemed right."

"It's okay." Mia took her cousin's arm. "Our little one is with the Father now."

After all of Mia's determination to soak in a bath, it was Jenna that Mia insisted use the upstairs tub first. While Kip visited with Marshall downstairs, Mia made sure Brian and Levi filled the cast iron monster in the bathroom with hot water hauled up from the stove downstairs—which needed a steady supply of wood as well.

"This hardly seems fair," Jenna argued once the two were alone in the bathroom. "You should go first. At least I won't be able to see the color of the water if I get in after you. I'm telling you—you won't like the color after me!"

"Oh, ye of little imagination!" Mia laughed. "As long as we have strong men to carry water for us, we'll each get fresh water! Soak it up. I'll be back before the water cools."

In the hallway, she positioned Brian outside the bathroom door. Candles flickered from the lamp stands where light bulbs once shined.

"Don't move from this doorway for anything," Mia instructed, "and this door better not open again unless I'm the one who opens it."

"Let me tell you something." He leaned over her. "I was protecting Jenna a long time before you came around."

"Well, now I'm here, and you'll do it my way, or you'll deal with Levi about it!"

A few seconds passed, and Mia tried to mask her swallow. Brian was inches taller, and in her condition, she couldn't fight off anyone. But Brian's face cracked a smile.

"Levi? I'm fine about dealing with Levi." He stood against the door, feet planted, hands folded before him like a sentry. "It's you who scares me."

Mia scoffed, but she allowed him to see her satisfaction before she turned away. Her heart softened toward the new man in that instant. She had no reason to suspect him after all. He was operating in the nature of Christ.

She left him there and descended the stairs with care. Her strength was still returning, and the walk that day had exhausted what few muscles she had. Although she desperately wanted that bath and then to pass out in bed, she knew God had given her the job of caring for others. It had first come with being a Caspertein, and now it was her responsibility as Kip's wife. Even at that moment, Kip was discussing the evidence of God with the lodge owner. Regardless of the risks and their own recent trauma, he was a witness for Christ, and she needed to remain like-minded.

Outside on the porch, Mia leaned against the roof support and wondered how Lena Travers was faring out in the woods. She was somewhere out there watching over them. At least she had Auggie with her. Levi sure knew how to pick them—she laughed to herself. Killers and persecutors, wicked and selfish. Now they were shepherds and guardians. Of course, she knew it had nothing to do with Levi's choosing them. He simply worked with what-ever people God brought down the trail.

The wind shifted, and Mia got a whiff of the pig pen beyond the garden. Pigs as livestock weren't as common anymore. Just as domesticated dogs had been turned loose after Pan-Day, many pigs had been released, too. Now several generations later, there were whole herds of swine foraging in the wild across the Midwest. Mia stepped off the porch and hopped across the rocks that led along the garden path, past a fish pond, and arrived at the pig pen. These were definitely not wild pigs. Two of the monstrous beasts tossed their heads in curiosity and excitement then ran to sniff at her through the low fence.

"Don't you eat me now!" She rubbed them behind the ears, narrowly avoiding dried mud halfway up their snouts. "Nice little paradise you guys have back here all to yourselves."

She guessed Marshall fed the pigs scraps from the dinner table and excess vegetation from the garden. Farther in the pen, other pigs were rooting around in the mud, digging up large clumps of roots or wood. Then she peered closer. Actually, it didn't look like mud or wood at all. It looked like a . . . *body!*

"Levi!" she screamed, turning only halfway back to the lodge without taking her eyes off the body. It was possible she'd lose sight altogether of the body in the mud if she looked away. "Levi! Get out here!"

She could hear him coming. Boots stomped and voices rose. The lodge's front door crashed open, and Levi's heavy body stamped off the porch and through the garden. When he reached her, his rifle was leveled and he bumped into her as he turned this way and that, searching for an enemy.

"What is it?" He gasped, aiming at the pigs, then back at the garden.

Marshall arrived, followed by Kip.

"That!" Mia pointed into the pen, then stepped back and watched Marshall's face. "That's a person in there!"

Kip leaned dangerously over the wire fence for a closer view. Marshall winced and made a face, his reaction conveying to Mia that he was seeing it for the first time.

Levi took off his rifle and hung the sling over Mia's head. One leg at a time, he climbed into the pen. In San Diego, some locals had raised pigs, so she was glad to see he wasn't skittish around the stout beasts. He waded up to his ankles in the muck and shoved two hogs aside to crouch over the body. Without hesitation, he thrust his hands into the sludge. In seconds, he found the person's head and wiped clear some of the gunk from the face.

"He's alive!" Levi scooped up the man in his arms, grabbing pounds of mud at the same time. "He's breathing!"

With his knees, he pushed past the curious pigs and climbed over the fence while holding the muddy body close to his chest.

"Marshall, you got water?" Levi asked. "That pond will do."

"No, over here!" Marshall hustled along the path, then led the way to the side of the house. "There's a hose. It's well water."

Setting the man down on the browning grass, Levi took the end of the hose as Marshall turned on the spigot. Levi used his thumb to pressurize the spray as he washed the man free of mud.

"Who is that?" Susan asked as she watched from the porch.

"You don't recognize him?" Levi asked. "Kip, help me."

Mia would've helped, but Levi was tearing off the man's clothes, and she was just as content to keep an eye on Marshall and Susan.

"No, I don't know him," Susan said. "Why should I?"

"He was in your pig pen!" Levi accused, then suddenly dropped the hose to cradle the man's head. *"It's Runner!"*

Mia glanced at Kip, then back at Levi.

"The guy who owned the dog?" Kip asked. "Auggie's old owner?"

Auggie seemed to realize who was in their midst as well, and she climbed on top of Runner, smothering his wet face with kisses.

"Look at this." Kip shifted the slender man. Since Runner was stripped down to his shorts, his white skin showed dozens of welts and bruises all over his body. "These aren't from the pigs."

"He was beaten." Levi glanced up at Marshall. "Some of these bruises are a week old. He couldn't have been here a week ago. We just left him in Tennessee right before we reached Ellijay."

"We didn't do anything to him," Marshall insisted. "Honest. I've never seen him before. I don't know how he got into our pig pen."

"I believe you." Levi touched Runner's neck, checking his pulse. "It's okay. We know him."

"Levi, look at this." Kip wiped Runner's left foot free of mud, but the color didn't come off. "His foot is black."

"This is bad." Levi rolled him over, checking the rest of his body. "He's probably gone septic. Mia?"

"Garlic." Mia touched Susan's arm. "Do you have any garlic in the house? It'll help him. Levi, carry him inside. We'll wrap him in a blanket and put him in our room, Kip."

No one argued as Levi picked up Runner, and Mia continued to give orders. Inside, Levi carried him upstairs. Mia was proud to see that Brian hadn't moved from the bathroom door, regardless of all the commotion outside.

"It's Runner," Levi told Brian in passing. "He's been beaten and dumped in the pig pen."

"Levi, wait." Mia stood next to the bathroom door, and Levi stopped at the door to her and Kip's room. "You rinsed him off with the hose, but he needs soap and warm water. All that bacteria . . ."

"What are you suggesting?" Levi shifted the half-naked man in his arms. "He ain't light as a feather, Cuz."

"Give me two minutes!" Mia slipped through the bathroom door behind Brian and closed it. She snatched up a towel and held it out. "Sorry, Jenna. You've got thirty seconds to climb out, because we need your bath water."

"I was feeling selfish, anyway," Jenna said.

Mia shared what had happened outside as Jenna quickly dried off. As soon as she was decent, Mia opened the door and waved at Levi to come in with Runner.

"Can I do anything?" Marshall asked as Susan showed up with a jar of dried garlic bulbs.

"More hot water?" Mia asked, then she guided Levi to the tub with Runner. "Kip, he'll need clothes that fit him. If he wakes up."

After a few minutes, only Mia and Levi remained in the bathroom with Runner. Brian and Marshall came and went with additional water as the unconscious man soaked.

Levi used his hand to apply pressure to Runner's foot as Mia held his head above water.

"He'll lose this foot," Levi said, "if it doesn't kill him first. Someone really did a number on him."

"Aunt Annette and Uncle Titus did some amputations." Mia looked away from the diseased foot. "I've never done one, though. You did Alice's arm, right?"

"The procedure is never pretty."

"You mean, it ain't easy?" Mia smiled, but she felt tears in her eyes. "This guy's bad news, huh?"

"It doesn't matter what he is. Or was." Levi looked into her eyes, and she saw pain there. "He's ours now. One-legged men aren't going to last long without help in this world."

"Are you saying we're going to take him with us?" Mia moved her leg as Brian poured more water into the tub. "We're wanted by every town in the South by now."

"Jesus was a wanted man in Judea, but He still went to Jerusalem for others."

"Even for His enemies." Mia took a deep breath. "Okay, so this guy stealing my bath water isn't the only sacrifice we'll be making for him."

"What's wrong with the hose outside?" Levi sniffed the clothes he'd gotten muddy from carrying Runner. "Phew. It ain't easy tolerating my stench unless I get to that hose myself!"

Rex shook his water jug next to the crackling fire. They were halfway through Iowa, and they were out of drinkable water. The farther west they traveled, the thicker the ash covered the ground, killing vegetation and polluting the water. But the ash that fell from the sky was whiter, composed of smaller particles compared with the ash from days earlier.

He sighed to himself as he watched Chloe sleep against a berm below a tree. Their pace across the country was most taxing on the older gal. Rex knew Chloe had once been one of COIL's elite operatives, so she wasn't one to complain, but Rex himself had removed her boots after she'd fallen asleep midday. She hadn't even stirred.

Even Alice was exhausted, sleeping at an awkward angle next to Chloe, the iron staff on the ground beside the one-armed woman. Alice was fit, but the miles and low water supply was building up acid in all their muscles, causing agonizing cramps and painful knots.

Miranda, the Chicago native, had been quiet for the last two days, and Rex sensed something occurring within her. Something spiritual. Rather than traveling with Bruno and Scooter, she'd chosen to travel with him, choosing almost certain death to the west rather than possible safety to the north. *For what?*

He was willing to die, if necessary, to find his family and meet up again with Levi. Such a reunion was worth his very life. Alice said she felt the same way. Chloe had simply admitted she was close enough to the grave, anyway, so west or north didn't matter much. Only Miranda hadn't fully explained her reason for continuing west, but Rex believed it had to do with him. Although this wasn't exactly a romantic vacation, he wasn't disappointed to have the hearty Christian survivor at his side, casting him little glances that lightened his heart.

Milo Rotham stumbled from the trees with an armful of firewood, his rifle over his shoulder. Rex rose to his feet to accept the wood from him. He set it down, then supported the weary man as he lowered himself next to the fire. It wasn't a cold day, but in their exhaustion, their core temperature had dropped.

"Found another dead deer," Milo said, his head hanging. "It didn't look like it had starved to death."

"The grass is dead," Rex said, "but deer can still eat bark off trees and other standing vegetation. Probably died of thirst."

"Speaking of thirst . . ." Milo tapped the water bottle below a plastic bag as it collected condensation. "Pure water?"

"Pure water." Rex hand-fed more tree leaves onto the shelf he'd built above the fire. "Even dry leaves have a little moisture we can draw out."

"Huh. The things you learn outside the city." Milo glanced at Alice who had snorted in her sleep. "You'd think she would leave that heavy staff behind."

"It's part of her." Rex chuckled. "I wouldn't know her without it. Fact is, I've never seen her without it. That's the way she arrived in Colorado with Levi, and after hundreds of miles, even a thousand, maybe it's become like the arm she lost."

"You think we can keep doing forty or fifty miles a day?"

"No." Rex looked at the sky. "It'll get harder. We're losing weight. Water will be tougher to purify if we can't find underground wells, and game will be scarce until we get into the foothills of the Rockies. It'll take everything that we—"

Rex leaped to his feet, knocking firewood into the fire. Milo caught the water bottle before it spilled, but Rex ignored the fire as he focused on two people who'd stopped on the hill above them, just thirty yards away. He didn't level his rifle at them, but he didn't swing it to his back, either.

The two figures wore gas masks to guard against the ash. Dressed in particle-proof suits and colored backpacks, they stood looking down at the humble camp.

They weren't carrying rifles, but Rex suspected they had handguns, like many travelers did those days.

He raised his empty hand in greeting. The nearest one glanced at his partner, then raised a gloved hand. Rex's face was covered only by glasses and a handkerchief, so his features weren't as hidden as theirs. Since they were concealed inside their suits, he couldn't even tell what gender they were.

After setting down his rifle near Milo, Rex started to climb the hill toward them.

"What are you doing?" Milo gasped through his own mask.

"It seems right," Rex said over his shoulder. A few yards below the strangers, he stopped. Now he could see through their plastic masks. They were two women, one older than the other. "We're sweating water out of some leaves. How're you set on drinking water?"

The nearest one looked past him at the fire.

"Is it clean?" she asked, her voice muffled. "How are you doing that?"

"I'll show you so you can do it yourselves. It ain't fast, but it works well."

He led them into camp. The younger one stayed close to the one Rex guessed was her mother. But once they noticed the three sleeping women, their posture relaxed some. They knelt together around the fire.

"You can use a raincoat instead of a plastic bag like this," Rex explained. "We're just dehydrating the leaves or bark or whatever we put on this shelf. The condensation collects on the covering, and I've got it dripping into this bottle."

"How much will you get from that many leaves?" the older woman asked.

"That many? Maybe an eighth of a cup if the leaves are a little damp, collected from the shade. We've been short on water since coming into Iowa, so we'll sit here until morning, feeding the fire and the leaves. We'll all have full canteens by morning if we stay at it."

The two strangers looked at one another, then the mother turned her face to Rex. Through the plastic face shield, Rex could see she was probably in her fifties. Gray hair hung in her eyes under the helmet.

"Thank you for this." She blinked rapidly several times, clearly emotional. "Our livestock died in Nebraska. Our pump was already running on its last seal. When it died from extra pumping, we knew we had to leave the farm. You've saved our lives."

"If I may be frank . . ." Rex glanced at Milo to see that the ex-colonel was listening closely on the other side of the fire. "I've only saved your lives temporarily. I'd rather we parted ways, knowing your *souls* are saved. Earthly water will fail us, but God sent His Son Jesus Christ to be Living Water that gives eternal life. I have that water. That's water I want to give to you. Have you heard of Jesus Christ?"

"Of course, but it was a long time ago." She stared at the fire. "You think the end is coming? That's what you're saying?"

"That's what I'm saying. We may have just met, but I can't pass you both on this gray day without telling you to pause and cast your lives on God's good mercy. Here, give me your water bottle. We can fill you up as we talk."

"My water bottle?" She shook her head. "We avoided the city of Lincoln because we heard people were killing each other for the last drinkable water. *Now, you're sharing?*"

"Sister, look what I'm sharing, would you?" Rex laughed aloud, making both women flinch like they weren't familiar with the sound. He pointed at the fire. "These are leaves and twigs. What kind of men would Milo and I be if we hoarded leaves and twigs? Speaking of which, we need a fresh batch. I'll be right back."

Rex walked out of camp, and at the north side of the base of a white birch tree, he dug at a thick layer of pine needles and leaves that had gathered from neighboring trees. He stuffed the debris into a tattered burlap sack, and rose to his feet, but nearly collided with Milo.

"We're going to die out here, aren't we?" He pulled down his mask, revealing more of his pointy face and worried eyes. "Give it to me straight. We're going to die soon. You know stuff. I've lived in the city my whole life, but you've been out here. We're about the same age, but you've had older men explain things to you that I've never heard before."

"Under these conditions?" Rex took a deep breath. "Yeah, Milo, we're going to die soon. We've got the OPT trying to kill us, and now this volcanic ash is falling. Who knows what kind of poisonous ash it is, or what it's doing to us? But it's no different than our lives have always been. Death has always been inevitable, but sometimes God opens our eyes to that reality in ways that makes us consider our eternal destiny a little closer. You don't want to die with a question mark hovering over your soul, my friend."

"I've been listening to you guys for weeks." Milo raised his mask again. "But I don't know what to do. My life has been nothing but war and fighting, and if I'm honest, I've never been alone."

"Well, you're talking about the right stuff now." Rex threw the sack over his shoulder. "Why don't we go back to the fire and talk about this in front of the ladies. They need to hear exactly what we're about to discuss."

"Actually—" Milo held up his hand to stop Rex. "There's something I need to get off my chest. Um, it's bad. And I'll understand if you don't want me to continue with you. I should've told you weeks ago, when I first joined you guys, but I was on the run and desperate."

"We'll work through it, Milo, whatever it is. I'm listening."

"It's about your cousin and the blind woman, Radiant Shade."

"Jenna Dowler."

"Yeah." He looked away, fighting an unseen conflict. "Before I left New York, I hired a bounty hunter named Runner. He was from out here somewhere. A killer. Eyes like ice. Some Federation scouts turned me on to him. They said he's got a reputation for killing his targets every time. He doesn't fail. I'm the reason Levi and Jenna never caught up to us. I . . . killed them. I'm sorry. I should've told you back when we were deciding to go west or not, after Chicago. I just . . ."

Rex studied the man next to him. Milo didn't seem much like a threat now. But he knew as a colonel, Milo Rotham had ruled eastern Pennsylvania for nearly a decade.

"I can tell it took a lot for you to tell me this." Rex noticed movement in camp. Miranda had woken, and she was visiting with the two strangers at the fire. "I was coming west, anyway, because my dad is in Meeker with Levi's mom. You don't know if this killer did what you hired him to do. Levi's easy to underestimate until you see him in action, but let's keep this to ourselves. Let's look at it as in the past. You wouldn't be telling me about this if you didn't regret it, right?"

"So, I've been wondering if I should go back and try to warn Levi. If he's still alive. The hunter isn't one to give up easily."

Nodding, Rex sensed the deeper change that was occurring inside the ex-colonel's heart. It was Rex's experience that people revealed their spiritual condition or readiness for the gospel by the way they spoke.

"You wouldn't know where to find Levi and Jenna any better than I would. I hope this hunter doesn't kill my friends, but that's not in our control right now. When you hired him, you did it in your ignorance. Ignorance is a consequence of being lost. But now, I believe God is bringing you into a place of turning. Let's not worry about what wrong has been done and just focus on doing what's right from here on out."

"I can't think of the future while I feel so . . . wrong about that past."

"Then you need to have a conversation with God about His forgiveness. But let's start here with us. Levi's my cousin. There are few people on God's good earth that I prefer to have beside me. If you did something to interrupt that, I'm plenty saddened. But I'm seeing the bigger picture right now, and that's this."

Rex dropped the sack of leaves and held out his hand.

"What?" Milo frowned at the hand, then looked up into Rex's face. "You want to shake my hand?"

"This is the hand of forgiveness, Milo. Shake my hand, and you receive my forgiveness. That's what God does for us, so we can do it for others like this. Forgiveness lets go and picks up. I'm letting go of what you did, and I'm picking you up to walk with you. Are you going to leave me hanging? That's your choice."

Milo hesitated, then slowly presented his hand. Rex clasped it firmly.

"There!" Rex boomed with laughter. "That's all you've got to do with God, too! Let's get back to the fire and talk to those ladies."

Rex picked up the sack and set his other hand on Milo's shoulder as they walked together.

"So, you're not afraid to die because you're forgiven by God?" Milo asked. "That's the trick?"

"It's not a trick, Milo. It's the truth. Come on. We have the evening to sort it out."

Chapter Five

It took Rudy two days to find a safe canyon once his family reached the area of Arches National Park. Sandstone cliffs and delicate arches painted a jagged yet pristine landscape. The night before, a thunderstorm had pounded the region with rain, washing the gray, thick ash away from the red, orange, and yellow terrain. The ash had finally stopped falling.

"And now a little green," Rudy said as he turned the horses loose to graze in the narrow canyon. The ravine ran southwest to northeast, which had offered very little opportunity for heavy ash to reach the canyon floor and kill the grass far below the vertical cliffs. Along the center of the valley, green grass grew in a thin strip where the sun shined the most.

The morning was cold and calm, and the sky appeared mildly overcast. Rudy walked to the mouth of the canyon and used binoculars to search to the east where Highway 128 wound along the Colorado River. He was concerned that he and his people had been seen from a distance leaving the highway, which had been packed with refugees heading south. Although he was trying to trust God to guard them from discovery by the OPT, he knew how travelers gossiped. It wouldn't take much for word to spread that a man with rifles and horses had turned off the highway toward Arches National Park.

"It's beautiful, huh?" Annette startled him from behind. "It's nice to see people can still sneak up on you Caspertein boys."

He kissed her lightly and put his arm around her.

"That's because you Caspertein women know our weaknesses. This view had me captivated."

"Don't try to hide it from me." She elbowed him lightly in the ribs. "You're worried about being discovered here."

"Like I said, you know my weaknesses."

"Titus used to say when people called him reckless, he was really just trusting God with what needed to be done and what he couldn't control. Then he would say something like, 'It ain't easy running in the dark, but someone's got to do it.'"

"Sounds like my reckless sibling." Rudy chuckled, then turned to admire their canyon. Their camp overnight was still pitched under a tarp where Vorca was lighting a small fire while Tilda and Gail slept. Caleb had wandered from camp, probably on some errand Vorca had given him to keep him busy. "With a little work, I suppose we could turn this into a temporary home."

"Unless we can't find water." Annette crossed her arms. "Then we'll have to move again. We can't count on collecting rainwater if it's mingled with ash."

"See the way the grass angles up toward the crack in that cliff? There's no reason it would do that, unless there's water just under the sand and rock there. I'll dig above and find the source, then dam it for a pool down below. We'll cover enough of it to keep the ash out, in case it starts falling again."

"Just tell me what you want me to do. And Gail and Tilda didn't come all this way to sit in the desert, either."

"We need to build a hedge out here so we can keep the horses in the canyon. This scrub brush can be gathered and woven together. The horses will nibble on it a little, but if you can make it about waist high, it'll keep them in like a fence."

"Sounds like something we can do."

"Great. Then while you three are working, I'll just lay around camp and—"

Rudy was interrupted as the ground suddenly shook. Up the length of the valley, the ground was rippling like water. The horses whinnied and galloped up to the far end of the box canyon. Caleb fell over and Vorca ran on unsteady legs to him. Gail and Tilda cried out as they rode out the earthquake from their resting place.

Annette clung to Rudy, and he lowered them both to kneel on the ground.

"No, no, no . . ." he growled as rocks the size of fists and boulders the size of cars shook loose from the canyon walls. "Stay here!"

He left his wife at the mouth of the canyon and dashed back into camp. The earth swayed and he stumbled as if drunk, but he reached Gail and Tilda as the rockslide was about to reached them.

"Come on!" He grabbed Gail's arm and wrapped his arm around Tilda's waist to get them moving. The tumbling rocks flipped and bounced down the side of the canyon walls and out onto the sandy floor, crashing toward them at race-car speeds. "Run!"

The two women found their feet and wobbled toward Annette. Rudy grasped at Vorca and yanked her to her feet from where she crouched to shield Caleb from the rocks. He grunted as a rock slammed into his back. As he fell to one knee, he saw a series of stones tumbling toward Vorca as her thick legs took two steps forward and one back. Caleb screamed. And Annette screamed. And the horses screamed.

Rudy lunged to intercept the last of the rocks before they could pummel Vorca and Caleb. He willed his aging body farther than he thought he could leap. At the final instant, the rocks battered his body, pounding him to stillness on the heaving ground. Out of breath, he watched Vorca scuttle to safety with Caleb where the other ladies were huddling.

Smaller stones trickled into Rudy's ribs, but he didn't move again until the earthquake was completely over.

Another thumping sound reached his ears. He lifted his head and held still as two of the three horses galloped past him and out of the canyon.

"Don't move, Rudy!" Annette shouted as she ran to him.

"Why? Are you going to call the paramedics?" He groaned and rose to his hands and knees. "This wasn't my first rodeo."

"That was a landslide, not a rodeo." She held his face in her hands. "You're bleeding."

"That's the least of my problems. My back . . ." He tried to take a deep breath. "Left side. In the middle."

Annette lifted up the back of his shirt to inspect him.

"Yeah, you've got something out of place. There's a big bulge next to your spine. It's like a hump."

"So, you're telling me we lost our horses, but gained a camel."

"You're joking at a time like this? How're your legs? Can you walk? You know better than anyone there'll be aftershocks. Come on. We need to get clear."

He leaned on his wife as she helped him out to Gail and Tilda, Vorca and Caleb. There, he collapsed in slow motion onto his back on the ground. When he found that position too painful, he rolled onto his side and breathed shallowly.

"I've never seen shaking like that," Gail said. "How big do you think it was, Rudy?"

"A high seven, maybe an eight. The way the ground swayed, it must've been shallow." He forced himself to breathe slower. "So much for the perfect canyon."

"The last horse looks injured." Tilda pointed up the canyon at the quarter horse limping heavily. "Looks like a broken leg."

"Annette, run back and grab the rifle and game ammo." Rudy checked his range of motion on both shoulders. "We may have gotten kicked out of our camp, but we'll at least eat steak tonight."

A minute later, Annette returned with one of the rifles and a magazine of hunting rounds.

"Just rest, Rudy." Annette slammed home the magazine. "This isn't my first rodeo, either."

"Look at us—a couple of rodeo clowns." Rudy fought a wave of pain. "Don't mind me. I'll just lay here a bit."

Vorca spoke in her native language to Caleb, coaching the child to cover his ears as Annette walked toward the horse.

Rudy closed his eyes and prayed. The only marginally safe place he could think of was no longer safe. Now where were they supposed to go?

The gun boomed and the horse fell. The earth shook with a strong aftershock, and Tilda bowed her head over Rudy, her hands on him, praying aloud for him and them all. She also prayed for Rex and Levi.

Levi had never before peddled a tricycle. He doubted they could go far on bikes, but it seemed the best way to leave Guntersville behind, and to transport Runner down the road. Also left behind was Runner's amputated black foot, cut off low above the ankle, and cauterized with white-hot metal that had left the slender man stinking like burnt flesh.

"Brings back memories, huh, Cuz?" Mia asked as she slowed to ride beside him. She spoke through her mask, the ash trickling down again in a sky filled with sparse clouds. "Except we're not running from the Brogdons now. I *am* a Brogdon!"

"It's been an interesting year." Levi glanced back at Lena, her face hidden behind the bridal veil. The cloth had lost its white sheen, but when Brian had cut new cloth for everyone's anti-ash masks at the lodge, she'd chosen to keep the old lace. "How's he look, Lena?"

"Aah-ah," she responded, keeping a wary eye on unconscious Runner, who sat backward on the wide seat between the two rear wheels. His one foot was held off the ground by a single strap, and a seat belt around his waist held him to the bike.

"Still asleep?"

"Aah."

"He's been through a lot."

Levi rode in silence not far behind Brian as he coached Jenna through the mechanics of riding a bike. She was a natural, balancing, peddling, and steering all on her own. Brian encouraged her to keep their speed low. Since Levi was peddling the heavy tricycle with no gears, he wasn't complaining about the pace.

That morning, they'd studied the map together, seeing the route across northern Alabama toward Mississippi. Backroads zigzagged through communities and forgotten towns. Long highways connected neglected fields for miles.

"Stay alert," he needlessly stated to Lena when they came suddenly upon an occupied town. "We're not stopping."

Auggie trotted comfortably in the grassy shoulder at Lena's side, the dog's tongue flapping wildly. The Lab veered away on some obscure scent and disappeared on another path.

"Auggie!" Lena called.

"Don't worry," Levi said. "She'll catch up to us."

A couple townspeople lifted their heads along the street where farmers and residents were bartering.

"What if they try to stop us?" Mia asked Levi, then turned to her husband. "I know you want to stop and preach, but we're on a schedule now."

"Yes, sweetie." Kip kept peddling.

"It ain't easy taking preaching cues from your wife," Levi teased, but he knew Kip was still recovering his strength and didn't need to be pushing himself too much. "Didn't the Servalites already come through here anyway?"

"In this world," Kip said sadly, "there's no such thing as too much of the gospel. The same town can change its whole population in a few months, and those we did preach to need some reminding. But we came through this area on a highway to the south."

Toward the end of the town, a black man in overalls jogged into the street, waving his arms. Brian swerved around the man, and stood up to peddle, urging Jenna to go faster. Mia and Kip went wide around the townsman, but Levi stopped peddling and coasted up to the man. He didn't appear to be armed.

"Aah!" Lena argued and pressed her brakes, taking the bike into the next lane. She wrestled for a few seconds to pull her rifle into readiness.

"What's with all the waving?" Levi rolled to a stop. "You need some help with something?"

"No, I just—" The man took a few deep breaths, winded from running out into the street. He was in his sixties, had a baritone voice, and shoulders wide like he knew manual labor. "I'm the newly-elected mayor. I'm supposed to stop and check all travelers for their OPT, uh, solidarity. There's some troublemakers around, word is."

"Did you hear that on the radio?" Levi turned and checked the rest of the street. A half-dozen people had stopped in front of the dark shops to watch.

"Yeah, the radio." The mayor rested his hands on his bulky hips. "So? The Oath?"

"You want me to repeat the Oath?"

"Or near best you can." He waved his sizeable palm. "You know, to do right by the OPT, so I know you ain't the ones they been talking about."

"Well, Mr. Mayor . . ." Levi leaned on his handlebars. "I'm not going to recite any Oath of Solidarity or allegiance to some ideas that contradict with my faith and allegiance to Jesus Christ. Me and my friends are probably the ones you've been told to stop or arrest."

"Uh. What?"

The mayor frowned at Auggie as she trotted up, panting and gazing around at the town.

"And that would be our hunting dog." Levi smiled. "But as you can see, she's no more of a troublemaker than we are."

"Oh." He sighed and glanced back at a storefront like he'd forgotten something. "You're the ones who won't take the Oath?"

"We're the ones." Levi grinned. "We're devoted to Jesus Christ, and you know you can only serve one master. My soul belongs to my Savior, and the OPT is a far cry from offering eternal peace or hope."

"Wait. I'm a believer, too. I'm a deacon at our church. Don't read too well, but I know who my Savior is."

"Then why are you enforcing the OPT's Oath? Don't you know it's blasphemous against God?"

"But it's . . . the new government rules, I thought. Unity will light the way. That's the motto."

"Maybe you should have someone read through that Oath one more time for you, Deacon-Mayor. Whenever the Oath says it replaces what Jesus Christ does for us, you know it's not something you should get involved with. It's their way or no way, but God says it's His way or there's another way—to hell."

"Never thought of this until now." He scratched his brow. "Best call a meeting. You can't stay and speak? You seem to understand something we don't."

"You've got Bibles, don't you?"

"Sure!"

"Well, there's where you'll get more wisdom than from me. Start in the Book of Acts, and it wouldn't hurt for you to brush up on the Book of Revelation, especially chapter thirteen about the deception of the government and chapter seventeen about the unity of the one world government. It's dangerous stuff, spiritually speaking. That should get you folks back on the right track, but you'd better have a heart willing to stand for what you find. The

OPT will come after you if you put your trust in God instead of the authority of the Oath. It'll cost you."

"I'm not afraid," he said. "We'll study more and plant our feet as much as we need to."

"Good man." Levi offered his hand. "Under the circumstances, you and I will have to wait to get better acquainted in glory. After all, we're just passing through."

"I do sorely wish we'd met sooner, Christian man." The mayor heartily shook his hand. "You may have saved this town from the wrath of God! What happened to your passenger there?"

"He was hired by the Federation government to kill me. His foot got infected, so we had to amputate. Now I'm waiting for him to wake up so I can teach him about God's love."

The mayor laughed a deep laugh that made Auggie tilt her head, as if she were trying to understand.

"You are an angel of a man for stopping, sir." The mayor moved aside and touched his brow in a slight salute. "It's one of God's mercies that He'd use a stranger to wake up a town!"

It took Levi all his strength to get the tricycle rolling again, and the mayor must've noticed, because he took hold of the back of Levi's seat and gave him a running push. Lena's critical eye swept the street once more, then she moved forward with Levi.

"Aah-ah?" she asked as Auggie trotted ahead.

"My wife would be proud of me." Levi grinned. "We actually passed through a town that was hunting us, and we left in peace without firing a shot."

"Aah." She rolled her eyes.

Runner suddenly groaned and Levi peeked under his arm at his passenger.

"How mad do you think he's going to be that it's us who found him? Think he'll be thankful?"

"Aah?" She pointed at her left foot. "Aah-ah!"

"Yeah. His foot. Okay, he's not going to be happy. Maybe when he opens his eyes, Mia should be the first person he sees. You know, a stranger's pretty face. But she'll still tranq him if he gets out of hand."

They slowly caught up to Brian, Jenna, Kip, and Mia. Levi shared his report about the last town, and Jenna prayed for more open doors in OPT towns. The longer they could use the bikes, the faster they could travel west and the easier they could transport Runner.

Levi realized he was putting them all at greater risk by traveling on roads—all with the intent to rescue Runner from his contrary heart. When he shared his concern with the others, they summarily dismissed the danger by pointing out that he wasn't alone in seeing Runner brought to Christ. They'd all taken him in, and they'd all see him cared for, which meant they needed to keep him with them.

Touched at their compassion, Levi prayed through the dread he felt about Runner gaining consciousness. Somehow, God needed to use the man's missing foot to reach his ugly soul. He said as much to Lena as they set up camp under a bridge east of Russellville, Alabama, that night.

"God did a miracle in me," Lena wrote on her tablet for Levi. She sat below camp at a creek's edge as Levi stripped Runner to his shorts and washed him. "God used my loss to show me what I needed."

"True." He waded back to the bank and held the man upright as Lena dried him off. "But not everyone's heart is softened just because they become aware of certain physical deficiencies. Some people never make that connection. They might get harder, not softer. I'm hoping that a little extra attention for this guy breaks through to his heart."

They dressed him in clean clothes, then washed his old clothes in the creek. Afterward, Lena picked up her tablet again.

"He might be more angry about his loss," she wrote, "than he is thankful for your love."

"It's possible. Some people focus on only the bad instead of seeing God's grace. Some blame God for uncomfortable circumstances in their lives or in the world, but then thank Him when they get their own way. We can't make people think differently, Lena, but by showing them Christ, we open up an alternative to their thinking that they may not have had before. Every situation is a crossroads. We can grow from it by submitting to God's love and planning, or we can whither from it in unbelief, thinking there's no hope or plan or purpose."

Levi lay Runner on a couple folded tarps they wouldn't be using that night since they had the bridge for cover. The small fire crackled softly as Lena fashioned a tripod of sticks to hang Runner's clothes next to the fire. Jenna was off to one side, reading a Braille Bible she'd brought from New York, and Brian returned with an armful of wood.

Kip and Mia were up the creek a short way. Levi was tempted to call them to hustle with the water for dinner, but it appeared they were in deep discussion.

Using her fingers, Lena tore up smoked deer meat from a previous hunt. The small pieces of food would be easier for her to gulp down. She'd also taken to feeding Runner, who still swallowed on instinct when food was trickled through his thin lips.

Taking his rifle, Levi climbed the bank to the bridge above. From there, he gazed down the bank at a few fish jumping at evening flies. Planning to wake early the next morning, he would fish for their breakfast. He relied heavily on those early mornings, waking before even Lena or Brian, to commune with God before the long days of cycling. And even better if he could spend that time fishing with God, too!

The road was a little traveled, and Levi knew the principal dangers of the OPT were limited to the towns and cities where authority figures were overstepping their God-given positions. Along the side of the road in the ditch, stagnant water had pooled, and water lilies were growing there. He picked a number of the plants, cutting them off low on the stem, to eat them raw or even cooked. But their flour was running low, so thinly sliced, the rhizomes could be ground into flour. The seeds could also be dried, parched, and ground into flour as well. Between Mia and himself, Lena was learning about edible plants all over the countryside.

"Levi?"

He glanced up to find Kip on the edge of the highway. The man's strength was growing daily, even though they were all exhausted each night from traveling.

"Mia's struggling," Kip admitted, and crouched down to pick at the lilies Levi had laid on the road. "She was doing well at the lodge. We all were. She had Jenna to dote over. But out here, Jenna's so self-sufficient, and Brian's stronger than I am and quicker to help Jenna with everything. I think it's left Mia to start looking inward. Not in a good way."

"Is this about the baby she lost?" Levi tugged up one last lily, then stepped carefully to dry land. "That'll take time and understanding. Lena and I were just talking about that."

"No, it's not just the baby." He stood and watched up the road to the east. "She's dealt with that pretty well. It's about what we went through in Ellijay. She's looking back, even though she's been hiding it from others."

"Those people will never catch up to you guys again."

"But the OPT is everywhere now. What we went through was . . . pretty bad. Mia's faith may not be strong enough to go through it again. If we're caught, which is a daily possibility . . . It's fear. She's afraid to a sickening degree. I mean, it's making her physically ill."

Levi collected his lilies in both arms.

"Though I've never been tortured for my faith before, I've read about many folks who have been." Levi sighed. "It's the world we live in now. If it makes it any easier, you know, the OPT won't be torturing too many believers anymore, not like Ellijay was doing. Their charter basically instructs the towns to just execute us and be done, since we're such a threat to their cosmic consciousness of unity and all that."

"I think it's mistreatment in any form that has her thoughts all twisted up." Kip wiped at his eyes, then faced Levi directly. "Ever since you led me to Jesus, I've been running full-out. Not caring about anything. I expected my faith to cover others. We went through hardships traveling east from Colorado the past year, but I thought Mia was seeing it all like I was for Christ. Now, I'm wondering if she was just bearing through it to be a good wife."

"But serving God for other people won't give us supernatural strength." Levi nodded. "I see where you're going. She's distracted by fear, and the weakness of her faith is showing. It might be lacking. But it can be strengthened."

"Yeah, I think so. And for that, I asked her if she'd be okay talking to you about it."

"Me? It sounds like you've got the situation figured out, Kip."

"But I think she just sees me as the problem right now." He shook his head. "I keep opening my mouth about Christ, and others keep paying the price. I mean, nothing is as bad as it was in Ellijay. I had no idea that new regulations were in place. At least we know what to expect when we start evangelizing in a town next time."

"Well, I can talk to her, but only as her cousin who's a Christian. You're her husband, her spiritual guardian, as Dad used to call a husband's place in marriage. I'm just going to talk to her about trusting in God's plan and trusting in what God's guiding you to say and do, no matter the consequences."

"I think that'll help her. She just needs to hear it from someone else."

"Hey." Levi shifted the lilies all to one arm so he could set a free hand on Kip's shoulder. "It ain't easy sacrificing our families to serve God, but that's what's required sometimes. We have to believe that God will hold us all together when obedience isn't free. This is coming from someone whose wife is hundreds of miles from him, so what do I know?"

"I think Lyla's happy to carry the cross with you."

"She knew what she was joining up with," Levi said with a chuckle, "and Mia knew, too, with you. The Lord will get her through it, but we can offer some reminders to help her along in her faith."

Together, they walked down to the camp where Lena was stirring two pots—a large one for the four, and a smaller one for herself and Runner. Levi checked Runner's pulse and breathing but found no change. His bruises were turning yellow, slowly healing, but there was no way of knowing what internal injuries or brain trauma he had. The infection in his blood was no longer growing since his diseased foot had been amputated, but irreversible damage may have been done to his organs.

Kip blessed the food, and they ate in silence, partially because they were aware that travelers could be moving over the bridge above, and no one was keeping watch. Even the fire was extinguished out of caution, after everyone had finished eating.

Lena felt Runner, who had already been a skinny young man, but now his hips and ribs protruded through his clothes.

Mia volunteered to collect everyone's dishes and went to the river to wash them out. Lena finished trickling spoonfuls into Runner's mouth, much like she did under her own veil, then took up her rifle to watch the road above.

Levi joined his cousin at the river, collecting the tins after Mia rinsed them. He prayed for the right words to encourage her.

"Remember San Diego?" He smiled at the stream. "When you were about ten, you used to beg Mom to let you leave the apartment with me. You didn't care about the danger, but they were worried about you."

"I remember." Mia didn't look up. "What makes you think about those days? That was like ten years ago."

"When they did finally let you leave with me, I remember you being so disappointed that all I did was take you fishing in the harbor."

"Sometimes I still smell fish guts on my hands."

"Someone had to clean those fish." He nudged her shoulder. "It didn't stop you from going again each week after that. You were my little business partner."

"Only because you'd take me hunting with you afterward, sometimes. Aunt Annette never really wanted me out shooting with you or Uncle Titus."

"They worried about you like they would their own daughter."

"Yeah, I know." She dried her hands on her jeans but didn't rise from the creek. "You think we'll really see Aunt Annette again? Colorado's so far away."

"I think so. But it won't be easy."

"When has it ever been easy?" She sighed, staring at the water. "I hear stories from you guys about the way life was before Pan-Day, and it sounds like a fairy tale. I see these cars by the side of the road and heaps of those computer gizmos rotting in the ditches, and none of it makes much sense. I can't imagine a time when nobody worried about what they'd eat or drink that day."

"How about you and I get up early and go fishing again? From above, I saw this hole downstream that looks promising. Catch some breakfast with me like old times?"

"Okay." She smiled. "I see what you're doing here. You're roping me in."

"I'm taking you fishing."

"You're going to talk to me about what Kip talked to you about."

"It ain't easy having my heart read by you." Levi grinned. "You know me too well. We can fish and talk before dawn, okay?"

"Yeah." She sighed again. "I really do want to get past this. I guess if anyone can help me, it's you."

"No, God's the one who'll help you."

"Well, you're His craziest and most courageous ambassador I've ever known, even more wild than Uncle Titus."

"I'd say the same about your husband."

"Yeah." She looked back at camp. "He's pretty special, huh?"

"Both of you are." He held her in a half-hug. "Come on. Early morning and long ride tomorrow."

In the night, Levi woke to someone mumbling in their sleep. He sat up and listened. It was Runner. Lena was also awake, leaning up on one elbow.

"Sounds like he's coming around," he whispered to her. "Should be conscious soon."

He lay back down, praying about the storm that would certainly come soon, since they had so many states still to navigate before reaching Colorado. And with Runner to care for, and Mia's fear of mistreatment, and their food and water always in short supply . . .

His eyes flashed open the instant Mia's hand touched his shoulder. In the predawn light, she held up a spool of fishing line in front of her puffy eyes and wild hair held back in a loose braid. He tugged on his boots, swung his rifle onto his back, and followed her downstream.

The fishing hole he'd spotted from above was so choked by briars that he had to doze his way through by force, making a path for Mia to crouch on the bank. From there, she could float a fly down the current. At her shoulder, Levi hung the line off the end of a short stick, while holding a second spool of line in his other hand. The stick gave him a three-foot advantage over the water.

"I just can't face again what they did to us in Ellijay," Mia suddenly opened the conversation. "They electrocuted me, Levi, trying to make me take the Oath. Said it was for my own good—for everyone's good. I've never felt pain like that. Worse than childbirth. And it was just me all alone with those people. Kip was locked up down in their dungeon. I was totally terrified. Then I went numb, and they dragged me back down to my cell to starve me to death. I knew misery to the point that I'd given up."

"But you held strong. You didn't give in. You kept the faith somehow."

"No, I gave up. I don't remember having any faith. I just remember refusing the Oath, and then I was too weak to talk, even if I'd wanted to. Their fists were bad, but it might've been the electricity that scrambled me."

Levi didn't rush to respond as he reached for words from God's own heart.

"Sometimes faith is unintentional, Mia, because it's something natural from who we are now. I think sustaining faith is more about who you are and less about trying to be someone you aren't—or trying not to do something you don't want to do."

"Accidental faith?" She pulled in her line and tossed it out again. "You're saying my faith was accidental?"

"Not accidental. More like automatic. Or natural. The faith we have now as believers who've experienced Christ's riches may not be the same confidence we directed toward God to be saved. I mean, faith and confidence are the same thing, but now our confidence is seasoned with the Spirit's own power because we're born again. Faith is voluntary, but there's a *being* faithful and there's *having* faith. Sometimes we have doubts, but we still trust that He's told us the best way to live."

"So, I'm doomed to resist the Oath every time the OPT arrests us and tortures us to death? I can't wrap my mind around what good that'll do if I've already shown God my loyalty. Haven't I proven it?"

"Of course you have."

"But I'm with you now. You're not going to let anything happen to us, no matter what the OPT tries."

"Mia, you know better than that." Levi frowned. "Chen Li and Nathan just died on my watch, but I know that's not on me. I think you know that the only way to stop the world's hatred of God's people is to either convert everyone or stop testifying altogether."

"That second choice is tempting."

"Sure." Levi felt a nibble on his line. "That's partially why we're in this mess. Many in America claimed Christ as their Savior before Pan-Day. But during and after Pan-Day, they shut their mouths and blended in with the world. Being a Christian never cost them anything. There are Scriptures that indicate that without dying with Christ, how could one ever really be born again?"

"How many times do I have to die with Christ?"

"Just once, Cuz, but there's more than one opportunity to show you live for Him. Christ lived to suffer for us in a world where He didn't belong. If you're really His—and I know you are—there'll be other opportunities for the world to see your life in Him contrasted with their lives as children under God's wrath."

"This isn't the Caspertein pick-me-up talk I was hoping for. What you call more opportunities, I call more torture."

"Can I tell you how I'm facing it? I mean, I think there are lots of Scriptures to stand on, but lately, I've been thinking on just one. Jesus told His disciples they'd be hated, tortured, and killed. But then He told them two things that hold my nerves together when it comes to facing mistreatment by the unsaved."

"What are they? You have a fish on your line!"

Levi jerked the stick back. The fish flew through the air and dangled from a bush where his line became entangled. He reached overhead to free both the line and his seven-inch catch.

"Okay, the first thing is this: Jesus said He was warning His disciples about mistreatment so they wouldn't stumble. How can we stumble while being persecuted?"

"By giving in, or behaving badly, in an un-Christlike way."

"So, if He was warning them ahead of time, it means He as God knew about it ahead of time."

"Okay . . ."

"And He knows about it now as well. It's planned out for us to live and behave and suffer like Christ. If it's planned, it's not an accident. There's a purpose for it all. So, I shouldn't stumble as a disciple when I'm mistreated. It's all according to the plan of showing the world an example of Christ. This is why we should still feel compassion and pity for our tormentors. Our lives lived in contrast to theirs condemns them, unless they repent."

"All that's the first thing that gets you through?"

"Yep." He held his recovered fish on a twig that was pushed through the gill. "Breakfast *de la pescado!*"

"We'll work on your Spanish later." She shook her head. "What's the second thing that holds you together?"

"The Holy Spirit's presence."

"Okay. Explain."

"The disciples became depressed when Jesus told them they'd suffer without Him and die for Him. But He said that His absence was actually to their advantage, since the Holy Spirit would be with them to connect all their faithfulness to Him and for Him. Nothing the disciples would ever go through for Christ would be disconnected from Christ, because the Spirit of Christ would be within them, like He is within us."

"His presence . . ."

"Imagine the Spirit in us encouraging us to endure a little longer. Everything we go through just brings us that much closer to appreciating Christ—and it strengthens His impression through us to the world."

"So, I'm just supposed to keep suffering and like it?"

"No, I don't think so." He chuckled at her sarcasm. "It's not the suffering that we like. It's the result and impact of the suffering that we like."

"Whoa."

"What? You get a bite?"

"No, you finally said something meaningful."

"Finally? Are you looking for a swim in the deep side of the creek?"

"No, I mean, you've been saying a lot of stuff, but then you hit it. God's not telling us to feel good about torture. Here I was feeling guilty because I wasn't—I don't know—*appreciating* the pain."

"Well, Cuz, that would make you mentally deranged, if you liked the pain."

"Exactly! But it's just . . . the other side of suffering, that's what we grab onto."

"You got it."

"This changes everything! I can work with this. It rings true. You know, on the inside. My eyes shouldn't be on the trouble, but on what the trouble brings to life! Whoa. A whole new world opening up to me right now."

"How about your whole new world including a fish on a hook?" Levi wound in his line on the spool, producing another fish. "It ain't easy catching all *los pescados* this morning."

"I can't think of fishing right now." She thrust her spool into Levi's hand. "I have to go tell Kip what I'm on to."

"But—" Levi looked from one full hand to the other. "Can't you at least reel in your line?"

"Nope!" She crashed through the bushes behind him. "No time. See you back in camp!"

Levi tucked the second line around a knot halfway up his fishing stick and leaned proudly out over the water with his new double-lined invention. Until he slipped and fell in. Sopping wet and tangled in fishing line, he climbed back onto the bank. It took ten minutes to sort out the lines and put one spool into a vest pocket. But not for a second was he discontent about the morning. God had answered his prayer from the night before. Mia was back. And her boldness was more securely in place based on God's invincible truth. That's all that mattered. They were ready again for the journey ahead!

Milo Rotham was so lost in thought over his newfound faith that he bumped into Rex from behind when the monstrous man stopped. Immediately, Milo stepped around Rex so he could better view the rubble of the city that had once been Des Moines.

"We're being watched," Rex said. Pointing with two fingers, he waved his left hand forward. "No sudden moves. We're just passing through."

Glancing at Chloe, Milo thought she appeared as tense as he felt. But she moved ahead of him, following Rex as the bearded giant led them through rusted and burned-out cars on the downtown street. Old battles and recent earthquakes had crumbled the once pristine and ordered buildings. Since the ash had stopped falling and the sky was clear, he could see for blocks where the streets weren't too cluttered.

Alice's heavy staff clunked loudly on the cracked pavement, which was windswept bare, except for weeds growing up in the cracks. The black woman's face appeared stoic as usual, even though Milo knew they were all tired, hungry, and concerned about water.

"You coming?" Miranda joked as she passed him.

"He said we're being watched."

"God is always watching."

"I don't think he was talking about God this time." Milo started after her, then raised his rifle at a flash of gray in an alley. "And he's not talking about that coyote that's chewing on who-knows-what, either."

They stepped carefully through the scrap metal of an overpass that had fallen. Highway signs were twisted in a mess of cement and rebar.

Milo had been closely watching his four companions the last four days since he'd come to believe in Jesus as his Savior. From reading Rex's Bible, he'd learned that he now had eternal life, but he couldn't imagine ever sharing their casual approach to disaster, danger, and death, which seemed to threaten them on all sides.

Then Milo saw them—scrappers, scavengers, and scroungers, as he'd called them in Philadelphia. Grim survivors in ragged coats. They carried rifles and other weapons. Two stood in plain sight on the roof of a building a block ahead, and another walked across the street fifty yards in front of them. They wore masks or cloth wraps around their faces. Milo turned around and noticed two more, a man and a woman, walking not far behind them. No, not walking—stalking, with their rifles in their hands.

"Maybe they have water," Milo suggested to Miranda, but she didn't respond.

Two blocks later, Milo noticed other gunmen on side streets, on both sides.

"Rex!" Milo called. "We're being corralled!"

He watched Rex turn and walk backwards, surveying through squinty eyes the locals who were moving beside and behind them. Milo could see Rex's face, and there seemed to be no concern.

"Should be okay," Rex said. "Just stay calm."

Milo was tempted to raise his battle rifle and start blasting, but lately, he'd been questioning every thought, motive, and plan. Rex had told him that the Holy Spirit was now working inside him, and he'd need to judge between what was fleshly and what was spiritual. So, Milo guessed his concern about the people closing in on them at that moment was simply fleshly concern. After all, Rex wasn't reacting to the danger of the Des Moines scavengers.

At an intersection on the west side of the downtown area, Rex stopped and unbuckled his backpack.

"Seems like a good place to take a break."

Next to them, a broken cement median from decades past lay crumbled beside a postal truck that was turned on its side. The tattered hide of a dead horse blew in the breeze, its white bones and the street's pavement showing beneath holes in the skin. Still, Des Moines citizens crept closer. Twelve were now closing in from all four side streets. Others stood on rooftops. Two held attack dogs on leashes, their fur patchy in places.

"This?" Milo asked. "This is the spot you think is a good place to take a break? We're . . . totally surrounded!"

Rex set his heavy pack down on the street, leaning it against the chassis of the postal truck. Alice walked a little farther out and stood watching the northern avenue. Chloe and Miranda dropped their packs and shared a canteen, the last of their water.

"Oh, I get it." Milo nodded. "You guys came through here a few months ago. You know these people and they know you."

"No, we traveled south of Des Moines when we came through here with Levi." Rex sat on the edge of the cement divider. His rifle rested across his knees. "Levi thought we'd save time if we avoided the bigger cities."

"And why didn't we do that?" Milo studied the closest Des Moines citizen, a man in an overcoat and dusty ski goggles. His lower face was wrapped in a scarf, and he carried a sawed-off shotgun. "We could've avoided bloodshed right now—probably our own since they're the only ones with lethal weapons."

"There won't be any bloodshed."

Rex didn't even check his rifle, which made Milo even more nervous. The big Caspertein man always checked his rifle before potential conflict.

But then he noticed the behavior of the others. Chloe seemed pretty nonchalant as well, seated on her own pack, and Miranda was inspecting the sole of her boot, which wasn't even on her foot. Alice leaned on her staff, watching the strangers approach, her rifle still on her back!

"This is supposed to be some faith lesson?" Milo almost cursed but caught himself. He wasn't that man anymore. God didn't like it when he swore. Gritting his teeth, he hung the rifle off his shoulder. "Fine. But I'm staying ready."

Their company seemed to coordinate to arrive around them all at once. They stepped around the postal truck and stood idly in the weeds and rubble on the street, completely surrounding the five travelers. Milo forced himself to hook his thumbs in his backpack straps. He knew Christians weren't supposed to be afraid of worldly threats, but this was ridiculous!

Now just feet away, Milo noticed some of the people had crossbows and not just firearms. One had a hunting bow, and two carried primitive spears. These were true survivalists, and their posture appeared threatening.

The one in the overcoat slowly unwrapped his face to reveal a salt and pepper beard around a mouth with a severe underbite. He took off his goggles to reveal the eyes of a man in his sixties. With his other hand, he kept the shotgun aimed in Rex's direction.

"Just the five of you?" he asked Rex.

Milo watched the man study each of them in turn. He seemed nervous, which surprised Milo. The man should've been stinking of confidence since he out-numbered the travelers by so many.

"Yep, just us." Rex nodded his shaggy head, then rose to his feet, which caused everyone to shift their gaze upward. "We were hoping we'd see someone friendly to trade with since we're out of drinking water."

"Trade what?" the man asked. Milo picked up on an eagerness in his voice. "I'm the governor here. Governor Treble. Treble Vickers. We've got clean water. You have, uh, something valuable with you?"

Treble licked his lips as he glanced at Rudy's monstrous pack.

"We have lots of valuables." Rex offered his hand. "The name's Rex Caspertein. When I was a boy, my folks scolded me when I'd play in the street. Why don't we go somewhere to talk and agree on a trade?"

"Bullets? Uh, cartridges?" Treble asked and shook Rex's hand. "You got any ammo?"

"Plenty—way more than we need to be carrying."

"Could I see them? The bullets? What kind do you have?"

Milo's eyes twitched. Bullets! Everyone used bullets for currency in the Plains Zone, but this was more than just a trade. The people were watching Rex for an answer like their lives depended on it. Of course! Their clothes, mostly patched and worn-out coats, hung off their bony frames. Treble's own wrists revealed at the bottom of his coat sleeves, were thin, and his cheeks were hollow. They were starving!

"Why don't you lead us to water first?" Rex offered. "And then I'll show you the ammo we have. You look like you have quite a few people to take care of here, so maybe I should help you with some hunting traps for the next time you run out of bullets, huh?"

Treble surveyed his people. Then he sighed and let his shotgun hang on a strap from around his neck.

"It's that obvious? You knew we didn't have any ammo for our guns?"

"We knew before we even saw you, my friend." Rex gestured down one street. "You've got deer grazing on grass on your city streets. Deer don't do that where there are people with functioning firearms. I think you were going to force us to give you our ammo, weren't you?"

"Saw no way around it." Treble looked away. "The ash killed off our gardens, and we can't eat if we can't hunt."

"Well, don't worry." Rex lifted his voice so everyone could hear. "God Almighty sent us here right on time. We'll spend the night with you and make sure you're able to get some game. In fact, Chloe? One of those does might be just the ticket for tonight's feast."

Chloe ejected one gel-tranq magazine for a magazine of hunting rounds, then she knelt and aimed her rifle southward. A couple seconds later, the muzzle boomed, and the people cried out and huddled together in small groups. Milo turned in time to see a middle-sized deer fall, start to rise, then lay still. Two other white tails flagged majestically as they bounded away.

"Governor?" Rex slapped the man on the back. "You have a couple boys who can dress that deer? Why don't you show us to your water?"

Treble signaled to two men, who immediately jogged off toward the deer eighty yards away.

"You're either about to take advantage of us for trying to take advantage of you," Treble said, "or you're the most understanding man I've ever met."

"It's called grace," Rex said. "God showed us favor that we didn't deserve by sending His Son to die for us. It shouldn't be too difficult to follow that example. Either that, or I'm as thirsty as you are hungry!"

Rex laughed, which attracted a few nervous chuckles from the people. Treble led Rex away to the north, and they all fell in step, walking in groups of twos and threes. Milo saw Miranda open her jacket pocket and draw out a pouch in which she kept whatever meat they'd smoked the night before. As quickly as he could, Milo produced several gnarled lengths of dry, darkened meat and offered them to the young men and women near him.

"Want some? It's just dog, but it's good meat."

In seconds, it was gone. They tore the strips in half, then passed it to others so everyone had some. Milo smiled contentedly, unable to ignore the joy in his heart, even though that was the last of his food, his canteen was empty, and they were certain to be killed sometime soon from a natural disaster, or by people who wanted to murder them.

"Feels good, doesn't it?" Chloe asked, settling in to walk beside him.

"I don't get it." Milo threw his hands up. "All these years, I thought I had to fight for my survival. Who knew that I could sacrifice myself and find more satisfaction? I can't believe no one's ever taught me this before. And I can't believe I'm only figuring this out now . . . the power of this stuff!"

"This *stuff?*" Chloe shoved him lightly. "It's not stuff. It's love. God's teaching you to love like He loves."

"And this is what the OPT is trying to kill us for? This is what Lena Travers and Obrador fought against for two decades!" He gasped. "It's what I fought against. It was right in front of me, and I couldn't even see it! This is the whole meaning of life—and I tried to destroy it!"

"Thanks to God, He opened your eyes."

"What God do you believe in?" asked a young woman beside Chloe. When she pulled back her hood, Milo saw she had blonde hair and big, blue eyes. "Sorry. I was eavesdropping. We don't get too many new people around here. Normally, we just, you know, make people give us what they have, then we let them leave the city. No one to talk to except the people I've known my whole life."

"I'll tell you what God we believe in," Milo blurted, sensing a confidence he'd never known. He'd only been a believer for four days, so he wondered what else he would learn if he spent more time with these Casperteins. But he knew enough! "You saw how Rex could've shot all of you for trying to ambush us? But he didn't. He was showing you the God we trust in; the God who doesn't ignore sin but rescues us from it—and from ourselves. I'm Milo."

He stepped around Chloe to speak to the young blonde face to face.

They trekked for ten minutes through a tunnel, old buildings, and into a basement shelter before Milo realized he'd been talking to her nonstop without even learning her name. He asked her forgiveness and took her gloved hand in his own.

"Giselle," she said, leaning towards him. "I've never met anyone like you before. You speak with such . . . passion and excitement about your religion. It makes me envy what you have."

"Oh, I'm nothing." He scoffed. "I'm just a fool who's learning about all of who God is. You can have everything I have in here, in the heart. And now's the time, too. God is going to judge the world soon. We've got to be ready. We've got to turn from evil and believe in Jesus. Come. I want you to meet someone."

Taking her arm, he led her through the basement shelter. Smokey fires burned in half-barrels, and bunks of sleeping survivors lined the walls. Chloe was busy with a young family, a child in her arms who wouldn't stop crying. Miranda huddled with other survivors who looked like teens, as they shined a flashlight on what appeared to be a disassembled radio transmitter. Then he spotted Alice who was supervising the arrival of the deer as it was hung and skinned for roasting.

"Alice, this is Giselle." Milo let go of his captive's arm. "Giselle, this is Alice. Go on. Tell her about how to do it."

Now, Giselle leaned expectantly into Alice. Alice backed up a step and frowned at Milo in the flicker of firelight.

"Tell her about what?"

"I want to be a believer like you guys." Giselle nodded. "Jesus died for me?"

"Yeah, but . . ." Alice sighed. "Um. Usually, it takes more time to understand what you're believing in. What do you know so far?"

"Milo explained to me that I've been an enemy of God." Giselle swept her hair away from her face. "I can't get right, but God can make me right. That's why Jesus died for me. Is there more?"

"Uh . . ." Alice pondered for a moment. "No, I think that's it. The Bible says if you admit those things about yourself, and you trust in God to save you from your sins, you receive eternal life."

"So, I have it?" Giselle looked hopefully at Milo.

"Does she have it?" Milo turned to Alice.

"Yeah." Alice nodded. "It's not that complicated. Now, live to honor Jesus, and learn about Him in the Bible."

"I have eternal life." Giselle grinned and grasped Milo's hands. "Yes, I can feel it! I never knew about this! You've got to tell me everything. Come on. I'll show you where my family lives. You have to tell them about eternal life!"

Milo's eyes bulged at Alice.

"Her family?"

An instant later, he was tugged away, just as he had led her along moments earlier. Then they arrived at a dim, damp corner of the basement where only one lamp was burning. Giselle knelt next to one bunk where a mouse scurried away from the limp hand of a person who lay on the bunk.

"It's my mom." Giselle touched the woman's hand, and guided Milo's hand to it. "And my brother's over there. He's sick, too. They both need eternal life. They have no hope, otherwise. Do you need a Bible? Will that help? Should I get a Bible?"

"You have Bibles here?" Milo asked as he squatted down and grasped the cold, clammy hand of the fevered woman. "Bibles printed on paper?"

"Yes, they're with the other books we saved from the fires. I'll be right back."

Seated on the floor, Milo was alone for a moment with several bunks and cots filled with presumably ill people. Some of them peered at him from under their blankets, their eyes sparkling in the dim light.

"What do I do, God? I'm just a soldier," he mumbled.

Giselle was back a moment later, her arms full of books. She dumped them on his lap.

"I think it's one of these," she said, then stood back. "Do you see it?"

He held up one book after another to the lantern light.

"Three of these are Bibles. These other six aren't. They're—" He studied her face. "You can't read?"

"No. No one ever taught me more than my ABCs. I know the alphabet, but when I was a kid, the pandemic shut down the schools, and nobody around me really, you know, took an interest in teaching a lot of us. They just wanted us to do what they said and think like they thought. After Pan-Day, it's always been about staying alive, keeping the garden weeded, and hunting when we had bullets."

"Well, everything you need to know is in here." He opened one Bible. "I don't know a lot, but I can teach you what I know. Honestly, I've just begun to read it myself a few days ago."

"If you teach it to me, I'll remember enough. It's about eternal life, right?"

"Yeah. And about the God who gives that life." He gazed across the basement at the distant gathering of people around other fires. "I wonder if I should check on my friends."

"I heard your big friend with the beard already talking to people about God, so they're just doing what we're doing." She tugged on his sleeve. "Come closer to my brother so he can hear, too. Wait just a minute. Let me get some others."

Again, she darted away, and Milo felt panic. *Was this even right?* Did he have the authority to share what he'd only recently discovered himself? He couldn't remember any warnings from Rex or Chloe that he couldn't tell others as much as he could. After all, if God loved everyone, then everyone needed to know about His love.

Four others returned with Giselle—three young men and another woman around Giselle's age, the mid-thirties.

"Start at the beginning," Giselle instructed Milo. "They can't read, either, but together, we'll remember. Tell us everything. Everyone's scared of dying, so they need to know especially about eternal life. Oh, it's amazing, you guys! God forgives us!"

Feeling completely overwhelmed, Milo pushed aside his feelings of inadequacy and even the pressing memories of his own sinful treatment of believers. Just a few months earlier, he'd been hunting the Casperteins! Now, he was a messenger of truth with them.

"What I have to tell you is completely true," Milo began. "Unless you accept in confidence what I'm about to tell you, you'll die in rebellion against the God who created you. Since I was born thirty years ago, this country hadn't told us the truth about our Creator. Somehow, most Bibles got lost or destroyed after Pan-Day. But now, I'm going to tell you about the God who became a Man and died for you and me . . ."

Milo lost track of time. After he told them everything he knew from his own experience, they ate some of the deer that others brought to them. Fresh water was also passed around in a container they all drank from. Then, he read from the Bible to them, and Alice joined his growing audience, for which he was thankful since she knew so much more about God than he did. Alice had a frank style of teaching, but the young people sat mesmerized. And as she spoke about prayer and heaven and the cross of Christ, Giselle's brother woke and listened as well.

They slept, ate and drank some more, then read together. Milo was on his way back from the latrine when Miranda walked up to him.

"You're not going to believe what just happened!" She was wringing her hands. "I don't know if I should be angry or happy. I just spent two days fixing their radio, and as soon as that Governor Treble guy heard the OPT's transmission, he broke the radio! Smashed it to pieces before my own eyes! I'll never be able to repair it now."

"Wait. Two days?" Milo couldn't see Rex in the crowded underground space. "It didn't seem that long."

"That's not the point. He broke the radio I just fixed!"

"Maybe you shouldn't have fixed it. As soon as you fixed it, even they recognized it wasn't good."

"So, contact with the world is a bad thing?" She abruptly raised her hand. "Don't answer that. I just heard it with my own ears. I thought . . . I was doing them a favor."

"By connecting them to the OPT." Milo thrust his hands in his pockets, realizing this was the first time in weeks he hadn't been carrying a rifle. "Sometimes what seems good turns out to be bad, or it can be used for evil. We could've used you to teach these people the Bible the last two days. From what I've seen, they've all been paying attention, some to me, and some to Alice, and the rest to Rex and Chloe."

"Okay, now you're making me feel bad." She turned her face away, but he could still see her bite her lower lip. "I've just wasted two days."

"Sorry." He backed away. "I need to get back."

"Milo," she called, "you're not wrong, you know."

He returned to his side of the basement where Giselle and the others were sleeping. While underground, he had no sense of day or night. With a sigh, he lay among the others, staring at an empty cement ceiling, thinking of the disagreement with Miranda. In his previous life, he would've gloated over winning an argument, proving himself right. But now that he wanted what was best for everyone, proving others wrong wasn't so satisfying. He guessed this was the Holy Spirit's safeguard against gloating altogether.

Sometime later, he woke and found Rex and Miranda filling their canteens from a spigot on the wall. Chloe was rolling up her sleeping bag to tie on top of her backpack.

"The blonde came to talk to me about you," Rex said to him as he watched them gather their things. "She asked if you could stay here. I told her that was your decision. Seems that we were able to help them some, huh?"

"Yeah. Giselle didn't say anything to me about staying." He looked toward her. "I haven't even unpacked my stuff. I've just been crashing on the floor."

"Well, we're pulling out. It's a new day outside." Rex stood in front of him. "The day of Christ's coming is near. Whether you come with us or stay with them—it won't be long now. Think of where you can do the most good for eternity."

"I'd already made up my mind to tell Levi face to face about Owen Travers. And there's that guy I sent after Levi and Jenna. That's some closure I need to see through."

"I know your heart about those things, Milo. I've seen the change in you. I can explain it all to Levi when we see him. Of course, it's possible we won't ever see him again. There's no point in going if there's a good reason to stay."

"What about you guys?" Milo felt torn. "You're done here, but I'm not?"

"I'm more obligated than you to get back to Meeker. Besides, I don't have a cutie asking for me to stay. You led Giselle and her friends to Christ. Milo, Levi will understand that you stayed back to build up a fellowship here. You two can catch up in heaven, and until then, I assure you, Levi will hold no hard feelings about the past. His wife was killed on my watch. I'm the one who really needs to have that talk with him."

"So, maybe I should stay." He looked around to see Chloe and Miranda listening nearby. "I don't feel like I'm ready to go on my own yet."

"You'll do fine." Chloe embraced him. "Alice said you're a natural teacher, and the things you don't know, you can read from the Bible and learn with them."

"What about the rifle?" he asked Rex. "It belongs to you guys."

"It belongs to the children of God," Rex said, "and you're a child of God. You already know how valuable it is, so keep it for yourself. The OPT will make it here sooner or later. Your rifle may be valuable, but the faith of these people is more important. Teach them to stand."

"And teach them to hunt," Chloe said. "No more hijacking travelers."

Milo felt a deep sense of loss as he walked outside and into the sunshine with his four friends. He kept clearing his throat, bravely holding back his emotions. Finally, while watching Rex's broad shoulders grow smaller down the street, he laughed at the memory of Rex first making him carry a goat during the people's daily marches.

"This is selfish of us to keep you here," Giselle said from beside him. "It's selfish of me."

He smiled down at her. In the sunlight, her face was pale, but her eyes were bright.

"I don't mind. God's given me new friends. And a new passion."

"No." Giselle looked after the four travelers. "I want you to stay, but I'd always feel guilty for making you stay."

"But I want to stay." He took her by the shoulders. "I'm going to teach all of you the Bible. I'll teach you to read, too. They're still my friends. I'll tell you that amazing story—how I met them first in Philadelphia. But I'm here now."

"You need to go, Milo. Please." She nodded her head through her unchecked tears. "Finish your journey. If our

God wants us together, then you'll come back. But not like this. I decided too quickly for you."

"I'm not staying just for you." He lowered his voice. "Your people need to learn to hunt game without firearms. I've learned how to do that, and I can teach you."

"We have enough bullets now to last a few months." She embraced him roughly. "I want you here, Milo, but not until you can stay without regret. Please go."

"But, I want—"

"Hurry back."

She pulled away from him, and a couple young men held his backpack and rifle for him. The moment was too much. He faced the risen sun and felt the tears on his cheeks. In all his years, he'd never before had a people who he wanted to be with, let alone *two* people. It took him several breaths to overcome his sobs of joy and sorrow and peace—all tied together. Some of the survivors of Des Moines were going to heaven because of him, but the possibility of seeing Levi again gave him an inspiration he couldn't express any other way but to live through it. It was even possible that he would see Radiant Shade— *Jenna Dowler!*

"I will come back." He held Giselle in his arms. "I will. All I'm doing is crossing Nebraska, see that my friends are safe in Colorado, then I'll be coming right back."

"Then I'll know it's for real . . . from here . . . you staying with us." She placed a hand on his chest. "I'll wait for you every day. Help your friends, then you won't be torn, and you'll come back to stay."

He accepted his pack, which Giselle helped to buckle across his chest once they'd lifted it onto his back. Then, they handed him his full canteen, and he swung his rifle over his shoulder.

"If Jesus doesn't come for us first," he said to the others outside, "I'll come back to Des Moines!"

For the first two blocks, he looked back and waved three times. Once out of sight, he jogged slowly through the rubble of the city until he caught sight of his friends ahead. At a fast walk, he overtook them within thirty minutes.

Chloe glanced at him as he steadied his breathing and walked beside her.

"Rex said we'd walk slow the first few miles," she said, "just in case you changed your mind."

"They changed it for me." He took a deep breath. "I need to finish what we started. Together."

"I actually thought you'd bring her with you." Rex looked back and winked. "Loverboy."

"Oh. I didn't consider that as an option." He frowned. "But her family is here. I'll come back in a few weeks. After we reach Meeker."

In minutes, he settled into the familiarity of his traveling companions. Ahead, Rex and Miranda shared a breakfast of bread and meat. Alice's heavy staff clunked methodically on the pavement. And he walked next to Chloe, the woman whose past intertwined so much with his own. Giselle and Des Moines were his future, but these Casperteins were his present. They'd always be his family now, even when he left them for good. Until then, he'd make the most of their time together.

"Tell me more about that COIL organization," he said to Chloe.

"COIL?" She smiled. "Now, there's a story worthy of the width of Nebraska!"

Chapter Six

A nnette was worried. Thunder rumbled across the Utah landscape as she walked under a limestone arch large enough to fit a locomotive. She'd lost the footprints of the two horses that had run away during the first earthquake, but that wasn't what worried her the most.

It'd been a week since Rudy had taken a beating from the rockslide in the canyon, and his condition wasn't improving. It was his back. The swelling hadn't gone down. Even Vorca had rambled aloud in her native tongue and tried ancient chiropractic adjustments, but the bulge along his spine wasn't going down and his pain wasn't diminishing.

Studying the sky, Annette realized she'd better call it a day before the storm moved in. She welcomed the rain. Anything was better than the ash! But with rain, visibility would diminish, and she needed to see afar to make directional changes by distant landmarks. Another wasted day, searching for the horses!

She held tightly to the rifle over her shoulder as she leaped from boulder to boulder. Nothing moved in the wilderness, but she'd brought the rifle anyway in case she came upon any game. Rudy's hope that the horses would return to the excavated pool of water in the canyon was unfounded. The horses were too afraid, apparently. Vorca had butchered the third horse that Annette had shot as mercy for its broken leg, but that meat wouldn't last more than a few weeks.

The rain fell without much prelude. The last of the ash that hadn't been swept away by the previous rain was now drained away permanently. The temperature was warm that afternoon, so Annette allowed her bare head to take the wet drops directly.

Happily, she picked up her pace when she noticed the opening of the canyon much closer than she'd thought. She hated to return empty-handed, but Gail and Tilda were keeping the camp upbeat. And Caleb wasn't a fussy child. He seemed content to play in the dirt. Vorca could always scout around for edible plants, and somehow, they'd make do.

The ground seemed to rumble under her feet, but it wasn't a quake this time. This was something noisier. The rumble grew in intensity, drawing nearer. She saw no tornado, and though the recent meteor showers had been loud, they hadn't shaken the ground like this.

She ran toward camp, and when she rounded the canyon mouth to find their small shelter built between limestone walls—instead, rust-colored water surged across the landscape. Annette saw no hope in outrunning the muddy flash flood. Gasping in dread, she darted to the right and clawed at the rocks, seeking a grip to climb above the torrent. Three feet up, the flood rose and tugged at her boots. A wave knocked her from the limestone and dragged her to the desert floor in gritty water.

Tumbling with sticks, rocks, and sand, she fought for air against the assault of water. In seconds, the flood spread out across the plain. Annette found herself lying on her back in a puddle of water, surrounded by debris from the canyon. Although the rain continued to fall, the burst of flood water soaked into the sand nearly as quickly as it had arrived.

Annette climbed to her knees and wiped her hair from her face.

"Rudy! Gail! Tilda!"

Gazing in every direction, she saw no sign of anyone moving amongst the uprooted bushes and unsettled boulders. Cringing, she felt a deep bruise on her upper arm and held it limply as she climbed to her feet. The canyon wherein the camp had sat had been altered again, this time by the flash flood.

"Rudy!"

She couldn't imagine that Rudy had survived the flood waters, not in his disabled state. That left little hope for the others.

"Vorca!" She screamed for the hearty native woman. "Anyone!"

Stumbling across the damp ground, she searched behind rocks and in sinking pools of water. There had to be some remnant of their camp—tins, canvas, or something! In the fading light, she traipsed into the canyon itself, searching the walls. Perhaps they'd heard the flash flood coming, and scrambled to safety?

Suddenly, she stopped and smiled. What was this? Feeling foolish, she wiped her face of rain and tears and laughed at her dread. *It was the wrong canyon!* But that didn't mean she wasn't worried. She returned to the desert and gazed northwest. Was it over there? Dusk was approaching, and she realized she'd made a rookie mistake. While searching for horse prints, she'd been looking down more than looking around. Now, she didn't recognize any landmarks.

In the fading light, she walked and sometimes crawled up limestone embankments. The rain stopped then started again, and with it came inky darkness and a terrible cold that she wasn't dressed for. She never meant to be away from camp more than the afternoon!

To hide from the weather, she found a bare outcropping, which sheltered only part of her head, back, and shoulders from the rain. With half her body exposed to the downpour, she shivered and prayed for God's comfort through another trial. She'd been through many adventures with Titus since their meeting in Israel. The model she'd once been as Annette Sheffield seemed like another woman now, decades later.

Dying of hypothermia at her age didn't seem like a terrible way to go—not that she had a choice! She sighed through a smile at the darkness all around her. Her legs felt the pelting rain the most. Though she hadn't given birth to Levi, she'd mothered him for over twenty years. They'd crossed half the country together, a trip that had forced her to recognize the man he'd become. He was her son, and not knowing his status left her heart unsettled. Even though Rudy was her husband now, and he wasn't doing well physically, it was Levi and Lyla that she kept praying for with intensity. If only she could see them again in her old age!

The distinct sound of metal striking rock reached her ears. Her eyes had started to close, but now she was wide awake and alert. How could anyone move in this storm? After a few minutes, she began to doubt that she'd heard the noise at all. Or maybe a stone had tumbled off the hillside and fallen in a puddle. The walls and canyons were known to distort noises.

But then she sensed movement in the darkness. She saw nothing in the night, but she could sense where rain was pattering differently, and the subtlety of air shifting. Was she imagining it? So far from civilization, this couldn't be a person. It must've been a wild animal! Her mind envisioned some grotesque apparition living in the deep Utah gorges, mutated from the virus, awakened by the quakes to feed on travelers who lost themselves searching for runaway horses.

Annette pressed herself closer to the limestone, the rough edges stabbing uncomfortably into her back. She could only hope to be ignored by whatever was out there, for she couldn't escape without being able to see. Blindly running, she would certainly tumble into a ravine or break her leg against a boulder. Wounded and dying seemed worse than shivering and dying.

Rudy would just have to make do without her. Vorca would keep them alive if she could find meat. Or Christ would come soon and they'd all be spared.

A sweaty, musky odor reached Annette's nose. It combined with her fear of a desert creature until her brain connected the smell to a wet horse, which she'd smelled many times. *A horse!*

"Hey there," she called into the darkness. With trepidation, she reached a hand into the rain. "You there, girl? Come here now."

She touched nothing but cold air, yet she realized the smell of wet horse—probably one of the two mares she'd been searching for—and sensed it wasn't far away.

Leaving her shallow shelter, she stepped like a blind woman across the desert floor. Her boots fumbled for footing over rocks and uneven sand. With almost an electric shock, she touched a living animal and jerked her hand back.

The horse whinnied softly, encouraging Annette to probe farther. Whether it was one of their horses or some other, Annette wasn't risking losing this chance company. *Chance?* No, there was no chance in the desert on this dark night.

"Steady, girl." She pet the neck of the mare and felt all over her back, trying to get a sense of the height and position she needed to reach. "Hold still now . . ."

After flexing her knees twice, she vaulted upward. Since she was naturally tall, Annette landed well on top of the horse's back, then swung a leg over. Laying up the length of the animal, she continued to comfort her. With a hand wrapped in the long mane, she urged the horse forward. The animal's body heat was a gift, but the rain still pounded down on them both.

The horse started walking, her head down, as if barely discerning the ground in the inky blackness. Her shod hooves struck rocks, but she didn't stumble. Annette closed her eyes, and prayed for God to guide this simple creature to some refuge.

But as the minutes stretched into an hour, then another hour, they reached no refuge. Annette dozed unintentionally on the back of the horse, only to wake with a start time and again, afraid she'd slip off and be alone again in the rain. For as long as she could, she remained awake, hugging the body of the animal that had come to her emotional and physical rescue.

As the night crept on and the rhythmic plodding of the horse continued, Annette was lulled into a deep sleep, her cheek on the mane. Her hands dropped limply to either side of the animal's neck.

When she woke, it was daylight, and discomfort plagued her body. The horse had stopped. She gathered her senses and pushed herself upright on the back of the horse. Before her, the desert terrain stretched in rusty colors, broken only by ancient boulders and distant plateaus.

"Annette?" a woman's voice cried.

She and the horse both turned to look down at the humble camp among puddles. Tilda stood up, throwing off a tarp from her and Gail, and rushed to the horse's side to clutch Annette's nearest leg. Just as surprising to Annette was the second mare standing idly a few feet away as well!

Less hurriedly, Rudy's head emerged from under his own tarp. Although the camp appeared waterlogged, it hadn't been swept away by the flash flood in the nearby canyon.

"Thank God!" Rudy sighed and lay his head on the tarp under him, which appeared as wet as the sopping tarp over him. "You found the horses."

"Oh, not quite." She slid off the horse and slapped life back into her legs before she attempted to walk. "The horses found me. I about died in the night!"

Gail looped a harness around one horse, and Vorca put a lead rope around the other, though both horses looked like they were too spent to run away again.

Annette knelt down to Rudy and kissed him. With her hand on his chest, she gazed into his eyes full of tears.

"I was wrong." He groaned under his breath. "I was wrong about Meeker and the volcano. It wasn't as deadly of an eruption as I thought. Now I've brought us out here like this. The rain has washed all the dangerous ash away. We need to get out of this desert or it's going to kill us. There's nothing for us here."

"Well, we didn't leave Meeker only because of the ash," Tilda said. "The OPT was rounding us up, too, remember?"

Rudy closed his eyes. Annette could see the pain on his face—more than just disappointment in their circumstances. His back was no better, and maybe even worse after the cold, wet night.

"We need to find a place where rocks don't fall on us," Rudy said, "where there's wood and water supplies, and some game. Without those three things, we're done."

"The closest place I know of," Gail said, "is back north. It means we'll have to get back on the highways, though."

"You can't travel," Annette told him. "You can't even stand."

"Then for you guys, I'll crawl." He grit his teeth. "We'll all die if you stay here with me."

Vorca spoke calmly in her tongue and gestured with her hands at the horses. Without waiting for their response, Vorca ripped the tarp off Rudy and walked over to Caleb. She sat down and began to knot a length of rope.

"Every time I think she doesn't understand English, she surprises me." Rudy could only gasp since it hurt too much to laugh. "Let's see what she's doing."

"Yellowstone could erupt again," Gail said as she righted a pot and blew sand out of it. "The earthquakes are probably not over, and that means that volcano isn't done belching, either."

"Nothing is perfectly safe anymore." Annette watched Vorca work. "If she's fixing something to take us all north again, then that's where we go."

"All the way back to Meeker?" Tilda asked.

"No, just to somewhere with woods." Annette shook her finger at Rudy. "That back of yours is the problem!"

"Tell me about it." He started to reach with one arm behind his back but winced and stopped. "It's like my whole spine is out of joint. I can barely breathe without screaming."

"None of us have enough strength to push it back into place," Annette said, "if that's all it needs. Maybe in the next earthquake, you could get in the way of another boulder and knock it back into place."

"Funny." Rudy panted. "I was thinking one of the horses could kick me right on that spot, and things would be miraculously better."

"Equine chiropractic adjustment?" Tilda laughed.

"Even if we've never heard of that . . .," Rudy groaned, "I'm about ready to let you try it . . ."

With concern, Annette watched as Vorca hitched the horses side by side, then fit a sling between them. Gail and Tilda picked up camp as Annette understood Vorca's plans and helped to secure the sling so it would indeed support a heavy man such as Rudy.

"I think that was the easy part." Gail chuckled as the four women looked from Rudy to the sling and back to Rudy. Even the horses seemed uncertain about what was to happen next.

"There's no way you're getting me into that contraption." Rudy shook his head a little. "You'll need a crane. I'm nothing but dead weight as long as I can't—"

"What are we—weaklings?" Tilda rolled up the sleeves of her sweater as the sun climbed higher. "You guys ready?"

"Maybe we could have the horses kneel," Gail considered, "like camels do, so their riders can climb on."

Rudy cried out as Vorca roughly forced him upright, her arms under his arms from behind.

"Take a deep breath, Rudy," Annette said. "Let's do it quickly, everyone. One, two, three!"

Vorca and Annette supported Rudy's upper half, and Gail and Tilda tried to carry his legs, but they ended up only carrying one. The other leg dragged awkwardly behind as they shuffled him headfirst to the sling.

"Use your arms, Rudy!" Annette shouted under strain. "Pull yourself!"

Vorca jabbered her own unintelligible instructions, setting off Caleb with his own directions accompanied by gestures.

Halfway into the sling, they all paused to reposition. Vorca and Annette each climbed onto a horse to help Rudy from above. Rudy's face was white as they heaved him more fully onto the sling. When all was finished, his head rested half off one end, and his legs dangled at the knees off the other end. The horses stepped closer together, drawn by Rudy's weight, sandwiching him between them.

"There." Annette slid off the horse and walked to the rear of the horses to pat Rudy's head. "Comfortable?"

"Do I look comfortable?" he asked as he lay partially sideways.

"There's no way we can reposition you unless we lift you up somehow." She kissed his forehead. "Northward bound?"

"Northward." He closed his eyes. "Where's the rapture when you need one?"

Their belongings were piled onto the horses and carried on their own backs. Annette led the way east out of the desert, with Vorca leading the horses. Caleb was once again on her back like their previous journeys, and Gail and Tilda brought up the rear.

"Everything's temporary," Annette whispered as she picked her way through boulders and up a slope. She chose not to despair about what seemed like a fruitless attempt to survive in the desert. They'd lost gear and Rudy was now crippled. "But everything's temporary . . ."

Desert Highway 128 appeared in the distance as a ridge line that spanned north to south. Moments later, Annette stomped her boots on its sandy pavement to ensure there was indeed pavement underneath. One of the many deep canyons nearby held the Colorado River and its bounty of water, but they were high above now, where sand flats and scenic viewpoints hosted only dry land.

"Annette," Gail called, looking to the south.

Following Gail's gaze, Annette saw there were travelers approaching them on foot up the highway.

"They're a couple miles back." Annette wrapped her hand once around her rifle sling to hold it tighter. "Let's stay in front of them. Maybe God will spare us from meeting anyone on the highway until we get north of the river. Hang tight, Rudy. We're on our way."

"Hang tight," Rudy repeated from his squished position on the sling. "Very funny, Mrs. Caspertein."

Setting a fast pace north, Annette looked back only twice the first mile. Vorca's short legs were moving as fast as Caleb was talking to the horses in Vorca's tongue, and Gail and Tilda marched at their own quick pace farther behind.

The highway angled northeast for miles, and the sun brought back memories of the uncomfortable journey the year before, when they were heading in the same direction and crossed the Mojave. The Colorado River was on their left, winding sometimes closer, sometimes out of sight. But by nightfall, the river had rejoined the highway, and Annette chose a plateau above the two lanes where they could camp for the night. The trail up to the plateau was steep and narrow, but Vorca seemed to understand that they had to get Rudy up by horse or they'd have to leave him on the highway, exposed to passersby.

Side by side, the horses scrambled up shale and bare limestone to reach the plateau, which was about the size of a basketball court. From below, Annette watched Vorca with the horses.

"We'll never get him down that way," she admitted to Gail and Tilda. "We might need to roll him down."

"Oh, Annette!" Tilda laughed and slapped her arm. "Just build a hang glider and strap him to it. You won't even need to take him out of the hotdog bun he's so fond of."

The ladies laughed together and helped each other up the trail. The top of the plateau was level and out of sight from the road only thirty feet below. Annette stepped to the edge of the table.

"Those people behind us must've pulled off to camp somewhere else." She unclipped her pocket for her binoculars. "It's almost too dark to see anything out there now. If we light a fire back far enough—"

"Annette!" Gail screamed. "Get down!"

She dropped to a crouch on the edge of the plateau but realized an instant later she was still in plain sight of the road below—in view of two trucks driving slowly from the north!

Their brakes squealed just fifty yards up the highway. Annette prayed she hadn't been seen. Too afraid to move, she glared north, her palms sweaty against the stock of the rifle. It was the OPT. It had to be. No one else would have the resources to fuel vehicles in the field.

Figures in tan and green fatigues climbed out of the vehicles and stood in the cover of their Humvees. Annette could see about six of them. A smaller person who appeared to be a woman—maybe OPT Advocate Veronika Kane—spoke in low tones to her subordinates. A man set his rifle on one Humvee hood and stepped clear of the vehicle.

"Come down from there!" he called.

Shrinking against the ground, Annette hid her rifle from those below, offering only her head to the OPT patrol's view. She checked the horses, then Gail, and Tilda. Vorca's arms were outstretched, holding everyone back. The horses pranced nervously, crowded against the wall of rock at the other side of the plateau. Rudy was no doubt more squished than ever, but she couldn't think about her husband's comfort or his lack of involvement at that moment.

Instead, she imagined what Titus and Levi would have done in similar moments. With them both, more than Rudy, she'd witnessed tense situations reduced to back-slapping laughter and celebration—even among strangers.

Rising to her knees, Annette allowed her rifle to dangle from her neck and shoulder. She lifted an arm.

"It's okay!" she yelled back. "We're just camping up here. Pass on by in peace."

She tried to control her breathing as they discussed her words. By offering them passage, she hoped they would be settled about moving by without threat of ambush. For sure, the two-Humvee convoy had been assaulted by anti-OPT bands of survivors.

"We're with the One Planet Trust," the woman announced herself, whose voice Annette recognized as Kane's. "Please come down and introduce yourselves. We're sweeping this region for resistance fighters."

"That's not us," Annette said. Again, she waved her arm. "We just came up from Utah. You can keep going. We have no ill will toward the OPT. We can all move on in peace."

Kane spoke several words to her men, and two went to the back of one Humvee. Annette couldn't see what they were doing as they stood at the rear.

"We're requiring all citizens to comply with OPT procedure," Kane informed. "It's for the health and safety of all Americans that we stand together. We have a standardized exam for all citizens in this area. Please come down. You won't be harmed for cooperating."

"Yeah, right," Annette mumbled, hoping Rudy could hear what she was up against, even though he was immobilized. The spare rifles were on the horses, but Vorca, Gail, and Tilda weren't sharpshooters. Then she responded, "We won't be coming down. The path coming up here was too steep to go down again without problems. Move along, OPT. You or anyone else you're working with won't be harmed."

"If you don't come down," Kane moved farther back, "we'll be forced to make you comply. We're giving you that free choice."

"Free choice!" Annette grumbled, then turned her head. "Rudy, can you hear her?"

"Yeah," he answered, his voice muffled from his place between both horses. "How many with her?"

"Looks like about six, but it's getting hard to see in this light."

"Do you have a shot? Maybe if you open fire, you'll send them on their way."

"This is a bad idea," Annette said, "but I can't think of any better one. We're cornered up here, and they know it!"

"Come down now!" Kane shouted. "Or we'll respond as if you are hostiles!"

Annette lifted her eyes to where the last rays of sunlight touched distant rock formations and scattered forests. Finding a new campsite in the dark would be near impossible. All she could hope for at that moment was that she could see them better than they could see her.

She leveled her rifle, holding it snug against her shoulder as she had many times before, even though it had been a year since she'd been in a battle. Barely had Kane's image filled her scope than she had pulled the trigger. Without waiting to see if Kane fell, Annette shifted to other targets. In those seconds, she didn't care too much about where she placed each round. If someone was visible, she fired as fast as she could. Six to one, she could make no mistakes!

But then the edge of the plateau spit chips of rock in her face. She tasted blood on her lip as she dropped to her belly. Their guns were thundering back nonstop. The zip of bullets overhead sounded like lethal wasps, and the ricochets off rock like whining bees in search of a victim.

Rolling over twice to change position, Annette then rose just high enough to scope for another shot. That's when she saw a man at the back of one vehicle raise a short tube and aim it up at the plateau.

"Grenade!" Annette screamed, and rolled into a fetal position.

The explosion washed over her, the concussion taking her hearing and disorienting her for a few seconds. She even started to rise to her feet when she remembered she was in the middle of a gunfight. And there was pain in her neck. She touched the muscle behind her right ear and felt blood. Smoke and dust choked her.

Her hearing returned to the sound of screaming, but it wasn't hers or her family's. It was one of the horses. One of the mares was bucking wildly, probably wounded and terrified, while still strapped to the other horse with Rudy's sling between them!

Vorca was wounded and down, whether by horse or shrapnel, she couldn't tell. Caleb was still on Vorca's back, but he was silent, hopefully uninjured. Gail and Tilda were lying motionless off to the left.

Regardless of the danger from below, Annette could think only of Rudy now—giant, loveable, immobile Rudy! He was at the mercy of the spooked horses. Annette started to raise her rifle, but her right side, from the neck down, wasn't responding. If she could just tranq the horses . . . Stubbornly, she panted as she crossed with her left arm to grip her rifle. But the wild horses, dancing in a wider circle, crashed into her. Her head bounced off one horse's flank, which sent her sprawling onto her back.

She clawed at the ground to avoid several hooves, and then the horses dropped off the plateau! No, she suddenly realized. They were galloping down the precarious trail to the highway!

Scrambling back to the edge, Annette watched as the horses charged down the slope, still playing tug-of-war against the sling between them. She prayed Rudy wasn't even in the sling anymore. Maybe he'd had the wits to climb off or he'd been thrown free already.

With horror, Annette watched the horses somehow reach the highway without tumbling, but they didn't stop. At full speed, they crossed both lanes, vaulted over the guardrail, and then they were gone. The dimensions of the gorge below were difficult to gauge in the darkness, but Annette knew the river was far, far below.

Now, there was only silence. Annette stared at the place where the horses had disappeared, not believing what she'd seen. Her arms hung at her side. Her neck was leaking blood and pulsed in pain.

Caleb started to cry. Annette staggered sideways over to her friends and fell down next to Vorca. With fleeting hope, she surveyed the otherwise empty plateau for any sign of Rudy, but he wasn't there. Rudy Caspertein was gone.

"Don't cry, Caleb." Annette held the child's hand where he wriggled on Vorca's back. Vorca remained still, laying on her stomach. "Gail? You still with us? Tilda?"

"We're still here," Tilda stated calmly. Annette could see her reaching for Gail. "We're a little worse for wear, but we're still here."

"Rudy . . . He . . ." She couldn't finish.

"I know, honey. We just have to—"

Tilda didn't finish as flashlights blinded them.

"Don't move!" men shouted. "Stay down."

Resisting the soldiers' hands, Annette fought them out of pure desperation in an effort to draw their aggression to herself rather than toward her friends. But they were strong, and she was wounded. In seconds, they pinned her down and zip-tied her wrists behind her back.

"Can you manage her?" one man asked another as they yanked Annette upright. "Get her down to the trucks. No need to be gentle."

Annette was tall enough to look face to face with the man who held her arm. Then, he slapped her on the side of the head.

"I've got her!" he barked back.

She was shoved to slide and trip down the trail from the plateau to the road. The headlights of the Humvees shined in her eyes, but she could squint past their brightness to see two other people moving around the vehicles. As she was escorted closer, she was disappointed to see Kane awake and alert. In all of her shooting, no one appeared to have been tranquilized.

"What a mess!" Kane cursed and rested a booted foot on a boulder at the front of one Humvee. "We're on foot unless we can clear this out!"

In fascination, Annette stared at the disaster around the Humvees. The grenade they'd fired had caused a rockslide. Thousands of pounds of rocks as large as truck tires surrounded the vehicles. Some had tumbled and bounced high enough to break windows and crush at least one hood—maybe even an engine!

"Sit there and don't move!" Annette's escort kicked at her leg. "Sit!"

Annette sat cross-legged on the rock-strewn pavement. From that angle, she could see the boulders would need to be removed to drive away, if their engines would even start.

Then the others from above arrived with Vorca—and Caleb on her back—and Gail and Tilda in restraints. The three women were forced to sit beside Annette.

"Don't talk!" Kane ordered her prisoners, then assigned one of her men to guard them. "If they talk, shoot them. We don't have time for this! We have to get to Dove Creek by noon tomorrow."

Intent on hiding her identity, Annette kept her head down. She recognized Kane from her meeting in Meeker, but Kane had probably been visiting with hundreds of people in a dozen cities during the last month.

Near the vehicles. Kane discussed their options with her men, but Annette could hear only a little. It was night, and the six probably had limited camping resources in the Humvees. Kane was concerned about additional hostiles in the area, finding water to drink in the desert, and a defensive position for the night. She wasn't willing to leave the vehicles quite yet, not until daylight when they could assess their problems better.

Turning her head, Annette saw where the headlight shined on the guardrail. That was about where Rudy had gone over with the horses. If his back hadn't gone out, he could've handled this differently, maybe even saved them all and humbled Advocate Kane altogether. It was too much to hope that he'd somehow survived the fall. At least he was out of pain now. Soon, she'd be joining him in glory.

Tilda wept quietly beside her as the man with the gun stood over them.

Levi felt his tricycle wobble and he glanced back at both back tires, expecting to see flats as before. But the wheels were fine this time.

"I'm stopping!" he called to his five companions. "Again!"

Farther ahead, Brian coached Jenna beside him to brake gently. Jenna had been riding accident-free since Guntersville. Rather than Jenna, Levi had been the drag on the party's progress, along with Runner in the boot behind his seat.

"He's awake." Mia braked with Kip and circled back to her cousin.

Hanging his rifle on his handlebars, Levi climbed off the tricycle, which he likened to climbing on and off a buckboard.

Auggie emerged from the border highway grasses, looked both ways, then bee-lined for Runner.

"Keep her back, Lena," Levi ordered.

Lena dropped her bike and intercepted the Lab before she could investigate her previous master.

Levi gazed down at the skin and bones figure of the young man he knew only as Runner. He was fighting against the wrapped blankets and tarps in which Levi had bundled him to keep his limbs from tangling in the back wheels. More than once, Runner had flailed in his sleep, but now he flailed while waking.

Runner grunted and finally freed his arms. He blinked up at the bright sky and squinted at the faces around him, settling on Levi.

"You!" Runner cursed, then weakly fought his lower half free of wrappings. Suddenly, he froze and observed his audience closer, even Auggie. He was panting from his exertion. "Am I your prisoner? Why are you idiots just standing there?"

Swinging his legs off the tricycle, Runner massaged his thighs as if the blood flow had been lacking.

"Yeah, you're sort of our prisoner," Levi said, "and sort of our . . . patient."

"What's that supposed to mean?" He rubbed his scalp. "Oh, my head. What'd you guys do to me? Come here, girl."

Lena looked to Levi, and he shrugged. She let the dog go, and Auggie's nose went straight to investigate Runner's missing foot. Runner pet his dog, then accepted water from Kip's canteen. After several swallows, he coughed and winced. His hand went to his throat, and Levi noticed fear and recognition cross the young hunter's face.

"How long have I been—?" He gave the canteen back to Kip. "Things are . . . a little . . . foggy. Um, I'm not sure what . . ."

Levi crouched down so his head was level with Runner's.

"You've been out of it for at least a week and a half. We found you in pretty bad shape. In a pig pen. Do you remember how you got there or what happened to you?"

"A pig pen?" Runner scoffed, but an instant later, he fell sideways.

"I've got you." Levi caught him and held him upright. "Take your time. You're with friends now. Think back. Someone gave you a pretty good beating, my friend."

"Friend?" The word sounded like a whimper. "I must be pretty messed up if you're calling me your friend. Stop staring at me!"

"No, you're not giving the orders here." Levi's voice was soft, his hand still on the man's shoulder to steady him. He could feel Runner's body trembling. "We've been nursing you back to health for days, keeping you alive, but just barely. Lena's been your nurse. You don't remember any of it?"

"It's . . . fuzzy." He rubbed his brow. "Are you letting me go?"

"He's not thinking clearly," Mia voiced.

"Coma patients need a while to get their senses back," Jenna said. "Just give him some time."

Runner held up his left hand and watched it shake. He closed it into a fist and dropped it into his lap.

"What's wrong with me? What'd you guys do to me?"

"When we found you," Levi said, "you'd been badly beaten. And your foot had turned gangrene. It was black, Runner. We had to remove it. I removed your foot."

"My foot?" Runner chuckled and studied their faces. "This is . . . bizarre. I'm having trouble, uh . . . What you're saying is . . .? I need to go home. I'm going back to River Camp. I've had enough of this."

Levi tried to steady him as he started to rise, but Runner batted his hand away. Heaving forward, Runner planted his one foot on the road. When he rocked upright, he tipped onto his amputated stump. Too quick for Levi to catch him, Runner fell to his left with a horrific scream.

An instant later, Levi held his head but Runner was unconscious again.

"He's delirious," Mia said. "He's not processing what's going on."

"It's okay." Levi lifted him up and set him in the carriage of the tricycle. "We'd hoped this day would come, that he'd wake up. Now we all need to help him through it, because we can't keep going the way we've been going."

"That tricycle's the problem," Brian said. "There's no way we'll reach Colorado with that thing."

"We're close to Red Bay." Levi tucked the loose gear around Runner to hold the unconscious man in place. "Maybe we can pick up a couple new bikes there, even one for Runner."

"What about the OPT?" Mia asked. "I'm not worried. I'm just hoping you have a plan to deal with them."

"Is using my wits considered a plan?" Levi asked.

"Let's just stay together, please," Jenna said. "We can face a town together. Maybe they'll be like the last, and people won't have the heart to arrest us."

"So, we go through town instead of going around it on the highway?" Levi checked their faces for opinions. Lena answered by tapping a couple fingers on her rifle. "Then let's make this our last stop for supplies for a while. It ain't easy praying for strength to go through fire rather than avoid it."

"Here we go, Jenna." Brian touched her arm. "Let's lead them out. Steady now. Get your speed up."

Levi stood on his pedals to start moving, once again at the back of the group with Lena.

"With Runner coming to," Levi said to the mute woman, "we don't have a choice but to stop in Red Bay. I want to avoid problems if possible. We'll first need a place to sleep. You want to go ahead and tackle that?"

"Aah-ah?" she asked.

"Yeah, you. Just use your pencil and paper to communicate. Helen Keller was born around here. They might remember what it means to work with people who are different."

She sped forward, and Auggie joined her, the dog probably thankful for a faster pace than the one set by Levi.

"What about Jenna saying to stay together?" Mia asked him.

"Lena is like Alice was on our last journey. A good scout keeps the group safer. Jenna wasn't on our last journey."

"Actually, I think you liked Alice warning people you were coming more than scouting ahead."

"Either way works for us." Levi slowed as they strained up a gradual hill. "With a little warning, folks have time to act rationally instead of in a panic."

"Yeah, well, they're going to act with a yawn if you don't peddle faster."

"A cousin who cared would get off her bike and push." Levi panted. "Or how about towing me up this hill?"

"Okay, I'll tow you." She held out her hand just beyond his reach, then sped faster. "Take my hand. Come on. I'll pull you along. Here's my hand. You've got to want it."

"Now, that's just cruel," Levi said to Kip. "No pity from you, either?"

"What? Sorry. I was praying."

"God will see us through, even if Red Bay is where we breathe our last."

"Oh, I know He will. I wasn't praying about our safety. I was praying for Runner. I want to see him saved."

Levi knew they were in trouble when they rode out of the broad oak trees onto Main Street and saw OPT banners hanging from two different building fronts. His travel companions slowed to ride behind him. Townspeople moved about the sidewalks and street, and gave the travelers furtive glances, but Levi saw no weapons or an OPT greeting party yet.

"Where's Lena?" Mia asked.

"You don't see Lena?" Jenna cried. "Levi, we have to stay together!"

"Lena was a Regulator and now she's a Christian with a tranq gun." Levi steered them to the sidewalk where a small department store stood dark at that late hour of the morning. "She'll be okay."

But Levi surveyed the street more carefully for some sign of her. He realized he needed to work out some signals with Lena if they were going to work like this all the way to Colorado. She needed to leave him some sign on the road or an indication of where she was.

Everyone climbed off their bikes and stretched their legs.

"A town loyal to the OPT didn't attack us," Brian said quietly to Levi. The others crowded as close to both riflemen as their bikes would allow. "You know what that means?"

"Lena is probably entertaining them for us already." Levi smiled and studied the storefronts under the two banners. "Well, we can't all wander around like a circus act in town, especially with him."

They looked down to see that Runner was awake.

"We'll be fine." Brian's thumb was tucked under his rifle sling.

Levi recalled the first time he'd met the sharpshooter. "I know you will be, Brian."

"Don't leave us, Levi!" Jenna snapped. "Stay together!"

"Now, I'm just going across the street." Levi unbuttoned his jacket to access his holstered .22 sidearm. "I'll be back with Lena in five minutes. She's just finding out where we can stay the night. Maybe she also found a couple more bikes for Runner and me to ride."

"You chopped off my foot!" Runner growled. "I'm riding no bike. I refuse!"

"Oh, yes, you will, young man," Levi said in his most fatherly tone, and jabbed his finger at the man. "I'm twice as ornery as you think you are, and I'll whip your backside like a spoiled child if you're going to give the adults your attitude."

"I have no foot!"

"Then I'll hop on one foot to make us even while I'm whipping you."

Jenna gasped in amusement while holding onto Mia.

"Oh, I'm sorry, I'm sorry!" Jenna recovered. "I just had a flashback of a much younger Levi being the one with the attitude."

"Maybe that *was* me." Levi smiled, then straightened his face for Runner. "But I learned to be a man for God under my dad's discipline, so you mind your mouth."

Levi marched across the street. Behind him, he heard Runner speak.

"I don't like him calling me a young man," he grumbled. "I'm not a child!"

Below both flags, Levi found a shoe store with the One Planet Trust words freshly stenciled on the front. Like many small towns, the local administrator's office had been repurposed for the OPT seat. Along the street, a few buildings had been burned down, so Levi guessed one might've been the courthouse or police station. Civil authority had been the first to be attacked during the Pan-Day riots. It had been easier to loot and kill with the police undermined in the chaos.

He opened the door to hear soft piano music through the ceiling speakers. Whether the source was from battery-power or electricity, Levi didn't bother to investigate as soon as his eyes settled on Lena standing in a back doorway. The shoe store had been gutted of shelves, and four desks were spaced out against two walls. When he reached Lena, he peered over her head to see she was holding three men at gunpoint in the storeroom. All three were kneeling, facing the wall, their sidearms and belts at Lena's feet. Auggie sat calmly on her haunches, off to the side of the captive men. The dog panted happily as though she would rather wrestle and play than bite or fight.

"Aah-ah, ah-hah ah."

"Yeah, I figured you were holding down the fort until we showed up." Levi moved past Lena and walked over to the wall that the men were facing so closely that their bellies were touching the plaster. "I'd like to apologize for our caution upon entering your town. It ain't easy getting jumped by the locals. You guys okay? You can rest your arms at your sides now."

The men sighed and dropped their arms. The closest and oldest man was portly and sweating. He turned his head and acknowledged Levi.

"Whatever you want, there's no need to hurt anyone. We're a fair-trade town of good people."

"And we're fair-trade travelers, all good people, too, so we should get along famously, right?"

The heavy man hesitantly nodded his head.

"There are seven of us in town, not counting this ferocious-looking Labrador. She's like me—she prefers to cuddle, not kill. But you can see we're armed, yeah?"

"Yeah."

"I've been known to leave a town in ashes when they're hostile to travelers, but we're not going to have any problems, are we?"

"No." The man shook his head.

"We want to stay the night in peace. It doesn't have to be a nice place. Even a garage would do. Do you know where we can spend the night?"

The heavy man turned to the middle one, a slender but fit-looking twenty-year-old with a light beard.

"Yeah, you can take the old flower shop," the young man said. "We put up visitors in there sometimes. There's running water and a bathroom."

"That sounds perfect for us. We've picked up some ammunition in our travels. Can we pay you, say, thirty .223 rounds for the lodgings? Those should work for some of your hunting rifles, right?"

"Thirty's good," the first man said.

"We also need to trade in a tricycle for two mountain bikes. We'll pay the difference."

"The Onion Man has a whole rack of bikes," said the young man. "I can take you to him. He grows onions, that's why we call him the Onion Man."

"Sounds fitting." Levi nodded. "You're my kind of townsfolk, I can tell. Now, one more thing. My people have been traveling for a while. Some of them are women like Lena here. They're tough as wolverines, but they'd rather just mingle and do some trading for supplies if that's okay. Can we all get along?"

"Yeah." The sweaty one wiped his brow. "No one'll bother them."

"Well, now, we need to talk about the OPT." Levi leaned closer. "We're not big fans. It ain't gonna be easy holding back my trigger finger if you're forcing your Oath of Solidarity on my people. So, tell me now: who's the OPT Advocate here?"

"That's me," said the heavy man.

"Stand up, guys. Introduce yourselves."

The three men rose to their feet. Levi shook their hands as they stated their names. The portly one was Jerry Mantello, and although he was the Advocate for the town of Red Bay, Levi noticed there was confidence missing in his life. Of course, the OPT may have chosen him because of that fact.

The middle man in his twenties was Ryan Pulloy, someone the regional OPT Advocate had deemed worthy to make an armed Oath Defender.

The last man was named Zach Sparks. The middle-aged man hesitated to shake Levi's hand at all. Fear wasn't the reason for the hesitation on his well-groomed bearded face, but of disapproval. Blatantly defying the OPT wasn't to his liking.

"I'm not giving you much choice," Levi said after he'd met them all. "I've warned you about the wrath I'm willing to pour out on this town if we're abused. In a land that's usually lawless, I hope you understand I'm only setting mutual standards I will meet as well. We respect each other, and we can trade, stay the night in peace, and we can leave as friends in the morning. I'm Levi Caspertein, and I won't be ashamed to shake your hands as good hosts from this day forth."

Only Mantello and Ryan nodded in agreement. Sparks just glared at him—a glare of which Levi took note, though he didn't return.

As the three men recovered their weapons and belts, Levi moved with Lena out to the main room of the shoe store.

"Watch Defender Sparks." Levi touched the corner of his eye. "He could be trouble. Good thing we're here for only one night. You, Brian, and I will pull guard shifts tonight. But we've got a few hours of daylight. I'm going to find the bikes we need. Can you see everyone safely to the flower shop?"

She accompanied Mantello across the street, and Levi left with Defender Ryan to investigate bicycles. But from down the sidewalk, Levi looked back at the shoe store and saw Sparks watching him. All three men wore their sidearms again, which wasn't too rare in those days, but

Sparks was the only one Levi was concerned about using his.

He could smell the Onion Man's residence before they reached the house. Ryan walked into the carport where two rows of bikes stood side by side. Although they were under cover from rain, the humidity had visibly rusted many of the gears and joints.

"It's like anything in life," Levi said. "Everything falls apart and fades away."

Levi checked one bike after another.

"Pick the two you want," Ryan offered. "The Onion Man is usually in his garden in the back. I'll take his payment to him. He trusts me."

"It's an honorable thing to be trustworthy." Levi found a sturdy bike, but to pull it out, the ones on the end needed to be lifted out of the way. "You wouldn't have your position as a Defender if you weren't dependable, right?"

"I didn't even want the job." His face was downcast. "The back wheel on this one is missing spokes."

"Let's swap the wheel with another. Why didn't you want the job? Lots of power, running things for the OPT."

"They only picked me because I'm the Pan-Day generation."

"That's how people in authority often try to influence society, through spokespeople who can relate to the crowd."

"I know why they want to use me, but I could never shoot anyone. Everyone in town is my friend. I'm not shooting them for the OPT or anyone else."

"Would you have tried to make us take the Oath of Solidarity?"

"Well, I'm supposed to make everyone take it, or arrest them. But Jerry—you know, the Advocate? He isn't even that concerned about some of those who haven't taken the Oath yet. We're supposed to write their names on a list and put them in lockup. Between you and me, the Birmingham Advocate said he'd execute anyone we didn't want to. Zack Sparks wants to follow the new rules, but Jerry and I aren't turning anyone in."

"Here, hold this one." Levi sorted through the second row of bikes. "You know, God is pleased with those who show favor to the humble. I think you're doing the right thing by protecting those others in town."

"How do you know God is pleased with me?" Ryan squeezed the brakes on the handlebar. "These brakes are good."

"Since I read the Bible a little every day, I've learned over the years what God says and feels about all kinds of attitudes and situations."

"I didn't know people could know that stuff about God. How about this bike trailer? The tires are flat, but you can put regular bike tires on it."

"Good thinking." Levi removed several bike parts and inspected them on the floor. "If you don't know how God views things, then you're not learning His will about your life. We should all be living in God's will, each of us. You never read the Bible?"

"Um, I thought it was just an ancient religion, outdated like other anti-science religions. That's what I was told, anyway."

"God isn't anti-science, and He certainly isn't outdated, even if He's not popular today. Are there tools in that box? True science was historically a study of the wonderful creation God created. People used to learn about God by discovering how and why He created things. Have you ever thought of the power necessary to create a single sun and put the moon in orbit around the earth? If God can do that, then He must be more powerful than the objects He's created. Someone that powerful, I want to be on his side. How about you?"

"I never really thought about it." Ryan held the bike frame of the first bike as Levi loosened the bolts. "Would you have shot us in the office?"

"Without hesitation." Levi looked into Ryan's face, which showed disappointment. "But I'll tell you a secret. Our guns are loaded with tranquilizers. You'd only take a nap and wake up with a little bruise. I wouldn't ever kill anyone intentionally. Every person was created by God and we're to love them."

"Tranquilizers?" Ryan smiled for the first time. "Are you serious?"

"I'm serious. My dad designed them because he knew we'd need special weapons for battle situations, but he also knew God doesn't want His people killing anyone. Why would we kill people when we're supposed to be training them for eternal life? Here. Sit on this. See how it feels. Ride it out to the street and back."

Ryan climbed onto the bike, but he didn't peddle away. Instead, he stared at the ground in silence for a long minute, then looked up.

"You say these things like you really know for sure."

"I do know for sure. I'd die before I denied that Jesus Christ is my Lord and Savior, the Man who was and is God, and who died for me."

"Well, I have no idea what any of that means, but I'd like to know something worth dying for."

As Ryan rode out to the street and back, Levi wondered if his eyes were watering from all the onion fumes in the air or from joy at the openness of Ryan's heart.

Together, they sat on the floor of the Onion Man's carport and took apart the bikes and trailer piece by piece, talking about Jesus' sacrifice for sins. Levi even drew out his sweat- and blood-stained Bible to show Ryan verses like Romans 5:8 and Romans 6:23.

"Something tells me this is all true," Ryan admitted soberly, staring at the open Bible in his lap. "Life has had no meaning until right now. I'm old enough to carry a gun and defend the OPT, but no one's ever told me what happens after death. Until now. It makes a lot of sense. I mean, what I've felt inside since I was a little kid. God hasn't been happy with me."

"All that can change right now."

"You mean, that symbol of getting cleansed by water?"

"Baptized?" Levi shrugged. "If you believe that Jesus died for your sins and rose again to give you new life, I'll baptize you right now. But like you said, it's only a symbol. It's what you believe in your heart that changes who you are."

"Then I should get baptized."

"You have a lake or creek nearby?"

"Bear Creek and Gum Creek are pretty much dried up. But there's the horse trough out front of the flower shop where you're staying. Sometimes people from the country come through on horses. You think God will mind if it's a filthy horse trough?"

"I know God pretty well," Levi said, "so I can say with good certainty that He won't mind a dirty horse trough. After all, Jesus was born in an animal shed. So, you're ready? You believe?"

Ryan grinned, then tried unsuccessfully to straighten his face.

"Yes, I believe. I'm . . . going to heaven when I die. I'm okay with God now. This is . . . more than I expected when you were holding us at gunpoint in the shoe store!"

Levi laughed and pulled the young man into a rough embrace, clapping him hard on the back. Leaving the bikes and tools, they returned to the town center and entered the flower shop, anxious to announce to the others about Ryan's choice to believe and to now be baptized.

Instead, Levi was struck in the face by flying camping tins when he entered the door.

"I'm not playing this game with you guys!" Runner shouted at Lena who sat before him, and Mia, who was setting out their meal for that night. "I'm not your patient!

I'm not going to get shot for your stupid beliefs! I'm taking my dog back, and we're leaving you guys!"

Ryan stood wide-eyed next to Levi, gazing at the mess of gear Runner had strewn across the floor. Brian stood near the bathroom where a faucet was still running. He held Jenna protectively behind him in case more objects flew toward them. Lena looked up at Levi. The woman held a gel-tranq in her fist, clearly ready to tranq Runner.

"If you want to leave, Runner," Levi said, "that's your choice. But Auggie is Lena's dog now. That was Auggie's decision, not ours. You could ask her if you want, wherever she is."

"For months, I've been putting up with this!" Runner shook his fist at Levi. "I'm not asking my dog who she wants more! I've known you for one day, and I'm already sick of you. You're a coward, Levi Caspertein. You never say anything straight. You always have to hide behind your sarcasm. I'm leaving with Runner, and I'll kill anyone who tries to stop me!"

"Ryan," Levi said softly, "it ain't easy dealing with ungrateful people, but you can't change their hearts. You gotta let them go if that's what they want. That's part of loving them like God loves them."

"There is no God!" Runner spat. "I grew up with that nonsense. I am my own god, and I want nothing to do with your weak-minded fantasies that do nothing for anybody!"

"Well . . ." Levi scratched his jaw. "I guess if that's what you want, I'll send you on your way. No one will ever say a Caspertein held you captive."

He walked briskly over to where Runner sat on the floor.

"What are you doing?" Runner slapped at his hands. "You stay away from me!"

Levi easily overcame the obstinate man's flailing hands. He picked him up from behind, pinning his arms under Levi's right arm, and carried him out of the flower shop as Runner screamed curses. Reaching the street, Levi walked down about a half-block, then dropped Runner in the middle of the dusty roadway. As soon as Runner rolled over and sat up, he swung wildly at Levi's legs, punching, clawing, and swearing.

For a few moments, Levi accepted the abuse, but Runner wearied quickly, and with exhausted gasps, he hung his head, breathlessly panting. Levi walked away, back to the flower shop where his companions had gathered to watch. Up and down the street, citizens of Red Bay had emerged to see what all the fuss was about.

Setting a hand on Ryan's shoulder, Levi gazed at his friends.

"Ryan here has placed his faith in the gospel of Jesus Christ, and he says he's ready to be baptized—in that." He pointed at the horse trough which sat alongside the sidewalk and next to a railing that appeared to be a hitching post. "Ignore Runner for a few minutes. He's on a time-out while he realizes he's not a god."

"You're just like Uncle Titus." Mia smiled, then elbowed her husband. "Isn't he?"

"A mixture of gristle and heart?" Kip sighed. "I sort of wanted to see Levi spank him, but I guess a time-out could work for a man with one foot."

Dragging a hose out of the flower shop storage room, Ryan connected it to a faucet with low pressure. As he dangled the end over the trough, Advocate Mantello walked up with a glaring Sparks at his side.

"What's this about?" Mantello asked.

"I'm going to be baptized! I'm a follower of Jesus now. I don't know much about it all, but I'm gonna learn."

"This is against the OPT!" Sparks complained to Mantello. "You allowed this, so you have to do something!"

"Why don't you do something, Sparks?" Levi said from the sidewalk. His rifle remained over his shoulder, but his pistol holster was already unclipped. He glared daringly at Sparks as more townspeople drew closer. "I'll baptize you, too, if you cast down your pride and humble yourself before Jesus Christ your Savior."

"He's not my Savior!" Sparks declared. "I'm with the OPT!"

Levi took off his jacket, holster, and rifle, and gave them to Mia and Kip. He knelt behind the trough and waved Ryan over. The young man threw down his gun belt and stripped off his outer shirt and boots. In seconds, he was seated in the trough, the surface of the water lapping at the metal rim.

"Do you believe Jesus is the Son of God?"

"Yeah." Ryan's face was beaming. "You already asked me, remember?"

"I know, but this is for them, too." Levi nodded his head and raised his voice, his hands placed on Ryan's chest and back. "Do you believe Jesus Christ died for your sins and was buried and rose again the third day, according to the Scriptures?"

"Yeah, I believe!"

"Then I baptize you in the Name of the Father and of the Son and of the Holy Spirit."

"This is ridiculous!" Sparks shouted. "You can't do this in a horse trough! It doesn't count. Jerry, this is the town's trough. That means it's an OPT horse trough. Stop this right now!"

"Aah-ah!" Lena hushed him, her rifle held before her.

"This is amazing!" Jenna, standing with Brian, held her folded hands up to her smiling lips.

"Buried with Jesus in the likeness of His death," Levi continued, "and raised with Him in newness of life!"

He guided Ryan backwards under the water, then lifted him all the way up to stand in the trough on his own two feet. For a moment, Ryan stood there, staring at his hands, then at the crowd of his friends.

"Congratulations, Ryan!" Levi shook the young man's hand.

"You can't believe all this stupidity, Ryan!" Sparks griped.

Levi looked past the crowd and noticed Runner had crawled closer to watch and listen.

Ryan was again beaming as he climbed out of the trough. Barely had he received a hearty pat on the back from Levi when Lena thrust her weapon into Ryan's hands and climbed into the trough herself! Levi blinked in surprise for a few seconds.

"Okay." He finally nodded. "Let's do it."

She sat down fully clothed, not even removing her veil, and Levi took her arms, crossing them before her. He asked her the same questions, which she affirmed with boldness in her throaty way, and he baptized her.

Dripping wet, Lena nearly leaped out of the trough to hug Levi. He laughed and squeezed her back, realizing she was trembling, though probably not from the cold since it wasn't a chilly afternoon. Instead, Levi thought she was relieved, and the Spirit of God in her was overwhelming her emotions. Lena was usually not one to express herself in public.

As Lena stood on her own and took back her weapons from Ryan, there was another splash in the water. Brian nodded at Levi from the trough. The old Regulator was somber though he firmly revealed his determination to join the other two believers in baptism. Levi knew Brian was older, in his mid-forties, and a little more mature, having ventured into the faith through those first months in New York, often alone, reading the Scriptures underground and privately with God.

Brian sat down, and Levi's own voice cracked with emotion as he spoke a few words. After he baptized the man, Levi bowed his head over the trough and embraced him as he stood. Kip was beside them a moment later, helping Brian step out of the trough.

Levi lifted his head and stood tall before the townspeople who were watching in silence, except for Sparks'
occasional criticism.

"Anyone else ready to express their faith in believers'
baptism?" he asked. "Judgement awaits the sinner. There
is no escape except for trusting in Jesus Christ, God in the
flesh, who died for all of us. Who will receive this free
gift?"

No one moved or spoke until Sparks slowly lifted his
arm and pointed at Ryan.

"Ryan Pulloy, you're a traitor to the OPT! If you're not
gone by morning, I'll arrest you myself. This town will not
be punished for your fantasies about God and crosses and
saviors!"

"Nobody mentioned crosses," Levi responded, "but
I'm glad you've heard the truth before, Sparks. If that's all
you've got to say, then remember what you've seen here,
and perhaps their testimony to the salvation found in
Jesus Christ today will bring you to repentance later on.
Especially you, Sparks. It ain't easy for a proud man to
humble himself before his Savior, but I'd be first in line to
shake your hand if you did."

Sparks cursed and shoved his way out of the crowd.
In moments, the people had dispersed, and Levi took back
his weapons from Mia.

"Well, I think I just got kicked out of my own town,"
Ryan said, but there was no disappointment in his voice.
"Where are you guys going from here?"

"Colorado." Levi smiled and shook the young man's
hand. "Looks like you'll be picking out another bike from
the Onion Man, this time for yourself."

Kip and Jenna embraced those who'd been baptized,
and Levi moved out of their company to the street, where
he knelt in front of Runner.

"I cut off your foot, but it was to save your life." Levi
frowned at Runner's downcast face. "There's no shame in

having one foot, but it would be a shame for someone who was offered help to refuse it. What's your name, Runner?"

Levi offered his hand. Runner visibly fought through indecision. Finally, he weakly accepted Levi's hand.

"Andy. Andy Radner."

"Well, Andy Radner, it's a pleasure to meet you. Let's see if this town has some crutches for you, and then we can talk about you peddling your own bike."

"What are you—?" Andy started to question.

But an instant later, he submitted to Levi's touch as Levi picked up the young man in his arms. This time, Andy didn't fight Levi as he carried him into the flower shop.

Chapter Seven

R ex used his binoculars to gaze west. Nebraska seemed to go on forever, but Colorado was just the next state away. He'd been driving his four companions hard each day, encouraging them onward with promises of veal and cool water from the White River Valley.

"I can't tell if those are trees," Rex said, "or if it's a town out in the middle of nowhere."

"It could be a place called Schuyler," Miranda said. "It's supposed to be on this highway somewhere."

"Um, I'm not liking this, Rex," Chloe said, binoculars also against her brow, but viewing northward. "I think I can see flames now. That fire's definitely moving this way. The grass and brush that the ash dried out is going up quickly."

Milo came forward to stand beside Rex. The black smoke from a grass fire had been visible for two days, but now the front line of the fire stretched as far as Rex could see, east to west.

"There's no outrunning it," Milo said quietly. "Going south accomplishes nothing. How do you westerners live through a prairie fire?"

"Jump in a river or run for our lives." Rex checked on Alice to his left. The stoic one-armed woman didn't appear too bothered by this latest threat. She leaned on her staff, her fit frame looking thin in the evening sun. The pace west had cost all of them several pounds, but it had built up their endurance as well. They were averaging just over thirty miles a day—and plenty of nylon thread to patch their boots. "If it's just burning grass, we might be able to run through the flames to the other side, but if that's a town up there, the buildings are doomed."

Alice led them away along Highway 30, which paralleled Interstate 80 a few miles to the south. They'd agreed on the country highway to avoid many travelers and bandits. Rex started after her with Chloe at his side. Miranda and Milo brought up the rear.

"You're thinking something," Chloe said. "Come on. You Casperteins are always drumming up some brilliance. What is it?"

"If this is a town up here, I was wondering how we could save it."

As they walked, Rex prayed quietly to himself that this wasn't a town. The flames were two stories tall, even though the fuel was only grass. Or, if it was a town, he prayed that it was empty, otherwise the residents were about to lose everything to the fire.

When the buildings ahead began to take shape between several cotton trees, Rex began to jog, his gear jostling on his back.

"This is gonna be close!" he said to Alice as he passed her.

The flames were moving steadily southward, but Rex tried not to look at them as he studied the town through his bouncing gait. The community consisted of shops and broken-down homes on both sides of the highway. About a dozen people were gathered in the road when Rex jogged up to them. Most were adults, but he noticed two children and one infant.

"The fire's close!" He unclipped his chest strap and dropped his backpack to the pavement. Then, he shifted his rifle sling across his chest since he guessed he wouldn't need it. "Get your tools! You have rakes? Shovels? Quick!"

"Thank God!" An older man with a red beard stood before Rex. "You're with the OPT? We knew you guys would come and save us!"

Alice and Milo collided with Rex from behind. Then Miranda and Chloe arrived winded.

"Show me where your tools are!" Rex pressed the man. "Hurry! We have little time. We can try to save some of these buildings."

The man with the red beard introduced himself as Don Cullen as he led Rex through two boarded-up shops to a garden out back.

"This is all we have." The man opened the door of a shed to reveal a rake and hoe, but no shovels or picks. "Is it enough?"

"I don't know." Rex grabbed the tools, but the hoe handle was rotten and broke in two. Nevertheless, he took the broken hoe and the rake, which seemed sturdy. "Come on. We need to cut a fire line in an arc around the town. Bring everyone with us, anyone who can get their hands dirty."

Rex returned to the highway.

"It's three hundred yards out." Milo hurried up to him. "It's coming fast!"

Miranda, get my shovel from my pack," Rex instructed, then addressed all the people. "We'll build a fire line to protect the town. Men come with me. Chloe and Alice, stay here and organize the women with buckets to put out any embers that drop on the houses."

"No, wait." Don Cullen held up a hand to his people. "We signed up with the OPT for this very reason. We deserve to be protected. Why should we put ourselves in danger?"

"*Deserve?* Sorry, pal, but we're not OPT." Rex tossed the full-handled rake to Milo and kept the half-handled hoe for himself. "If you don't fight for your homes, you'll lose everything. Let's go!"

Rex ran after Miranda, who was carrying his short entrenching shovel, usually used for digging latrines and graves. Milo yanked the short hoe from him and thrust the tall rake into Rex's hands.

"Shorter tools for shorter people," Milo explained. "How far are we going out?"

They emerged on the north side of town and kept running into the grass another twenty yards. Rex stopped and tried the ground. It was dry and crusty, with loose soil on top.

"This'll do. Milo, cut the lead line, and we'll widen it." Rex lifted his head after only a few strokes with the rake and saw that no one was with them from town. "Where is everyone?"

"Maybe they're getting more tools," Miranda guessed.

The three bowed their backs to the task, trying to avoid looking at the closing danger. Milo cut a slim line down a hundred feet, then came back to help Rex and Miranda widen the tilled ground.

"It's not long enough," Rex gasped at Milo. "We've got to cut it longer. You haven't gone even half the length of the town."

"We can cut a short, effective line," Milo said, working behind him, "or a long ineffective line. What do you want? No one's helping us."

Rex didn't answer. After a day of marching, they didn't have the energy to debate, only to work.

Feeling the heat a few minutes later, Rex was panting as he acknowledged the wall of flames creeping closer. Then he judged their fire line only a hundred feet long, but ten feet wide.

"If they would've helped us," Miranda shouted over the roar, "we could've cut it the length of the town!"

Resting his rake over his shoulder, Rex pulled on the back of Milo's faded uniform, nearly dragging the man from his feverish work.

"That's enough." Rex backed the three of them away from their line as the fire reached its edge. "It's holding at least but look."

They watched the flames barely hesitate as they licked at the grasses around the end of the fire line, then continue to rampage unchecked toward the town.

"Well, that was a failure!" Miranda swung her shovel in the air like a bat. "What a waste!"

"Not trying at all would've been a waste," Rex corrected. "Come on. We'd better get the people to safety."

Rex led the way back through the buildings where he found all the people still crowded together. Alice saw him coming and approached him first.

"The people won't do anything without the OPT. Apparently, the OPT promised them the moon."

"Well, they've slightly under-delivered." Rex stopped in front of the townspeople, who grew silent at his presence. "Your town is about to burn to the ground. You could've saved it, but now it'll burn. Now, you have about two minutes to grab whatever you can and hide down here on the highway. Hopefully, the flames will pass over us— or stop at the highway. Go! Get some clothes and water jugs and food if you have any!"

The people scattered, all except Don Cullen, who stood defiantly, his arms crossed.

"If you're not the OPT, what gives you the right to tell us what to do?"

"You've trusted in the wrong ideas, old man." Rex dropped his rake on the pavement. "Now, your people will suffer the consequences. Don't you have anything to save before the fire comes?"

"The OPT will replace anything I lose. I can tell just by listening to you that you're not one of us. You don't stand with humanity. You don't know the resilient human spirit. We can overcome anything we put our minds to. Together, we are—"

Rex walked past the man to help the woman with the infant. She emerged from a house, the crying baby in one arm, and clothes and plastic containers in the other.

Although Rex was willing to take her possessions from her arm, she instead gave him the baby.

"Everyone, to the end of town!" He waved toward the east end. "Move!"

The flames licked at the side of the structures on the north side. The rest of the people joined them, with Milo, Chloe, and Miranda carrying what they could. Alice stood with her staff in the middle of the highway a few yards out of town.

"Gather around me!" Alice instructed the people. "Lie flat on your bellies on the pavement! Hurry! Cover your heads!"

Handing the baby back to its mother, Rex approached Chloe.

"Go ahead and lay down. Milo and I will stay up to watch for embers."

"Wrap every part of exposed skin—your faces, arms, and neck!" Alice continued. "We'll pile your belongings on top of you once you're on your bellies."

"No one's going to do what you say!" Cullen complained even as he complied. "The OPT is going to hear how you've treated us. They'll hear of it!"

Once all the people were down, Milo and Rex stepped among them and covered their bodies and limbs with their possessions. As the fire reached the edge of the highway, embers flew like bees toward the sky. Rex wrapped his face and put his shoulder to the heat blasting from the nearest building, now a roaring blaze.

Milo suddenly leaped through the people to slap at a smoking ember that had landed on someone's belongings. Rex watched more embers glow like fireflies over their heads, then drop onto the south side of the highway. There, the dry grass offered fresh fuel as the fire continued.

When the fire was hottest and Rex couldn't bear to keep his eyes exposed, he leaned down on his knees over the woman and her infant. Miranda was somewhere near, praying aloud. Others were sobbing in fear and whispering their love to those nearest.

Then, the flaming grass by the road was gone, left only as whispering black ash, and the fire burned southward. The heat from the buildings was intense, but manageable. The danger was past, and Rex started to help the people up. Together, they backed farther away from the heat, watching their town crackle and burn. Every building was on fire. The two children were crying and some adults with them.

"A few people don't even have their shoes." Miranda supported a woman whose scalp showed through singed hair, but she wasn't burned badly. "We'll have to get them to another town."

"Absolutely not!" Don Cullen forced Miranda's hand off his townswoman and shoved her backward. "The OPT definitely saw the smoke. We want no more to do with you!"

Rex caught Miranda before she fell from the man's violent push. After he steadied Miranda, Rex started toward the spindly man, intent on pulling him straight up by his red beard, but Miranda took his elbow.

"It won't help. This isn't our fight." She looked around with him at the blackened faces of the disheveled people. "You were right. This wasn't wasted effort, but it also wasn't successful."

Alice returned from scouting the damage as structures collapsed behind her.

"There's still a functioning well over there." Alice pointed with her staff. "It wasn't damaged."

"Then you can get your fill of water and leave us alone," Cullen declared.

Nodding, Rex surveyed the ruin and the townspeople. When his eyes reached Milo, his heart lifted. The man shrugged as if to say they were out of options except to move on. How far the ex-colonel had come spiritually! The despair Rex felt for the lost town and ignorant leadership vanished in the rays of God's potential, displayed by Milo.

"We'll leave you in peace, my friend." Rex offered his hand to Cullen, who frowned at the gesture. "I wish we could've been more help, but you've made up your mind about these OPT people."

"Enlightenment isn't a state of mind, young man." Cullen shook Rex's hand briskly. "It's a state of reality!"

The travelers collected their gear and walked away from the smoldering town. From a distance, the five turned to look back at the black spot where buildings had once stood.

"The OPT will never care for them the way they want," Chloe said. "They could die out here, waiting for people to fulfill their hopes."

"Big promises," Miranda said, "don't mean big ability. I learned that in Chicago. All of their faith in wrong things is wasted faith. Only God can deliver on His promises."

"I don't care what reality people live in," Rex mumbled, "fire is fire, whether here in Nebraska or below in hell. The OPT won't save them from that."

That night, after a meal of wheat bread, honey, and dog meat, Rex stood outside camp and stared at the dark western sky. They'd found a stand of a dozen trees in a shallow draw in which to tie a tarp, but there was no water except what they'd brought from the burned town.

The wind blew in gusts and the tarp he'd tied at three corners flapped violently. Such was the noise and darkness that Rex didn't hear or see Miranda approach him until she nudged his arm. Behind them, Chloe and Alice scrambled to build a guard for their campfire. Milo leaped to catch hold of the corner of the tarp that whipped overhead.

"Thinking of home?" Miranda asked over the wind.

"Yeah." He glanced down at her, her effort earlier that day fresh on his mind. "It can be your home now, too."

"With you?"

"Um . . ."

"Are you proposing to me? That we make a home together?"

"What?" He faced her and held up his hand. "Wait. I was just saying—"

"I'm teasing you, Rex." She laughed and hooked her arm in his, turning him back to face the west. "I know what you meant, and I'm thankful for a place to go."

"Sometimes I don't say things right." He shook his head. "It can really get me into trouble, obviously."

"A home with me would be trouble?" She leaned closer. "Again, I'm kidding. I'd be happy to live anywhere around you Casperteins. Somewhere to call home for a little while. Until Christ comes. I've got that vertical view now, ready to leave all this, you know. Chicago was a pretty lonely place."

"Some tough years, huh?"

"At the beginning, with all the flooding around the city since the river locks weren't managed, it was pretty bad. After the burning and chaos, things settled down. I grew a garden on the roof. Hunted in the city until they took my rifle and passed out ration cards for everyone."

"Rifles for ration cards? That was the OPT?"

"No, it was before them. I knew our independence was being attacked when they wanted us to rely on the Chicago Administration Authority. Not everyone submitted to their idea of freedom—which seems to be the way all governments sell their brand of forced compliance nowadays. When the OPT sold their own philosophy, it caught on. Most people saw outsiders offering unity and blind tolerance as the answer to their struggles. Some of us didn't agree, so we left. I'm glad I did."

Rex turned his back and shielded Miranda in his arms as the wind gusted harder.

"This isn't good. I didn't see anything for miles around that could shelter us from this kind of weather."

"Can I ask you something?" she voiced louder, even though she was still in his arms. "Have you been avoiding me since the others turned north in Iowa?"

"It wasn't intentional." He staggered against the wind. "Don't take it personal. With Milo coming to the Lord, I've been talking to him a lot. And I want us all to get to Colorado as soon as possible."

"You're worried about your dad?"

"The OPT must've reached Meeker by now, at least by radio. They're everywhere."

"So, you're saying I would've been a distraction to you?"

"I guess that's one way to put it."

"Maybe you could use the distraction." She clutched his coat, pulling her head up to his chin. "I know I could."

"Rex!" Milo shouted.

But Rex wasn't able to look up right then. He dipped his head and kissed her. An instant later, leaves and sticks in the wind pummeled his back and made him stumble against Miranda.

"Rex! We need you now!"

Holding onto Miranda, Rex returned to camp. The fire had blown out, and the five of them grappled for their ash goggles to guard against flying debris.

"We need to take it down!" Rex shouted as he untied one corner of the tarp while Milo was still trying to secure it. "It'll never last in this wind."

Milo pulled on a slipknot, and the last rope broke that held the tarp to the thin tree. Before either man could catch the canvas, it was gone like a kite in the darkness. Rex felt the wind pushing even his bulk off balance.

"What do we do?" Alice called from where she knelt on the ground. As the lightest among them, she seemed to be a shadow clinging to the ground to avoid being swept away. "This is the worst I've ever seen!"

Rex couldn't recall such a strong windstorm, either, not in Colorado, nor on the road with Levi. One of the trees around them fell over their camp, bruising and scratching them under its branches before it, too, rolled away in the wind. Grass, rocks, sticks, and soil battered their bodies.

"It's a tornado!" Rex yelled. "Gather your stuff and huddle up on the ground!"

Lightning crackled, and in the dimness, he saw the others grope for their packs. Miranda didn't leave his side as he held her in one arm and rolled his heavy pack across the ground.

"Get behind me and Milo!" he instructed the ladies. Miranda helped him put his pack onto his back. "Milo, lay down with your pack on!"

"My pack is gone!" Chloe shouted into his face. "I was unpacking, so it was almost empty. The wind—"

Communicating was too difficult at that point. Milo's head crowded close to Rex's, huddling close, while both men held the three women in their arms. He heard Miranda talking loudly, but he couldn't make out the words.

The wind ripped at their clothes and hair. Rex kept his eyes tightly shut, even though he wore goggles, as if he didn't want to glimpse even a lightning flash of the horrors around them.

Then, in a matter of seconds, the wind became still, and he lifted his head. He realized suddenly how fast he was panting when Miranda touched his bearded cheek. Maybe she meant to calm his heart, or maybe it was a gesture to say goodbye in the midst of a fallen world of strife and storms.

"Don't be fooled," Chloe said. "It's just the eye."

"Alice, you good?" Rex asked.

"I'm on top."

Rex had never been through a tornado, but he trusted Chloe's long life of experience.

"Brace yourselves!" he roared as the sound of a freight

train seemed to thunder toward them. "God is still with us!"

The wind velocity rose, and he felt Alice being pulled away. She roughly laid her heavy staff over Miranda, striking Rex's arm. He tucked it under his arm and prayed that Alice hung on tight.

Minutes later, the twister moved on, and the five travelers were left listening to the roar fade away. It was replaced by a cool breeze from the north.

Letting go of Alice's staff, Rex lifted his arm from Miranda.

"Everyone okay?" Milo asked.

"I think I'm going to need stitches," Chloe said as she rose to her feet, holding her head. "Something cut my head open. It's bleeding."

"Let's find wood for a fire." Rex thanked God for a little starlight to help discern shapes around them. "Once we have some light, we can check out the damage."

As others gathered wood, Rex chopped down a tree that had broken off ten feet above. In minutes, they had a fire blazing, and they surveyed each other's faces. They were all scratched, bleeding, and bruised. But Chloe's gash above her left brow was the most serious. Miranda accepted Rex's suture kit to work on Chloe while he, Alice, and Milo took torches around the vicinity to collect anything left of their camp paraphernalia. But they recovered nothing more than firewood that had blown around.

Back at the fire, Miranda heated water to wash their scratches.

"Miranda and Alice, your packs are gone," Rex summarized. "Chloe, you have half your pack, whatever you hadn't pulled out before the wind started. Milo, you're light on what? The tarp?"

"The tarp and a couple shirts I had hung on that tree there."

"I've still got one large tarp, and Chloe, you have the small one in the bottom of your pack?"

"Yeah." She eyed Miranda and Alice. "Sorry, girls. Looks like we share the one holey shirt I've got to spare, or wear whatever the guys offer us."

"Rex's flannels will double for tarps, too," Milo said.

A few seconds passed, then they all erupted in laughter. But Rex didn't mind that it was at his expense. They'd lost a few possessions—almost half of the gear they'd accumulated. But they were alive, and they were together. Their faith was intact, and they were nearly to Colorado.

Miranda sat a little closer to him as they shared a mug of hot tea. When they bedded down, it was next to a low fire, Miranda on one side of him, and Alice on the other. The night wasn't too cold, and Rex didn't sleep much on account that he was listening for another tornado, but the night was pleasant regardless.

He prayed for the refugees who'd left with the other COIL operatives, and he wondered if he'd see Levi again before heaven. It was the only depressing thought he had that night, because he didn't see how he'd reunite with his cousin with so many obstacles to overcome.

Meeker was close now, the lowlands before the mountains already visible in the distance. Soon, he'd be home. And Miranda—the woman he was beginning to love—was at his side.

Rudy opened his eyes to the sound of tumbling pebbles. An instant later, his eyes focused on a ground squirrel not a foot from his face. He shivered at the cool air where he lay in the shade, but the sky was blue far above the limestone canyon wall.

The ground squirrel darted into a burrow below a bush that grew out of a crack in the rock. The little creature's movement started more small rocks tumbling down the cliff.

Cliff?

Shifting his shoulders, Rudy was apprehensive about what injuries he'd find. His memory seeped back, enlightening him to his situation. There had been gunfire. The horses had been bucking and screaming—while he'd still been strapped between them!

"Thanks, Vorca," he scoffed, vowing never to allow anyone to transport him in a horse-suspended sling ever again.

And then the horses had charged into darkness and weightlessness. Then . . . *here?*

He moved his head from side to side, searching his upper spine for tenderness. It didn't seem reasonable, but he felt no severe pain after such a fall. Unless . . . he was *paralyzed . . .?*

After wiggling his toes, he dismissed the idea that his pain-free condition was from being paralyzed. Then he smelled the odor and sat up stiffly. The guts of one of the horses was splashed across the rock under him. *Under him?* He rolled off the dead horse to kneel and rest his hand on the animal's head. The second horse must've landed elsewhere.

Scoffing no longer, Rudy pieced the puzzle together. He and the two horses had fallen into the canyon together. Except he'd landed on one of the horses, cushioning him from the otherwise deadly impact. But that wasn't all. *His back!* By curling his shoulder forward, he could feel his spine was sensitive to movement, but the severe pain was gone! Whatever bulge had afflicted his spine, the fall had adjusted it back into place!

"Sorry, ol' girl." He pet the neck of the mare. Her eyes were cloudy, but her body wasn't yet cold. He hadn't been lying there unconscious for days, only hours.

Turning his face skyward, he guessed he'd fallen about sixty feet from the highway—a back-breaking distance under any other conditions. With care of his back, he climbed to his feet and stepped closer to the ledge nearby to look down at the river two thousand feet farther down. The shelf he'd landed on was twenty feet wide and seemed to stretch as a layer of hardened sediment along the cliff for a mile in both directions. And unless he wanted to start cutting horse steaks and searching for a water source, he needed to find a way down the cliff. Or up.

He studied a few angles, not liking the lack of hand and footholds up the vertical face. But of course, he had to go up. Annette and the others—but there was no point dwelling on them. Or hoping against hope. The OPT would've killed them by now. Annette, Gail, and Tilda would've never caved in and denied their Lord and His gospel. Their loyalties—and exclusively so—were set in stone, hardened by years of faith, quickened by Christ's everlasting love and presence. Vorca probably would've stood with Annette, even though she couldn't answer an OPT Advocate with an intelligible word. Only Caleb would probably escape whatever execution the OPT would exact.

Rudy picked through the horse pack that had burst upon impact. He couldn't take much if he was to climb up to the road. Or maybe he could! The rope from his pack was possibly long enough for him to tie to his waist and pull up his pack after him. But his pack was split up one seam, and the internal frame had torn through the supporting fabric. Without mourning the loss, he set about to construct a new pack using a needle, nylon, and a leather palm. The ground squirrel emerged and investigated the scene, but Rudy ignored the critter. His mind was on climbing the cliff.

In an hour, he had built a decent pack, using the shoulder straps off his old one. He filled it with gear he'd need to camp in the woods—or support his small family, if he happened to find them somehow alive.

Finally, he chose one of the battle rifles from those Annette had packed onto the horses and stuffed his old ammo jacket into a pack strap.

Among all the gear he had at hand, he had no canteen, and the water containers that had been on that horse had burst. With nothing left to do but to climb, he tied one end of the rope to the back of his belt and the other end to his pack and rifle. The horse and remaining gear he left to the vultures and the ground squirrel.

"Steady hands," he prayed as he started up the wall. "Steady feet. I wouldn't mind a few good footholds along the way, Lord. Or a ladder."

But he didn't chuckle at his own joke. Another fall could kill him and ruin any chance to find his family.

Uncharacteristic to sedimentary rock, there was a diagonal crack that his fingers found about ten feet up. He wondered if such a crack had opened up from recent earthquakes. He didn't miss the irony—that an earthquake had debilitated him for days, but now a crack caused by an earthquake would be his passage to escape the canyon.

A few inches at a time, he slipped his fingers into the crack, then felt with his booted feet for a meager step up. He wasn't a rock climber, since his body had never been flexible, but half the battle he thought was mastering his fear, staying calm, and breathing shallow breaths. In moments when his boots felt no toehold, he merely paused to consider God's watchcare. Each time, he decided afresh that if God wanted him to die and depart the earth, then he would find no foothold. But if God wanted him to make it up that rock face, then He would provide them.

And each time, with a little blind foot searching, he found a protrusion or dip or an irregularity on which to support his weight. Higher and higher he crept, until suddenly the diagonal crack for his fingers ended, and he was left with bare rock.

Fighting panic, he felt above and to the side with his left palm. Then he remembered how far God had already brought him. Clinging only with his right hand and his left foot, he strained his eyes down and to the left. His positioning was so precarious that he dared not lift his head to look up. Yet, down to the left, he saw the shelf he'd left behind—about thirty feet below!

"Halfway," he breathed, and closed his eyes, begging God that his taut muscles wouldn't begin to tremble or shake.

When he opened his eyes, while still peering downward, he noticed the tendrils of a plant or root system trailing like hairs up the cliff face. Rudy walked his fingers across the rock to the roots. Expecting the roots to be brittle and weak, he found they were only thin and stringy. He gathered more of them into his hand until he'd collected a finger's width of roots. As much as he dared, he tested the strength of the roots by yanking lightly on them. Gasping from the emotional tension, he acknowledged that there was no way to know if the roots would support his weight except by giving them his weight.

It was a test of faith that his reason argued against. But there were absolutely no other handholds. And once he fully grasped the roots, he would automatically swing over to them. There seemed to be no foot placement at all on the bare face.

He released the roots and the foolish notion to trust them with his bulk and searched to his right for another route. With care, he even backed down a few inches, clinging to the crack with his fingers. However, there seemed no other option, so he returned to the roots. One by one, he gathered them in his left hand again, collecting them until he had a bundle to twist tightly with his fingers.

The roots perhaps weren't roots at all, he pondered, but vines. A single strand or even a few strands would break quickly, but could a handful truly support his weight?

A little at a time, over several seconds, he shifted his weight from his foot and fingers to his left hand and the vines he grasped. Finally, he passed the point of no return, when he'd placed more weight on the vines than on the rock. If the vines broke, he'd fall. There would be no recovery.

But they didn't break. With a gasp, he let go of the crack entirely, and his left boot slipped off the tiny bump he'd relied on. His elbows grated briefly against the limestone as his body swung a foot to the left. His right hand grasped the vines as well. Sand and pebbles sprinkled on his forehead from whatever heights the vines found as their anchor. When the dust stopped falling, Rudy risked a glance up. There was a bump in the rock ten feet above, and the vines disappeared over it.

Because of his weight, Rudy couldn't climb the vines by using his hands alone. Testing the vines' strength even further, he planted a knee against the rock, then a flat foot against it. He laughed to himself about his unbelievably helpless situation. There was only one thing to do—proceed.

Hand over hand, he climbed the vines, and crouching against the wall, he walked up the cliff. He reached the bump above and scraped his fingers against gravel as he followed the vines over the berm.

There, the vines were secured in a small cleft where an ancient nest had been left by some bird. Below the cleft was a forty-five-degree span of rock where Rudy gathered his feet to rest while squatting, trusting the Lord and his boot soles to grip the rock.

When he looked down, he couldn't see the horse or the shelf that he'd left behind. When he looked up, he wondered if the next outcropping of rock would indeed lead to the road, or if it was merely another obstacle in a series up the vertical rock.

The limestone above was more weathered and pitted. Several handholds and bulges for his boots offered him a couple yards of advancement at a time. He paused only twice to catch his breath and shake out his aching limbs before he reached the top.

Panting, he crawled onto level ground and set his meaty palm on top of the metal guardrail on the shoulder of the freeway. *The Lord had delivered him!*

His celebration was checked an instant later when he noticed the rear bumpers of two Humvees twenty yards to his right. He ducked behind the rail when he saw movement. Three gunmen were standing at the front of the vehicles. But the Humvees were fully engulfed in rocks and sand. A rockslide had immobilized their convoy!

Annette and Vorca came into sight as they labored together to roll a boulder off the road. *They were alive!* The two women leaned the boulder against the rail, then a gunman gestured with his rifle to urge them toward another boulder, and they passed out of sight.

A small blonde woman walked around the rear vehicle. She stretched and used a cloth to wipe her neck. Rudy could see only her profile, but he recognized her easily enough—Veronika Kane, the OPT Advocate from Denver. So, she was behind his demise.

Rather than risk discovery behind the guardrail, Rudy untied the rope from his belt and looped it around the nearest rail post. He tied a knot to make a stirrup in the end of the rope for his foot, then he backed off the ledge, lowering himself with his homemade pulley back down the cliff a few feet.

With one hand, he held the doubled rope from slipping, then, a few inches at a time, he drew the backpack and rifle up to his position until he could grasp one pack strap. Finally, he shifted the strap over his shoulder, causing his rifle to bump into his tender spine.

For a few still seconds, he stared at the rock face, considering how his crazy brother should've been the one doing those acrobatics, but here he was. Although he'd been shooting a rifle since his childhood in Arkansas, the battle rifle wasn't his weapon of choice. It was too short, too light, and too powerful. But he knew it could be a determining tool in the hands of a master. He wasn't a master, but he could aim and shoot.

"How many, Lord?" he whispered. "How many are there?"

He licked his lips and climbed back up to the guardrail again. It couldn't matter how many enemies were above. Whoever was there, he'd need to defeat them. Two vehicles? There could be five men per vehicle. Maybe some had been injured in the rockslide. They'd need medical attention. But Annette needed to be rescued first so she could help him secure the scene. Even if they had mistreated her, she wouldn't hesitate to help the wounded. She had the heart of Christ.

One leg at a time, Rudy climbed over the rail, his rifle leveled at the rear of the Humvees. With one hand, he loosened his waist from the climbing rope, and stalked forward. Vaguely, he recalled the brief battle from the night before. The enemy had grenades. He'd lose a prolonged battle, and he didn't want to put Annette in the middle of a hostage situation. There could be no negotiating. It was time for sudden and overwhelming force, which worked for him, since he was holding a cannon in his hands.

Stepping through boulders to reach the closest Humvee, he glanced in the back window, which was cracked. Caleb! The child lay asleep on an assortment of gear and munitions. No sign yet of Gail or Tilda.

Since he wanted to advance swiftly on the OPT personnel that were in front of the vehicles, he checked the pavement for the path of least resistance. His efforts would be wasted if he charged forward shooting, only to trip over one of the boulders alongside a Humvee. The route between the vehicles seemed best, which would put him immediately in the middle of the enemy. Two men were sitting on the hood of the other Humvee. But where were the others?

"Sometime today, ladies!" a man shouted. "We've got miles to drive still."

Rudy gazed through the cracked glass of the vehicles as Annette and Vorca struggled with another boulder. There seemed to be at least one other OPT soldier on the ground on the other side of the farthest Humvee, but he was out of sight. And he hadn't seen Advocate Kane since he'd returned from the cliff.

He took a couple quick breaths, then steadied his breathing. The stock of the rifle was braced firmly against his shoulder, and he lowered his head to view down the short barrel, though he'd be far too close to his targets to use the scope.

When he rounded the back of the rear Humvee, his feet found a path through the rocks and over the uneven soil. He made no sound until his elbow brushed past the rearview mirror on the passenger side of the front Humvee. Although he could've reached out and grabbed the arm of the nearest man who sat on the hood, he instead fired a tranquilizer point-blank into the ribs of both men.

Now his peripheral vision identified all of his targets. Three more, including Kane, sat on the ground below the cliff on the side of the road, and one man with a baton in his hand stood over Annette and Vorca, forcing their labor.

Rudy stepped clear of the front of the Humvee to fire down at Kane and her two companions. Such was their surprise to see him that in the thunder that followed from Rudy's barrel, only Kane managed to draw her sidearm, but she failed to raise it in time.

Lastly, Rudy spun on the soldier with the baton. Now he saw the man was young—probably not yet thirty—and though he wore a sidearm, he hadn't reached for it. His baton was half-raised, his eyes were wide, and his mouth seemed to struggle with the right response to the threat of Rudy.

Annette stood poised, looking from Rudy to the soldier. Vorca muttered a few native words and attempted to roll away a boulder without Annette's help.

"Drop the baton," Rudy said, "and you won't receive the biggest bruise of your life."

The young man was clearly inexperienced, and Rudy wasn't about to shoot the poor soldier frozen in fear, his eyes on the battle rifle aimed at his chest. Rudy lowered his weapon and took three steps to reach the soldier. He gently took the baton from his hand and drew a gel-tranq from his ammo vest.

"This is for your own safety." Rudy slammed the gel-tranq into the man's shoulder.

The soldier let out a squeak, then collapsed on the gravel-strewn pavement.

"Is that all of them?" Rudy turned, covering the vehicles. "Just six?"

Annette didn't answer. She rushed to him. Rudy turned this way and that to finish taking in the scene. One Humvee was too crushed by rocks to drive. The other appeared operable, but it was still captured by the rock-slide.

"Gail and Tilda?" he asked, his body stiffening in dread of the answer.

"No." Annette stepped back and eyed the guardrail. Dirt smudged her face, and her hair was loose. "Kane wouldn't waste even a bullet on them in the night, once they refused the Oath. They went without a whimper, Rudy. You would've been proud of them."

Rudy climbed over the guardrail to peer over the canyon. If they'd been thrown over in the night, they would've fallen while he'd still been unconscious. He hadn't seen anyone else on the narrow shelf below, so the women must've fallen all the way down where the second horse had gone.

"Your back?" She guided him away from the rail. "I mean, this is a miracle!"

"I landed on one of the horses. Now, *that* was a miracle! The force knocked me out but realigned whatever my spine needed. It doesn't feel too strong yet, but I can move okay."

"So, we've lost everything—and half our family."

"I brought up some gear with me." Rudy set a hand on Vorca's shoulder. "Vorca, that's enough. Leave the rocks alone. Can you get my pack over there? Thanks."

"They have some gear in the trucks." Annette eyed the six. "What about them?"

"Drag them clear and burn everything we don't take with us. Did they get a call out of this canyon?"

"I think they tried, but the mountains blocked the signal. Either way, Kane will be coming after us now. She'll have the whole OPT army coming after the Casperteins."

"Yeah, but I'm not about to make it easy for her."

Annette collected her rifle that'd been confiscated from her the night before, and Vorca woke Caleb from the back of the truck. Since his back was weak, Rudy had Vorca and Annette help him move the unconscious soldiers away from the Humvees and lay them down the road. The two women were exhausted, but Rudy saw no advantage in sticking around. He used fuel to douse the vehicles after removing any armaments. The weapons were thrown over the cliff, and the Humvees were set ablaze.

From Vorca's back, Caleb conversed with her about the fire as she walked away. From a distance up the highway, Rudy put his arm around Annette and watched the trucks burn.

"You think Caleb will be able to translate for Vorca someday?" Rudy chuckled. "He's got to be picking up English as well, right?"

"Maybe when he's a little older, he'll learn he's the only one who understands her, and he'll help us out." She looked up at him. "Are you thinking of Gail and Tilda? They're with God now, Rudy. They didn't suffer long."

"But I led us down here. We should've never been caught out here like this. Gail and Tilda are a loss I feel, even if God gained a couple more saints."

They walked slowly after Vorca, but once they rounded the next bend, Rudy picked up the pace. Annette carried some of the OPT gear, but they were an undersupplied party now—who needed to find a safe hiding spot indefinitely.

"Returning to Meeker isn't an option," Rudy considered aloud to his wife. "Wayne won't hesitate to arrest and kill us. And we can't expect Trapper to hide us either, though he'd certainly try. We'll need to find something in Colorado, maybe a cabin in the mountains. Or build one."

"And then what? Just hide out? The boys will never find us."

Rudy didn't answer. She was right. In all their running and hiding, if Rex and Levi made it back, there would be no reunion, not on this side of heaven. He wouldn't be able to embrace the mountain of a man his son had become or laugh with Levi at his wit that reminded everyone of his father.

His emotions broke right then, and he couldn't hide his weeping from Annette. They stopped together, knelt in the middle of the canyon highway, and prayed for God's strength.

During a swim in the Coldwater River, Levi couldn't help but tease Brian about a belly flop he'd just performed. The flop left Brian breathless, and those watching were left just as breathless from the sight and Levi's subsequent jokes and open-air reenactment. But their laughter ceased the instant Levi noticed Lena, who was scouting ahead, wave them off the bridge. As rehearsed a dozen times before, Brian guided Jenna on her bike to the side of Highway 278 and into the grassy ditch. Kip and Mia ran with their bikes at an angle into the grass, and Ryan Pulloy followed them. After ditching his bike beside the pavement, Levi held his rifle in one hand and crouched next to Brian and Jenna on the side of the road. Andy Radner was the last to pull off the highway where he carefully tugged his stump out of a sleeve attached to his bike's left pedal.

"Defending your diving prowess, Brian, may have to wait." Levi peered through his rifle scope at Lena two hundred yards ahead. "She's signaling us. Something's definitely going on up in front of us. Ryan, move everyone into those bushes. Brian, cover me. I'm going to Lena."

But before Levi left his travel companions, he gave Ryan the .22 pistol to go with his rifle, then he hustled back to Andy who was sitting in the grass, massaging his stump.

"How's it feel? Did you bump it?"

"I feel those phantom pains like you said I would." Andy plucked off the sock he wore to examine the tender skin beginning to grow over the amputation. "The sleeve you built grips my calf up here, so there's no pressure where it feels the weirdest."

"You'll be ready to pedal and tow me in the trailer in no time." Levi smiled and slapped Andy on the shoulder.

"Very funny," the ex-bounty hunter said.

An instant later, Auggie emerged from the bushes and collided with her old master. She slobbered all over Andy's face long enough to leave the young man sputtering, then the Lab was off down the road toward Lena.

Levi was more stealthy in his approach to their point person than the dog was. He remained in the ditch and crossed the highway to her when the way seemed clear.

She'd dropped her bike against a tree well off the road where she stood next to a lightning-struck spruce.

"What is it?" Levi asked.

"Aah-ah." She touched her ear, then made the sign for a gun.

Sure enough, two pops drifted through the afternoon air.

"Gunfire." Levi used his binoculars to scope ahead. "That's the town of Marks up there. I see the exit. Looks like the town sits off to the left a bit."

"Aah-ah?" Lena motioned that they could pass the town on the highway.

"We could. Waiting until dark might be best." Levi checked on the others. Only Brian was visible where he knelt on the shoulder, ready with his antique rifle at his shoulder. "But we're not the kind of people who ride past people in distress."

Lena nodded, her eyes seeming to frown. He knew his wife would've been just as apprehensive about making stops where they could avoid people altogether, but Levi couldn't do it.

"Ryan has the .22," Levi informed, "and Brian can hold here if we need to fall back. Let's you and me go on foot."

They moved out of the trees as more gunfire popped sporadically. The small town of Marks, Mississippi, spanned to the south on the west bank of the Coldwater River. But immediately off the highway, Levi and Lena spied upon the conflict that had drawn them. A giant barricade of garbage had been erected across the whole street, barring any vehicle from entering the town.

One hundred yards in front of the barricade sat a parked Suburban. Behind the vehicle stood two men with rifles and a third man with binoculars. As Levi watched from his elevation, the men behind the Suburban each fired a shot from their rifles over the hood of the vehicle. On top of the barricade, a body rolled out of sight on the far side. More townspeople lay prone against the block-ade, and others mingled behind it. Levi saw no firearms in their hands, but they did carry clubs, and a barrel was burning on the street farther back near shops and houses in disrepair.

"That's got to be the OPT Suburban, probably coming to enforce their policies." Levi scanned the highway and nearby streets. "I see only those three. Probably an Advocate and the two with rifles are Defenders of the Oath. Feel like a little target practicing?"

He and Lena knelt on the highway behind and above the men with the Suburban. Lena was ex-military, so Levi knew he didn't need to tell her which enemy to target. She was on his left, so she was responsible for the left-most man, the Advocate. Levi aimed at the rifleman on the farthest right. The middle man would be fair game for whoever put down their first target the soonest.

Lena fired an instant after Levi, and he allowed Lena to fire on the third man. The three crumbled on the street next to the Suburban.

Levi stood and raised both arms, holding up his rifle for the townspeople at the barricade to see him. Hesitantly, a couple men climbed over the blockade and approached the Suburban.

"Let's go." Levi left the highway and cut across a burned-out, weedy lot where he and Lena reached the street and Suburban. "Howdy, neighbors!"

The two townspeople were black men about in their thirties, wearing machetes on their belts.

"Are we neighbors?" asked one man. He had a large gold earring in his left ear. "I've never seen you before."

"Jesus taught that neighbors don't need to be familiar with one another." Levi stopped at the rear of the Suburban. "We only need to identify people who need to be treated neighborly."

"Interesting philosophy," Gold Earring said.

"Hey, these fools are still alive!" his friend announced, a white bandana tied around his head and another around his neck. He checked the pulses of the three downed men.

"We only tranquilized them," Levi said. "Figured they were OPT. I see an Oath of Solidarity marker on their dash there. Seems we figured right."

"Always some white fools trying to take over Marks!" Gold Earring spit at the OPT men. "Marks don't bow to no white man."

"This ain't about race, my friend." Levi noticed more townspeople skirting the barricade and approaching. "Whatever battles you've had in the past, the OPT is all about subjecting everyone under the controlled unity of the worship of humanity and the planet. They'll kill me just as quickly as you if we don't take their Oath."

"Well, we just wanna be left alone." Earring jutted his chin at Levi. "Where you from, Shooter?"

"I'm just a pilgrim these days. Headed to Colorado right now. Listen, these OPT people are driven by a pretty strong desire to rebuild America their way, and they'll be back here, no matter what happened today."

"We'll string these fools up by the highway. That'll be a warning for the others."

"That won't do anything to stop them. They'll come back with a whole unit, and they're well-armed. This may seem like a conflict over your small town, but this is a spiritual battle, my friend. You won't win any other way but through trusting in the God who created you, the God of the Bible. And you might even die, but Jesus Christ overcame death when He was resurrected the third day. If you want to save your people from these guys, get them to trust in the Lord God Almighty. These are the end times we're living in. Don't make it about race and territory when it's about souls in sin and ruin."

"Easy for you to say." Earring cursed. "You're white!"

"Neither of us chose our skin color. It's sad if Marks has a history of prejudice, but the oppression of sin knows no color. If there's to be hate passed around, make sure it's a hatred of evil in all of its colors. That's just some friendly advice from your pasty-white neighbor, okay?"

Levi offered his hand to Earring. The man eyed it for a moment.

"I never shook no white man's hand."

"It's just a hand."

The man flexed his fist.

"Well, I suppose there's a first time for everything." He accepted Levi's hand.

"That's right!" Levi laughed and pulled Earring into an embrace and back slap, which the man only slightly resisted. "It ain't easy makin' friends in this day and age."

"So how long these people sleeping for?" the bandana man asked.

"Just an hour, and you don't want your town getting caught with their vehicle. We'll take it and the three prisoners with us. You guys keep any gear and weapons. Sound fair?"

"We want the vehicle."

Moving past both men, Levi opened the passenger side doors and the rear door. He unloaded a duffel bag and a heavy assault rifle.

"Nah, we're the ones on the road," Levi said, "but you can help me load them into the back here. Come on. Let's get rid of them—the sooner the better. Grab his legs."

Levi and Earring grabbed one OPT man, then another, while Lena and Bandana piled the third into the back.

"You're a strange one, Shooter." Earring stood with his hand on his machete handle. "I never met any fool quite like you."

"Well, you find a Bible and take care of these people God's way, and you and I can get to know each other better in eternity."

Lena climbed into the driver's seat, for which Levi wasn't disappointed since his driving experience the last two decades was scarce. After a wave to the inhabitants of Marks, they drove onto Highway 278. There, they found other vehicle tracks coming from the west, so they knew an OPT presence was somewhere ahead. However, Lena turned right and raced east.

Only Auggie was in sight as she bounded out of a ditch where Lena slowed to pick up their friends. She swerved the Suburban in a tight U-turn, and even honked the horn, but still, no one came out of hiding. Not until Levi himself climbed out did Kip move from his cover in the bushes, and Brian came running from up the highway.

"We'll never get everyone in that!" Mia said. She and the others picked up their bikes from the grass. "How do you expect this to happen, Levi? Leave half our gear behind?"

"Gear in the back, bikes on top, strap Brian to the hood." Levi opened the back. "We'll make it work."

"I heard that." Brian arrived and picked at the vehicle's rusted body. "You'll only want me as a hood ornament if you're trying to make this baby appear more rundown than it already is."

Levi shared the news from Marks and how they'd acquired the Suburban. As he spoke, he groaned under the weight of the sleeping captives whom he carried one at a time to the ditch. There, he laid them in the grass where Jenna furtively touched them. Andy studied the three men, then crawled up to one, unlaced and took only his right boot.

"It ain't easy waking up with only one shoe, huh?" Levi laughed and held out his hand to Andy. "I'd like to stick around and see their faces when they try to figure out that one."

"Believe me," Andy said, accepting Levi's hand. "I'd take both boots if I had use for two."

"Did you ever hear the one about the one-legged man hopping down the road?" Levi picked up Andy and carried him to the back door, held open by Lena. "He stopped complaining when he saw the man with no legs."

"You really do have an answer for everything, don't you?" Andy shook his head, and Ryan handed him his crutches. "Do you ever get tired of winning at everything, even arguments?"

"There's only one thing I want to win at right now, and that's getting to my wife in Colorado." Levi closed the door, the glass in the window missing. "And this rolling contraption is going to get us there in a hurry."

"Strap in, Andy," Jenna added from beside him. "I think that means he's driving."

They loaded the gear in the back. It took ten minutes to tie the pile of mountain bikes and trailer to the roof. Two bikes had to be strapped to the hood, then the other eight climbed into the front and rear seats. Auggie made nine.

"Phew!" Levi gasped from the front passenger seat where he rode shotgun. "Who forgot to give that mutt a bath?"

"Be nice, Levi," Jenna said. "You'll hurt Brian's feelings. He doesn't like cold water unless he's practicing his swan dive."

"Oh, Lord!" Brian yelled out the window next to Jenna. "Save me from this car of clowns!"

But with all the levity, Levi glanced back to see that Mia was holding Lena's weapon while the mute woman drove. Like Mia, Brian held his rifle in his hands as well, his elbow on the windowsill. Having a vehicle meant they could cover the miles, but it would also make them an easier target.

"Take us home, Lena," Levi said, and glanced back at the ditch as the Suburban pulled away. The three OPT soldiers would wake up in about thirty minutes. If he were alone, he would've stayed behind to confront them about their need for the Lord.

"Some people," Kip said from beside him, "have to be left in God's hands alone to be dealt with."

"What're you talking about?" Mia asked.

"Levi knows," Kip answered.

And he was right. Levi did know. He wanted to help everyone, but there were some who couldn't be helped. Those were wounds he carried inside, while on the outside he cared for those God had given him to see safely home.

Chapter Eight

Chloe Azmaveth was on point this time instead of Alice as they walked through another town in Nebraska. Some of the towns had names, but most didn't. Since leaving the burned-down remnants of Schuyler, one town after another had been abandoned or destroyed. Except this one.

She stopped in the middle of the street and surveyed the sea of tents and plywood shacks. Blank faces and empty eyes stared back at her. Hundreds of people, their faces filthy, their clothes in rags, their hair long and knotted—sat or limped along the street. In one gutter, a stream of foul water ran toward a drain where a carcass half-blocked the grate. Chloe didn't approach the carcass for fear of what she'd find. She was afraid it could've been human.

But Alice, coming up behind her, wasn't as squeamish. She used her staff to scrape away the remnants of bones and flesh. The thing came apart when it was moved, but Alice didn't walk on until the drain was cleared and the water was flowing free. She caught up to Chloe at the same time Miranda and Rex reached her. Milo was a few steps behind, his rifle held with vigilance, but Chloe couldn't see anyone who looked like a threat.

"Refugees from the volcano," Rex guessed. "We're getting closer to Wyoming. They look like they ran for their lives with nothing."

"Why'd they all stop here?" Miranda wondered.

"Sometimes stopping is contagious." Rex adjusted his pack strap. "When one person gives up, it discourages others from continuing."

"That sounds like something from the Bible," Milo said.

"Numbers thirty-two." Miranda turned in a circle. "Maybe that's why God never gives up on us. He's never discouraging because He always finishes what He starts, Philippians 1:6."

"Maybe we should keep moving?" Chloe said, trying to read Rex's face.

She'd expected the giant man to shudder under their losses during the tornado, but he hadn't balked at all. He'd been walking beside Miranda all day, but his steadfastness couldn't be attributed to puppy love to impress the woman who'd stolen his heart. His stamina was from something deeper, more driven. Like God, he wasn't allowing them to quit. Chloe's smaller pack was nearly empty, and some of Milo's gear had been shifted to Rex's back as well. Alice, slender and stoic, hadn't complained when Rex had taken her light pack to carry in his left arm. But she refused to put down her heavy staff.

"Alice and Miranda, see if you can find a place to camp," Rex said. "Chloe and Milo, find us clean drinking water. And stick together. We're in a land where hunger makes stronger appetites for evil."

"What about you?" Milo asked. "You'll be alone."

"Don't be ridiculous." Rex grunted. "Nobody wants to tangle with an old work mule."

"He's right." Miranda slugged him lightly on the shoulder in passing. "I've seen him kicking like a plow horse at night."

"That's the Caspertein jig I'm dancing, getting ready to get two-stepping in heaven. It takes practice to do it in your sleep."

The pairs separated in opposite directions. When Chloe looked back, Rex was kneeling next to a tent where a child clothed in a burlap sack accepted a piece of meat from him.

"You knew the Casperteins before Pan-Day," Milo said as they turned a corner, following the dirty water ditch upstream. "Are they all like Rex?"

"Stubborn and dry-humored?" She laughed. "Only the Caspertein men. The women are graceful, courageous, and beautiful. Annette, Levi's mom, was a clothing model. And their Aunt Wynter was a gorgeous woman who was an archaeologist."

"Was?"

"Levi said she died in the Sierras a few years after Pan-Day. She had a child named Mia. Rex will have to tell you the story sometime. It's worth hearing—how God has used that whole family for decades."

On the north side of the town, Chloe and Milo emerged from the buildings to stand at the edge of a stinking pond. Plastic and clothing blocked a culvert to the west, so the reservoir was overflowing, forcing the foul stream to flow through the town. On the opposite side of the pond, a family of giant boars with tusks were tearing at an elk carcass. A few feet away from the animals, two men with a rake and a two-by-four were prodding and shouting at the boars.

"This is actually to our favor, isn't it?" Milo smiled at Chloe. "You ready? We can completely fix this town right now."

"Fix?" Chloe shook her head at the water and the grunting swine. "This is disgusting! There's no fix here, short of a bulldozer excavating this whole place."

"What're you guys always telling me?" Milo ejected the non-lethal gel-tranq magazine from his rifle. "You've got to see what God is doing, even in the ugly times of life."

Milo slapped a magazine of hunting cartridges into the rifle, then knelt in the mud to aim across the pond. Chloe jumped as Milo fired, and a boar on the far bank dropped where it had been wading in the water. In swift succession, Milo fired at the other three swine, perfect heart shots to put down the beasts.

"Get them out of the water!" Milo yelled at the two men who suddenly stood with their hands empty and raised. "And get some others up here to clean up this mess!"

Chloe followed Milo around the pond to the shore where the two men still refused to move. Only now was she seeing Milo's plan, and she stepped around her abrupt partner to address the men.

"It's okay. We're not here to hurt you. Pull these pigs out of the water and go get more men to help. Then get that dead elk out of here. Go ahead. We'll try to get this water flowing again."

They backed away then ran into the shanty town. Chloe stood next to Milo admiring the hogs, each of them at least seven hundred pounds.

"I think we'll be eating good with these people by sundown."

"Yeah, I think so." He passed his rifle to her. "Throw me a life preserver if you see me go under." He waded into the water toward the blocked culvert.

"If you were wearing waders, I'd feel better about this." Chloe gagged as she eyed a soiled diaper on the bank. "This isn't safe, Milo."

"Isn't the Christian life all about self-denial?" He picked up a roll of chicken wire and tossed it to shore. "If you're volunteering to come do this instead of me, I might take you up on that right about now."

He threw two plastic bags of garbage onto dry land. They tore in midair.

"No, no." she laughed and kicked the bags of trash farther away from the water. "You're doing just fine."

More men arrived from the town. Chains and rope were tied onto the hogs to drag them away. More downcast people wandered up to the pond to watch, and someone shouted for a barbeque pit to be dug. No one cheered or smiled, but Chloe sensed at least an attitude of curiosity among the observers. Alice and Miranda walked up and stood with Chloe as they coached Milo from the diseased water.

While the townspeople were taking the hogs into town, a number of teenagers arrived, some with tools, and stood on the shore to help Milo. The teens appeared too slender to be strong and healthy, but Milo moved submerged debris closer to them to involve them in wrestling it ashore.

Across the pond, others removed the elk, and when Milo had sufficiently cleared the culvert, the pool began to flow again. The foul stream ceased flowing through town, and Milo splashed back to shore to stand next to Chloe.

"Don't think you can dry off yet," Chloe said. "As soon as the water clears, you're going right back in there to wash out your clothes!"

"Might just have to burn them!" Miranda said.

Milo sniffed at his clothing, amusement on his face as they watched the stream that fed the pond wash away the stagnant water. Rex was missing out on what they'd accomplished together, but Chloe wondered if maybe that was for the best. They'd been relying too much on him. He needed a break from being involved in everything.

"There's an abandoned shack on the east side of town," Alice said to Chloe. She allowed Milo to use her staff to wade back into the water that was less polluted and remove more garbage. "It doesn't have a roof, but it has walls and a door."

"I'll be glad to sleep indoors," Chloe said. "Who knows if we'll get another chance before we reach Meeker."

"If Meeker still exists," Miranda said.

Chloe glanced at Miranda.

"We'll keep that between us, but it is a possibility."

"So, you've thought about it, too?"

"Meeker is just a location." Chloe smiled. "Heaven is our destination."

"That sounds like something Rex would say." Miranda turned away. "Where is that human semi, anyway? We've saved this town's water supply, and he's not even here to see it."

"He could probably use the break. He's been our luggage porter for a hundred miles."

"Ladies, a little help?" Milo called.

Alice took back her staff as Milo splashed ashore, dragging a fishing net.

"What's an ocean net doing in a landlocked Midwestern state?" Chloe asked as she took hold of the net.

"What's a soldier from Philadelphia doing in western Nebraska?" Milo asked. "Some things we'll never understand."

The four of them tugged on the net that trailed into the pond but couldn't budge it until the teens from the culvert came to help them. Ten strong, they heaved the net ashore. Tangled in its line were more unlikely items found in the Nebraskan pond: a scuba tank, a snowboard, a model airplane, and an assortment of rotting clothes and wood.

The teens picked over the treasures as Milo signaled with his hand.

"Smell that?" Then he pointed to Chloe. "No, it isn't me this time. It's that barbeque! I haven't smelled anything like that since I was a kid!"

Chloe trailed after her friends, joining the flow of other townspeople who were drawn by the aroma of pig on a spit. All around them, people emerged from inside sheds, from under tarps, even from holes in the ground. The promise of food had awakened the broken town of refugees.

When they arrived at the excavated house site of which all that remained was the cement foundation, Chloe discovered not one but three of the pigs were cooking over flames.

"We have to take advantage of this," Milo said. "Where's Rex? He should do the speaking."

The four glanced about for the man who would've stood out, but when they didn't find him, Milo took a deep breath and went to the men who were tending the meat. The crowd continued to grow, their filthy bodies pressing closer, their eyes staring at the sizzling flesh, their mouths agape over the juicy meat.

"How long until this feast is ready?" Milo asked a man with a drawn butcher knife.

"Twenty minutes or so." The butcher shook his head. "Look at the size of these beasts! It could take longer, but don't worry. There's enough for everyone here."

"Oh, I'm not worried about the food," Milo said. "I just wanted to know how long I have to speak a few words."

"Speak?" the butcher eyed the people. "To this bunch?"

"We might all eat some pig now," Milo said, "but what about in a week? What'll keep us going then?"

"I don't know. Go back to eating dog, I guess, when we can catch one."

Milo raised his arms to the people.

"Everyone! Please, listen. I have something important to say."

Chloe smiled at the man who'd once commanded Philadelphia's Citizen Army. He'd spoken to hundreds of warriors before, but now he was speaking to hundreds of orphans, widows, and wanderers.

"Hey, I'm worried about Rex." Miranda whispered to Chloe. "I'm going to look for him."

"Yeah, I'll go with you." Chloe wanted to hear what Milo had to say, but not at the expense of the safety of one of their own. She leaned over to Alice. "Miranda and I are going to look for Rex. He should be here. He's missing out on what's happening!"

Alice nodded, then turned back to Milo.

"Brothers and sisters," Milo shouted, "in a few minutes, we'll all be eating pork to our stomach's delight.

It was my honor to have shot these wild beasts for you, and if you're close enough to smell me, you'll know I just cleaned out the pond outside of town as well. By tomorrow, the water should be clean enough to boil and drink. But right now, we need to consider the future—not just tomorrow's food, but our safety for the rest of time. We need to talk about our hearts . . ."

Chloe followed Miranda out of the crowd where darkness had settled upon the town and Milo's loud voice was difficult to hear.

"See that?" Miranda pointed to the shimmer of another fire that reflected off the wall of a building east of town. "Someone's not interested in all the food available."

They set off together, stepping over drying puddles from the polluted water that no longer ran through town.

Not knowing who they'd find, both women crept forward cautiously toward the fire. Chloe sniffed the air.

"The fourth pig!" she whispered. "Back there, they were only cooking three. Someone else has the last pig."

Miranda nodded under the moonlight and peeked around the rubble of an old shop. She waved at Chloe to look as well. A man's voice carried on the night breeze, but Chloe couldn't make out the words until she moved around the corner.

"You see?" Rex was saying to a group of youths seated around a wide but low fire. "Slow but thorough cooking. Do this right, and the meat will last longer. We could even smoke what we can't finish tonight, and it'll keep for a couple more weeks. Now, where were we? Oh, yeah. I was telling you about a shepherd boy named David . . ."

Chloe bit her lip, then grasped Miranda's shoulder.

"Look at them! There must be forty kids here!"

"Probably mostly orphans," Miranda said, "or they'd be with the adults."

"I thought Rex was missing out on what we were doing." Chloe scoffed. "It looks like he hasn't been missing out on anything."

"Let's sit in the back." Miranda pointed. "He probably won't even see us. Let's just listen. Sounds like he's teaching them about King David."

Chloe looked back toward the larger fire where Milo was speaking to the adults. No one seemed to be left out in the whole town. They'd all receive physical food as well as spiritual food. In a town that had been entirely overlooked by the OPT, God wasn't overlooking anyone.

At the back of the circle of teens, next to some of the kids Chloe recognized from the pond, she and Miranda sat down to listen and watch Rex. Between acting out complete scenes from David's life, he rotated the pig on the spit, which must've taken twenty kids to hang the pig up onto the two forks.

As she listened, Chloe tilted her head back and gazed up at the blanket of stars. She couldn't help but release her emotions, and tears ran from her eyes. So near the end of their journey, God was blessing them with this opportunity.

Miranda put her arm around Chloe and laid her head on her sister's shoulder.

"My sentiments exactly," Miranda whispered.

When Chloe looked at Miranda's face, the younger woman was smiling, her teary eyes on the sky as well— their Lord's amazing starry sky.

Somewhere north of Grand Junction, Colorado, Rudy led his small band of survivors on foot into the woods. On the edge of a clearing, he gazed back at the freeway and sighed. Other travelers were pointing up the slope at them, but Rudy was too weary to care at that moment. Of course, word would reach the OPT, and Advocate Kane would come with a vengeance, but some things were out of his control.

Within the trees, Rudy caught up to Annette who was waiting for him. Vorca moved ahead, straight up the ridge.

"Are we okay?" Annette asked. "You look worried."

"Worried. Tired. Sore." He smiled and took her arm in his. "It all blends together for me now."

"You said you've hunted along this range before with Rex, right?"

"Years ago, after Pan-Day."

"So, you know of a safe place to stay?"

Rudy passed several trees before he answered.

"No. I would be wrong to promise you safety at this point. We have each other right now, and we know God's promises in Christ are unchangeable. Sometimes those are the only guarantees we have."

"It's been enough for generations before us." She held his arm tighter. "I'm not asking you to tell me that it'll get better. I know it'll only get worse, and once believers are removed from the earth, the world will suffer tribulation for seven years. I know all that."

"So, if you know that," Rudy said, "help me understand what you're asking me to say."

"I want you to tell me what's impossible to know— that we'll be together a little longer."

"How about this?" He stopped and turned her to look back down at the freeway and the Colorado plain beyond. "As long as we're together, we'll enjoy our time under God. If we're separated for any reason, we'll look forward to being together with Christ in glory. No matter our circumstances, we'll live and trust in God's goodness."

For a few moments, they stared at the specks of people moving east and west.

"Everything's been stripped away." Annette sighed, then smiled sadly up at him. "We have nothing left but to rely on God."

"See? We have that going for us."

"You Casperteins always turn losses into gains."

"Oh, that's not a Caspertein thing. It's a Christian thing. Blame Paul's letters to the Philippians and the Corinthians. Weakness opens the door for us to find strength, and loss opens us up to realizing all there is to gain."

From up the slope, Caleb shouted at them in Vorca's tongue. Although Rudy didn't understand the words, he understood the tone.

"I think we're being encouraged to remain together." Annette laughed, and the two hurried to catch up to Vorca and Caleb.

When they reached an adequate elevation, Rudy turned them east to traverse the mountain until they found a narrow stream.

"This'll do," Rudy said, admiring the surroundings. "A nice meadow below us. Water. Woods."

"But it's the nice range of fire for our rifles that you really like," Annette stated.

"It does offer an advantage over an enemy. And being on the south slope, the sun will shine on us all day long."

"Again, you mean the warmth and dry air will do your old joints some good."

"You know me too well." Rudy whistled to Caleb, who was attempting to lift a boulder that Rudy guessed weighed a ton. "Caleb, this is our new home. Can you collect some firewood for a cook fire?"

"Fire!" Caleb cheered, then scampered off to pick up finger-sized sticks.

On the edge of the green meadow, Rudy walked along the tree line, picking out trees to chop down for a small cabin. The ground needed to be leveled. With winter coming in a few months, firewood and game would need to be gathered.

From across the meadow, he looked back at what remained of his family. After losing their horses and gear in the river canyon, all that remained were the things he'd recovered in one pack and what they'd taken from the Humvees. One axe and his entrenching shovel were more valuable than his battle rifle now, even though they were low on food. So much needed to be done and their old bodies were capable of only so much. At least they could count on Vorca to help with cooking and caring for Caleb. She could identify edible plants, too.

"If this is our end, Lord," Rudy prayed, "let it be an end that pleases you."

He didn't bother praying to see his son and Levi again. His hope seemed better aimed on eternity rather than on what was so unlikely in the current chaotic world.

Levi was at the wheel of the Suburban as they drove down the winding road of Mount Magazine State Park in northwestern Arkansas. The Arkansas River Valley lay before them, and behind them were the charred remains of Little Rock. Lena had been at the wheel a few hours earlier as they had crawled through the sprawling metropolis, its bridges and overpasses barely negotiable. Although Levi knew his father had grown up somewhere near, where the Ozarks and the Ouachita Mountains met, he didn't feel nostalgic like he thought he might. Pan-Day had changed the world. The Caspertein family home was probably gone like so much else in the area.

They'd found no fuel since leaving Mississippi, and Ryan, their latest addition, had emptied their last gas canister into the fuel tank. Levi decided to switch off the ignition, stay in neutral, and coast down the northern slope of Mount Magazine. He wanted to use the vehicle for as long as they could since they were covering so many miles so quickly, but it all depended on fuel.

Wherever they went, concerned townspeople shared the news, and they heard more details about the volcano. There'd also been a terrible earthquake somewhere to the west, so Levi knew resources would be stretched thinner as they traveled toward the setting sun.

He drove into Paris, Arkansas, with a sharp eye out for an ambush, since the town appeared to be inhabited by several hundred people.

"I don't see many with rifles," Mia said from the back seat.

"Aah," Lena agreed from the passenger door where Auggie stood half on her lap, head and tongue hanging out the window.

"We need to find fuel here," Brian said from the back seat next to Jenna, "or we bike the rest of the way to Colorado."

"Nobody goes anywhere alone," Levi stated. "Remember that we're pulling up in an OPT vehicle."

"Yeah, with bicycles piled on the roof," Jenna added. "That's probably not OPT procedure."

"Let's hope they don't notice." He parked the Suburban in front of the town courthouse, its once-white four columns now gray and chipped in the afternoon light. "It ain't easy pretending to be bad guys, but it's a means to fuel in this case. Trade what you can for food, too. Keep your weapons ready."

Levi himself groaned as he climbed out of the vehicle. Auggie leaped out and brushed past him, her nose to the dusty pavement.

"So, what do I do?" Andy asked, sliding past the steering wheel, careful not to bump his stump on the door.

"Can you and Ryan stay near the vehicle?" Levi asked.

"We don't have an intimidating weapon like you do," Ryan said. "People might bother us."

"I don't think they will." Levi eyed an open-air market in a square across the street where townspeople eyed him back. "Just be friendly."

"What if they ask us about the Oath?" Mia wondered as she and Kip paired up. The battle rifle looked natural in Mia's hands. "We shouldn't lie."

"Right, we don't have to lie." Levi browsed over his friends. "When you're in command of the moment, you ask the questions to put others on the defense. And if you can, sow seeds of doubt about the OPT's stability and authority. When you can, explain the gospel."

"But we're supposed to be the OPT?" Kip smiled. "Levi, they're not going to buy this. Us? Jenna's blind, Andy's got one foot, Lena can't talk, and we're Christians in OPT territory. Why can't we just be ourselves?"

"Fine." Levi lowered his voice as several men approached from the market. "Lena and I will pretend to be OPT, and the rest of you are passengers heading west with us."

Levi turned in time to smile at the men from Paris. A large, older man with thinning blond hair pushed ahead of his companions. None of them appeared to be armed.

"Welcome to Paris!" He held out his hand, a smile that reached his blue eyes. "I'm Advocate Boone. We're the city council at your service."

Most of the population in the market had stopped their activities to watch the interaction.

"The name's Levi Caspertein." He firmly shook the Advocate's hand. "The OPT is making contact in person with some outlying towns. We're transporting some cyclists and kind people along the way. Glad to see some friendly faces, Advocate Boone."

Boone clasped his hands, his smile remaining broad, but his eyes lingering on the weapons and ammo vests.

"Well, let's get acquainted, shall we, Mr. Caspertein?" He turned to his people. "See that our friends get what they need—water, food, anything to see them on their way."

The man took Levi by the shoulder and turned him toward the market, but they stopped a few steps later in the middle of the street. Lena remained protectively close. Levi allowed his rifle to hang from the shoulder strap as he hooked his thumbs in his pockets.

"We're glad you're here in person, sir," Boone said. "Jacksonville said we'd need to execute our anti-OPT people ourselves, but we're just not executioners, Mr. Caspertein. You're some sort of official, right?"

"I'm more of what you'd call an ambassador." Levi nodded.

"But you can take these prisoners off our hands? Maybe execute them yourselves? We're trying real hard to abide by all the new OPT laws, but I'm risking a riot here if we start executing relatives and friends. Even if you were to say that you're assisting on the execution yourself, that'd help. I mean, half of you guys look like you're soldiers. Nobody will react in town while you're here."

"It's a tough situation—these executions." Levi glanced at Lena, stalling. She'd turned her back on such gruesomeness. If he let her, she'd storm the jail herself right now to free the victims. "I'll take them out of town with us, and you don't need to give them another thought. How about that?"

"Oh, thank you so much! I'll tell the people you insisted, if you don't mind."

"If that keeps the pressure off you." Levi shrugged. "How many anti-OPT people are we talking about?"

"Eighteen now." Boone gestured at the courthouse. "They're in the holding cells in the back."

"I'll need two things for all this to work." Levi lowered his head, as if he were truly scheming for the Advocate's favor. "We'll need more fuel for the Suburban, and a trailer to transport eighteen prisoners. How about a horse trailer? We can hitch it to the back, take them down the road a piece, and deal with them. Fuel and a trailer. You'll bring them out of the jail bound and hooded, you hear? I don't want a revolt on my hands as we head out with your prisoners."

"Nobody in town will revolt." His eyes widened. "You're the ones with all the guns! We have some fuel, but I'll need to talk it over with the council. And the trailer— we'll need to find one. We really want to comply with the OPT."

"Sounds like we have a plan." Levi slapped the man on the shoulder. "Let's not drag it out longer than an hour or two, understand?"

"Yes, sir. Thank you, Mr. Caspertein. I'm loyal to the OPT, you see? I assure you, we're slowly adjusting to this new normal, like they used to say. We have to conform to this One Planet Trust—this global consciousness."

"I prefer to consider the renewing of the mind," Levi said, his eyes narrow and critical, "rather than conforming to the world, but I'll leave that to you."

Boone hurried back to his waiting council to discuss the situation in private. Levi approached Ryan who was leaning against the Suburban, waiting with the doors open. Andy sat casually in the driver's seat.

"Can you set the gas cans out here on the ground?" Levi asked Ryan. "They'll give us fuel if we do them a favor."

"You want me to look for hose and horse trough?" Ryan asked, grinning. "Another public baptism would be a nice favor in this OPT town."

"It certainly would be." Levi chuckled. "It ain't easy running covertly through these towns. A good gospel message should be shared at some point. Maybe we can find a way to let them know before we leave."

Boone walked up to the Suburban. The council behind him dispersed.

"They've agreed," the Advocate said. "A mechanic will get a horse trailer ready for you, and we'll give you enough fuel to get you to your next OPT destination."

"Very good." Levi raised his chin. "Now, let's have a look at those prisoners."

As Boone led Levi and Lena up the courtroom steps, he explained how they had required the Oath of Solidarity from everyone in town, and then under threats and pressure, they had examined them further. Only when a citizen decisively refused to take the Oath, were they locked away for execution.

"The prisoners are mostly families." Boone led them down a corridor of offices. "A couple idealists, but the rest are those Christians. They've never been a problem for our community, to tell you the truth. That's why this is such a difficult time for us—getting rid of people who have been good neighbors."

"Christianity spreads hope in God in the midst of adversity," Levi said as they paused for Boone to fit a key into the door. "It's understandable that the OPT wants them gone since the Trust wants people to put their faith in the opposite of God."

"Science, right?" Boone guessed.

"I think science is just their excuse. The OPT wants to establish trust in mankind." Levi nudged Boone jokingly. "Like mankind can be trusted to do anything reliable or trustworthy, right?"

Boone chuckled nervously and continued to a metal door where he fit another key. Lena glared at Levi, communicating her disapproval of his comments. He guessed she thought he was being too obvious about his displeasure with the OPT, but he couldn't leave Boone in Paris without planting some sort of seed.

"Here they are." Boone opened the metal door wide to a window-lit expanse. "Eighteen is the most this town has ever had arrested at one time, so it's a good thing this is a temporary situation."

Lena swept past Levi to examine the prisoners, some in enclosed cells and others packed into a Plexiglas drunk tank. Instead of stepping up to the cells, Levi turned to Boone and stood close enough to put his hand on the man's shoulder.

"We may be leaders during a hard time in America, Mr. Boone, but I commend your compassion toward these people. You've clearly not lost your sense of humanity through all this. The OPT has an agenda that is pretty dark under the surface of all its promises. As one family man to another, you keep treating everyone with dignity, you hear?"

"Mr. Caspertein," Boone said, pausing to swallow, "you're not speaking like the OPT officials we've talked to on the radio. If I didn't know better, I'd think you disapproved of the way the OPT is telling me to do things."

Levi looked into the man's eyes and prayed to God as he measured the leader's heart. He took a deep breath.

"Aah-ah!" Lena called him, then shook her head, urging him not to reveal their identity.

But he couldn't resist.

"You're in OPT territory, Mr. Boone," Levi said. "You've got to put up a good show of complying with their new laws, but your heart is clearly not into murdering good and innocent people like these."

"Well, I mean . . ." Boone shook his head and looked away. "I try to adjust, I think, and . . . to make the, uh, right—"

"Don't worry. I've got your back. We can keep it a secret that neither of us approves of executing good people."

Boone blinked, then shifted his gaze to Lena.

"Uh, I don't know what you're talking about, sir."

"Oh, don't worry about her." Levi waved his hand at Lena. "She's as much of a Christian as I am. This is a rescue, not an execution."

The man's mouth fell open.

"I . . . can't believe what I'm hearing. You're OPT!"

"No, I've never taken the Oath. I'd die before I did. We'll take your prisoners a safe distance by trailer then let them go. You can tell the Jacksonville OPT that you got rid of them. In the future, you can 'get rid of them' yourself. Got it? The OPT won't know the difference, at least for a while."

"Yeah, but eventually they'll figure it out! I can't go against the OPT or the Oath. It would mean my death!"

"Who wouldn't want to die for a good cause?" Levi held out his arms. "Come on. What better cause is there to die for than caring for God's people who won't deny the Lord who bought them?"

"The Lord?"

"I know you're old enough to know the story of the cross of Jesus Christ. You said yourself, these are good people. What do you think made them good? It was their faith in a good God. No other way. You can quietly keep up this facade, all while secretly saving the lives of Christian people who would do the same for you."

"But . . . the town would think I was killing them."

"Maybe at first." Levi leaned closer to him. "You let the town think that, but privately, you can let a couple people know here and there that you've just sent their relatives and friends off where they're safe from the OPT."

"So, you're not really OPT?"

"No, but we need to be mindful of their presence. I'll be gone in a couple hours, and you'll still be in charge. Can you remain a leader while secretly caring for others? Place your faith in God, and even if you're found out one day, you'll know you pleased the heart of Jesus Christ by looking after His people. It ain't free being a hero. It's costly, but it's a worthy cause—an eternal cause."

Boone stood speechless, so Levi joined Lena at the cells.

"If that backfires on us," Levi mumbled to her, "I'll gladly admit you were right. Hopefully, that won't be in a blaze of gunfire or at our own executions."

Lena scoffed and walked to the next cell where she looked in through a narrow window.

Levi stared at the blank faces of the prisoners in the drunk tank. A couple men rose to their feet as if to stand in defiance of him and the OPT, but the rest of the women and children remained seated on benches or lay on the linoleum floor. He assumed they thought he was their executioner, and for now, he couldn't let them think otherwise.

Suddenly, he pointed into the tank.

"Hey, they have—?"

"Bibles?" Boone sounded exhausted as he came to stand beside him. "Yeah, I figured it didn't matter if I let them keep them. They have a few belongings, too, since I didn't know how long they'd be in here. Not everyone in town has felt sorry for them, though. Some of their residences have already been looted. They have little to return to, so I guess it's good they're leaving town."

"The OPT really isn't messing around, are they?" Levi frowned. "Kids, too? Come on, man."

"I was told if they're old enough to understand the questions, they're old enough to be held accountable for their answers—when they refuse the Oath."

"Aah!" Lena waved him over to the third cell.

Levi looked in on five women who shared a cell built for one.

"You've got a pregnant woman in here!" Levi growled under his breath. "She's ready to pop, Boone! The sooner we get them on their way, the better. Do you have enough handcuffs and hoods to make this look good outside?"

"The council is on it, but trust me: they're no happier about this than I am. You might get some hateful glares, but no one'll probably do anything."

"Hmm. Now I'm hoping these believers don't react in a way that reveals our facade. It may be less risky to tell these folks what's happening. Give them a little hope."

"What're you going to tell them?" Boone's eyes were wide. "You can't open the cell doors without risking a situation."

"Lena? Look." Levi traced a cross on the glass of the nearest cell. The heat and oil from his finger left a smudge. Then, he winked at the pregnant woman who was facing the door. Her eyes narrowed and her lips turned up slightly. Covering her mouth, she whispered to the others in the cell. "There. That'll do it. Pass it on to the others, Lena."

"That's it?" Boone asked. "That's all you're going to, uh, communicate?"

"Nothing else is necessary. They already know God is with them. A little indication that some of God's people are out here is all the encouragement they need to remain cool while we load them up."

"But you've never met these people before!"

"We're kindred at heart."

Levi watched Lena enjoy the honor of signaling to the other prisoners. She went a little further by touching her heart, pointing at them, and making the cross sign.

"I don't know whether to be impressed or terrified," Boone said.

"Maybe a little of both!" Levi laughed.

Prisoners inside the cells conversed and pointed at the two armed strangers.

"They'll know I was in on this," Boone stated sadly. "It's dangerous. Someone could come back to Paris and turn me in or report me to the OPT in another town."

"If saving lives didn't make us vulnerable in some way, everybody would be doing it, Boone."

"I assume you've done this sort of thing before. How are you still alive?"

"Like I said, when you look to the God of the Bible, Boone, you're not too concerned about safety. You're more concerned about other things, since your life is hidden with God in Christ."

"Man, I don't even know what that means." Boone threw his hands in the air. "This is all so crazy."

"We'd better get back outside to help with arrangements." Levi opened the outer metal door. "But after we're gone, you should devote your life to the plain reading of the Bible and put your faith in nothing else—especially not the OPT!"

"Oh, we're all gonna die," Boone cried. "I wish I had some assurance this was going to work out today."

"Let me tell you about the assurance of heaven, Boone, and you can move forward from there."

By the time they'd reached the street, Levi had given Boone the gospel in its elemental form. Out on the street, both men returned to their former roles and went to their people.

"This looks good for us," Levi admired through the opened back door of the Suburban. Mia and Kip had done most of the gathering of water and food. "But we need ten times this now. Trade and barter everything we can spare for more camping gear, hunting gear, and food supplies."

Ryan and Andy listened from the side of the vehicle as Levi explained how he'd taken on eighteen more travelers—including a pregnant woman late in her third trimester.

Brian, Jenna, and Lena banded together, and Levi agreed to stay with Andy so Ryan could join Mia and Kip on a broader hunt for supplies.

"You risk your life too much for others." Andy stood on his one leg in the open driver's door, leaning back on the seat. "It'll get you killed someday."

"The best people I've ever known or heard of died for others," Levi said softly, crouching down to pet Auggie. She'd returned with a prize in the form of a dead squirrel. "Sacrificing for others doesn't make you weak, Andy."

Andy swore, then said nothing for a few minutes. He scowled at Auggie as the dog ignored her former master.

"Mia said you and Lena kept me alive while I was unconscious. And Brian, too."

"Everyone helped." Levi looked up at the young man. "If you remember, I'd tried to get your attention a number of other ways. You were persistent about trying to kill me."

"It was a job. I had a contract." He sighed loudly. "But you . . . really bathed me? With Lena there? Man, that's humiliating."

"Lena's old enough to be your mother, Andy. As a Christian now, she has a compassionate heart. We all nursed you back to life."

"Yeah, after you cut off my foot."

"Sometimes we need to leave a piece of ourselves behind to start over. You know what that's all about. I remember you said you were raised with people who taught you the Bible."

"Yeah, I thought I'd left it all behind." Auggie finally went to him. "Hey, girl! Looks like our running days are over now."

"With a bike and crutches, there's nowhere you can't still go, just slower maybe." Levi stood and smiled at the sky. "You can go back to Wyoming, and I'll go back to Colorado. My wife must be there by now. They had a straight shot on the interstate."

"I can't go home." Andy shook his head. "I burned that bridge."

"Never underestimate the love that family has for you, regardless of your mistakes."

"They're not even my real family. Eric and Gretchen adopted me, a few years after Pan-Day. I idolized Eric at first. Everyone loved him, depended on him. Some said he was protected by God to protect the rest of us. But when I got older, I knew it was all make-believe."

"And you think it's make-believe what's happening between me and you?" Levi asked. "Think of everything that's happened since we crossed each other in New Jersey. That's not make-believe to me, my friend. It ain't easy admitting God is really directing our lives, but believing in coincidences or finding no purpose or reason for any of these events is even more ridiculous. You and I were meant to stand here like this in Paris, Arkansas, and talk about the Lord's sovereign hand over our lives."

"I see it, all right?" Andy nearly shouted, startling Auggie. Then his voice softened. "I just don't like being out of control."

"God's already taken your foot for your stubborn-ness." Levi walked into the street. "What else are you daring Him to take so He can give you what's best for you?"

Brian walked up with Jenna on his arm as he pushed a wheelbarrow full of camping gear.

"Had to trade some more hunting ammo," he grinned, "but I'd say we scored, huh?"

Andy drew a crutch from the truck and hobbled up to inspect the contents of the wheelbarrow.

"This tarp has a tear in it, and this fishing reel is rusted solid." He held up an axe head with no handle. "This is all junk."

"So, it fits us perfectly." Levi nudged Andy on the shoulder hard enough to make him stumble into the wheelbarrow. "The biggest critic volunteers to turn this useless junk into useful gear. You've got one hour to mend that tarp, get that reel spinning, and find a handle for the axe."

Brian picked through several of the other items in the wheelbarrow.

"We've got some old rain slickers, and a tent, too. They're in fair shape. Some camping tins and a wind-up light."

Andy growled at Levi, then set the items on the pavement for assessment. Kip and Mia came and went with two townsmen who'd been appointed by Boone to fill up the gas cans, then Boone himself returned to share the news that the trailer was ready. Lena drove as Brian rode shotgun to hitch up the trailer, which was on the next street west. Jenna, Levi, and Andy remained in front of the courthouse with the bartered gear.

"You really think you can pull this off?" Boone asked Levi, then glanced at Jenna and Andy. "Should we be talking in front of them?"

"If we can get those eighteen out here and into the trailer," Levi said, "I'll get them safely down the road and out of your jurisdiction. What happens after that is out of our control."

"It's a better chance than others have been given," Jenna said. "Mr. Boone, you're part of this, Levi says, because you care about the people you were forced to lock up. Now it's time to become dedicated to the entirety of the situation."

"More dedicated?" He gasped. "Giving you the eighteen, and the trailer, and fuel isn't enough?"

"But you're doing all that for us." Jenna moved closer, feeling up the man's arm to his shoulder. Then she set a hand on the Advocate's chest. "It's time you gave this—your heart—to God. He'll help you with your fear by opening your eyes to His love. Let Him lead you, Mr. Boone."

"I . . . want to." Boone wiped at his brow. "I really want to. You guys are just so . . . strange, that I know what you have must be real."

The Suburban rolled up the street, towing a four-horse trailer. Lena parked it at an angle, so the back of the trailer was closest to the courthouse.

The tension built as hundreds of townspeople from the market entered the street. Levi assigned Lena to stand on the roof of the Suburban amongst the heap of bikes where she could act as crowd control. Her masked face and brandished battle rifle drew many concerned glances.

Meanwhile, Boone and Levi lead several sturdy men prisoners from the courthouse with Brian, Kip, and Ryan as escorts for the eighteen. The men captives were cuffed behind their backs and hooded, but the women and children prisoners had their wrists zip-tied in front, and they were spared a hood. Regardless of Levi's earlier encouragement to the Christians, several of the women and children wept along the trek through the courthouse, as if they still thought they were being marched to their deaths.

Levi made a point to be the one to take the pregnant woman's arm as her escort. Her wrists were bound in front, so she held her belly and walked slowly at the rear of the column. She was a young brunette, and the top of her head reached only as high as Levi's shoulder.

"How're you doing?" he asked her in a low voice. Brian and Ryan were nearest him with other prisoners. "You gonna make it?"

"So, it's true?" She panted between her words. "You really care? You're here to help us?"

"That's the plan, but we've got to make it look good." Levi checked her face. "You're not in labor, are you?"

"No. I'm just carrying a basketball-sized suitcase. Every move takes some effort."

"Is your husband one of the prisoners?"

"Yeah, right." She stumbled and fell into Levi until she recovered her balance, then she continued. "He took the Oath and ran off with his sweetheart. Left me and this kid on our own. They said we were going to die, that our faith interrupted the collective consciousness of the Trust."

"It's not the first time authorities have spouted nonsense to justify murder."

"So, this isn't some elaborate game to get us to walk peacefully to our own deaths? You're really this nice?"

"I would rather die than hand you over to be hurt." Levi shook his finger at her. "You're not getting out of having that kid, young lady! Quiet now. No smiling. Let's do this."

The evening cast a shadow upon the town of Paris. Boone and his people loaded the first prisoners into the dome-shaped horse trailer. Though most of the crowd stood silently nearby, some of them were crying, and some were clapping. Levi was the last to reach the trailer. He figured at this point, there was no harm in allowing the pregnant woman to take her time, even though everyone was watching.

She used his arm to steady herself as she stepped into the back of the trailer. Levi looked up the length and found most of the prisoners seated against the outer walls. There was room for ten more, but instead, Brian and Ryan were quick to fill in the rest of the space with additional gear.

Levi helped the woman sit against the wall. He knelt next to her, his back to the trailer door.

"Give us time to get out of town," he said, "then we'll stop and undo everyone's wrists, okay? Hold tight."

As he backed out of the trailer, his eyes on the condemned prisoners, Boone himself closed the wide door and loudly latched it with a chain. Levi's mind was still on the bound pregnant woman he'd just abandoned in the back of the horse trailer, but then he turned and fixed his eyes on the crowd of men, women, and children. Some of them may not have been comfortable about their Christian neighbors being executed, but all those before him had sided with the OPT. They had abandoned the prisoners long before Levi had driven into town.

"Do we have everyone?" Levi asked Brian. They walked together to the Suburban. "We're done here."

Brian did a quick head count and helped Jenna into the back seat. Lena hopped off the roof and sat behind the wheel. Mia rode shotgun, her battle rifle muzzle resting on the window frame.

"You've got it from here?" Levi shook Boone's hand.

"Yeah, I think so." He leaned closer. "Seeing how you're doing this gives me confidence to do it, too."

"The OPT will continue to tighten their policies as they gain more control. Until the Lord comes for His Church, you'll have your hands full—if you're faithful to Him."

"I don't know how to do that yet." Boone checked over his shoulder for eavesdroppers. "But as long as I'm Advocate of this town, I'm not executing anyone."

"Find a Bible. Read it."

"I will. Take care of our people."

"You have my word we'll set them up somewhere before moving on ourselves."

Levi climbed into the back seat behind Lena and tapped the side of the vehicle. Lena rolled the loaded Suburban and trailer forward, slowly gaining speed as they approached the west side of town. Several of Levi's companions glanced at him as if they could sense his eagerness to tend to the prisoners.

"Who'll volunteer with me," Levi asked, "to ride in the trailer to give our seats up here to the women and children?"

Jenna's hand went up first, and everyone else followed suit. Even Andy, though he raised his hand last, but his face showed concern.

"We're not far enough down the road to turn them loose," Kip said.

"Yeah, I know." Levi touched the back of Lena's seat. "But we can still undo their cuffs and give them a ride up here. Lena, go ahead and stop. Jenna, Brian, and Lena, I want you three up here with the women and children. The rest of us can ride in back. Lena, you drive. Jenna, remind them of God's love."

"I will." The blind woman bravely stared toward him, not hiding her tears. "Do the same back there."

The Suburban stopped, and everyone piled out. Levi was the first to reach the back of the trailer. He threw off the chain like it was a poisonous snake, and Brian tugged open the gate. Brian, Kip, and Mia climbed into the trailer and began to remove the bindings of the captives. Levi claimed the pregnant woman for himself, cutting away the zip-tie with his blade.

"What's wrong?" He touched her shoulder. "Are you in pain?"

"Are you blind?" She squeezed her eyes closed and screamed. "It's coming!"

Everyone in the trailer froze for a few seconds. Mia was the first to react to the woman in labor.

"Levi, we need to heat up some water—boiled water." Mia knelt beside the woman. "I was midwife a couple of times with the Servalites. We're going to help you through this. What's your name, honey?"

"Brandy!" She grit her teeth. "Is that important right now?"

Mia fixed her eyes on Levi, who still hadn't moved.

"Cuz, set up a tent, start a fire, boil some water and find clean clothes for her and the baby." She looked up the length of the trailer. "Has anyone else done this before? I need a second pair of hands to help me."

"Aah." Lena waved her hand from where she hovered over Levi's shoulder.

"There you go." Levi backed out of the way, not doubting Lena's diverse experience at her age. "We'll get the, uh, stuff together. Come on, you guys! Get the wall tent up. We need firewood and boiled water!"

Just beyond the ditch, a barbed wire fence was cut to access a pasture where cattle and horse grazed no longer. The Parisians stood idly around the Suburban with Levi and his people as they stared at the wall tent hastily erected in the pasture. Brian tended a fire outside the tent with Kip and another woman from Paris, following Mia's orders.

"I feel useless," Jenna said as she held onto Levi's elbow. "I've never delivered a baby before."

Levi put his arm around her.

"Once we're loaded back up, you'll be doing what no one else can do. These people need Radiant Shade's heart. They have difficult times ahead of them. We can't take them all the way to Colorado with us, not with the OPT closing in. They'll be safer if we leave them somewhere in Oklahoma. So, they need to hear from you about how to prepare themselves for what's ahead, comfortable or not."

"I'll tell them." She nodded. "The Lord can't be far away now, can He?"

"No. It won't be long."

A few minutes later, the cry of an infant interrupted the anxious observers, and they cheered together. Levi wandered over to where Andy stood alone, leaning on one crutch next to the Suburban.

"Exciting evening, huh?" Levi sighed. "Just think. You would've missed all this if you'd killed me weeks ago."

"But I'd still have my foot." He acknowledged Auggie digging up a rodent in the grass. "And my dog."

"Maybe. But you wouldn't be on your way home. You'd still be trying to please the Federation or someone else."

"Don't tell me." The aggravation in Andy's voice was ripe. "You think God did all this?"

"We just took away eighteen people who were slated for execution because of their faith in God. Without firing a shot. We just allowed the town's fears and assumptions to lead the way. You could say today has been practically effortless—just us obeying God and serving Him by caring for others. And you think God's not fully involved?"

Just then, Mia ran up to Levi, her coat sleeves rolled up to her elbows.

"Cuz, um, there's something . . ." She moved closer so no one around the trailer could hear. "It's a boy, but she doesn't want him. She wouldn't even hold him."

"Doesn't want him?" Levi blinked. "I don't understand."

"Hey, Levi?" Ryan called from the other side of the vehicle. "Pass out food to everyone?"

"Yeah, go ahead." He waved at him. "Whatever we've got, Ryan. Okay, Mia, explain."

"Brandy just said she doesn't want him. Something about him reminding her of how she's alone and even her own husband doesn't want her. I don't know what to do. Lena has the baby with her in the tent still."

"How could she not want her own baby?" Andy whispered harshly. "Isn't she supposed to be a Christian?"

"These Christians have been through a lot." Levi frowned at the pavement in thought for a moment. "She's not thinking clearly. We have to help her through this. No matter what the mother thinks she wants right now, we're not going to split a baby from his mother."

"She just needs to know she's not alone," Andy said. "That's all it's about. It's her deadbeat husband who abandoned her. Now she's acting out because of him, and the baby is paying for it."

"We have to get back on the road." Levi gazed to the east. "We're only a mile outside of town. Someone could've heard us all cheer a minute ago."

"What about the baby?" Mia asked. "We're not set up to take care of an infant. Diapers and nursing, Levi. Remember Caleb?"

"Believe me, I remember Caleb. Can you keep her near the baby? Sit in the vehicle next to her. Maybe it's like Andy says. She just needs to realize she's not totally alone and abandoned. Maybe she'll start to bond with the baby, if she begins to bond with others."

"I can sit next to her, too," Andy offered.

"You?" Levi questioned. "You can't stop complaining about your foot. How're you supposed to help her?"

"I'm just saying, I know about losing things like she's lost things." Andy shrugged. "I lost my parents, my foot, everything. Come on. I'm not doing anything else."

"They're about the same age," Mia said to Levi. "Brandy's around twenty."

"If your heart was right with God," Levi said to Andy, "I'd feel better about this. You'd better not play any games with this woman and her baby! Remember, you can't run away from me if you slip up."

"Yeah, rub it in, why don't you?"

"She won't even name the baby," Mia said. "What do we call him?"

"I gave Caleb his name because the mother wasn't around to tell me." Levi sighed. "But this mother's still here. Use the name-choosing to draw her in to caring, maybe. That's my suggestion. Beyond that, we've got to trust God to do a lot of healing. Brandy's not the only one who was just ripped out of her home in Paris, though. Seventeen others are in such a state of unknown, relying on us, that Andy's missing foot is small potatoes in comparison."

"Okay, I'll stop talking about my foot," Andy said, "if you stop talking about my foot."

"Hey, we agree on something!" Levi laughed. "Let's load everyone up. You two with Brandy in the back seat. That'll just make more for me to meet and visit with in the trailer. Come on, Auggie! Your stinky breath is back in the trailer with me."

The tent was torn down, and Mia returned with the baby in her arms. Brandy walked with Kip's support.

"Drive for another hour or two," Levi said to Lena, "even in the dark. If you see lights ahead, turn off your headlights, stop, and we'll figure out what to do. Either way, it's going to be a long night."

"Aah." Lena nodded and climbed into the driver's seat.

Levi was the last to step into the back of the trailer. He held Auggie back with one hand, and with the other, he latched the door from the inside. Holding his rifle in his lap, he slid to the littered floor of the trailer. Night had fallen, so he couldn't see the faces of the many strangers near him who seemed to be an even mix of men and women.

He cleared his throat after the trailer started rolling. Those who'd been talking hushed themselves.

"The first thing I think we should do is pray together," he said over the rumble of the wheels on the road. "Somewhere ahead, you'll be given a new place to settle until the Lord comes for us. But I'd be lying if I said I thought you've seen the last of the OPT. This isn't just about leaving one place and going to another. I realize you have nothing, except what we're able to give you from our own short supply. As I understand it, you're believers in a sovereign and loving God. In the weeks to come, contentment in Him may be your only satisfaction since more of us are unlikely to find any peace or rest in the things of this world any longer."

"I'd like to start, Levi." Kip's voice came from farther back, where he'd found a seat among the Parisians. "Dear Father, You know our individual situations because You know all things. You have promised not to abandon us, and we rely on that promise now . . ."

Leaning his head back on the wall of the jostling trailer, Levi listened to his brothers and sisters take turns, praying in the darkness to the Father of Lights. His heart felt heaviest right then, thinking of his own plight, wishing more than ever that he had Lyla there beside him. Soon, he prayed, the journey would be over, and he would hold his wife again.

Chapter Nine

Rex led his companions into Meeker from the same direction Levi had led them out a year earlier. They'd covered the last hundred miles in three days, which seemed like record-time since they'd hidden in creeks and canyons a dozen times to avoid OPT patrols on the rural roads of northern Colorado.

Chloe was on the verge of collapse, and Miranda had stopped talking two days earlier, as if she were reserving all her strength to keep walking. Alice had ceased taking the lead since leaving Nebraska. She'd asked Rex to strap her staff onto her back since she could no longer hold it or lift it while walking. Such was her attachment to her heavy staff that she'd rather carry it on her back than leave it by the side of the road.

Milo had cast off most of the provisions he'd been carrying in his pack, now only toting his rifle, canteen, and three blankets. Alice and Chloe carried no packs, and Miranda had insisted she carry one tarp. Rex carried the rest, though he'd left extra clothes and unnecessary gear in the Nebraska border town where he'd cared for the refugee youths in the muddy unnamed town. Only by sheer determination had he not thrown away his hatchet and shovel.

When they limped into familiar acreage northeast of Meeker, Rex barely recognized the forest of his youth. There were no longer any birds or cattle or sheep. The larger trees appeared to have been shaken so hard by a giant's fist that they'd snapped off midway up. The smaller trees were standing skeletons, devoid of leaves, needles, and cones. The combination of earthquake and volcano blast-wave had stripped the land bare. It had rained in the past month, however, and any ash that had settled on the ground was now washed away or blown like sand in small corners of the natural world.

Before he reached the cabin his father had built, he weaved through the carcasses of cattle, now shriveled heaps of bones and hides. Not even wild predators had feasted on the remains.

Moments later, he stood in front of the cabin. Only two walls were left partially standing. The huge logs had splintered and toppled. The roof seemed mostly intact, though collapsed now, slanting against part of one wall, while the remainder rested on the ground. The corrals and barn were in no better shape.

"You know this place?" Milo asked, stopping beside him.

Miranda, Chloe, and Alice trailed behind another twenty yards.

"Dad was building this place before we left last year. See those horse corral posts? I pounded those."

"So, we're in Meeker?" Milo's head lifted, his eyes searching the grazeland until he spotted the town in the distance. He turned to Miranda and the other two weary travelers. "Hey! We made it!"

Chloe dropped to her hands and knees, then shook her head at the cabin.

"Rex? This is what we came hundreds of miles to find?"

Alice walked into him, and he took her in one arm to hold her upright. Her face was blank, her eyes hollow.

"A lot has happened while we've been gone." He reached for Miranda, and she came to stand with him, accepting his other arm around her. "We made it. I don't know what we arrived to find, but this is home."

"It looks abandoned," Miranda said.

"The OPT is probably in town. Dad might've led the Christians into hiding, whoever the OPT hasn't captured yet. Or, Dad was captured, and this place was just left to fall apart."

"If Levi made it here," Chloe said, "he would've left a message for us. He'll be looking for Lyla."

"A message . . ." Rex left Alice and Miranda to enter the cabin wreckage. "There's enough left behind to live off. Milo, check the well. It's over there. I don't see any recent tracks. We're probably safe from the OPT if they're in town. At least until they realize we're out here. We'll keep our fires low and hide in those trees."

"Unless everyone in town went the way of those cows," Miranda said. "This isn't the Caspertein homecoming I was hoping for."

"I knew it would be bad." Rex left the remnants of the cabin. "But I wasn't expecting this. Meeker has been home to the Casperteins for decades. There's got to be someone in town who can tell us what happened. Maybe Dad is living in town now."

"With the OPT?" Chloe tried to climb to her feet, then gave up and stayed on the ground. "I'd like to say I could back you up, Rex, but I can't take another step."

"It's okay," Rex stated quickly. "We'll camp here. Rest and recover. Tomorrow's a new day."

Milo returned from the well.

"I think the well's okay," he said "Tastes okay, at least."

"Let's get a camp set up before dark." Rex helped Chloe to her feet. "We've got all kinds of stuff from the cabin to help us now. Dad left plenty of firewood, too."

Rex felt a second wind that evening as he and Milo set up a simple camp and started a fire for the women who lay motionless on a tarp, while a second tarp was fashioned as a lean-to sheltering their heads in the clear, starry night.

"Why don't we boil the water, anyway," Rex said quietly to Milo. "Keep them drinking and don't let anyone come after me. If I'm not back by dawn, head back east. Return to Iowa. Giselle is waiting for you."

"We're not leaving you behind." Milo grabbed the front of Rex's coat. "We came this far, Rex, we have to finish together."

"It may already be finished." Rex took Milo's hand off his coat and gripped his hand tightly. "Cling to Christ, Milo. I'm in His hands. Don't cling to anything else, my brother. Dad and the others may have already passed on. I'll see if there are any people around and if I can find out something, okay? A year ago, I knew everyone in Meeker."

"You led me to Jesus." Milo dropped his hand to his side, where his rifle hung. "We're supposed to see all this through—about Levi and meeting your father."

"I know." Rex pulled the weary man into an embrace. "Some adventures have no closure. They just end, and we may not find out why until we get to glory. Right now, your job is to keep these three safe and together. Remember, I'm too ornery for anyone to bother with, right?"

Rex took only his canteen and rifle. As darkness closed, he looked back from a distance. Their fire was low enough that he couldn't see it. When he turned back toward Meeker, he felt the exhilaration of youth once again. This was his land, the pastures of his childhood. Death had ravaged it, and the tribulation years were approaching, but he was still there. The Casperteins hadn't yet been wiped from the land!

He knew every inch of the White River Valley, so even in the dark, he ran full-out, the night breeze touching his face like a familiar friend. After leaping a crumbled wooden fence, he jumped a stream and found the road into Meeker. The closer he crept, the more lights he saw ahead.

Past Barone Middle School, he cut across a field to reach the outskirts of town. Using Park Avenue and staying against the buildings instead of walking up the street, he pushed deeper into town. No dogs were barking.

No singing or laughter drifted in the air. Meeker had become a ghost town. Nearly.

Arriving behind the courthouse, he then eased up to Main Street to spy on Hotel Meeker where lantern light glowed from several windows. It flickered like firelight, so he knew the town's electricity was out. The earthquake must've damaged the whole electrical grid.

For a long while, he watched the street, praying about what to do, pushing away memories of a joyful childhood, and then of Levi's arrival and deliverance a year earlier. His instruction to Milo still rang in his ears—not to cling to the fleeting things of this world, since all of it would be burned up eventually.

A door slammed, then a lone figure walked by the light of the moon down the sidewalk from the courthouse. Rex recognized the man's frame, someone he'd known since they were boys.

Wayne Sullivan was a tall man, wiry and strong, but Rex was unburdened, so he was able to attack swiftly and silently. Inches taller than Wayne, Rex covered the other man's mouth from behind and dragged him down to the dead grass off the sidewalk. As soon as Wayne was down, Rex straddled him, his hand still over his mouth. Something hard stabbed into Rex's knee, and he drew a sidearm from Wayne's side, then tossed the weapon away.

"Relax!" Rex whispered, sitting on top of him. "Be still! It's me, Rex Caspertein. Relax, Wayne. Don't scream, okay? I'm going to take my hand away."

As he removed his hand, Rex climbed off Wayne, and drew him to his feet.

"I didn't know who to trust," Rex said quietly, glancing around the street. "Tell me what's going on here, Wayne. Where's my dad?"

"Rex?" Wayne turned his head in the direction Rex had thrown his pistol. "What are you doing back here? The whole country is looking for you guys!"

"What're you talking about?" Rex scoffed. "The whole country? I just got into town a couple hours ago. Dad's ranch is abandoned, and I don't see a single animal left out there, not even a coyote!"

"Listen to me, Rex!" Wayne cursed and shook his head. "The volcano hit us hard. Your dad thought the ash would fall for weeks, so he convinced others to leave. Some ran west, some east. Your dad and others went south. Last I heard on the radio, your dad had attacked Colorado's OPT Advocate Kane and her convoy. And he and his wife aren't the only Casperteins on the wire—"

"Wait. Dad's got a wife?"

"Annette. He married Annette."

"I knew it!" Rex smiled. "It's that Caspertein charm."

"The OPT isn't too charmed by all of you. Levi is leaving a trail of destruction across the south. The radio says he's traveling with an army of resistance fighters, slaughtering anyone in their path who's taken the Oath, even women and children. Rex, every Caspertein in the country is being hunted down right now. They're calling you domestic terrorists. If anyone sees me even talking to you—"

"Where's Levi right now?"

"Last I heard, he was somewhere in Arkansas, maybe Oklahoma by now. The OPT is putting the pieces together. They know he's coming back here. Between him and your dad, every OPT Defender in the region is hunting you guys!"

"Come on, Wayne. You know we're Christians. Levi isn't slaughtering anyone. But Oklahoma? He could be weeks away still."

"Not if the last rumor is true. He killed a convoy of OPT aid workers and stole their vehicles."

"I'm not buying it." Rex lifted his finger. "You're eavesdropping on the OPT intel? They just let you listen in? How do you know all this stuff?"

"Rex, everyone is OPT now. Haven't you seen the Oath? No one can buy or sell anything without taking the Oath. "I'm . . .OPT, Rex. I'm the Advocate of Meeker."

"You?" Rex loomed over him. "What've you done to Meeker, Wayne? You're doing their bidding now?"

"I let your dad leave, honest! He and Annette had those rifles. Me and the boys would be no match, so we just let them leave. The ash was still falling when he headed south. They're making me arrest Christians, Rex. I don't have a choice."

"Oh, you have a choice!" Rex checked his voice and his wrath, then backed away from the weak man. "You were once a student of the Bible, Wayne. What happened to you?"

"I learned better! I know now that science is going to get us through this period. You'll see. The OPT is going to resurrect this country better than it ever was."

"The OPT is against God, Wayne. Don't you see? They've taken a role that must lead right up to the seven-year tribulation period in the Bible. The rapture must be close—and you're playing Advocate for these clowns?"

"I'm staying alive!" Wayne wiped his nose on his sleeve. "If you help me, we could turn things around, get your dad to come in peacefully. The Oath isn't evil, Rex. It's the right way to live, to think of our communities under the regulation of the Trust. Think of the planet, Rex. It needs us to do this!"

"So, you've sold your soul." Rex shook his head. "You've bought into their lies as they crumble with the very world they claim to control. The OPT isn't in control, Wayne. Mankind doesn't control science. God does! And until you submit to Him to rescue you from sin and death, you'll go the way of the prince of this world."

"Now you're the one who's delusional." Wayne shook his fist. "I listened to those stupid lies my whole life. Superstition, all of it! We're a new race, Rex. We survived the Meridia Virus. We're the builders of our own destiny, identity, and purity. We don't need God anymore. We don't need religion. We're stronger than that now. We're more evolved. At least, some of us are. You're missing the bigger picture, and those who insist on missing it, the OPT has an answer for that."

Rex sighed and partly turned from Wayne—but he didn't take his eyes off the man.

"How many have you arrested?" Rex asked.

"A few. Just the ones who wouldn't leave when I told them to go somewhere else. I didn't want to execute anyone, Rex, but it's the law now, for those who refuse the unity that the Oath brings."

"How many have you executed?"

Wayne didn't speak for a moment.

"I know you won't kill me, Rex. You think I'm a bad person, I know, but it's you who's holding us all back from moving forward."

"How . . . many?"

"Um, I don't know. A few. It's the law. The OPT comes here once a week now to check on us, besides radio contact. If I didn't follow the law, they'd arrest and execute me as well. This is survival, Rex, for everyone and this planet."

"Well, some things are worth dying for. Some people are worthy of dying for, Wayne! Did you kill your dad? I know Trapper would never take the Oath."

"No, Dad's out at his ranch. He stays away from town. Some people who're still here would make me arrest him if he's around too much. They know he's a Christian."

"The things you've done, Wayne . . ." Rex cleared his throat. "The people you've killed and justified it, convincing yourself that it's for the greater good—the righteous dead are in a better position than what awaits you in eternity unless you turn from this nonsense."

"You're the one who's rejecting the unity the whole human race is moving toward."

"I'm done trading threats with you, Wayne. You stay clear of me while I'm here, or else."

"Or else nothing," Wayne snapped. "You're not doing anything. You're just like your old man. All you Casperteins are as good as dead. I'm walking back into that courthouse right now and telling them that one of the Casperteins has reached Meeker. Even if you're not your father or your cousin, you're a dog they'll enjoy putting down, just because you're from the same family."

"The radio's in there?" Rex nodded toward the courthouse. "Oh, Wayne, you know I'm not too sharp. I always lacked the marbles in my skull, but your own arrogance makes you more foolish than me. Let's go pay that radio a little visit, huh? Then I'll go have a chat with your dad."

Although Rex was weary, he wasn't about to be overpowered by whiny Wayne Sullivan. He gripped his collar and drew a gel-tranq from his vest. With more force than necessary, Rex slammed the cartridge into Wayne's ribs. Wayne squealed in surprise, then the tranquilizer took effect. Wayne went limp, and Rex pulled the man over his left shoulder.

"What do you think, Wayne?" Rex asked as he opened the front door. "Shall we have a little chat with the OPT before the radio has an unfortunate accident?"

Before Rex entered the dark courthouse, he came upon electrical cords laying across the threshold. When he looked to his right, he noticed a generator sitting in the open against the side of the building. He set Wayne on the ground and fumbled in the dark until he found the generator had a push-button starter. The motor rumbled to life, and lights inside the courthouse blinked on.

For a moment, Rex eyed the street, waiting to see who would come to investigate the loud noise. However, nothing moved in the night, as if those who remained in the town were used to the noise from the courthouse.

Rex picked up Wayne and entered the unlocked building. Inside, filth littered the historic courthouse and Rex followed the cords and the occasional light bulb to the right, then straight back to the courtroom itself.

Two lamps stood over the judge's seat, and where the desk must have once stood, it had been removed from behind the low wall. There, Rex found the radio sitting on stacks of mildewed boxes. Rain had seeped into the building, and Rex glanced overhead, wondering if the structure was actually safe to enter when so much else seemed to have suffered damage from the quakes.

He turned on the radio and adjusted the headset to fit over his large head. Weeks earlier in New Jersey, he'd heard from Levi himself how he'd sent disinformation over the radio to the Federation. Now, it was Rex's turn to do the same—to the OPT.

Voices filled the headset.

"Roger that, Buford74," a man stated. "If you can't repair that superstructure, tear it down and bring us the parts for our side of the river. Over."

"Sweetwater23, this is Glenwood16. Do you copy?"

"Glenwood16, this is Sweetwater23. We read you five-by-five. Over."

"Sweetwater23, Glenwood16 needs a confirm on those 10-15s you found in Gypsum. What's the count? Over."

"That's nine in restraints, Glenwood16. Over."

"Thank you, Sweetwater23. Glenwood16, out."

The radio was silent for a moment. Rex didn't know who was behind the call signs, but he recognized the towns of Buford, Glenwood Springs, Sweetwater, and Gypsum. He pressed the transmit button, hoping a made-up call sign did the trick.

"Glenwood16, this is Meeker77. Come in. Over."

"Meeker77, this is Glenwood16. How are you doing up there after that raid? Over."

Rex stared at the radio a moment. Wayne hadn't said anything about a raid. It could've been a raid of the OPT against some sort of resistance, or a raid of survivors against the town, looking for supplies.

"Glenwood16, every day is an adventure as we're rebuilding up here. Do you have an update on the Casperteins? That's what we're still recovering from. Over."

"Meeker77, there's something happening in the west on the 70, last I heard. Grand Junction is where the Denver Advocate is staging. Didn't you get the status report? We don't know more than that. Over."

Rex's eyes narrowed. Grand Junction! That was two days south!

"Glenwood16, I read you. Did anyone see that five-car convoy heading north from Wolcott? Those weren't OPT troops. They looked armed to the teeth for something. Over."

"This is Yampa34. What's coming our way? Please repeat your last. Over."

Rex froze, wondering what else he could really effectively say without sounding obvious. Wolcott was in the other direction from Grand Junction.

"This is Eagle81. Yampa34, he said there's a five-vehicle convoy heading north from Wolcott. You better brace yourselves for action just in case. Over."

"Yampa34, this is Glenwood16. We have a chase vehicle and a little fuel. We can cruise over there and back you up . . ."

Taking off the headset, Rex figured a subtle distraction about a phantom resistance convoy would keep the state talking for a couple days. But he needed to get to Grand Junction. Whatever update had been posted, it had to be about his father, since the only other Caspertein Rex knew about was Levi, and Levi was somewhere in Oklahoma. According to Wayne, at least, which wasn't saying much.

Grand Junction was less than a hundred miles southwest of Meeker, across the Roan Plateau. It hurt Rex's feet just thinking about setting off across that wild land, but it would save him thirty miles if he went over the plateau rather than the road. And the roads and towns sounded like they were heavily trafficked now. If the OPT was staging something at Grand Junction, his father was probably their target.

Rex smiled at a memory. About fifteen years earlier, Rudy had taken him on horseback to hunt the mountain range north of Grand Junction. Although Rex didn't know that wild land too well, his father had surveyed out there as a seismologist, so he must've had a place in mind to lay low for the winter.

After cutting off the power to the radio, Rex lifted the console and dropped it on one corner three times to crack the cover. He widened the crack by smashing it with his heel, then used his hands to tear the metal plates apart. Rex wasn't wise to electronics, so he ripped everything from the motherboard that looked important. Finally, he took his deer knife and slashed cords and gouged components until he felt certain he had disabled the radio permanently.

As a last touch of sabotage, Rex carried Wayne into the back where he knew there were holding cells. Upon entering, Rex choked at the smell of death. He propped open a door to allow light into the jail section, only to find there was no dead body in the cells, but the smell of death would be hard to remove without proper chemicals. Blood had seeped into the linoleum of the floor, staining it purple.

In one of the cells, Rex dropped Wayne onto a cement bunk, then slammed the cell door closed. If he'd had more time, he would've found a way to break the lock, trapping Wayne inside until someone came along to cut him out. But he needed to go before someone else came upon his mischief.

On his way out of the courthouse, Rex broke the light bulbs, and outside the front door, he opened the gas cap of the generator and tipped the motor on its side. With the fuel draining out, Rex stomped on a few fragile exterior components, then walked away the way he'd come.

Weariness had left him, and righteous anger had given him a fresh mission. His body desperately needed rest, but his will was as determined as ever. He couldn't wait to get back to the others and report what he'd found out. Milo especially would be excited to hear that Levi was on his way!

Outside town, Rex walked through the dark night toward Old Man Trapper's ranch. A dozen times, Rex paused to search his back trail, concerned that someone might have been following him from town. But he doubted anyone knew that land like he did, able to walk confidently under the starry sky, the moon having set, with no light to illuminate the way forward.

Unlike the past, no sheepdog barked to greet Rex as he walked up to the Sullivan residence. He knocked loudly on the door and listened to the house. Trapper had been like a grandfather to him, taking him reel fishing and teaching him about sheep herding. Rex preferred flyfishing, but Rudy had told his son to learn from the old man, anyway.

"Who is it?" Trapper's gravelly voice called from deep within.

Rex opened the front door, knowing Trapper didn't know the definition of locks in a land where he refused to live in fear.

"It's Rex, Trapper. It's Rex Caspertein." Then he added, "Don't shoot. I'm coming in."

"Come in at your own peril, young man, but not because I'm armed. The floor is covered with hay bales."

He walked inside and closed the door as Trapper lit a candle and held it up.

"Let me look at the man you've become." Trapper squinted at him. "I prayed the Lord would let me live long enough to see you come home. You made it all the way east and back, did you?"

"Yes, sir, and it was some adventure."

"I wish I could've gone along." Trapper grinned, his mouth missing more teeth than Rex remembered. "But someone had to look after Meeker while you were gone. Get over here, young man!"

Hay bales weren't the only things crowding the living room of the Sullivan house. Two milk cows chewed the cud where they stood and lazily gazed at him from behind an oval dining table.

"Ranching has changed some since I was here last!" Rex laughed and embraced the old timer. "Don't tell me you brought them in here because you're lonely."

"Nah." Trapper sat on a bale and set the candle on an empty bookshelf. "It was all that ash. Killed off the grass just like your dad said it would. The water table seems okay, but I couldn't let the animals range free with people starving so bad. Wild animals were killing and eating everything they could find."

"I didn't see any sign of cats or bears coming in from the northeast."

"They're still out there, just fewer." Trapper nodded and sized up the large young man beside him. "You bring back that cousin of yours? You should know your father married Annette, so I guess that makes you and Levi brothers now."

"No, Levi had to go another route. I was just in town and talked to Wayne. He told me about Dad and Annette."

"Wayne? Oh, Rex, I've nearly given up on him. He killed the last of the believers who were still in town, the ones who arrived last year and didn't want to leave again. Did he tell you he killed Dathan a few days after the volcano?"

"Tentmaker's dead?" Rex frowned. "I thought he would've left with Dad."

"He wanted to, but Wayne's thrown in with those Trust people. I never thought I'd see the day that my own kin would become a tool of the devil."

"Wayne said Dad went south, and he let him go with a few people."

"Only because God put some holy fear in Wayne. Wayne wanted him gone, so he let him leave. I spoke to Rudy right before he left. He said to tell you he's going down to the deep limestone canyons in eastern Utah. There'll be water and protection from the ash. Of course, the ash has stopped now."

"It seems Dad only made it as far as Grand Junction. At least, that's where he is now, maybe in the mountains north of there. The OPT is on his trail, trumping up charges against him to put him down. Dad's not afraid to die at the hands of evil men, but I don't think he'd mind if I showed up with a blazing battle rifle, do you?"

"Who you got with you?"

"Alice is back. Remember the one-armed woman?"

"The dark lady with the hard eyes. She has a good appetite, if I remember from the wedding."

"The wedding. Right." Rex sighed. "Lyla didn't make it, but Levi doesn't know yet. If he shows up here, someone should tell him so he's not looking for her."

"How'd she go?"

"Two cowards murdered her. God avenged her, though. Those were hard days, Trapper, running for our lives and hiding every night. But they were fruitful days, too. New friends were made. New brothers and sisters."

"But can they shoot those stumpy guns of yours?" Trapper jabbed a finger at Rex's rifle. "That's what matters if you're planning on running down to help out your dad."

"Yeah, they can shoot." Rex grinned. "We've had a long trek, but it sounds like it isn't over yet. Dad and Aunt Annette need us down at Grand Junction."

"Could you use some meat?" Trapper rose to his feet and picked up the candle. "I've got steers in the barn that're eating more feed than they're good for."

"Beef steaks?" Rex slapped his midsection. "Now you're speaking my language!"

An hour later, Rex was walking back to his dad's demolished cabin carrying twenty pounds of raw steaks wrapped in paper. It was after midnight now, but he was feeling energized by Trapper's good news as well as a time of prayer with the old saint.

Beyond his father's cabin, Rex moved toward the trees with caution, calling out twice to the low fire as he approached. He received no call back, but no one opened fire at him. Chuckling to himself, he walked up to the fire and lean-to to find his friends all fast asleep. Milo was beside the fire, rifle in his lap, his head tilted to the side as he snored. Alice and Miranda were laying on either side of Chloe under the lean-to.

Though Rex thought of waking them to share his news, he figured they needed their sleep more than an update. Until dawn, at least, he'd need to hold it all in. Still smiling, he lay the steaks on a rack he quickly fashioned, then stoked the fire and lay down across from Milo. He fell asleep thinking of how far God had brought them, and wishing he'd met Miranda during a time that they could've settled down together, even raised a family. Now more than ever, such luxuries needed to fit into the shifting backdrop of the events leading up to Christ's coming.

"Ouch!" someone exclaimed.

Rex was startled awake in the daylight by Milo as the man shook his fingers to cool them down. Having not learned his lesson, he used the same fingers to pluck a bronzed steak from the rack over the fire and tossed it onto a dinner plate that Chloe must've recovered from the ruined cabin.

"Steaks?" Miranda slapped Rex on the leg. "My stomach was rumbling all night, and you've got steaks on the fire?"

"That's not all I brought back." Rex sat up and stretched his back. Morning dew covered the grass in the clearing to the west. "I spoke to an old timer not far away, as well as the OPT Advocate, a guy I know named Wayne."

"So, the OPT knows we're here?" Chloe asked.

"Hold it." He lifted a hand to the COIL operative. "That's not the real news. Yeah, the OPT is onto us being here, but they also shared some intel. Dad's holed up somewhere down around Grand Junction, about two day's walk away. I need to get down there before the OPT pounces on him. He needs to know the good news."

"What's the good news?" Alice asked. "Oh, you mean the news that you're back?"

"Sure, that's good news, but I mean news that'll probably change everything for all of us—even the OPT." He licked his lips, searching their faces. "What've we been hoping for? What would change the tide of the OPT cornering the Casperteins up here in Colorado?"

"Uh, the rapture?" Miranda offered. "Quit playing and tell us!"

"Okay, okay." He raised his eyebrows. "Levi's on his way!"

"Levi's here?" Alice stopped chewing on her steak. "Where?"

"This changes everything!" Chloe gasped. "Yeah, tell us where!"

"I guess he's driving up through Oklahoma."

"Driving?" Milo asked. "Now that's the way to travel!"

"The OPT has been trying to catch him every step of the way through the south. Between Dad and Levi, the Caspertein name isn't a pleasant one on the ears of the OPT Advocates."

"I've asked this before: how could your cousin change everything for us?" Miranda asked. "We're still going to die if we're caught."

"You've never met Levi." Chloe sighed, munching on her steak, holding it with her bare fingers. "He's so much like Titus, his dad."

"He's fearless." Alice pounded her staff on the ground. "He's not afraid to run when it's time to run, but you've never seen anyone stand like him when he chooses to stand. He doesn't care about the odds."

"When I saw him on the bridge . . . that day in New York . . ." Chloe shook her head. "I knew we'd be okay. Somehow, having all of you Casperteins there to save us, I knew we'd make it, even though a whole army had us cornered."

"But he's just a man," Miranda insisted. "You talk about him like he's Moses or something."

"You're right," Rex agreed. "Levi would be the first to tell you he's nothing special. It's just that God gives him special things to do."

"And then he says stuff like . . ." Chloe cleared her throat to speak deeper. "It ain't easy being a nobody called to do something for somebody!"

They all laughed.

"Oh, you have to do that impression for him!" Alice laughed. "It'll make his day."

For a few moments, they ate their steaks in silence.

"I need to leave right now to get to Dad by tomorrow night, if he's where I think he is." Rex wiped his fingers on his pants. "Hopefully, it takes a few days for the OPT to get their forces together, too. We can regroup here with Levi and figure out where to go. Levi might even want to go on the offensive against the OPT. He'll have a plan in mind, even though he pretends like everything he does is spontaneous."

"It's a hundred miles down to Grand Junction?" Miranda asked softly, touching her calf muscle. "I'm not sure I can make it, Rex."

"We'll need to move quickly, even jog most of the way." Rex looked to Milo. "You up to it?"

"The way I feel, I think I'd just slow you down."

"Rex, how are you able to walk even a mile?" Chloe turned her head away. "We haven't eaten well in weeks. I wouldn't trust my legs to walk from here into Meeker right now."

"Well, you don't want to go into Meeker," Rex said. "Wayne may be an old friend, but he's fully OPT now. He's even executing Christians, so steer clear of town. If you see them coming out here, do like last year. Levi put someone up on the rimrock above and sent the Federation running. Alice was there."

"No problem." Alice nodded. "We'll hold 'em off."

"Then, it's decided." Rex wrapped two cooked steaks in paper and tucked them into his shirt. "Rest up here and be ready to receive the rest of us when we show up. It might be with the OPT on our tails. I'll fire a warning shot if we need cover fire."

"I can go up to the rimrock," Alice said. "If it takes you two days down and two days to get back, I'll be ready by then."

"A friend named Trapper says Dad married Annette, Levi's mom. I'm guessing she's with him, and knowing Dad, he'll have a few others under his wing, too."

"We'll be ready." Milo's weathered Federation uniform was worn through on the knees and elbows, but his eyes showed genuine care and readiness. "I can work on some defenses around here. With Chloe."

"Of course," Miranda stated, "if Levi arrives, we can just sit back, and he can handle everything."

"It won't be like that," Rex said, "but you'll see a real leader in action if he makes it here. You'll see."

"I've been with him the longest," Alice said. "He up-ended whole towns just by telling them about the gospel and helping them set things in order."

"Pray for me." Rex tightened his near-empty pack onto his back, then picked up his rifle. "And pray I get to Dad in time."

Rudy smiled at Annette as they shared a canteen during a break from constructing a small cabin on the side of the mountain far above Grand Junction. For a week and a half, they'd cut down trees and excavated the hillside to accommodate their needs. It had rained only once, so Rudy had fashioned their tarp as a cover over a temporary shelter to stay dry.

"Why are you smiling?" Annette asked.

"Do you think our bodies used to move faster than this?"

Annette choked on her water as she coughed and laughed. She wiped her mouth and passed the canteen back to her husband.

"I know for a fact my body is moving slower. I don't even remember needing so many rests."

"My body hurts all over." Rudy gazed down the hill at Vorca and Caleb as they walked across the grassy slope. Vorca stopped often, pointing out things for young Caleb to inspect. "A one-room cabin for the winter for four people."

"Yeah, I'm not laughing anymore." Annette followed his gaze. "This isn't the retirement home we dreamed of, is it?"

"Maybe we'll need to wait until heaven to retire."

Rudy picked up the tarp, which was to act as their waterproofed roof for the winter, supported and held down by wooden poles. Nearby, a long and narrow smokehouse crackled and snapped as they smoked the meat of a small deer Annette had shot two days earlier.

The stream gurgled quietly as it trickled into a rock-rimmed reservoir that Vorca had built with Caleb.

"Caspertein!" Vorca suddenly yelled. "Caspertein!"

So surprised was Rudy to hear Vorca say his name, that he guffawed and started to point out to Annette that he'd never heard Vorca call his name before. However, the words stopped in his throat as he realized the terror on Vorca's face. She stumbled over the uneven ground, catching up Caleb in her chubby arms.

Dropping the tarp, Rudy walked quickly to the side of the smokehouse where they'd heaped what few belongings they had until the roof was on the cabin. He picked up his rifle and threw his ammo vest over his shoulder. Only then did he browse the mountainside and tree line below for a bear or lion.

Vorca arrived at camp, speaking wildly in her native tongue to Annette. Only when she pointed down the mountain and over the treetops did Rudy feel the same dread that Vorca's face revealed.

"Rudy?" Annette turned to him.

"Stay here."

Calmly, he walked west to where Vorca had first called his name. His nerves were on edge and his stomach was in knots, so he intentionally resisted the urge to run, which would probably result in a fall over the rocky ground. When he reached where Vorca and Caleb had been studying plants, he gazed southward through a gap in the trees.

Grand Junction was in sight, as well as the brown plain to the east. The specks of travelers in the far distance seemed a normal sight. What wasn't normal, though, were the eight vehicles creeping up the grassy slope. They'd be forced to stop when they reached the field of boulders and tall trees, but then they'd come on foot.

Lowering to one knee, he used the rifle scope to study the enemy. The OPT wasn't leaving him alone. He guessed that tranquilizing Advocate Kane back in the gorge was something he wasn't getting away with. Days earlier, people on the highway had seen him leave the road and head into the mountains. The OPT had surely questioned pilgrims in and around the towns, describing Rudy's size, weapons, and traveling companions. Now, they were coming for him. No, they were coming for *all* of them, even Vorca.

Rudy glanced back at Annette on the mountainside. She was holding her rifle as well but was staring in his direction. Vorca was crouching behind the smokehouse with Caleb. Besides the smokehouse and the log cabin, Rudy realized he hadn't actually built anything that could be considered defendable fortifications. The logs of the cabin would stop a small caliber bullet, but he hadn't stacked rocks, or mounded earth, or dug any trenches.

Below and behind the eight vehicles, about forty foot-soldiers were marching, streaming slowly from other vehicles left on the highway. If they charged, they could reach his position in thirty minutes, maybe less. But there was no need for them to hurry. They had him trapped now.

He walked back to Annette, trying to steel himself with thoughts of Gideon, David, and Elijah.

"They're coming?" Annette asked. "How many?"

"Fifty or sixty. Too many." He turned toward the mountain. "We could head up, try to lose them on the plateau."

"In our condition?" Annette looked down at her hands, stained with pitch and weathered with callouses. "I could try, but I'm afraid I'd slow you down. You want me to pack up our stuff? We can live under the tarp during the nights. Why aren't you saying anything?"

"I didn't plan for this very well." He frowned. "It'll take time to climb that mountain. We'd be exposed. Those are real soldiers down there. They'd probably shoot us in the back as soon as they realized we were running away.

We're not worth the chase. Kane was just going to execute us, anyway, remember?"

First fury, then sorrow washed over Annette's face. Angrily, she wiped at her tears.

"They won't kill Caleb." Annette went to their gear and started packing a small pack. "Vorca can take him. She can live off the land better than anyone. You think?"

"Yeah." He picked up the tarp and hastily rolled it into a lumpy bundle. "We can cover her escape."

"Vorca? You're going with Caleb," Annette explained, pointing uphill. "Go. Run! Go back to Trapper Sullivan. Remember Trapper? You know Trapper. Go back to Meeker."

She forced the pack onto Vorca's back, then the young woman submitted to Rudy's hurried tying of the tarp onto the top of the pack.

"We'll be praying the whole time," Rudy said, wondering if she understood a single word. "Remember to trust in God. Tell Caleb about Jesus when he's old enough to understand."

Annette embraced Vorca, then directed her to flee. Vorca started and looked back several times before she seemed to accept that Rudy and Annette weren't coming with her.

Rudy set his jaw as he watched the woman leave with the child he considered a Caspertein as much as any other family member. Caleb was Levi's son as far as he was concerned.

"They'll be okay." Annette patted his arm. "Vorca will take care of him, even if she doesn't get back to Trapper."

"Yeah." Rudy faced the enemy, who were still not in sight from that position behind the treetops. "Let's do this."

"We have water and food," Annette pointed out. "We can wait them out in a standoff."

"But they have dozens of people." Rudy gestured uphill. "They'll get around and behind us. There won't be any standoff."

"Then what do we do?"

He smiled sadly down at her eagerness to fight, then took her shoulders in his hands.

"We know what to do. Kane is coming to make an example of us. So, we'll be an example for Christ."

"This kind of ending really stinks." She fought tears again and whipped her hand in the direction of the OPT. "I mean, *they're going to win!*"

"You know better than that." He chuckled. "In the end, we know who really wins. Right now, we face the final test. Then we stand in glory."

"How bad do you think it'll be?" Annette sniffed. "I mean, the treatment and all. The execution. You know me—I'm a whiner over a leg cramp."

"Just remember who this is for." He raised her chin with his finger. "That's who we focus on. Jesus died for us. This is our honor. We won't deny Him. That's what this is about. It's spiritual. Let God make our hearts soft right now, not hard. Maybe we can even touch some of their hearts through it."

"We'll see Titus soon." She smiled.

"That rascal? Wait a minute. Now I'm having second thoughts!"

They laughed together as he held her in his arms.

When the OPT emerged from the trees below, they did so all at once, coordinated. Rudy and Annette sat behind the smokehouse, which had a rock base and wooden sides, but they didn't duck down yet. Nor did Rudy use his rifle scope to look closer at the approaching troops, since he didn't want them to misinterpret his actions.

"Gel-tranqs?" Rudy asked Annette, and they both made sure they'd switched magazines from their hunting rounds back to non-lethal rounds.

At some unheard command, the line of soldiers below stopped, and Annette pointed to a smaller figure to the right of center.

"I think that's Kane. And look. They have a couple grenade launchers. That's what got us last time."

"She probably won't risk anything this time." Rudy studied them, counting to himself. Fifty-seven. "This is definitely overkill for two young women, a child, and an old man."

"There's an extra crown in heaven for you for calling me a young woman."

Squeezing her arm, he prayed aloud for them and for Vorca and Caleb. He mentioned the troops as well, who were about to kill them. Maybe they would see Christ through their deaths. As he was praying about their submission and trust in God's will, even in death, a trickle of rocks above alerted him. He glanced up to see Vorca with Caleb in her arms descending the mountain slope. *She was returning!*

"Vorca!" Annette gasped. "Why's she—"

"Look." Rudy pointed at a lone figure farther up, a man with a rifle standing on the ridgeline. His silhouette revealed that he was a large man, his shoulders like boulders. "They already got around and above us."

"Rudy," Annette said, "I don't think that's OPT."

Confused, he looked down at Kane, but she hadn't advanced. Instead, several of her nearest infantry had gathered around her. He turned back to the mountain and risked raising his rifle to scope past Vorca.

"That's Rex!" He shouted. Twice, he lowered the scope and checked the figure again. "That's Rex!"

Vorca reached them, jabbering an explanation not even Annette could decipher. Rudy stood and kept looking from Kane and her troopers then to Rex, who had descended the mountain to their position.

"She doesn't know what to do," Annette said of Kane.

"Rex might have more people with him. I don't think Kane was expecting other people to be with us."

"That makes two of us!" Rudy could barely restrain himself from running to his son, but he waited until the image of his younger self reached the camp and Rudy embraced him, laughing through his emotions. For a moment, thoughts of martyrdom had vanished, and the presence of his son overwhelmed him.

"Either this is a terrible time for you to reunite with us," Rudy said as Annette wept and clung to Rex as well, "or this is perfect timing. You see we have company?"

Rex laughed at his own emotions and dried his eyes.

"Yeah, I see that. Quite a party." Rex gazed from one end of the line of soldiers to the other. "Good thing I brought backup."

"You did?" Rudy grinned and subtly eyed the slopes of the mountain above. "Levi? Alice? The whole COIL army?"

"Well, no, not quite." Rex rubbed his bearded jaw. "The short version? Levi and Nathan Isaacson sort of beat down the Federation in New York, then took a southern route from there. Alice and I came across on I-80 with a bunch of refugees as far as Iowa. I haven't seen Levi in months, and I had to leave Alice and three others back in Meeker. It's been a hard journey, let me tell you! No, today, I came alone."

"But, you said you had backup," Annette's voice cracked.

"Oh, it's more in the form of good news." Rex nodded. "I got it out of Wayne Sullivan and the OPT that Levi is on his way by vehicle. He must be across Oklahoma by now and into Colorado."

"By vehicle?" Rudy smiled. "So, Levi is here."

"Levi!" Annette covered her mouth with her hand. "He's okay? Oh, praise God!"

"Yeah." Rex lowered his eyes. "But Lyla was killed back in New Jersey. A couple of snakes in the grass murdered her. Levi doesn't know yet. I'm not happy to be the one to tell him. He was trusting me with her life."

"Not Lyla!" Annette cried. "Oh, poor Levi . . ."

"Lyla was a strong Christian." Rudy set his hand on his wife's shoulder. "And Levi will understand you did what you could, Rex."

"So, what do we do now?" Annette asked.

The three faced the OPT.

"Now, I'm feeling some inspiration," Rudy said. "We warn Advocate Kane about the wrath of God."

"Mixed with a little Caspertein justice?" Rex offered.

"I don't see why not." Rudy considered their position. "Why don't you two spread out and cover me? I'm going down there to talk to Kane."

"What're you going to say?" Annette's face showed her worry.

"Would it be a bluff to say Levi is about to come through here like a tornado?"

"About Levi, you don't have to bluff." Rex scoffed. "He's probably already harnessed the whirlwind and he's about to let loose on the OPT himself."

"Then he won't mind that I'm about to bring him into our fight here?"

"Knowing Levi," Annette said, shaking her head, "like his dad, he'd be disappointed if you didn't!"

"Well, the Lord knows we need a bit of an Arkansas-style whirlwind right about now." Rudy waited a moment as Rex walked out onto the mountainside to stand where he had no cover, his hand on his rifle. Annette remained next to the smokehouse with Vorca and Caleb. "Now would be a good time to start praying."

"Start?" Annette adjusted her rifle sling. "Have we ever stopped?"

Rudy picked his way down the slope toward Kane. When he got close enough to see her face, he noticed that she didn't look worried, and her sidearm wasn't even drawn. And why would it be, Rudy thought sarcastically. She had fifty men aching to shoot him for her!

He stopped about twenty feet in front and a little above her. Rudy's rifle hung loosely at his side, but none of the soldiers moved to disarm him.

"I'm assuming you have terms of surrender?" Kane offered. Her red and black cape was clipped tightly under her chin, and her blonde hair appeared washed and recently trimmed to frame her face. "The OPT doesn't negotiate with administrators of instability."

"You're not really my enemy," Rudy said. "In more ways than one, I'm here to protect you from digging yourself into a deeper hole."

"What's that supposed to mean?" Kane shifted on her feet. "My patience is wearing thin after you ambushed us down by the river."

"Actually, I'm surprised you're bothering with me at all, Advocate Kane. You've got bigger problems than me to deal with." Rudy liked hearing the humor in his voice. It reminded him of Titus. "Levi Caspertein is on his way here."

"So, all you Casperteins are rallying from all over the county?" She tilted her head. "Others are dealing with him, I assure you. What other stall tactics do you have?"

"You really think someone's dealing with Levi Caspertein?" Rudy chuckled. "See that big kid up there? Well, he's not a kid anymore. That's my son. That's Rex Caspertein. Until he arrived from New York City a few minutes ago, my wife and I were all set to give in to your little army here. But then Rex came with news that Levi is in the area. Now, that changes everything."

"It changes nothing!" she spat.

"Well, you don't really know the facts yet." Rudy held up his hand. "Listen, this is Levi Caspertein, son of the world-famous gun smuggler, Titus Caspertein."

"Where's Titus Caspertein?"

"He's dead now, but he taught his son everything he knows. I mean, tactically. And then he taught him all about Jesus Christ and the power of the resurrection."

"So, he taught him. Big deal."

"Oh, it is a big deal. Levi's got a special hand of grace from God on his life. Just in the past year, he's brought the Pacific States to their knees and turned the Appalachian Federation inside out."

"So, he's a saboteur, nothing more." Kane pointed at Rudy's rifle. "If he shoots tranquilizers like you do, he's no real threat."

"No, of course he's not a threat as far as life and limb are concerned. I mean, he has phosphorus acid rounds that'll turn your vehicles into smoldering puddles of metal, but he won't kill anyone. I would think you'd be more concerned about his testimony—you know, if he speaks to your people."

"That shouldn't be a problem. There's a shoot-on-sight order for Levi Caspertein after the chaos he's caused in the south."

"Shoot-on-sight? That won't stop him. He's too agile and even more cautious. And he can out-shoot anyone you put against him. This is Levi Caspertein. When he walks into hostile towns and they hear his compassion for their lives, he brings them over to his way of seeing things. He shows God's love to strangers in unexpected ways, and just like that, people know they're serving the wrong authority. They turn to God when they hear him share what Jesus did on the cross for us all. If this sounds familiar, then you've probably already gotten reports about him. I can see it on your face."

"What reports?"

"Why shoot Levi Caspertein on sight?" Rudy smiled knowingly. "You know he's a threat, that's why. He's come through the south, like you said. That means all along Levi's route, he's ruined towns for the OPT. Those towns have witnessed Jesus' love in action, and they've thrown down their Oath of Solidarity to pick up their Bibles. Am I right?"

"You can't know that."

"But I do know that. People are starving inside for hope, and science won't give them what their Savior can. Remember, I'm a scientist, Ms. Kane. Have you forgotten? Tell me what you've heard about Levi over the months. Give me something. He's my nephew. What's the harm?"

"They are just rumors, nothing more." She scowled. "There's no way he's all you say he is."

"Let me guess, since you won't tell me specifics. Towns have witnessed extraordinary acts of self-sacrifice and even mercy coming from Levi."

"Shut up. Those things will fade away."

"Levi has cared for people who expected something horrible, and now their hearts are changed. That means you've stopped hearing from some towns, or they're no longer cooperating with regional Advocates. They're harboring Christians, or they've become believers in Jesus themselves, setting aside the unreasonable demands of the OPT to have exclusive trust in science and humanity's failing progress."

Rudy could see that his words were having an effect on Kane. She licked her thin lips, in obviously concern.

"No religion is that powerful," she said.

"Of course not. God is a Person, not a religion. Jesus is God in the flesh, sovereign and holy and loving. He's not an idea that can come and go. You can't execute a truth. He's Jesus eternal, and people learn by connecting themselves to Him in faith so they're rescued from their own mortality forever. We may die, but we'll be resurrected to live in glory forever. That's why it's called resurrection power. Yeah, it's that powerful. That's the weapon Levi is marching here to wield like the sword it is. And you're wasting your time with *me?*"

"So, you don't have the same power?"

"The Lord is in me, but I'm an old man now. God gave me a different path than He gave my brother, Titus, and now Levi."

Her eyes drifted past Rudy, and he saw her take in Rex's position, then Annette's.

"And now you think because Levi is here that I won't remove you from being a headache?"

"You can spend the time removing me." Rudy nodded. "That's what I'd expect you to do. Every minute you spend with me buys Levi more time with whoever you sent to face him. I'm no ballistics expert like Levi, but I'm pretty sure my wife and son up there, who have elevated positions and a little cover, will have tactical advantage over you."

"We'll flank you and go higher."

"We'll go higher still." Rudy tapped his finger on his rifle. "My objective is to tangle you up here, not defeat you. Levi's crippling your forces as we speak. He's winning them over. The kid's got charm, I tell you. If you stay on the path you're on, you'll meet him yourself, and you'll see."

Kane stared at him for a few seconds, then turned away. From her belt, she drew a handheld radio and put it to her mouth.

"Timbrook, come in. This is Kane. Do you read me? Timbrook, come in."

While Kane wasn't paying attention to him, Rudy spotted his moment to leave, shrugging at the many soldiers standing nearby. They looked to her as she busied herself with the radio. Rudy wondered if the army would do anything without her orders.

"Do you read me, Timbrook? This is Kane! Do not engage Levi Caspertein. I repeat, do *not* engage Levi Caspertein! Stand down. Do not communicate with him, and do not fire upon him. Timbrook, do you read me?"

Rudy turned his back on her and started climbing the mountain, careful not to get in Rex's line of fire with Kane.

"Timbrook? Does anyone on I-70 read me?"

A garbled communication came back. Rudy kept climbing, distancing himself, expecting a barrage of automatic gunfire, but hoping it wouldn't come.

"Repeat your last! This is Advocate Kane. Come in, anyone on I-70. I need to relay a message to Defender Timbrook!"

After a few more seconds, Rudy was high enough where he could no longer hear her attempted contact on the radio. He focused on reaching Annette and the smokehouse.

Then, he arrived, and turned around to face down the slope. At that moment, Kane spun toward him. He couldn't see her face at that distance, but by her body language, she was startled to not find Rudy still standing there. She spoke wildly to those nearest her, clearly reprimanding them for allowing Rudy to return up the mountain.

"She's mad about something," Rex hollered at him from the mountainside. "Should we take cover now?"

Rudy sidestepped toward Annette but kept his eye on Kane and the line of soldiers.

"Nice and easy, Rex, walk toward me."

"Sorry, Dad. It's not time for nice and easy. They have fifty guns, and we have three. Aunt Annette, you take out the rocket launchers, Dad and I will start on the ends."

"The ends?" Rudy eyed the soldiers skeptically, their own uncertainty obvious from that distance. "What's that mean?"

"The ends! The ends of their column. Take out the ends, and you'll stop them from flanking. You'll force their center to retreat or advance."

"I didn't teach you that."

"No, but spending a year with Levi did. Aunt Annette, now!"

Her rifle boomed next to Rudy, and he ducked momentarily. But an instant later, he rose over the smokehouse and aimed at the left-most soldier. Rex was already firing, hardly taking time to aim, it seemed, but soldiers were dropping on the right.

Rudy gauged the distance downhill to be about two hundred yards, so he knew from shooting caribou in Alaska and deer in Colorado to aim low. Unfortunate for the OPT, they didn't seem to know that shooting uphill required a huge adjustment for gravity. Their bullets started to smack the dirt and rocks far short of the smokehouse, and with so many firing, no one was correcting their aim.

It was several more seconds before Rex reached cover behind the nearly-completed cabin. By then, eight soldiers had dropped, and only three of them by Rudy's rifle. One last grenadier fumbled with his firing tube until Annette put him down, then she pivoted to help Rudy.

"Get down here!" Annette ordered him, yanking on his sleeve. "You're too exposed up there!"

"We're all exposed!" he shouted over the firing.

"No, look." She pointed at the east end of the smokehouse. "You're needed to shoot at only one man at a time on the end, so you expose yourself to only one gun at a time. I'll fire first. While I reload, you take over. Got it?"

So impressed was Rudy, he could only nod once sharply. Then she turned and started firing systematically. He expected no less from a woman who had lived with Titus for twenty years, but he hadn't realized her actual combat expertise until then.

Sure enough, when he looked back at the cabin, Rex wasn't even in sight, revealing himself only to the next target on his end, one at a time.

Before Annette tapped him to take his turn, Rudy checked the center of the OPT line. As predicted, they were retreating, firing with Kane as they stepped away and into the trees.

When Rudy moved into position, he patted Vorca on the shoulder, making sure she knew to stay down. She protected Caleb with her whole body, her hands covering his ears. Any other child would've been screaming from the noise or danger, but Caleb wasn't one to cry often.

Rudy fell only two more targets, then realized there was no one left.

"Careful!" Rex called. "They managed to grab one grenade launcher while they retreated into the trees!"

As he scoped the trees, Rudy felt dread in his heart. One grenade would decimate the smokehouse along with the four souls behind it. But the tree boughs were low and their cover so dense that a launcher would need to step from cover to fire. He searched for such a grenadier until he lowered his rifle and looked back at Annette.

"They won't be any better at firing grenades uphill," he said, "than they were at shooting uphill. I think we'll be okay."

A breath later, Rex's rifle thundered, and a wayward grenade hissed across the slope and exploded three hundred yards downrange. The whole mountain shook.

"I got one," Rex called, "but someone else might pick it up and try."

Both Annette and Rudy watched the trees for another attempt to fire the launcher. Then, out on the plain, Rudy noticed about a dozen soldiers moving away, back toward the vehicles, abandoning those that were unconscious in the clearing.

"Kane probably went back to her truck for a radio with a longer range," Rudy said. "She's worried Levi will influence the soldiers she sent to confront him."

"Wonder who gave her that idea." Annette cast him a knowing look. "Levi can take care of himself, but we don't need to make it unnecessarily difficult for him."

Rex rushed from the cover of the cabin to the smokehouse. No one fired at him. He skidded to a stop against his father.

"We've got an hour until sundown," he said. "It'll take that long for those twenty or thirty to wake up. I suggest we prepare to evacuate in the dark."

"And go where?" Annette asked.

"I'm pretty sure Kane won't follow us across the upper plateau," Rex said. "Alice and my other shooters are at your old cabin. They'll hold that position using the rimrock until we show up."

"But Kane will expect us to return to Meeker," Rudy said. "It's our familiar ground. Wayne's there, and Kane will know she can trap us there."

"She doesn't know we have Alice, Chloe, Milo, and Miranda there waiting." Rex grinned. "And we're not even counting yet what Levi's bringing to the fight. You know that's where he's going. He's going home."

"Then we go home, too." Rudy nodded and confirmed the decision in each of their faces. "We're going home."

Levi never thought he'd be involved in a car chase two decades after the collapse of America. It was a low-speed chase to conserve fuel, but it was a chase nevertheless.

"I think they're gaining on us," Mia judged as she gazed out the back of the Suburban. Since they'd left the trailer with the released Christians back on the Arkansas-Oklahoma border, they could see the headlights of another vehicle far behind. "What do you think, Cuz?"

From the very rear of the Suburban where Levi lay on top of their gear with Auggie, he passed a pair of binoculars to his cousin.

"Try these," he said. "Tell us what you see. Slow and steady, Brian, Keep it under forty. Watch for washouts or bridge collapses."

Brian didn't respond as he drove with both hands on the wheel. At the moment, Jenna wasn't seated beside him since Levi wanted everyone in the front seat to help Brian keep an eye out for danger. Their headlights were low and dim, casting an orange haze only twenty yards ahead.

"Wait a minute," Mia said. "I'm seeing glimpses of more than one pair of headlights!"

"That's what I thought." Levi drew his battle rifle under him, laying prone in the back, but at an angle to accommodate his size. "Change of plans, Brian. Slow to a stop and turn off our lights. No brake lights."

"Cover your ears, people!" Brian warned.

He stopped the Suburban, and Kip walked around outside to open up the back gate. Auggie jumped out, and Levi settled into his position a little better, resting his muzzle past the threshold of the vehicle door so he didn't blow out the windows. Ryan took Brandy's newborn to the front of the vehicle where the noise wouldn't be as loud.

"They're about a quarter-mile back right now," Levi reported softly. "Kip, wind?"

"I don't feel any," he said from the side of the Suburban. "But I can't even see the grass or trees around us to get a read."

"Everyone's covering their ears?" Levi warned. He aimed between the headlights far away, then adjusted for the distance by a few feet. "Three, two, one . . ."

When the gun boomed, his own ears rang, but he shook his head and applied his eye to the scope. No one spoke as he observed the situation. He'd fired a phosphorus round straight into the grill of the lead vehicle.

"It looks like they're stopping." He smiled. "And there's vehicle number two pulling alongside."

"They probably think they just blew a radiator hose or something," Jenna said. "Levi, give us another countdown again if you—"

"Three, two, one . . ."

Boom! Levi watched the second vehicle's headlights as the first vehicle's lights blinked out. He imagined the acid had eaten through wiring and shorted out the electronics in front of the grill.

A moment later, the second vehicle's headlights went out, and two or three smaller lights hovered over the dark scene. They were flashlights, he guessed, held by personnel inspecting the damage.

"That's a wrap." Levi ejected his phosphorus magazine for the safer gel-tranqs. "How about we get a few more miles in, Brian, then find a camping spot?"

Ryan climbed into the backseat with the crying newborn, and Auggie leaped into the back with Levi when she was called. Kip closed the back gate and Brian continued ahead, the headlights on now that the pressure was off from behind.

"Anyone seen a sign?" Andy asked from the backseat where he sat beside Brandy. "We must be in Colorado by now."

"We could reach Meeker by tomorrow night," Jenna said. "Are they ready to take in nine wanderers and a fusser?"

"Come on," Levi said. "I don't fuss that much."

"She was talking about my baby," Brandy said, "but he doesn't fuss that much."

"They know," Andy said softly. "They were just joking. I bet he'd cry less if you held him. He's already known you for nine months. That's nine more months than he's known any of us."

Levi put an arm around Auggie and pushed the dog's head away from his own to breathe in another direction. Along with everyone else, he waited in silence for Brandy's response. Andy actually hadn't been too bad at encouraging her to accept her baby, but she'd remained distant.

"I guess it wouldn't hurt," Brandy finally said. "You know, to help him stop crying."

Smiling in the darkness of the back of the Suburban, Levi thanked God for a prayer answered. There were already enough orphans in the world.

"Where are we at with a name for this little bear cub?" Ryan asked as he passed the baby to Brandy. "Now that I think of it, Cub isn't a bad name!"

"We've all had our say," Mia said. "I think Brandy should decide the winner. She's his mom."

"Well, I . . ." Brandy cradled the child, then turned to Andy. "I sort of like your idea. Weston, because we're going west."

"Weston Sorvino?" Brian asked. "I was rooting for Nathanael, but I can work with Weston."

"Weston, going once," Mia said. "Weston, going twice. Sold to Andy! Weston Sorvino it is. Winning comes with perks, Andy. You have to change little Weston for the next week."

"Oh, no, you don't!" Andy protested. "I changed a diaper back at River Camp and couldn't wash the stink off me for two days!"

"Then you were doing something wrong!" Jenna laughed. "It's the baby you're supposed to clean up, Andy. I'd change him, Brandy, but I'd just make a bigger mess."

"So, I think all the name-picking losers should change him for a week," Andy voiced. "What do you think, Brandy?"

"I'll change him," she said quietly. "If I feed him, I guess I can change him."

"Well, we'll all help you," Ryan said. "I think I'm the one he smiles at the most, anyway."

"Speaking of changing," Levi said, "this is probably far enough, Brian."

"Oh, Weston!" Kip gasped. "Phew! This is definitely far enough. Must . . .breathe . . .fresh air."

They found a shallow gorge off the highway that showed the promise of a creek nearby, but after inspecting the area in the headlights of the Suburban, Levi and Brian found none. Nevertheless, they set up camp and planned to just go to sleep rather than use much water for washing.

Ryan had been proving himself useful, and that late night he strung a rope overhead and hung a tarp for the four women and the baby. However, when Levi bedded down partially under the front of the Suburban, Lena unrolled her bedroll behind the front wheel a few feet away. Brian made sure the women, especially Jenna, had what they needed, then he lay down at the far end of the vehicle, his antique rifle at his side.

For a moment, Levi watched Andy use his crutches to scout the edges of the clearing they'd chosen. Then, he knelt to lay out a blanket Levi had given him. After a while, Auggie joined Andy, groaned through a yawn, and lay down next to him.

"I remember when you were where he is," Levi said to Lena. "Remember those weeks? You were struggling between leaving one life and accepting your new one. You could never go back to the Federation. That's where he is right now. He can never go back to what he was. But he's still fighting the Lord's calling."

"Aah," Lena agreed. "Aah-ahah, hagh-aah."

"Yeah," Levi said. "The Lord will break him down. He broke each of us down."

In the morning, the dawn was cool but clear, and Levi walked out to the highway while the others picked up camp. Out on the pavement, he found Andy on his crutches. Levi gazed to the east, looking for signs of the OPT, but he noticed Andy studying the pavement where the Suburban hadn't yet driven.

"Old habits die hard." Levi joined Andy, acknowledging the tracks on the dusty road. "See anything?"

"Some habits never die." Andy's voice wasn't hard like it had been a few days earlier. "I don't need two feet to read sign."

"What do you read?" Levi passed Andy a stick of dried meat.

"There's a vehicle ahead of us." Andy looked back at where the Suburban tracks turned off, but the other tracks continued. "We were behind it in the night. They may have seen us while we were so concerned about who was following us."

"They definitely saw us," Levi said.

Andy was quiet a moment.

"No, I can't tell that from the tracks."

"I can." Levi pointed. "See? Someone walked really careful inside those tire prints, probably to see where we were camping, then they walked back."

"Impressive you saw that."

"My dad trained me to read sign like your dad trained you."

"My dad trained me to track elk, bear, and cats." Andy frowned. "I took that a step further later on."

"Yeah, I guess you did."

"You know," Andy said, "I'm not bad like you think. "I'm a whole level worse than you could ever imagine. The things I've done . . ."

"If you think I care, you're misunderstanding God's *agape* love that I have for you."

"No. I'm telling you because I can't go home. People like my dad would be able to tell. I won't have to tell him. He'll know I've killed people, tracked them down for favors or supplies, and cut them down with my bare hands."

"He might know, or he might not know," Levi said. "What matters is who you are now, not what you've done or who knows it."

"I'm the same person—minus that one thing you're tired of me talking about."

"Who do you want to be?"

"It's pointless to fantasize." Andy's lip trembled. "I can't erase the past."

"Maybe you can't, but our God can."

"So, I just move on?"

"No, you die to yourself and turn toward God for life. I know you know what it means to be born again. You just lack the proper humility to let God make you new. If your dad really is a Christian, then he won't care about the remnants of your past. He'll rejoice to see what God has done inside you, no matter what it took."

With his crutches, Andy went up the highway twenty paces, then turned around.

"Weston will need a father. You know, Brandy picked my name for him. That's got to mean something, right?"

"It means something, but I've told you before, I don't think you'll be the man you should be until you allow God to have His way in you. That includes fatherhood. Or being a husband, if you have that in mind."

"You think she'd take an old bounty hunter for, you know, to marry?"

"Brandy's a Christian, Andy. That's why she refused the Oath. She's upset about her ex-husband abandoning her, and she was reacting wrongly with Weston. But she's pulling herself together, partly because of how you're helping her. But marriage—she'll want a Christian example for Weston, and someone who loves her through the ups and downs of being that close to someone. And she might be more concerned about her own baggage than you are about yours."

"I hadn't thought of that. Huh." He scuffed one crutch at the tracks on the highway. "What're we gonna do about this truck in front of us?"

"What would you do? You're part of this now, Andy."

"Hmm, I don't know." He gazed to the northwest. "The OPT knows we're coming."

"Seems so."

"So, they're waiting for us. Somewhere."

"Probably."

"Whoever these prints belong to, it's probably a scout for them."

"Could be."

"It's an ambush," Andy stated. "We're driving into an ambush!"

"Or we'll walk into an ambush if we run out of fuel in the next hundred miles."

"I can't go across land. I'll need to get on the bike, but being on a bike won't solve anything. Ryan's got the .22 rifle. Brian, Lena, Mia, and you have rifles. It's not much against a whole unit, depending on what the OPT can put together. Then again, in the right area, you could use the range of your rifles against them. You just disabled a couple trucks at a quarter-mile. I've not heard of anyone doing that."

"Distance is our advantage. If we're close, their numbers will overwhelm us. So, how can we control the battlefield wherever they're choosing to fight us?"

"Drive slowly so we see them ahead of time. If I was paying attention, I'd know what to watch for. I'd see a trap before we got there."

"Okay." Levi nodded. "Let's tell the others."

Kip didn't protest when Levi asked him to drive. Although Kip had been trained with the Pacific States, he hadn't fired a gun in over a year, but Levi wanted someone with calm nerves at the wheel. That left the five shooters ready to pile out the doors and take up their positions. Levi and Ryan were to take the center, while Mia took the left flank, and Brian took the right. Lena would be the last to get into position, moving as far behind the enemy as she could.

Levi had known they'd have to face off against the OPT sooner or later. For days, they'd been squeaking through the towns they'd had to stop at and avoiding other locations where they knew the OPT had a larger presence. With the exception of not having Rex, Alice, and Lyla at his side, Levi was confident with the team he had with him. Lena was army-trained, and Brian was a natural marksman with years of Federation experience. Since Levi had trained Mia to shoot, he knew her skill the best.

Jenna agreed to ride in the very back and keep Auggie company with the gear. Levi didn't mean to exclude her, but he knew she'd understand that she couldn't be in the way during the urgent activity that could occur. However, there were things that Jenna could do better than others, even at that moment, and it was her sweet voice of calm that prayed for them as Kip drove slowly northwest through Colorado. Everyone's eyes were focused ahead for the earliest possible warning of danger.

"Maybe there's no one out there after all," Brandy suggested after two hours of driving.

"No, they're out there," Andy insisted from his position next to Kip where the tracker's keen eyes could help spot danger. "That's what an enemy wants you to think—that there's no danger. But they're waiting. They have a hiding place. They've picked something where we'll be blind to their presence until we're suddenly right on top of them. It's what I would do."

Due to a bridge washout, Kip backtracked a mile where the party was forced to take I-25 north. They came upon the small town of Trinidad.

"Earthquake damage." Andy pointed at a ramp ahead. "We'll need to go through town."

Kip pulled off the freeway and cruised through at only twenty miles an hour, spying empty neighborhoods and deserted shops. In some lanes, the pavement had fallen away, and garbage and cars that had been abandoned twenty years earlier blocked whole avenues.

Parts of Trinidad had been burned or dismantled for firewood, but Levi noticed curtains on windows and laundry lines, which gave evidence that there were still inhabitants.

At the Purgatoire River, Kip stopped, and Levi ran down to the water to check it. He returned to the Suburban a moment later.

"Too polluted." He climbed back into the passenger seat. "No point wasting the few filters we've got left on that sewage. We'll find something cleaner out in the country."

At the turnoff to Highway 12, Kip stopped again while Andy, Ryan, and Levi studied an old highway map in the front seat. Brian leaned up from the backseat. Since he'd traveled that way before, his input was essential. Otherwise, the passengers were silent and tense. Even Jenna's quiet voice of prayer from the far back had ceased.

"We could take the 12 west," Brian said, "then take the 285 north. But if we run into another washout, we'll be stranded out in the middle of nowhere."

"Our fuel's low, too," Kip reminded.

"So, our choice is between a smaller, safer highway that may be a waste of time because of earthquake damage," Levi said, "or a larger, riskier freeway that'll get us closer to Meeker in hours."

"The OPT will be more frequent on the interstate," Mia said. "How eager are we to get into a face-off with them?"

"I don't know that it's altogether avoidable." Levi looked away from the map. All he wanted to do was get across Colorado. He was certain Lyla had already reached Meeker. "No matter what the OPT may be doing, I've got my own reasons to go north the fastest way. But you all need to decide for yourselves. Kip, tally the vote, and that's the way we'll go."

Before they continued their discussion, Levi climbed out of the Suburban and walked back down the interstate a few yards. The journey was almost over, but he couldn't shake the sense that God was bracing him for the most difficult hurdle still to come.

"Give me strength, Lord, " he prayed, "and mercy. Don't let me be selfish. If I die, let it be for a purpose. Let me see the opportunity for You through it. Don't waste my death, Lord, please."

He returned to the vehicle.

"It's unanimous," Kip announced. "We'll take the fastest route to Meeker, and we trust God to go before us when it comes to danger."

"Then onward." Levi closed the door and turned in his seat to look upon the faces of his friends. "Either way, we're meeting the Lord soon. Everyone's ready?"

They nodded solemnly. Levi knew they were taking spiritual inventory before God and were ready to enter eternity in a state of submission, liberty, and consecration. No grudge was held, and no charge was felt. In the arms of Jesus, they were His faithful saints. They had taken no Oath, and they served no other god. With a clear conscience, they were all facing the next stretch of road together.

Except for Andy. But Levi didn't pressure the young man. As the exception in the vehicle, the tracker and hunter had the necessary instincts to know he was the odd one in the cab of evens. Instead, Levi watched out the window and prayed for the man who'd been hired to kill him.

At Walsenburg, everyone agreed to take the 160 west to avoid Denver, but privately, Levi wondered if they had yet again chosen the predictable route. They passed La Veta and Blanca, which weren't abandoned, but Levi recommended they not stop. When they turned north on 285, the Suburban lurched. The gas gauge had finally dropped below the *E*.

"Stop!" Andy shouted, and Kip obeyed.

Everyone was jostled around in their seats as the Suburban halted on squeaky brakes. Levi leaned forward to peer through the windshield. There was a high bluff with vegetation on top, and the highway curved around a blind bend to the left. On the right was an open plain.

"Ambush alley," Levi acknowledged. "We don't know what's around this bend, so everyone prepare like this is the real deal. Mia, handle that ridge. Brian and Lena, go wide to the right. Ryan, you're with me."

The five shooters climbed out of the vehicle. Brian and Lena hopped the ditch and jogged away, straight east.

"Mia, here." Levi gave her the pistol with the built-in silencer. "If there's someone on the ridge, I think we're too close to the bluff for them to see us right here. It's probably just one or two people, if this is where they're springing a trap. Take them out silently from behind."

"You should be doing this, Cuz!" Mia was shaking. "Really, you want me to go alone?"

"If you're quiet, they won't see or hear you coming. Look, they're probably already watching to see what Brian and Lena are doing. And they'll be watching the road, too, not the back door."

"Okay. I can do this. You're counting on me."

"We all are. I'll give you a couple minutes, then we'll go around that curve."

She hefted the handgun's weight in her hand a couple times, then stuck it in her belt. Though she was still slender from her days of starvation, she didn't seem to lack in energy as she charged off the highway and up the wooded hillside.

"I've never done anything like this before." Ryan licked his lips. "Deer, pigs, and dogs are all I've ever shot at."

"The enemy doesn't know that. If there's anyone around that bend, and they start shooting, you take the left ditch for cover and I'll take the right. We have sharpshooters who'll cover us. Then we can return fire. The gel-tranqs will fire like real bullets, so make sure you're in range with that .22 rifle."

Ryan and Levi started walking up the center of the highway. Kip turned off the engine to conserve the last of their fuel and stayed back with the vehicle. Levi resisted the urge to look up to the left to check on Mia's progress on the ridge. He knew this wasn't her first gunfight.

Levi was the first to round the bluff and see the three vehicles parked on the highway. He stopped in the middle of the road, only eighty yards from the blockade.

"Good thing Andy spotted this possibility," he said to Ryan. "We would've driven right into them. I count . . . about twenty."

"Some guys on the sides, too."

Squinting, Levi could see the OPT soldiers standing behind the vehicles, only their heads and shoulders visible. One man was standing on a doorstep of a Jeep with binoculars aimed toward the two approaching gunmen.

"Our shooters probably aren't in place yet," Levi said to Ryan. "Let's buy them a little more time and sling our rifles."

"They could start shooting!"

"Well, they're not shooting yet." Levi moved his rifle behind his shoulder to hang on its sling. "Maybe they won't shoot if we don't antagonize them. Keep your hands in sight, palms open, and walk real slow. The longer we take, the better position our cover shooters will find."

"What if they saw our cover shooters run out there?"

"Our people will stay out of range of small arms fire." Levi took small steps forward. "They won't seem like a threat until they start firing. The OPT probably doesn't know about our range superiority yet."

"Except you and I are in the OPT's range," Ryan said. "What about that?"

"Somebody's got to be the rodeo clowns." Levi laughed. "It may as well be us who know where we're going if the bull wins the rodeo."

"You have a weird sense of humor."

"It's just my nerves," Levi said. "You can ignore me. Everyone else does. I don't mind."

They advanced on the OPT blockade until they were fifty feet away. The man who'd been on the radio stood up taller behind the hood of one vehicle.

"That's far enough!" he yelled.

Levi and Ryan stopped side by side.

"I don't like this . . ." Ryan said under his breath.

"Be cool," Levi said. "It ain't easy being brave while looking down the muzzles of twenty guns."

"What do we do?"

"Offer them grace. They need it." Levi noticed the great caution the OPT was using. "They're in much more trouble than we are."

"They have more guns."

"Doesn't matter." Levi narrowed his eyes. "They're afraid of eternal judgment and we're not."

"So that's it?" Ryan's voice broke. "Your plan is to beat them to eternity?"

"No." Levi chuckled. "They may have more guns, Ryan, but our guns are bigger. They're at our mercy."

"I think . . . we're at *their* mercy. I'm not sure—"

"Just listen." Levi waved his right hand at the men. "Hello there. It's a pleasure to meet you. My name is Levi Caspertein."

"We know who you are, Levi Caspertein!" The leader barked back. From what Levi could see, his face was leathery, his eyes squinty. On the belt of his leather pants, he wore a bowie knife. "We have orders to shoot you on sight!"

"Well, you haven't fired a shot," Levi yelled. "So, I'll assume you're surrendering before I decimate your unit and destroy your vehicles."

"Surrend—?" The man glanced at his people. "We're not surrendering! We're not shooting you because you're the ones who're surrendering!"

"No, I thought you were surrendering," Levi pressed, "because you realized we've got the high ground and we have you surrounded. The one who's surrounded is the one who usually surrenders. Didn't they teach you that in OPT military school? What's your name, soldier?"

"Uh, Timbrook. Just a minute. Don't you move, Levi Caspertein!"

The Defender conferred with his nearest men and a

few women. One rifleman set down his weapon and used binoculars to peer up at the high bluff.

"My people already took the ridge," Levi said. "I also have other shooters north and east of you. They're sharpshooters, firing a .308 caliber. They can hit a watermelon at five hundred yards. Do you know what phosphorus is?"

"No." Timbrook gazed far to the east into the plain. "What's phosphorus?"

"One phosphorus round into the front of your Humvee will ruin the engine block. It'll eat away the whole thing like acid. If I know you OPT people, your vehicles are more important to you than your own lives. We won't kill you because we want to show you the love of Jesus. But we'll sure as the sky is blue burn your vehicles to the pavement if you open fire."

"If you do anything," Timbrook shouted, "I will shoot you dead where you stand!"

"Timbrook, you're not hearing me." Levi rested his hands on his hips. "I've already told you I'm not going to kill you. You're hearing from my own mouth that I'm not your enemy. My rifle is on my back. Step out here and let's talk before this goes south. I don't want to die, and you don't want to lose your vehicles. It ain't easy getting stranded on foot in the middle of Colorado's wilderness, so let's talk this out."

"I don't believe," Timbrook said, "that you have shooters out there."

Nodding, Levi guessed only Timbrook's man or two on the bluff had seen him deploy shooters into the plain. By now, Mia would have tranqed the hidden soldiers.

He was close enough to see Timbrook turn his head and speak quietly to those around him. Levi couldn't hear what was said but he wasn't taking chances. Timbrook's command to his people looked like an order to open fire.

Shoving Ryan to the left, Levi leaped to the right. Gunfire blasted from Timbrook while Levi dove through midair. He landed on the inside slope of the ditch, rolled over, then belly-crawled back up to the edge of the road. Keeping his head and elbows down, he moved his rifle from its sling to his arm, even as dirt bit his scalp from ricocheted bullets.

The popping of small arms fired from Timbrook's soldiers became scattered as a louder and more distant thunder rolled across the landscape. Mia had opened fire from the bluff, and there was Brian's antique rifle barking at intervals in a lower pitch since his barrel was longer. Then from the north, Lena's rifle boomed once, then again.

From the ditch, Levi raised his head to see what his ears had already heard. The OPT had begun to drop. Those still conscious scrambled for cover, but there was no cover. Mia commanded the scene from on high. Brian was raking their left flank, and Lena was nearly behind them. To make the OPT's situation worse, Levi heard Ryan open fire, which meant the young man with the .22 rifle had reached his ditch safely.

Levi leveled his rifle only high enough to fire over the ditch and under the vehicles at the exposed soldiers' legs. He tranqed them where they knelt, stood, huddled, or cried in fear. They screamed as they were shot with tranquilizers, and Levi pitied them as they feared their deaths that weren't actually occurring yet.

Two final soldiers were hiding where two of their three vehicles gave them minimal cover from the long-range shooters. Levi rose to his feet, a fresh magazine in his rifle, and prowled closer to the nearest Humvee. One soldier spied Levi's approach and called a warning to his friend. Levi's rifle was already raised, so he fired three shots rapidly over the hood, tranqing both men.

Ryan rushed up to Levi's side.

"Check your head," Levi said.

The young man rubbed his fingers on his hairline and his hand came away bloody.

"Oh, it's nothing. I fell." Ryan grinned. "All those bullets, and I almost killed myself on a piece of farming equipment down there in the grass."

"It ain't easy leading with your head." Levi pointed at the farthest vehicle. "Circle around that way. Watch out for anyone who may have scattered."

Until Ryan finished his sweep, Levi held his ground and remained vigilant. When Ryan shook his head, signaling that he'd found no other conscious OPT soldiers, Levi waved the others in from their positions.

"Go get Kip," Levi said to Ryan. "Bring the Suburban up here. We'll pick the best two vehicles and push north. We're almost home."

Ryan jogged down the road, and Levi collected the rifles of twenty-four OPT personnel. When Lena arrived, she climbed directly onto the rear Humvee and kept watch with her rifle.

"Good shooting, Lena," Levi said.

"Aah."

"I tried to get them to surrender."

"Aah."

"I'd guess we're probably not done with these OPT characters."

"Aah."

"Unless you want to take the Oath of Solidarity and make this life a bit easier?"

She scowled at him, which made him chuckle.

Kip drove the Suburban up and everyone piled out. Andy was one of the last as he fit his crutches under his arms and hobbled up to Levi. Auggie zipped from downed soldier to Humvee wheel, her nose investigating the latest scents.

"What I would've given to have been here for this!" Andy whistled at the scene of battle. "How are you still alive?"

"The same way I'm still alive from your shenanigans," Levi said.

"Of course." Andy rolled his eyes. "God."

"You can't call it luck. This happens too often." Levi shook Brian's hand as the shooter walked up. "But don't worry, Andy. I'm not invincible. When the Lord is finished with me, I'll die like any other man, except I'll have a smile on my face."

"Going to heaven?" Brian asked. "I didn't hear your whole conversation, but I'm ready to go with a smile on my face, too."

Andy put his head down and said nothing more. Brandy stood beside him, cradling Weston in her arms.

When Mia arrived from the bluff, Levi put his arm around her as she admired her handiwork. Kip and Ryan were taking inventory of the vehicles, and Brian took Jenna aside to tell her his part in the excitement.

"I'm a little nervous to see Aunt Annette again," Mia said to Levi. "She'll want to know about the baby, but I'm trying to move forward with my emotions."

"You've taken your time to grieve," Levi said. "Now you might need to help her take her time to grieve, too."

"She was so against me marrying Kip." She blushed. "You remember why."

"Yeah, I was there." Levi sighed. "By now, Mom'll see God's hand in things. Losing the baby isn't something we'll fully understand this side of heaven, but you've learned to trust that God knows why, that He's still loving and has a purpose in this madness."

"So, you think this'll be bad?" she asked. "I mean, when we get to Meeker?"

"Seems we're expected. The OPT might've already taken Mom and Uncle Rudy."

"It's possible, I guess, that we're walking into that, too, isn't it?"

"I'd say so."

"Maybe God wanted me to help you against the OPT." She patted her rifle. "I couldn't have done this with a baby in my arms, Cuz."

"That's true."

"Does that make me a bad mother for saying that?"

"No. It makes you a mother who's open to God's reasons in the wake of losing her baby." He pulled her into a hug. "You know, you're not the only one who's nervous about the end of this journey."

"I've thought about it. You said Chloe is with the other group. Lena and Chloe will be meeting?"

"There's a bad past there." Levi lowered his voice. "Lena killed Corban Dowler. I hope Lena has grown in the last few months to get along with everyone. And I hope the refugees are able to accept her. She's responsible for most of them being in those cages in Manhattan. You've heard about all that."

"But Jenna's forgiven Lena," Mia said. "They were enemies."

"Yeah, for years." Levi grunted. "God's in the healing business, if we'd all just get out of the way."

"I'll help where I can." She looked up into his face. "You taught me to forgive Kip. He's only alive because you forgave him. I know that. And he knows it, too. That's why he's such an evangelist in every town we visit."

Two of the Humvees were in better condition than the Suburban, so everyone but Andy, Brandy, and Jenna helped divide the gear between the two vehicles. The bikes from the roof were the last to be tied down. Brian used a bungee on one roof, and Levi used a rope on the other.

"She brought us over a lot of miles," Levi said to Andy, and patted the hood of the Suburban. "We've drained the fuel, but it just doesn't seem right to leave her behind. Why don't you do the honors?"

He offered Andy the key to the Suburban.

"What do I do with this?" Andy moved one crutch to his other hand and accepted the key. "This key's not good for anything if the vehicle has no gas."

"Come over here to the edge of the road. I know you can throw a hatchet, but I wonder how far you can throw a key. It's a symbol, you should know."

"A symbol of what?" Andy studied the key in his palm.

"We're letting go of the Suburban. She represents our past. It's been through a lot of miles, and wear and tear. But we have a new future to look forward to. We're letting go of the past and trusting God about our future. There's a new key for us now. It's time to throw the old key away."

"You're using the Suburban key to tell me I need to be born again." Andy scoffed. "You're not very subtle, Levi."

"I wouldn't be your friend if I was too subtle." Levi smiled and took one crutch. "Here. I'll hold this. Don't throw it until you're serious about casting it away. Dead to the old, and alive to the new. You already know everything Jesus did for you, Andy. It's time to give up to Him, so when we all die rolling into more OPT territory, I know every person in the vehicle with me is going to the same eternal home."

Weston sneezed, and Andy turned his head to see the whole group gathered behind him, listening, watching.

"Oh, you're all in this together, huh?" Andy felt the weight of the key in his hand and faced the plain. "I'm not sure when or why I started hating God, I just did. Maybe I was just rebelling against what Eric raised me to know. Every minute he was awake, he talked about Jesus. It got to the point that I knew there had to be something different out there. Out here."

"So, you ran away." Levi leaned on the extra crutch. "What'd you find?"

"Literally and figuratively?" Andy lifted his eyes to the sky. "It all ended in the pig slop."

"Even if you don't return to Wyoming," Levi said, "you can return to the feet of Jesus. He'll wash that pig smell off you and take you back. The Lord will wrap you in His own clothes and welcome you to His table."

"Now I'm the prodigal son?" Andy hung his head. "No, I have to go home. I have to find a way."

"I'll get you there," Levi assured. "We can roll through Meeker, spend the night, and keep right on rolling until you get back home. There's enough fuel for it now."

"We'll make sure you get there, too," Brandy said, moving closer. "I know there's a good man waiting to be born. The potential, anyway. But Jesus needs to be yours, Andy."

Andy tightly closed his fist around the key, and for a few seconds, his closed fist was pressed against his brow. No one moved, until suddenly Andy whipped his arm back and hurled the key far out into the field. It was such a wild and desperate throw that Andy's one leg wasn't enough to keep his balance. Levi caught him and pulled him into an embrace. The young man shook as he sobbed. Behind him, Jenna found Brandy to hold her as they wept together, while Kip and Mia held hands. Brian nodded at Lena, who nodded back, and Levi's eyes blurred with tears of his own.

Everything seemed so right in that moment. Except Lyla wasn't there, Levi thought sadly.

Before the soldiers woke, the believers drove off in the two Humvees. The Suburban and third OPT vehicle were left ruined for transportation, their tires slashed and fuel taken. A mile up the highway, Kip pulled over the first Humvee, and Levi dug a hasty grave for Brian to bury several armfuls of weapons and ammo the OPT wouldn't be needing anymore.

A few minutes later, Kip drove on, with Andy in the passenger seat of the first vehicle. Ryan and Levi sat in the backseat, their rifles in their hands and windows down. Lena drove the second vehicle, with Brian in the passenger seat. Mia, Brandy, and Jenna sat in the back. Auggie rode in the rear with fuel cans and half the camping gear.

Levi felt the somber mood in the first Humvee, as if they all knew they were driving to their deaths. No one spoke as they listened to the garbled chatter on the radio. Indeed, their situation was grave, for the radio was alive with mentions of the Caspertein name and someone named Advocate Kane who was wildly searching for Levi. Since Levi couldn't think of any wisecracks to cut the tension, he left the radio on and remained silent.

They rolled through Saguache, which hadn't been inhabited for years by the look of the buildings, and by noon they reached Highway 50, where they stopped for a bathroom break. Highway 24 lay north of them, and Lena, Brian, Andy, and Ryan gathered around Levi, who stared up the highway, wishing he could see what lay ahead.

Brandy and Mia changed Weston on the hood of the second vehicle. Auggie scouted a gopher hole, and Kip stood aside, content to listen and pray from a distance.

"I know what you're all thinking," Levi finally said. "We just drove a few miles, listening to the OPT radio. They're looking for us, and they're looking for Timbrook. It seems where Timbrook set up that ambush for us, he was out of range of anyone else with the OPT."

"Timbrook probably had a call sign on the wire," Brian said, "so we can't safely pretend to be him."

"A hundred and fifty miles to get to Meeker," Levi said. "Can we use the radio to our advantage?"

"We need to use it before we run into anyone," Andy said, "and before we reach I-70. We're getting uncomfortably close to Denver now."

"There's an eastern route into Meeker," Levi said, "but we still need to get down the 70 past New Castle."

"Aah-ah," Lena called their attention to her notepad, where she'd written, "Don't wait to get caught or ambushed again. Pick the spot to stand. Use rifles."

"Interesting." Levi eyed her with a sly smile. "Am I rubbing off on you?"

"A little," she wrote, "but I add reason to your wit."

They all laughed, but Levi was the loudest, appreciating the jab from his otherwise mute sister in the faith.

"Okay, let's consider this option," Levi said. "We can hope to reach Meeker by slipping through the OPT ranks, which is unlikely since we'll have to drive on the interstate. Or we can determine the next battlefield ourselves. Do we draw them into a fight, or try to avoid it?"

"We're not looking for a fight," Brian said. "Can we look at it as an attempt to reconcile? I read in Second Corinthians that's our ministry."

"OPT won't reconcile!" Lena wrote.

"I'm trying to think like a, uh, a Christian now," Andy said. "Can we convert the ones who are trying to kill you? Us, I mean. Oh, man. This is going to take some time to get used to. I just know how you guys broke me down—and that worked."

"You want us to cut off their foot?" Ryan asked. "I mean, in a spiritual way?"

"We just tried that with Timbrook," Levi said. "I showed that he was outgunned, but he wasn't convinced and still tried to kill us."

"Were you using the power of the gospel?" Brian asked.

"Well, I mentioned we were Christians." Levi leaned against the hood. "But I guess I wasn't trying to win them; I was just trying to intimidate to get past them. What you're proposing—this will require some real faith in what God can do. If we get on that radio and call them out, their fighters will probably come out in greater force than the few Timbrook had with him."

"Yeah, with grenade launchers," Brian said, "heavy artillery, and snipers of their own. That's a possibility."

"So why would we do this?" Ryan asked. "I don't have a death wish."

"A fight's inevitable," Andy said. "We can stumble into a fight or decide where the fight takes place. If it has to happen, the Jesus way is to use it all to preach the gospel. That's what my dad usually did, and it worked for him. He's still alive."

"That sums it up." Levi turned to welcome Mia, Kip, and Jenna into the conversation. Brandy was feeding Weston in the other Humvee. "We'll need everyone in the right position if we do it this way. The right position for me may not be up front, but somewhere that I can put the rifle to use. But I'm also not going to put anyone else in danger up front to do the sharing of the gospel."

"I'll do it," Jenna stated. "You're talking about giving the gospel message to the OPT?"

"Lena's recommended," Levi said, "that we get the fight over with by inviting them on the radio to come to a face-off. That means they'll come with an army."

"Greater is He who is in me, than he who is in the world," Jenna recited. "I'll speak to them. Whatever army they have—I won't see it, so I won't be impressed or afraid of it. We already know there'll be an army of angels surrounding us."

Levi studied their faces, which revealed their concern and excitement.

"So, we're serious about this? We could race toward Meeker right now and get there easily with the fuel we have."

"The OPT would still try to arrest us in Meeker," Brian said. "I'm not taking their Oath. They may come to meet us with guns. That's fine. We have weapons, too. Our ammunition is undeniably merciful, and now we'll speak to them about Jesus. I'll cover Jenna with my rifle if she wants to be the one who speaks to them."

"Aah-ah," Lena seconded, slapping her chest.

"Count me in," Mia said.

"You guys are gonna get me killed!" Andy scowled, but as he glared at Jenna, his gaze softened. "I guess it would be something to see a one-footed cripple leading a blind woman up to speak to the commander of the OPT army."

"I accept." Jenna smiled and found Andy's arm. "Those who are weak in the flesh are strong in the Lord's might. The rest of you can figure out what you'll do, but Andy and I need to talk to God and each other about our parts."

"Oh, no!" Andy stiffened. "I'm not talking! I'll be there for moral support. Everyone else is risking their lives, so I'm not staying back with Brandy and the baby. I'm no coward, but I'm not ready to speak for God."

"Don't worry," Jenna comforted. "I'll speak to the OPT, but if we're going to stand together *for* God, we first need to speak together *to* God."

"Maybe I've changed my mind," Andy said. "Give me a rifle. Someone else can plan this out with Jenna."

"No, you don't!" Jenna tightened her grip on his arm. "It's you and me, Andy. All alone, you and I are a testimony of God's miraculous love and forgiveness. We're the right team for this."

"Don't look at me," Brian chuckled at Andy's panic. "Everyone here knows Jenna and I are close in a certain way. But for this, she's teaming up with you for another mission. You're on your own, buddy."

"What do you want me to do?" Kip asked. "I don't have a rifle."

"We might have something special for you," Levi said, tapping his fingers on his chin.

"Uh-oh." Mia set a hand on her husband's shoulder. "I've seen that look in Levi's eyes before. It's that Caspertein creativity again. Hang on to your hat, Kippy."

They laughed, then Levi shared his plan. It was a plan for a night operation, and he read approval in their eyes once he'd explained it fully.

"It's just crazy enough to work," Brian said.

"Easy for you to say." Andy took a deep breath. "You're not the one standing in front if this goes south."

"If the shooting starts," Jenna said to Andy, "you have my permission to hide behind me."

"No way!" He stood up taller. "I'm not hiding behind anyone!"

"Good, then I'll hide behind you!" Jenna poked him in the ribs, drawing some chuckles.

"It ain't easy walking into battle," Levi said, "but I'm glad I'm with all of you to do it."

"Here, here," Kip said, taking his wife and Lena's hands. Lena took Levi's hand, who took Andy's. Jenna held Andy's hand, and took Brian's hand with her other, and Ryan completed the circle. "Let's pray that whether we live or die tonight, we die well, ready to meet Jesus face-to-face with love in our hearts, even for our enemies. It would be something to see a few of them come to the cross because of this."

They prayed together, and Brandy joined them as they laid out their fears before the Lord. And as they spoke to the Father, their plan shifted into place, and Levi could sense God's blessing on it all. After all, Jesus Christ was the Centerpiece.

Andy Radner shifted nervously on his crutches where he stood in the darkness of a field in central Colorado. A train of headlights wound down the brown-grass valley toward him. There were so many! The OPT must've summoned every soldier in Colorado for this meeting.

"The Lord is our strength and our refuge," Jenna reminded from his side, her hand hooked under his right elbow. *"He will never leave us nor forsake us."*

Nodding, Andy watched as the first headlights swept over them, blinding his eyes. Long-gone was his bravery in his abilities. He couldn't fake his courage even for the older but still beautiful woman at his side. With only one foot, he couldn't run away. With no weapons, he couldn't fight. Now, he could barely stand. Oh, how he regretted volunteering to involve himself! It was that Levi Caspertein—motivating him in strange, new ways.

But no, he decided. Levi was just a man made of flesh and bone. God was using Levi, and now God wanted to use him—a one-footed, terrified ex-killer who'd pushed his own family away.

"I feel like Gideon," he mumbled to Jenna as more vehicles pulled up. "Afraid, but willing to face an army with only three hundred men. Even if it kills me."

"The dead will rise and live forever." Jenna's voice was soft. "Stand steady now, Andy. I'm counting on you. I'll be the voice, but you've got to be my sight."

Andy lifted his chin, angry at himself that his eyes were brimming with tears. He wasn't sure if it was happiness at being part of this terrifying enterprise, or if it was terror at being in the hands of the OPT. Or maybe it was the lights in his eyes.

"You're trembling," Jenna said.

"Nah, I'm crying," Andy admitted and used his left sleeve to wipe his eyes. "I can't believe this. The things I've done . . . I shouldn't be like this!"

He was glad Levi couldn't see him. Levi wouldn't tease him as someone in the world might, but he wanted to be as stoic as their leader. Andy guessed Levi cried at appropriate times, like at funerals, but not at the moment of action and danger.

Behind the lights, the shapes of men and women climbed out of their vehicles, mostly Jeeps, Humvees, and a few SUVs. Andy resisted the urge to turn his head to see if any of Levi's shooters were visible. Of course, they wouldn't be visible in the darkness. Even in the daylight, they would be hard to spot since they were so far away. Ryan was nearby as his .22 rifle didn't have a great range. He was supposed to cover Kip, who was also close at hand, hidden in camouflage like a lump of earth.

The odor of gasoline seemed too strong to miss. Levi had soaked the ground in a circle around where he suspected the OPT would park. Kip was responsible for lighting the fuel at the right signal from Jenna. When the circle of fire was to be started, Andy knew what he was going to do. He was going to pull Jenna to the ground and cover her with his body. She was Brian's woman, but for the first time in his life, he truly wasn't afraid of dying and facing God. Surprising himself, he had surrendered to God—the God of his father, Eric, the God who had somehow kept him alive after he'd wandered the country, lusting for blood and a reputation. God had kept him alive long enough to come crawling to Him. Now, he could die. His outer man was scared, but inside, he had more courage than he'd ever known.

A short woman marched from a Humvee toward him. She wore a beret and a cape. Her blonde hair was short, framing her pale face and small mouth.

Gunmen in green and black jackets backed her, then fanned out beside her. About twenty vehicles had parked in triangle formation, and the nearly hundred soldiers with rifles now formed an oval around him and Jenna. Andy looked into their fierce faces and considered their muscled frames, shadowed by the headlights behind them, and imagined Levi and Lena already choosing their targets. Brian and Mia were on the opposite two corners, forming a box around the soldiers, with Ryan on the north side.

"Here I am," the woman said. "You called for me. I'm Advocate Veronika Kane. Where's Levi Caspertein? I know you're not him. The Casperteins have a look about them that I'd recognize on a darker night than this."

Andy realized she was looking at him, apparently expecting him to answer. Instead, he turned his head to look at Jenna, then shifted his arm to signal her that it was time for her to speak. But Jenna didn't move, except to open her mouth, allowing a few more suspenseful seconds to pass before she spoke.

"My name is Jenna Dowler," she stated, her voice like a song of calm in the tumultuous moment. "I've been blind since I was a young girl, but I'm one of the oldest friends of Levi Caspertein. He's waiting for me to signal him to show himself as soon as I've spoken to you."

Kane shifted her feet and eyed the darkness.

"He's out there now? No, you tell him to come out. I've been warned not to give him a chance to speak. I'm extending that warning to you. By the authority of the One Planet Trust, I order you to comply, or I'll shoot you this minute, whether you're blind or not!"

"You, Ms. Kane, won't allow me to speak?" Jenna asked. "Where is your understanding and compassion if you won't hear the heart of the people under your government's authority?"

"Compassion? I'm not discussing anything with you!" Kane fumed. "I know Levi has . . . some sort of influence. I won't permit it. Now, bring out Levi Caspertein!"

"If you want Levi," Jenna said, "I'll show you Levi. But after this is finished, you *will* hear one of us speak to you, and you will listen."

"I'm not listening to your—"

"Quiet!" Jenna silenced Kane, surprising Andy since he'd never heard the gentle woman raise her voice before. She lifted both her arms. "Hold your fire! Everyone, hold your fire. None of you will be shot except for Ms. Kane."

Kane reached for her sidearm but didn't draw it.

"Prepare to fire!" Kane shouted, her eyes wild, perhaps realizing for the first time that they were surrounded by darkness but standing in full light of their own headlights. "Hold your ground! They won't kill you!"

Jenna lowered her left hand to take hold of Andy's arm again, but she extended her right arm forward. With precision that a seeing person couldn't have improved, Jenna pointed at Kane's face. It was one of the signals Jenna had been given by Levi for just such a situation.

Andy flinched as the sound of a bee zipped past his head by a few feet and slapped into Kane's shoulder. The commander fell backwards and lay still at the feet of the second row of riflemen. The very distant sound of thunder rumbled an instant later. It was so far away that it hardly seemed to belong to the bullet that had struck Kane.

"Hold your fire!" Jenna shouted again. "I'm unarmed. Hold your fire and no one move! Advocate Kane wouldn't allow me to speak, but I must. Calm yourselves. I am your friend. Be still. My love for you is greater than your fear of me. Stand still and listen, then you will know the choice that is before you."

The soldiers jostled with one another for a few seconds, but Jenna's words pierced their dread of the unknown out in the darkness. They didn't lower their rifles, but they gazed once again at her rather than at the night where they hadn't even seen a muzzle flash. Andy's heart pounded against his ribs, so glad that Jenna had the words to speak, because he couldn't gather a single thought!

"That's better," Jenna said, her voice softer but still loud enough for all to hear. "I know that you are all strong men and women. You've joined the cause of the OPT because you want to feel hope and purpose and order in your lives. I commend you for your courage to fight for what you want. Because I'm a blind woman, you may think my life is empty. But I'm here tonight to tell you how complete my life is. I must tell you what has given me peace about tomorrow, joy indescribable, and love that can't be separated from me."

Mesmerized, Andy stood in the spell that Jenna cast upon them. Her openness to God's will had made her so much stronger than these mighty soldiers.

She told them of Jesus Christ, who loved them enough to die for them, and of a just God who had to punish sinful mankind. In simple words that reminded Andy of his father, Jenna explained the path of deliverance from the penalty of sin, then she spoke of the deliverance available from sin's strong draw. No one interrupted her, and Andy guessed that Jenna would've signaled that person for a gel-tranq if someone had. Levi was waiting for just such a moment.

It wasn't the only signal Jenna had in her arsenal. Her final signal to Levi loomed closer as Andy recognized the gospel message winding down toward the approaching ultimatum. Andy saw no way that the ultimatum wouldn't conclude in a gunfight, but he was also personally aware of God's power to turn hearts that seemed untouchable.

"So, if you're ready to enter God's love," Jenna concluded, "and turn your back on the fulfillments of this world's pleasures, science, and self, you'll find God's shepherding arms ready to receive you. Becoming a child of God won't make you a friend of this world, but it's far better to pass into eternity as a friend of Jesus, your Savior. Who will accept this truth? Will you? If you have believed what I've spoken, come forward to me and separate yourself from your past. Come now. Stand here beside me. This is the moment to trust God. Don't trust me. I'm just a blind woman. But trust in what God has done for you. Walk up here to me now so I can meet you."

Two men immediately approached, then a woman from the back stepped over Kane on her way forward. Andy looked at the ground. The three had crossed over the gas-soaked circle.

"Andy?" Jenna asked. "How many have joined us?"

"Three. Two men and a woman." He gestured to them. "Stand over here behind us."

They moved behind him and Jenna.

"The rest of you are free to go!" Jenna announced. "Go to your homes, go to your families, and go to your neighbors. Tell them what happened here tonight. Perhaps, you'll turn from your sins and trust in Jesus' forgiveness, and you'll receive eternal life. Go now."

A few from the back started toward their vehicles, but the rest stood their ground. Andy read their faces. They couldn't leave, not without Kane, and not without responding. Since they hadn't joined Jenna, there was only one other response in their souls. The Holy Spirit seemed to have released them as a captive audience. They were back to the flow of their OPT pursuits.

"Uh-oh," Andy said, shifting his crutches to step backward.

"Don't retreat," Jenna said. "Just kneel with me. Down on your knees."

Jenna knelt, and Andy turned to the three behind them.

"Throw your weapons clear and get down on your knees with us. You'll be safe."

Andy was the last to kneel, and for a moment, he felt like he was alone before a firing squad as the OPT soldiers chambered rounds and cocked their weapons.

Holding out her left fist, Jenna suddenly opened her hand, holding her fingers open and erect. The soldiers knew she had signaled someone, but they didn't know who and Andy wasn't about to betray where Kip was. A few seconds later, fire flashed from the west, and a wall of flame spread in both directions. Like a train, the gas fire arced toward Andy, then it turned and divided him and Jenna from the crowd of soldiers.

The soldiers shouted and backed away, then argued for direction.

"Get down!" Andy told Jenna and the three others, pulling them from their knees to lay flat on the ground. Before he could see the fire complete its wide circle around the parked convoy, he dove on top of Jenna to shield her, and his hand found the three newcomers, two grasping his hand and arm in return.

He wasn't sure who shot first. Gunfire popped and zipped, and Andy squinted through the blazing fire at the headlights still beaming. People were running in front of those lights, no doubt searching for cover from shooters too far away to see—on all sides. Soldiers were shooting at unseen targets into the night, but Andy knew their team was hundreds of yards away, where even a muzzle flash would be hard to spot with the naked eye.

"Andy!" Jenna screamed. "Get us out of here!"

Immediately, he saw why. Two bullets, whether intentional or accidental, spit dirt beside them.

"Stay low!" Andy gathered his crutches and pointed to the southeast, where the two Humvees and Brandy waited beyond a hill. "That direction! Help Jenna!"

The two men who'd left the OPT each grabbed an arm of Jenna and hauled her away. The woman crouched and ran after them. Andy was more cumbersome, crawling a good distance, dragging his crutches alongside until he could finally stand.

"Wait for Andy!" Jenna ordered from somewhere in the dark. "Andy's coming. Stay together! He'll get us to safety."

Andy fell over them where they were huddled. He looked back at the ring of fire and blazing battle in the night. The gas was burning itself out, but some of the grass had ignited. Two vehicles had driven off, but Mia had been left with enough phosphorus rounds to cripple the engines as they roared away. They wouldn't get far.

"Follow me," Andy said. "We don't have far to go. Watch your footing."

With Andy in the lead, they climbed a gradual hill. He could hear more clearly now Lena's rifle booming off to the right and used her position to guide them farther east. When they topped the hill, he saw by moonlight the two vehicles parked in a small bowl in an empty field. When he looked back at the battle, he smiled. It felt good to be on God's side for a change, even if they were quite out-numbered.

For just a moment, he wondered what it would be like to return to River Camp and tell his father this story. Eric had a history of standing faithfully for God against all odds. Andy never thought he'd ever be doing the same. Living as one of God's men in such a volatile world, maybe this was simply how Christians lived. For the first time, he regretted not realizing earlier the wonder of Christian courage.

Conclusion

Levi walked through the battlefield of unconscious OPT soldiers and smoking vehicles. He was distinctly aware that the enemy would begin to wake up in about thirty minutes. There was much to do before they ran away, leaving Advocate Kane's crippled army on the Colorado plain.

In the beam of one of the vehicles, Mia dressed a bullet wound on Kip's left side. He'd bled badly, the bullet passing between his ribs and out his back muscle, but he would live. Next to them, Lena used an OPT first aid kit to wind gauze around Ryan's head. His right ear was now missing. Since Kip and Ryan had been the only two close enough to dangerous gunfire, they were the only two who'd been wounded. Their wounds weren't grave, but Levi still felt it was his fault for not planning better. Both men had risked their lives for a gunfight that the group had welcomed.

Brian met Levi in the middle of the carnage where he threw another armload of rifles into the back of one of the only functioning SUVs of the twenty vehicles. The rest were sizzling from phosphorus rounds, or their tires had melted from the grass fire. Levi tossed his own collection of OPT armaments into the vehicle and coughed from the drifting smoke.

"Jenna got three, huh?" Brian's face showed his satisfaction. "You think they're okay?"

"They looked like they made it out without injury." Levi gazed toward the southeast, but he could see only darkness in the direction of their parked Humvees. "You want to get a couple tanks of gas? I think we'd better head out."

"We haven't seen the last of her." Brian looked down at the small figure of Advocate Kane where Levi had laid her on safe ground already charred from the fire. Her nametag on her uniform identified her. "There's probably an armory in Denver or somewhere. They'll regroup, find more vehicles, and come after us again. The OPT can't allow us to coexist anywhere on this continent. You know what they believe—Christians are a stain on their canvas."

"Yeah, maybe. But they'll have to walk back to Denver. We'll be in Meeker by dawn, and with a couple days' lead on them, we'll know our next move before they catch up. I'm going to run this winter gear back to our vehicles, then come back for Kane. Can you pick up some gas and get the others on their way?"

"Sure." Brian nodded. "You think you can get through to her still?"

"I have to give it one last try."

With about sixty pounds of food rations and heavy-weather gear, Levi walked onto the plain. Climbing the slope, he arrived at the two Humvees where Brandy, Jenna, and Andy were waiting. The three ex-OPT soldiers were with Jenna when Levi walked up. He turned on the headlights of one vehicle to illumine the area for Brian and the others to find them. After setting the gear in the back of one vehicle, he let Auggie out to run free and turned around to find Jenna in front of him. She wrapped her arms around him.

"That was amazing, Levi." She lifted her face up to him. "You don't know how overjoyed I am that you let me do that."

"Let you? Since when does Jenna Dowler need anyone to allow her to do anything?"

"You knew it was dangerous, but you didn't hold me back."

"Well, you were the best person for the job." He patted her shoulder. "And I had your back through my scope the entire time."

"I know you did, but it was still dangerous."

"How are our guests?"

She introduced the soldiers to Levi, and he shook their hands.

"They'd all heard the gospel before," Jenna explained, "but they didn't know they were going against God by taking the OPT's Oath until I explained it to them. But they won't be going far with us because they have families in Silt or Parachute."

"We can drop them on our way to Meeker. Just a little longer, and we'll get going."

"I'm preparing them to walk for the Lord on their own," Jenna said, "and to stand strong even if it means their deaths."

"Good." Levi took a drink from his canteen. "There's one more I'm going to try to prepare for the end."

He jogged back toward the scene of battle. When he passed Lena, Brian, Mia, and the wounded, he told them to be ready to leave when he got back.

"They'll be waking up in minutes, Levi!" Brian called after him as Levi continued toward the fallen OPT soldiers.

Once on site, Levi dumped a can of gas on the rifles they'd piled in the back of the last SUV. He started the engine and aimed it at the plain. As it rolled away, he tossed a flare in the back window. Twenty yards later, the gas caught fire, and the vehicle became a rolling ball of flame.

Levi picked up Advocate Kane over his left shoulder and walked halfway up the hill toward his friends. There in the darkness, he set the OPT woman down and sat a few feet away. Far to the east, the SUV started to pop and bang louder as ammunition exploded. The weapons in the back would be ruined, and the last functioning vehicle would be destroyed.

The moon was close to setting, and without it, only starlight lit the landscape. He heard men's voices in the direction of the battle and knew the soldiers who'd been tranquilized first were waking up and feeling around in the dark. Kane was a small woman, so the tranquilizer in her system affected her longer. She stirred well after an hour and sat up slowly.

Calmly, Levi sat next to her, waiting for her to gather her senses.

"Who's there?" she asked a moment later.

"It's me," Levi said softly, knowing she could see only the shape of him. "It's Levi Caspertein."

Seconds passed.

"Am I your prisoner?" Her clothing rustled. "You shot me. I can't feel my arm."

"Oh, it's just bruised. It'll heal and you'll be fine."

"I can hear my men. Those are my people over there."

"Yeah. They're over there about three hundred yards."

"I could call for them."

"You could."

"They'll come for me."

"No, they won't. They have no vehicles, and we took all your guns. They're probably not committed enough to you to charge toward a blasting rifle. What do you think?"

She sighed and shifted her arm.

"The feeling's coming back already. Can I leave, or what?"

"When we're done talking."

"Oh, I'm not talking to you."

"Then, I'll talk and you can listen."

"I was warned about you. This is why I told everyone to shoot you on sight."

"Come on." Levi chuckled. "I'm not even dangerous. Don't you realize the lengths I've gone to, to keep you safe?

Even while you were unconscious, there were burning fires around you, and I moved you twice to safer ground. Does that sounds like someone who wants to harm you?"

"You're harming us all, our whole planet, by refusing to take the Oath of Solidarity."

"Because I serve the God of the Bible, I'm a responsible steward of my environment. On the other hand, you exchange the truth of God for the worship of the environment. Your Creator has made the creation for you, my friend, not you for the creation. Your religion is destroying the people around you and your relationship with your Creator."

"I have no religion. I'm an atheist."

"Atheism is a belief system, and your belief system in the infallibility of your science and global consciousness has blinded you to the One who is offering you salvation from your fear."

"Your anti-human ideals are the only things I fear."

"No, you fear annihilation as a species, so you've created a cause of self-preservation to give you a figment of hope and purpose. But it won't work, Advocate Kane. God has allowed mankind to see its own inability to save itself. He's been waiting for us for thousands of years to give up as individuals and just trust Him to save us. There's much more happening than what you identify as a climate out of control. It's a spiritual curse, and death can't be avoided. This is why Jesus Christ—"

"Well, you're wasting your time. All of your God-talk is ridiculous to me."

"Right now, that may be. But later, when you realize the OPT really isn't the answer, you'll remember this conversation. If I'm still around, you can find me. And I'll embrace you as a sister in the faith. But what you really need to do is trust in Jesus Christ who was a real Person who came to earth and died for your sins. He defeated death, and He wants to pull you away from your bondage to the creation and into the love of the Creator—God

Himself. The OPT won't resurrect you after death. The planet doesn't love you or acknowledge you. But Jesus knows you and loves you and wants you with Him forever. It's not too late, Kane. What's your first name, by the way?"

She was silent for a moment.

"Veronika."

"Veronika." Levi climbed to his feet. "That way, I can pray for you by name. When you realize God is trying to get through to your heart, that's Him responding to my prayers, just as He wills. Give me your hand."

Hesitantly, she gave him her small hand, and he drew her to her feet. He enveloped her in his arms, holding her head against his chest. She didn't hug him back, but she gripped his coat with her fingers.

"I'm a married man. I'm not holding you now because I want you, Veronika. I'm holding you now because these arms may be the last bit of kindness you'll ever know for eternity. You are deeply loved by God, but you are wrapped up in ideas that hold you in bondage apart from God. Don't die without opening yourself up to all that He has for you."

Then, he released her. Although she hadn't returned his embrace, her hands went to his right hand and held it tightly.

"There's something about you, Levi Caspertein. I wish it were light out and I could see what it was in your eyes."

"It may show in my eyes, but it's my heart that Jesus has touched. You can have what I have. No one is too far gone on this side of the grave for His amazing grace."

He stepped away and she let go of his hand.

"Your Uncle Rudy said you were more dangerous than I knew."

"You met him?" Levi felt a chill. "Did you . . .? Is he still alive?"

"Yes, but I would've killed him yesterday if he hadn't distracted me with rumors about you." She cursed. "Your cousin Rex was with him. They all went back to Meeker, I'm guessing, where you're going."

"Why are you telling me this?"

"I don't know. Maybe to get all of you Casperteins in one place instead of running all over the country. The OPT can't allow this cancer to spread any longer."

"Then, you and I may meet again soon." Levi walked away. "I'll always welcome another chance to talk to you, Veronika. I won't forget you. Stay safe."

Saying nothing, she only stood there. He felt that her heart was torn between the strange compassion he had shown her and the devotion she had to the OPT. Tearing herself from one or the other was a choice he couldn't make for her.

He walked up the hill, and when the Humvees came into sight, he smiled at his friends who were waiting for him. But it was a sad smile, for a sadness that so many were still refusing the God who had created them.

Midway in his trek to join the others, his left leg wobbled. Instead of fighting the motion and risking injury, he allowed his knee to buckle, and he rolled to his side. Only then did he realize his leg wasn't the problem, but the ground itself was rolling and heaving!

"Brian!" Jenna called. "Where are you?"

The others with the vehicles cried out for each other as well, but Levi rode it out on the ground. It lasted forty seconds, then the earth was still. He stood and marched swiftly to the lead vehicle.

"That was a big one," he said. "There'll be aftershocks. Let's get to Meeker to see what the damage is. Rudy and Rex are waiting for us."

Their three OPT guests piled in with them, and since Kip was injured, Levi drove the lead vehicle. He roared onto the highway doing fifty, knowing they had fuel to spare now. They reached Interstate 70 minutes later.

"For how long do you think we crippled the OPT?" Ryan asked from the backseat.

"Probably just a few days," Levi said loudly for the young man since one of his ears was gone and bound with a bloody bandage. "But we all might have more to deal with if that earthquake means what I think it means."

"Yellowstone again?" Andy asked.

"Could be." Levi glanced at the dark sky. "If it was Yellowstone, we'll see for ourselves the same thing that happened here weeks ago."

While he drove, Levi told Kip and Mia what Kane had told him about Uncle Rudy and Cousin Rex.

"More Casperteins?" Kip joked. "That's all we need in this world!"

At the town of Silt, Levi dropped off one of the men who'd left the OPT that night, and a few miles later, he let out the last man and woman who were returning to their families in Parachute. They were sent on their way with Jenna's blessing, and the three were eager to get back to their homes and flee with their families before the OPT could track them down.

Levi drove swiftly up Highway 13 toward Meeker when he suddenly had to turn on the windshield wipers.

"Snow?" Andy asked. "No, it's ash."

They crossed the White River and zoomed through a gulch along the Meeker Ditch until the town came into view.

"Stay alert." Levi slowed his speed and checked the mirror. The second Humvee was on his bumper. "From what Advocate Kane said, the OPT has been around here."

Rolling up Main Street, they parked in front of the courthouse. Levi noticed several lights on in the Meeker Hotel windows, and up the street, he saw people on the side of the road, even though it was the middle of the night.

"The earthquake woke everyone up," Levi said to his passengers. "Keep your eyes open. I'll see what's going on. Stay inside."

He left the engine running, and walked to the rear vehicle, which Lena was driving. At her open window, he looked in at his friends and brushed ash off his head.

"Sit tight. I'll see where my family is staying. Someone's got to know."

A tall man walked out of Hotel Meeker with a flashlight and a gas mask on his face. Levi passed between the vehicles and approached the man. It'd been a year since he'd been in Meeker, and he hadn't spent enough time in town to get to know many of the citizens.

"Good timing!" the man shouted, his voice muffled through the mask. "We've got even more buildings damaged this time. I hope you brought, uh . . ." His flashlight beam shifted from the vehicles to Levi's face. "You're not OPT. You're Levi Caspertein!"

"Do I know you?"

The man took off his mask and aimed the light at the ash-covered ground.

"I'm Advocate Wayne Sullivan. Now, don't attack me! Right now, I don't care who's OPT and who's not. Your uncle and cousin have been nothing but problems for me. I remember you, so I'm not going to try to arrest you, either. Here I thought you were the OPT coming from Denver with supplies. We've not even recovered from the last eruption, and here we go all over again!"

"Where's my family?"

"Out at Rudy's place north of town in the woods. I don't know if they're still there, but they were a couple days ago. Hey, what're we gonna do for food now? You can't see it here, but the grass was barely growing back. Now everything is gonna die again!"

"Pray about it," Levi said, "but don't count on the OPT. We just decimated their largest force in the state and ruined all their vehicles. It ain't easy relying on people who can't keep promises from one day to the next."

"You've ruined the only people who could help us!" Wayne shook his head and turned away. "We're dead. We're all dead."

"How dangerous is this ash?" Levi asked.

"Your uncle said it could be radioactive. I haven't brought a Geiger out tonight, since it's not as thick as it was last time, but I'm taking no chances."

Wayne fit his mask back over his face.

"Have you got more of that gear? Masks and suits? Where's your stash?"

"We have just enough for emergencies from the hardware store."

"Me and my people are outdoors, so that makes it an emergency for us. You've got houses to hide in. Where's your gear?"

"In the hotel." The man scowled. "Follow me."

"Brian!" Levi waved at the vehicles. "Help me for a minute."

Wayne led the two inside. Men, women, and children were moving around, their arms loaded with clothes and cookware.

"Some of the rooms upstairs are too damaged to live in now, so people have to find new quarters. This earthquake couldn't have come at a worse time. Hey, make sure you guys don't clean us out, okay?" Wayne opened a room that was stacked with trunks and crates, plastic-wrapped gear and weapons. "Half this stuff we don't even know how to use. I've never shot a grenade or assembled a launcher. I don't even know what this is."

When Wayne held up a mortar tube, Levi took it from him and set it back in its place.

"Best not touch it if you don't know what it is. Point out the protective gear and masks."

He showed Levi stacks of about one hundred biohazard suits, thirty masks, and fifty sets of filters. Levi loaded Brian's arms with enough for their ten, then added a few more for Rex, Annette, Lyla, Alice, and Rudy.

Outside, Levi and Brian dispersed the gear, then donned the suits and masks themselves.

"What about us?" Wayne asked, standing beside the vehicles. "We had three commit suicide in the last week. I don't know what to do if the OPT isn't going to help us."

"You are the OPT," Levi said. "What did you think was going to happen? Governments have always laid down laws, Mr. Sullivan, but you should know by now that laws have never improved our lives. We have a responsibility to submit to God's grace and be patient about the end days here. The Lord could come for His Church any minute. Don't you know Jesus Christ?"

"Yeah. I mean, your uncle taught me some, but it's just fairy tale stuff."

"Then you already know the truth." Levi climbed into the driver's seat. "If you want to reject the only gospel that brings hope in this life of suffering, that's your decision. If the OPT shows up, you'd better send them elsewhere, and not out to the ranch, or I'm coming for you, Wayne Sullivan."

Wayne stepped away as Levi drove up the street, Lena following him. With the ash falling in gray-white clumps, Levi felt like he was driving through a winter snowfall.

He turned onto the road that led out of town, where he'd led an assault on invading Federation troops a year earlier. A new enemy and a new disaster now greeted him. This wasn't the homecoming he'd envisioned when he'd boasted to his fellow travelers about the safety of Meeker that awaited. In a way, he was glad Nathan and Chen Li had been spared this disappointment.

His headlights finally swung across the remnants of the log cabin with only one wall standing and its roof collapsed upon the logs. It was about three in the morning now, so he wasn't surprised that he wasn't greeted by his friends. Even his wife would be suspicious of a couple OPT vehicles arriving at that hour.

Levi took the radio transmitter and spoke into it.

"Lena, everyone stay in the Humvees, including Auggie. My family must be nearby, but they don't know who we are."

"Aah," Lena responded over the frequency.

With the headlights still illuminating the cabin, he climbed out. He walked over and stood in those headlights, then took off his mask and unzipped his suit. After folding down his suit to his waist, he turned in a circle, his arms out, showing himself in the headlights for whoever might be observing.

There was a whistle from far away. In the falling ash, the origin of the whistle was difficult to discern, but Levi still knew the landscape. Someone had probably been stationed on the rimrock. Even in low visibility, he'd be hard to miss in the headlights.

Closer, beyond the cabin and near the woods, there was a shout, then a scream of excitement. Levi smiled. Advocate Kane had said he'd been expected, so his family knew he'd been on his way. That had to be his wife screaming.

He zipped up his suit to his neck but left the mask off.

"It's okay!" He waved at the two Humvees. "Everybody out. Leave the headlights on in the front vehicle, but it's safe."

Levi rounded the cabin rubble at the first glimpse of movement. In the light, he recognized a masked woman, slender and older, too short to be Annette. When she drew closer, she pulled down her mask.

"Chloe." Levi grinned and embraced the woman, her curly hair sprinkled with ash. "You made it. We all made it."

"Oh, Levi!" She sobbed against him. "So much . . ."

"Yeah, it's okay." He chuckled and patted her on the back, surprised at the emotion from a woman he'd barely met a couple times in his life. "It's okay now. We're all back together."

Movement behind her made him lift his eyes, expecting to find Lyla, but instead he saw two more masked people, a man in a tattered green uniform and a brunette woman with a COIL rifle. He shifted Chloe aside and stepped toward the strangers.

"Where's Lyla? And Alice?"

"Levi?" Chloe touched his arm. "A lot has happened in the past few months. I know Rex wanted to be here when you arrived. We've prayed about this the whole way."

"What happened?" Levi's throat felt dry and constricted. "Tell me. Where is everyone? Where are all the refugees?"

"Bruno and Scooter led the refugees into Canada to avoid the ash after the first eruption." Chloe wiped at her face, smearing gray ash under her eyes. "We lost Lyla, Levi. In Pennsylvania."

"Pennsylvania?"

She moved closer.

"We buried her in the woods where she was killed. Everyone loved her. We've been grieving the whole way. I'm . . . so sorry, Levi."

Levi's knees buckled for the second time that night, but he recovered and turned away. Breathing suddenly seemed difficult. He panted and took a few steps out of the headlights. The pain was unbearable. His heart felt like it'd been cut out. His hands went to his head, his fingers wrapped in his hair. Trying to scream, he only managed breathless words from an open mouth. *Not Lyla. Not Lyla!*

He stood there, losing track of time, then he choked as he began to breathe again. Doubling over, he sighed aloud. Then, he stood upright, his eyes closed, and his face turned to the dark sky. The ash brushed across his face like feathers.

"Take me now, Lord," he whispered to God. "I'm finished. I'm done. I can't do this. All this way . . . All this time . . ."

With nothing resolved in his heart, he remembered the others and what they'd lost as well. All of them had suffered. He couldn't be selfish. If Lyla had died, then he was alone now. But that didn't mean his friends didn't still need him. Exhaling long, he wiped his face and turned slowly to face his friends. On the left, his Humvee companions stood with their backs to the headlights, and on the right, Chloe and the two masked people stood facing him.

"All of us are hurting," he admitted softly, "in different ways. We lost Nathan and Chen Li in the first days of the OPT. I'm sorry, Chloe. I know you were close to them."

Chloe bowed her head and folded her hands where she stood. Her shoulders shook, but she remained silent.

The sound of running feet caused Levi to search the darkness. From the direction of the rimrock, one-armed Alice appeared through the ash. She skidded to a stop at the edge of the light. Her rifle was on its sling, but she held the tall staff like a warrior. When she rushed forward the last few feet, she threw aside the staff and collided with Levi, both of them moaning aloud. As he held her in his arms, he could tell that Alice had lost a tremendous amount of weight, so much so that he could've almost wrapped his arms around her twice.

"We made it." While still holding her, he looked over her head at Chloe. "Where's Rudy and Rex and my mom?"

"Rex went south three days ago to find Rudy and your mom." Chloe shook her head. "We haven't heard anything since then."

"Then they aren't back yet." Levi shifted Alice to one arm but didn't let her go. "I spoke to someone who said they're on their way back here. My mom's okay?"

"The only news we have is a few weeks old," Chloe admitted, "but Rex found out that your mom and uncle went south after the first eruption."

Levi nodded and focused on the two strangers behind Chloe.

"We have introductions to make," he said. "I don't want to leave anyone out."

"Everyone, Levi . . ." Chloe moved to the woman first. "This is Miranda Nelson. We picked her up passing Chicago when the OPT first laid down the Oath mandate. She's a Christian and sort of, well, she and Rex are close."

Miranda smiled and offered her hand.

"Welcome to the family." Levi chuckled as he shook her hand. "It ain't easy throwing in with a clan with so much history, huh?"

"I know," Miranda said. "I'm still learning everyone's names, but I've heard much about you."

"Yeah, we've promised her a lot with your arrival," Chloe shook her finger at him, "so you'd better not disappoint when you deal with the OPT!"

"It's too late." Brian stepped forward, guiding Jenna with him, both of them still wearing their masks. "He already ruined the OPT army after sundown tonight south of Highway 70."

"Already?" Chloe threw up her hands at Miranda. "See what I mean? You blink and you miss how God uses this guy!" She turned to the other masked person. "And you are . . .?"

Jenna lifted off her mask with Brian's help.

"Chloe." Jenna let go of Brian and felt for Chloe in front of her.

"*Jenna!*" Chloe shrieked and lunged to embrace the blind woman, laughing and crying together.

"Hello there." Levi held out his hand to the masked man in the tattered uniform. "Another Christian soldier, I presume?"

Levi saw hesitation in the man's eyes above the mask. Nevertheless, he pulled his mask down, and Levi was taken aback at the face of Colonel Milo Rotham. His second reaction was to search for Lena in the headlights. He saw her in the back of the group, where she'd retreated a step to the front bumper of the nearest Humvee.

"He's come to Christ, Levi. It's okay." Chloe held Jenna's hand, but extended her other to Milo's shoulder. "Milo's a believer now. He's even been helping to preach the gospel and save souls."

Looking the man up and down, Levi was torn between his loyalty to Lena and his yearning to accept the man in Christ. *This was the man who'd shot Lena!*

"The longer I'm alive," Levi said, "the more God impresses me with His love."

"I've come to know that love," Milo said, "and his forgiveness. Before I knew better, I had a hand in the deaths of the men who murdered Lyla. You and I were enemies back then, but I was real upset that they'd killed your wife, Levi. For some reason, I wanted to come all this way to tell you that."

"Thank you, Colonel, but right now," Levi raised his voice for all to hear, "we need extra grace, Lord, for more love. Milo Rotham, there's someone who has come a long way to tell you something as well. Like you, she has her own past."

Though Levi didn't look directly at Lena, he hoped his words were received by her. No one moved, and then Lena finally did. She walked forward, weaved around Brandy and Mia, and past Ryan. Before she reached Levi, she dropped her battle rifle in the ash. Alice took a step back, and Levi held out his hand to Lena. Her eyes were on Milo and no one else, but her face was hidden behind the plastic of the biohazard mask, as well as her bridal veil underneath.

Slowly, her hand went to the mask and lifted it off her head. She shook out her hair and stood there.

"I don't . . . understand," Milo said, glancing at Levi. "I don't recognize you."

Levi tensed as Lena's fingers found the end of the bridal lace, then she unwrapped her face. He'd never known her to intentionally expose her deformed face to anyone, but she let the lace fall to her shoulder. To Milo's credit, he didn't recoil, but looked closer.

"But I don't—" His words stopped and his mouth froze agape. "How—?"

"That day after she was shot, I carried her from the Bowery," Levi said, sensing the others drawing closer to hear and see. "God kept her alive. Eventually, she gave her soul to Jesus. She's a sister now, Milo."

Milo bowed his head and looked down at his hands. They were shaking. He clenched them and opened them again, but they were still shaking.

"I . . . never thought I'd stand before you again. I thought I'd . . . killed you."

"Aah-ah." She looked at Levi and gestured so he understood he was to translate. "Aah-hah gha-ah ah."

"She now forgives you," Levi said.

Lena held out both her hands to his trembling fingers. Milo dropped to his knees at her feet, and she embraced him there as he wept and held her.

"Phew!" Levi took a deep breath. "God is still good, isn't He? Jenna, Chloe might be interested in your friend there."

"Nah, I don't want to take away from this moment," Brian said. "I can wait."

"Well, I can't!" Jenna exclaimed, feeling up to Brian's face and mask. "Chloe, I think you lost a little puppy dog back in New Jersey, didn't you?"

Jenna removed his mask.

"Brian!" Chloe gasped and threw herself into his arms, laughing and shouting incoherently. Eventually, she held him at arm's length. "Rex is going to fall over when he sees you. *He buried you!*"

"He buried the guy who I took off my coat for to save his life. That didn't work out for him, but God kept me alive. I ran into Jenna and Chen Li a few days later."

Levi gave them space and found someone else by his side. Andy leaned on his crutches for a moment, then lifted his mask.

"I know him," he said to Levi, nodding at Milo. "He's the one who sent me, you know, after you and Jenna."

Milo overheard and lifted his head. Rising from Lena's feet, he extended one hand to Andy.

"Yes! You're Runner!"

"Not any longer." Andy held up his stump. "I'm just a cripple now."

"But you caught up to Levi Caspertein." Milo shook his head, his face full of wonder. "And?"

"We terrorized each other for a few weeks." Andy shrugged. "Then he let me tag along with him."

"Then?" Levi urged.

"Then, yesterday, I trusted in Jesus for the first time."

"Yesterday!" Chloe clasped her hands together. "I don't know whether to cry or celebrate!"

"Maybe a lot of each, sister." Levi frowned. "Okay, we've got others here. Everyone, this is Brandy and her son, Weston."

Levi continued to make introductions after everyone had welcomed Brandy and her newborn. He encouraged Ryan to tell his story, including his dunk in a horse trough, then it was Mia and Kip's turn. This was especially important to Levi, since Mia was family, and the couple was embraced all around.

Industrial masks and suits were passed to those with none, and Chloe wanted a look at Kip's bullet wound in his side. Alice led them into the woods where a small lean-to and tarp had been fashioned. Brian and Ryan went to work extending the shelter with two more tarps to keep off the ash. Milo and Miranda passed out cooked beef, and Brian prayed for them all before they ate. A fire crackled,

Weston cried, and the last hour of darkness gave way to light.

Sleep tempted Levi and his head dropped as he sat between Andy and Lena, listening to Chloe recount their trip.

"Hey, Levi." Alice nudged him with her staff, her voice a whisper. "Rex should be on his way back. We should set out a watch."

"Something up?" Brian asked, rubbing his eyes.

"Nah, stay put." Levi climbed to his feet. "We're just going to go meet my mom."

"Cuz?" Mia stepped over several people to reach him. "Don't tell Aunt Annette about me, okay? I want to surprise her."

"She's all yours." He patted her cheek. "I know she'll be thrilled to see you."

Levi nudged Lena on the shoulder. When she looked up, he held out his hand to her. She clasped it, and he pulled her to her feet.

"Suit up," he said, noticing that Alice was already suited and walking away. "For someone who has only three limbs, you'd be surprised how she stays ahead of everyone."

"Ah-hah?" Lena pointed at herself.

"Yes, you," he said softly. "Unless you want to stay. I could use a little hike myself."

Climbing into her suit, she pulled on her mask. From the fire, Milo approached Levi.

"I need you to know, Mr. Caspertein, that I promised someone back in Des Moines that I'd return to help her and her people."

"Okay, I understand, Milo. And call me Levi. We're family now. Whatever you've got to do for the Lord, I'll support you."

They shook hands, and Levi headed out with Lena.

"We can't stay in Meeker long," he said to her as he set a fast pace to overtake Alice. Auggie bounded out of a thicket and tore across the meadow to intercept them. "The ash will slow up the OPT, but I think the next rain will clear this out and they'll come hunting for us again."

"Aah."

"I had told Andy I'd get him up to his folks in Wyoming, but that was before I knew Meeker was so compromised. Now, I don't know what to do."

On the other side of Meeker, Alice stood outside a ranch house from which Levi understood they needed to cut through the property to get to the plateau. A man was walking beside a covered wagon drawn by two steers.

"Don't I know you?" Levi asked the man who wore only a cowboy hat and a scarf to ward off the ash. "Last year, we met at the wedding."

"Yes, Levi Caspertein." The man extended a rough hand that had seen decades of hard work. "Name's Trapper Sullivan. I've been expecting you. I'm glad to see you made it. Alice, I remember you, too. I was hoping to catch you all at Rudy's place before you left. I'm not going to die out here alone with these animals. I kept two steers to slaughter and loaded up everything I could to come find you guys. "

"God's still up to His wonders," Levi said cheerily, though the ache of losing Lyla stabbed at his insides. "Even the ash seems a little lighter this morning."

"It doesn't matter." Trapper surveyed the terrain covered in the gray and white blanket. "Your uncle could tell you better than I what's in this ash, but it's killing everything. After we eat these two beasts, I don't know what we'll survive on."

"Either it'll work out, old friend, or we'll push on to glory." Levi set his hand on the man's shoulder. "Which-ever way, the Casperteins are glad to have another believer with us."

The three continued on after seeing Trapper on his way east toward the camp.

"So, how are you handling things?" Alice asked as they walked beside White River. "Lyla was like a sister to me. Part of us died when she died. It felt like I'd lost you both. I was so lonely."

"Sounds like you know what I'm going through then." Although Levi knew Alice to be a private and solitary woman, she was surprisingly open speaking in front of Lena.

"You should talk more to Milo," she said. "He's been waiting for hundreds of miles to tell you about his part in catching Lyla's murderers. In a roundabout way, it played a part in softening his heart to join us and connect with Rex."

"How did it happen? Do you know how she died?"

"I don't want to say." She looked across at Lena. "Talk to Milo."

A few seconds later, Lena stopped and pulled at a pocket to bring out her tablet.

"Was it my brother?" she wrote and held it up for both to read.

Alice clearly didn't want to answer, but Levi stared at her until she did.

"Yeah. He and that chancellor guy caught Lyla alone and wanted her rifle because Rex and Bruno had taken their guns from them. Those two were pure cowards. But Lyla went quickly. Rex and I are the ones who found her. They just killed her, took her rifle, and ran away. Milo can tell you what happened after that. He was still with the Federation during that time."

"Aah-ah hah." Lena touched Levi's arm.

"I know you're sorry, Lena." He frowned. "But it's not your fault Owen was the way he was.

"And I'm sorry, too, Lena," Alice said. "Levi needed to know, but I didn't know how you'd take it."

Lena stuck her notepad into her pocket, then embraced Alice briefly. A couple seconds later, she stepped back and continued ahead.

"She's okay, then?" Alice asked.

"Yep, I'd say so." They walked after Lena. "The old Lena would sooner kill you than touch you. I don't think she was close with her brother, but now she knows what happened. These things can harden us or bring us closer to God. It's a choice. When Christ owns us, it's more natural for these things to soften us for Him. She's learned that."

As they walked, Alice told him about the way Rex had learned to lead without him, and Levi told Alice about their trek through the southern states.

Suddenly, Lena shouted in her throaty way and pointed ahead.

"It's them!" Levi could make out four adults.

Before he could draw out his binoculars to make sure, Lena rushed ahead to meet them.

"I guess we're running?" Alice laughed. It was a good sound to Levi's heart. "Does Lena even know your mom or Rudy or Rex?"

"No!" Levi laughed and started jogging with her. "But she's become like you after a few hundred miles."

"Like me? What's that mean?"

"Part of the Caspertein clan."

Their meeting was nothing but laughter at first. Levi twirled his mother around in the air. She'd lost weight and gained a few lines, but her smile was the same. Rudy was midway through a bear hug with Lena before he asked who she was. Rex threw off Levi's mask and ruffled his hair before Levi got behind him and jumped on his cousin's back to hold him in a headlock. Auggie immediately went to sniff out the youngest Caspertein traveler, and Vorca coached Caleb how to pet the dog.

"Hey, Uncle Rudy." Levi felt small in the man's shadow.

"Come 'ere, you!" Rudy enveloped his nephew.

Levi embraced Vorca last, taking a moment to hold

her hand and listen to her as she cried and jabbered to him in her native tongue.

"It's been a rough few weeks," Annette explained for the family nurse. "We've really counted on Vorca to help out. But you got the news? About Lyla? Rex told us. We're so sorry, Levi."

He nodded.

"Yeah, Chloe filled me in."

"Chloe!" Annette covered her mouth. "I can't wait to see her! It was Pan-Day in San Diego since I last saw her."

"She's back at the cabin. There are all kinds of people back at the cabin. And this is Lena." Levi put his arm around his friend. "Wait until you hear her story, Mom. Do you mind if I tell it, Lena?"

Lena rolled her eyes.

"Well, she's obviously used to you!" Annette laughed. "Why don't you let her tell us?"

"That's part of the story—why I have to tell it."

"Hey, guys?" Rudy called with his palms turned toward the sky. "Look at this!"

Levi studied the land and the sky. It wasn't blue, but the ash had ceased to fall. Those with suits took them off and rolled them up.

"We've got lots to figure out," Rudy said, walking between Levi and Rex, "the three of us."

"Four of us," Annette corrected, and elbowed her way between Rudy and Rex.

"Aah-hah ah-aah!" Lena corrected further and took Levi's and Alice's arms.

That night, Mia Brogdon sat next to her Aunt Annette in the circle around their fire in the forest. Upon finding Weston, Vorca had promptly abducted the infant from Brandy to build a carry-pouch for the young mother to carry her son. Brandy and Vorca were the only two adults not at the fire meeting, which Uncle Rudy was chairing, but everyone had a voice. They'd eaten a light dinner, and now it was decision time.

"We can't stay here without continued conflict," Rudy said. "I've tangled with the OPT, and now the rest of you have, too. The Casperteins are too much a liability for the OPT to leave alone in the country. The volcanic eruptions might continue, and they aren't to anyone's advantage. They make everyone's survival tougher."

"You've tried to go south," Rex said. "And Levi and I came from the east. The OPT might've been temporarily beat back here, but just about every remaining town or city has run into the arms of the One Planet Trust."

"And we can't go north," Annette said. "That's where the volcano is."

A couple side discussions started for a few minutes, and Mia grew disheartened that it seemed they had nowhere to go. At least they were all together again, she thought to herself, looking at Annette. Her aunt had received the news of her baby with tears, but there was no blame or anything but love. For a few minutes around the fire, it seemed that they would have nowhere at all to turn but to encourage each other through death—until she saw Levi and Andy exchanging a few quiet words where they sat across the fire. Mia sighed and looked up at the sky, realizing that God wasn't finished with them yet. Another adventure still lay ahead.

"What're you smiling about?" Annette asked her. "We're sort of backed into a corner here, you know?"

Everyone in the circle silenced themselves, and Mia realized she'd drawn the attention of the gathering. She knew most everyone except Milo and Miranda. Milo seemed to pal around with Alice, even though Alice said Milo had a girl back east to whom he was already preparing to return. And Miranda so mothered Rex, that the two were clearly an item.

With everyone's attention, Mia played coy.

"Don't look at me. I was feeling pretty uncertain about things like all of you until I noticed our God is wildly at work right now. We're not alone. As my cousin would say, it ain't easy coming up with a plan the day before the Lord comes back for His people, huh, Levi?"

"A plan?" Rex asked. "What plan?"

"Well, it's just an idea." Levi tossed a twig into the fire. "Andy was just telling me that going north might not be a total waste. His family lives in the remote mountains of Wyoming. Some pretty rugged canyons and steep hillsides all around. Rivers, forests, and lots of game. A place called River Camp."

"But it's so close to the volcano," Brian said. "And what about the ash? It must've killed everything up there."

"The ash didn't stick around the first time," Levi said, "and it'll wash away this time, too, unless there's a more drastic eruption. The canyons and gorges of the Wyoming mountains might offer us some shelter and a place to live."

"The OPT will just follow us, won't they?" Ryan wondered. "Unless they won't bother because it's so close to the volcano."

"There are no roads into River Camp," Andy said. "My dad, Eric Radner, settled there and built the first cabin. It's so secluded that different armies in the early days tried to invade. But the winters immobilized and killed off the invaders, and in the summers, my dad met them on their own terms and backed them down. Dad's pretty steadfast, and he did all that for years without your battle rifles. Imagine a wilderness with no access, where the woodsmen and hunters all around would see someone coming before the OPT could get within fifty miles of River Camp. That's where I grew up."

"It's a possibility," Levi said.

"It's the best possibility that I've heard," Rex voted. "Dad?"

"It could be the answer we're looking for."

"I was joining Andy on his trip there, anyway," Levi said, "so now we can all pile into the Humvees and go as far as we can on the roads. We've got the bikes, too."

"And the two steers?" Trapper added. "You'll not pile them into anything."

"Then we'll take two caravans," Levi suggested. "One by vehicle with women and children, and the second on foot with the two cows, the wagon, and the bikes. Camp along the way. It isn't that far."

"We can go up on Highway 13," Andy said, "then follow the 80 east to the 25 north. The Laramie Mountains are on the left."

"How far away from the volcano will we be?" Annette asked.

"Two hundred and fifty miles," Andy said.

The circle of adventurers looked to Rudy, the seismologist.

"Depending on the size of the eruption," Rudy said, "that could be far enough away to protect us, if the mountains are high and the valleys are low."

"The sooner we head out, the better," Andy said. "Dad will want to prepare for extra people before the snow falls."

"So?" Rex asked. "To River Camp?"

"To River Camp," Levi agreed.

Mia watched his face as he stared at the fire. Everyone else celebrated the River Camp prospect, but Mia felt guilty for having Kip, while Levi had no one. He'd lost Lyla. Saving everyone else had cost him so much.

It was agreed that both parties would leave the next day. Although Trapper was donating his cows, Rudy insisted the old man ride in the Humvee with him. Rex agreed to lead the second wave of travelers, which would consist of Alice, Milo, Miranda, Lena, Mia, Kip, Brian, and Ryan. Levi would be riding with Rudy, Annette, Caleb, Vorca, Jenna, Andy, Brandy, Chloe, and Trapper. Those walking were encouraged to hear that they could go cross-country to River Camp, cutting their distance in half. Andy showed Rex the southern route on a map, which would be only a five-day walk.

"That's hardly even a hike," Miranda joked. "Maybe we should pick some place farther away so we feel like we really earned it."

"Oh, we already earned it, sister!" Mia assured. "We earned it ten states back!"

The next morning, the vehicles were loaded, and those traveling by foot embraced the others as if they wouldn't be seeing each other until glory. It was a time that even a five-day journey was too unpredictable. Mia kissed her aunt's cheek and slugged her cousin on the shoulder goodbye. Levi was the last to climb into the lead vehicle when Auggie started barking outside the camp.

"Company!" Ryan warned, and set down his backpack to aim his .22 rifle.

Mia was shifting her own rifle into firing position when Levi ran from the Humvee.

"Hold your fire!" he shouted.

A lone figure outside town fell to their knees, then rose again to continue walking. The person's posture was that of complete exhaustion, which Mia recognized because she'd experienced it herself. Levi reached the visitor before he or she fell again. Mia couldn't imagine who it was. None of their people were missing, and Levi hadn't said he was expecting anyone.

"Of course," Rudy said next to Mia. He'd climbed out of the second vehicle to watch. "Leave it to Levi to bring *her* in."

"Who is it?"

"That is Veronika Kane," Rudy said. "She almost killed us a few days ago, and you guys wiped out her command, didn't you? It must've taken her a day and a half walk to reach us."

"That's Kane?" Mia smiled. "Levi had gone back for her later after our firefight."

"Looks like she just needed to be humbled a little more," Andy said, "before she could accept the truth."

Levi walked up with the small OPT Colorado commander in his arms.

"She's coming with us," he said. "We'll put her in our vehicle. She's done-in."

"Then she'll fit right in," Trapper said.

Everyone loaded back into the Humvees, plus their newest passenger. Levi honked, then they both pulled out.

"Yep, that's my cousin." Mia smiled and waved after them. She found Lena standing next to her. "It ain't easy following his act."

"Aah."

Lena saw to Mia's pack, tightening and fitting it onto her small frame.

"To River Camp?" Rex called out to those outside the collapsed cabin.

Brian stomped out the fire they were leaving behind.

"To River Camp," Miranda agreed, and took Rex's hand in her own.

Ryan led by foot the two cows that pulled the wagon. Alice walked far ahead, her staff pounding the ground at intervals, and Lena climbed onto the back of the wagon where Ryan couldn't see her. She winked at Mia, and Mia winked back.

"Until the Lord comes," Kip said, walking beside his wife.

"Maranatha," Mia said to him. "Our Lord come."

Eric Radner stood in front of his old mountaintop cabin and remembered those early years after Pan-Day spent in hiding and self-isolation. He didn't come up here too often anymore, but the earthquake two nights earlier had inclined him to leave his wife and friends at River Camp and return to visit the familiar mountain.

For years he'd maintained the cabin, but the recent earthquakes and subsequent aftershocks had broken down the log walls and caved in the roof. The water tank on the west side of the house had tipped over and the garden on the east side was overrun by ash-plagued weeds. It was hard to look at the one-room shelter and not think of the boy named Andy he'd taken in a few years after the pandemic. The cabin had collapsed, and his adopted son had run away. One now seemed to resemble the other.

As Eric walked down to the pond he'd built in the first year of escaping civilization, several rabbits darted into the underbrush as he crouched at the water's edge. The water level had gone down a few feet, but he was glad to see the containment walls were holding. The stream that fed the pond still gurgled quietly, but it seemed the rabbits were the only life on the mountain. There were no birds in the dying trees and no deer loping through the forest anymore.

From that height, he could see the mountains nearby as well. A layer of ash had coated everything, but the shockwave from the eruption had spared the lower altitudes. Ten miles west, where River Camp lay in its gorge, the forest had actually become a bit crowded since wildlife had migrated down to the safety of the still-thriving forest vegetation. The ash had also fallen in lesser extremes down below, and Eric thanked God that he hadn't been forced to relocate. Yet, at least. As long as his people didn't over-hunt the game around them, or over-fish the gorge river, they could sustain themselves off the land.

He climbed to the highest point of the peak where the HAM radio had weathered many winters under its protective box. The antenna wire had since tangled in tree branches, but he didn't bother to remove it. The radio that had been his source for news during those first years hadn't interested him for many years now. People from

River Camp had visited the nearest town and brought back all the news he needed to hear—a new government was being formulated worldwide called the One Planet Trust. Everyone in the world was being required to register and become a citizen. It was a global revolution. Most were excited, but Eric knew what it meant according to prophecy. God was still directing the slide of humanity in the world, so it was in God whom Eric trusted.

Eric smiled at the Wyoming rangeland far to the northeast. From those very woods, he'd seen armies come and go. Might and power and control seemed to be man's ultimate drive. But he knew that only God had the authority to actually call the shots. In fact, his body was covered with scars from those conflicts during hard days of learning from his Savior to stand steadfastly against the wicked. Some had repented, but many hadn't.

Perhaps this OPT would be the next force to try to tear his faith away. Maybe they would even kill him. He'd been there before, willing to accept death rather than deny his eternal Lord. But he wouldn't do it for a meager few more years of approval from mankind. No, he'd gladly die, and Gretchen, his wife, would be at his side. Many had expected the rapture to occur earlier, but the testing in America had refined God's people. God was still moving the world toward the Tribulation years.

His only regret was that Andy wasn't there to stand with him. The poor boy simply had to see the world out there, and Eric couldn't imagine that Andy had been able to avoid the OPT these last few weeks—if he were even still alive.

Below the peak, an animal moved, something black trotting through the leafless and pine-less trees. He flipped his open-sight deer rifle to his shoulder. Bears had found those mountains a paradise for the last two decades, and Eric carried scars from them as well. River Camp didn't need the meat, and besides, this far from his friends, he didn't trust his aging frame to pack a load of meat ten miles like he had when he was younger.

The animal moved out of sight, then Eric saw it again. It emerged from behind a boulder, trotting straight at him. He raised his rifle to defend himself but lowered it when he saw it was just a big dog. Nevertheless, he still backed up a few steps when it didn't slow its charge. Eric had dealt with enough wild dogs to know that this canine couldn't be wild if it was approaching him alone, wagging its tail.

"Hey, girl." He knelt and offered his hand to the bold animal. But the dog ducked right under his hand and yelped in excitement, running her head right into his legs, begging for attention. "Where'd you come from? You must be lost."

Stray dogs, even domesticated ones, didn't greet strangers this way! He held the animal's head in his hands. Andy had had a number of black Labradors after his childhood retriever had died, but this didn't look like the puppy Andy had left with. Of course, Runner would be a few years older now. Eric pulled back her cheeks to check her teeth, finding she was indeed about four years old.

"Runner?" He ruffled the dog's coat, which only excited her more, and she pounced with her forelegs, understanding that it was time to play.

With one hand extended to Runner's head, Eric stood upright and surveyed the trees below. If something had happened to Andy, it was slightly possible that Runner, now a meaty-sized adult canine, had found her way back home. However, Eric hoped it meant something else.

He left the peak and angled back toward the cabin below. After hopping the water trough, he froze at the sight of a crowd of people walking out of the trees into the clearing. The trunk of a tree stood to his left, so he ducked behind it. Runner put her nose down and dashed away, probably sniffing out the rabbits by the pond.

The visitors were talking, their tones not guarded but rather loud and open. Eric noticed several of them carrying compact assault rifles, but these weren't soldiers. A plump native-looking woman was carrying a jabbering two-year-old on her back, and a smaller woman was carrying an infant in a hide pouch on her front. Another woman, clad in an official uniform Eric had never seen before, was carrying a pack in her arms.

A bearded man—the largest person Eric had ever seen—held the hand of a tall brunette woman, his beard and her hair showing streaks of gray. Beside them, an older woman with long, curly hair tied back guided a younger woman who was clearly blind, her legs lifting awkwardly as she tentatively sought footing over the uneven forest floor.

But the most remarkable characters were the three who first reached the cabin. An old man with a walking stick was carrying a pair of crutches. Another tall, blond man with a muscled frame was carrying another man on his back, piggy-back style. The blond man set down the other to stand on his own, and Eric noticed that the one who'd been carried had no left foot. And he knew this man. His face had matured, but his shoulders were still narrow, his neck slender. It was Andy.

"There's a pond over there." Andy used a crutch to point down the slope. "The water's spring-fed, so it should be clean. My mom is buried over there, too."

Eric moved from behind his cover. He wasn't surprised that Andy spotted him first since the boy had been observant and cautious since his youth.

"It's okay!" Andy alerted his companions. "It's my dad, Eric Radner."

The tall, blond man didn't wait for Eric to reach them. He came forward swiftly with a smile, and when they were a few feet apart, he extended his hand.

"Glad to meet you, Mr. Radner. The name's Levi Caspertein. I hope you don't mind, but your son thought we might find shelter with you and yours at River Camp. We've heard a lot about you and your people. Glad to find there are still some devout people of God out here."

"Yes, um, welcome! River Camp's several miles away still, but we have plenty of room." Eric walked with Levi to the cabin. He approached Andy directly, ignoring for a moment the strangers with assault rifles. "Son, you came back."

"Yeah." Andy fidgeted on his crutches. "My eyes have been opened, you could say. God woke me up, Dad. These are the Casperteins. Good Christian people. You don't mind? We hid our vehicles off that access road by your old car, but we have more gear to fetch later. Our tracks are covered."

"It's all fine. Welcome home, son." Eric's voice broke. He held his arms wide, and his son moved into them. "Welcome home."

Milo Rotham looked back at the mountains of Wyoming, his heart already missing the people he'd grown to love in such a short time. He would never forget the Casperteins.

"Des Moines isn't going to come to you!" Alice called from ahead. She stomped her staff on the ground where new grass was growing. "You have to go to it! Giselle is waiting."

He smiled and started after her. Giselle hadn't been far from his thoughts in the few short weeks since he'd left her. Everyone else seemed to have found their place in Wyoming, and now it was his turn to return to Giselle's side.

In front of Alice, Mia and Kip walked side by side. The husband and wife had insisted that, as Servalites, their work in America wasn't finished yet. Milo hadn't expected Alice's company, but he was happy to have the dependable, one-armed woman with him. He'd heard her tell Levi that she couldn't settle down in River Camp quite yet, not when she was called to escort God's travelers in those last days. After he reached Des Moines, Milo guessed Alice would lead and guard the Servalites on to other towns and people in need of the gospel, whether the OPT was there or not.

Christ's coming was near, Milo knew, and America as a whole wasn't spiritually prepared for what was ahead. But as the Casperteins had touched his heart for God, he hoped to do the same for others with the time he had left. Next to Giselle. Even if, as Levi would say, *it ain't easy* . . .

I pray that *Dawn of Tribulation* and the *Last Dawn Series* have been great blessings to you! Please leave a review wherever you bought this book. That will help guide me in my next writing projects. Thanks for your kind help!

—*David Telbat*

About the Author

D.I. (David) Telbat is a Christian author best known for his **clean, Suspenseful Fiction with a Faith Focus**. This includes his bestselling and award-winning *COIL Series, Steadfast Series, Last Dawn Series*, and other Christian Suspense and End Times novels. He wrote his first book at age 14, and he hasn't stopped since!

David studied writing in school and worked for a time in the newspaper field. Getting into serious trouble with the law as a young man became a turning point in his life. The Lord used that experience to draw David into a personal relationship with Him. Re-focusing his life for Christ, he now seeks to honor God with his life and writing by doing what he loves most—writing and Christian ministry.

Subscribe to receive David Telbat's FREE, bi-weekly **D.I. Telbat Newsletter** with one of his Christian short stories, or an Author Reflection, or his Novel News Update. You'll also receive **exclusive subscriber gifts**, such as his *Three For Free*—three-novels-in-one eBook! You can join the adventure by visiting his site at books2read.com/DITelbat/ and click on the "**Follow this Author**" button.

www.ingramcontent.com/pod-product-compliance
Lightning Source LLC
Chambersburg PA
CBHW051315190726
48290CB00001B/166